"Takes you full force right away and doesn't let go until the very last page . . . has enough full-bore action to take your breath away, barely giving you time to inhale. The action is nonstop. Gilstrap knows his technology and weaponry. *Damage Control* will blow you away."
—*Suspense Magazine*

THREAT WARNING

"If you are a fan of thriller novels, I hope you've been reading John Gilstrap's Jonathan Grave series. *Threat Warning* is a character-driven work where the vehicle has four on the floor and horsepower to burn. From beginning to end, it is dripping with excitement."
—**Joe Hartlaub, BookReporter.com**

"If you like Vince Flynn–style action, with a strong, incorruptible hero, this series deserves to be in your reading diet. *Threat Warning* reconfirms Gilstrap as a master of jaw-dropping action and heart-squeezing suspense."
—**Austin Camacho, *The Big Thrill***

HOSTAGE ZERO

"Jonathan Grave, my favorite freelance peacemaker, problem-solver, and tough guy hero, is back—and in particularly fine form. *Hostage Zero* is classic Gilstrap: the people are utterly real, the action's foot to the floor, and the writing's fluid as a well-oiled machine gun. A tour de force!"
—**Jeffery Deaver**

HOSTAGE ZERO

NATHAN'S RUN

"Gilstrap pushes every thriller button . . . a nail-biting denouement and strong characters."
—*San Francisco Chronicle*

"Gilstrap has a shot at being the next John Grisham . . . one of the best books of the year."
—*Rocky Mountain News*

"Emotionally charged . . . one of the year's best."
—*Chicago Tribune*

"Brilliantly calculated . . . With the skill of a veteran pulp master, Gilstrap weaves a yarn that demands to be read in one sitting."
—*Publishers Weekly* (starred review)

"Like a roller coaster, the story races along on well-oiled wheels to an undeniably pulse-pounding conclusion."
—*Kirkus Reviews* (starred review)

ALSO BY JOHN GILSTRAP

SCORPION STRIKE

A JONATHAN GRAVE THRILLER

JOHN GILSTRAP

PINNACLE BOOKS
Kensington Publishing Corp.
www.kensingtonbooks.com

Kensington Publishing Corp.
119 West 40th Street
New York, NY 10018

All Kensington titles, imprints, and distributed lines are available at special quantity discounts for bulk purchases for sales promotions, premiums, fund-raising, educational, or institutional use. Special book excerpts or customized printings can also be created to fit specific needs. For details, write or phone the office of the Kensington sales manager: Kensington Publishing Corp., 119 West 40th Street, New York, NY 10018, attn: Sales Department; phone 1-800-221-2647.

PINNACLE BOOKS and the Pinnacle logo are Reg. U.S. Pat. & TM Off.

First printing: July 2018

10 9 8 7 6 5 4 3 2 1

ISBN-13: 978-0-7860-3980-7
ISBN-10: 0-7860-3980-9

Printed in the United States of America

First electronic edition: July 2018

ISBN-13: 978-0-7860-3981-4
ISBN-10: 0-7860-3981-7

CHAPTER 1

"So, let me get this straight," Annie Banks said, leaning in a little closer. Her eyes looked less swimmy than her words sounded. "You get to stay here as long as you want, eat the food, drink the booze, and you don't have to pay for it."

Tyler Stratton smiled and sipped from his Jack and Coke—his fifth of the evening. "Divorce isn't necessarily as traumatic for children as the talk shows lead you to believe," he said. "Paternal guilt is a powerful force." They sat at a table for two in the largely empty lobby bar, surrounded by mahogany and crystal. While the place didn't close for another half hour, all but the most stalwart patrons had headed off to bed. Truth be told, Tyler was ready for some tangled-sheet recreation himself, but Annie seemed resistant.

"Your father really owns all of this?" she asked, not for the first time.

"Stepfather," Tyler corrected, also not for the first time. Then he added new detail. "I was barely a toddler when my real father was killed in a robbery. When Baker Sinise married my mom, he took on the daddy role all the way. When things went south with their marriage, Baker was really broken up about leaving me." The lump that appeared in his throat surprised him.

"Sending you to military school wasn't exactly an act of love, was it?"

Tyler took another sip. "Well, yeah, it kinda was. I was what you might call an 'angry young man.'"

"Angry at your mom?"

"Do we really have to talk about this?"

"You never talk about your early years," Annie said.

"There's a reason for that."

"You want to get laid or not?" She sold that with just the right coy smile.

He laughed. "So, you're going nuclear on me." He prepared himself with a breath. "I was angry at the world," he said. "Not Mom, per se, but she took the brunt of it. I was pissed when my dad died, and then I was pissed when Baker and Mom started to fight."

"So, he left you guys and moved to the islands to buy a hotel?"

Tyler bobbed his head noncommittally. "You lose track of about six years in there, but yeah. And it's not just the hotel. It's the whole freaking island."

"You can own an island?"

Tyler laughed at the amazement in her face. "Who knew, right?"

"And he's okay with you bringing guests to share all the freebies?"

Tyler broke his gaze. Lying was never his long suit, and he had it on good authority that his eyes always gave him away.

"What?" Annie leaned in closer.

It was a question he hadn't expected.

"He knows I'm here, right?"

Tyler cleared his throat. "He'd be fine with it," he said.

"Then why—"

A loud crash terminated her words, yanked their heads back toward the ornate wooden door with its cut glass insert. The doors exploded open as if hit with a battering ram, ripping the auto-close hardware from their mounts. Before the panels could rebound, three men charged through the opening, identical assault rifles pressed to their shoulders. And they looked dead serious about using them.

"Hands up!" one of them yelled as he swept the room with the muzzle. "Hands! Hands! Hands!" The gunman's friends mimed his actions and echoed his commands.

Tyler thrust his hands high, while Annie just sat there, her face a mask of fear. Confusion.

"Annie!" he whisper-shouted.

An instant later, through his peripheral vision, he caught a fellow drinker and his date bolting from their stools at the bar, heading toward the doors that led to the beach. They'd made it maybe three strides when a burst of gunfire knocked them both to the polished bamboo floor and shattered two panels of the wall of windows. After impact, neither of them moved.

Annie screamed, drawing the muzzles of two rifles in her direction.

"Shut up!" one of the invaders ordered. "Shut up now, or shut up forever."

Annie clasped her hands over her mouth, as if it were the only way to halt the sound.

"Your friends were stupid!" the invader yelled to the

guests who remained in the bar. "They didn't listen and now they are dead. Do exactly as I say, and the same will not happen to you."

Tyler nudged Annie with his raised elbow. "Put your hands up," he hissed.

They moved from her mouth and stretched high over her head. At first, Tyler thought that maybe she was mocking the terrorists with such an absurd stretch, but then he realized she was just that terrified.

"Up!" the same invader commanded, gesturing with the muzzle of his gun. Since he was the only one talking, Tyler figured him to be the man in charge. "All of you stand where you are, next to your chair. Ladies, leave your purses and handbags where they are."

"What are you going to do?" asked another lady who was perched at the bar.

One of the silent attackers whirled on her and fired a single bullet into the front panel of the bar, missing her by only an inch or two.

"That wasn't bad marksmanship," the leader said. "That was a warning to listen carefully and to keep your mouths shut. Now, please stand, everyone, so I don't have to make you fall. Keep your hands up the whole time. It will feel awkward, but you can do it."

Awkward didn't touch it. As Tyler slid from his elevated stool and tried to push it back with his butt, it toppled with a clatter and a slam. He jumped, but his captors did not. Apparently, they'd been expecting that. Other chairs toppled, as well, but everyone complied.

"Well done," the leader said. "Now, gentlemen, I want you to move very deliberately and carefully to turn out your pockets. I want it all. Wallet, keys, cell phones, cameras, and even your wristwatches. Pretend that you are naked, but with clothes. You will be searched afterward, and you do not want to be found noncompliant with this."

Tyler complied, placing his wallet, room key, and phone on the bar table, then raising his hands again.

When the men were done, the lead terrorist said, "Ladies, the rules are the same for you. If your items are all contained in your purses, then you are done for now. If you have items in your pockets, empty them."

Tyler shot a look to Annie, who shook her head. She had nothing.

"You're doing very well," the leader said. "Now I want you all to move to the center of the room and join together." He motioned to a spot near the center of the wall of glass doors.

As Tyler's heart hammered, he felt his face flush. They were being herded into a smaller target. They'd taught him some of those terror tactics at Wilmot Academy, not as a lesson on what to inflict, but rather as a lesson on what to avoid. They were quickly reaching the point of no return, yet it would be foolish to even think about running or fighting. A simple glimpse at the bloody corpses on the floor was testament to that. Compliance was the only option. Victimhood. This was really, *really* bad.

When everyone was in the proper spot, the invaders pressed them progressively tighter into each other, until they were touching, shoulder-to-shoulder or chest-to-chest. Tyler counted eight of them altogether, and of the crowd, he and Annie were the youngest by at least ten years.

Beyond the shattered doors, somewhere out in the

night, more gunshots rattled the stillness. The hostages— is that what they were now?—all jumped, but no one screamed. A lesson well learned.

"Join hands," the leader commanded, "everyone facing each other. We will be walking all the way down to the beach. It is a full moon, and we can see you, so do not attempt to run. If one of you tries to run, I will shoot the entire group. Do you understand? I expect an answer."

About half of them said, "Yes," and the other half mumbled some version of "I understand." But everyone answered, and no one said, "No."

Tyler gripped Annie's hand in his own left, while a sweaty fat guy did his best to crush his right. Tyler nudged the guy and said, "Lighten up, that hurts."

When the guy failed to respond—he just kept his eyes locked to the front—Tyler rattled the guy's hand to get his attention. When Hand Crusher's gaze shifted, Tyler whispered, "You're hurting me. Ease up."

This time, the pressure eased.

"No talking," the invader snapped, and Tyler felt a surge as someone pushed the group forward.

The doors from the lobby bar led to the expansive veranda with its slate floors and gorgeous wicker furniture. Only five hours before, Tyler and Annie had enjoyed evening cocktails before dinner there. Two hours before that, the maître d' had sheared the neck off a bottle of Dom Pérignon as part of the resort's famous evening ritual.

Tyler found himself walking in shuffling half steps amid the crowd, the only way to keep his balance.

The veranda led to a wide flight of five steps that

grounded out at the perfectly manicured lawn, where earlier in the afternoon, hotel guests dressed all in white had engaged in a rousing croquet match. The pretentiousness of the Crystal Sands Resort made Tyler's skin crawl. But the ladies loved it, and it was free. Pretty high cotton for an unemployed nineteen-year-old.

A hundred yards ahead, there'd be another short flight of stairs down to the beach, where there'd be another hundred yards of flawless sand, and after that, a 100-mile swim through the Pacific Ocean to the western coast of Mexico.

Twenty-five yards short of the steps to the beach, their captor ordered a hard right turn. Linked as they were in a circle, some stumbled at the pivot, but no one fell. More gunfire ripped the night, this volley coming from far away, well on the other side of the clubhouse and the pool. Tyler thought he might have seen flashes.

"None of your concern," the leader said. "We are heading for the pool deck."

That meant another hundred yards or so of difficult footing. The circle of strangers navigated erupting palm roots and fallen coconuts as they made their way through the shadows cast by tastefully suspended lights that had been installed in the treetops. And because God had a wicked sense of humor, the in-ground sprinkler system was throwing water everywhere. Though the air temperature was likely still eighty degrees, the water and the slight breeze combined to make the night feel frigid. Within seconds, Tyler's khaki shorts and polo shirt were soaked, as was Annie's slinky little dress. He felt like a pig for noticing that she wasn't wearing a bra, and that, well, she was cold, too.

"Why is this happening?" Annie whispered.

"Just keep going," Tyler whispered back. "I don't know."

"Are they terrorists, do you think?"

"I don't know that, either," he said. Listening to the news, you'd think there was a very specific definition for what a terrorist was, but if these thugs didn't meet a commonsense definition, he didn't know who could. "Just do what they say."

The pool at the Crystal Sands Resort was unlike any community pool Tyler had frequented as a child. No rectangular construction and swimming lanes here. This was a pool that wanted to be a lagoon. The complex was actually a series of pools, split among four different levels, each linked by elaborate waterfalls and separated by flowers and palm trees. A lazy river circumnavigated the whole area, providing opportunities for guests to float on rafts through the bar and restaurant areas. The water in the river was dormant now, but the waterfalls still flowed. The normally soothing sound of rushing water provided no solace tonight as Tyler marched like a gulag prisoner to his death.

More gunshots in the distance.

As his cluster of hostages made their way up the gradual hill to the concrete lagoon, Tyler saw more of the guests being herded into the same spot. They, likewise, moved in clusters, hands joined as they shuffled along. The smallest group he saw was four people, the largest looked to be ten. Everyone wore varieties of nearly nothing, clearly having been rousted from sleep.

Terror and dread manifested differently among the terrified. Some people were crying—men and women alike—but most moved stoically, eyes wide and darting from compass point to compass point. Tyler saw the Rabinowitzes, the older couple from Indiana that he'd crossed paths with late in the day yesterday. Mr. Rabinowitz—Jacob, if Tyler remembered correctly, an ego-fueled executive with a trash company—was bitching to the poolside bartender about the blandness of his Bloody Mary. When he'd caught sight of Tyler watching, the old guy had said, "Mind your manners, shithead." The wife—Tyler didn't catch her name—rolled her eyes, his clue that this was common. It must be tough going through life living with an asshole for a soul mate. The enormous rocks adorning her fingers and ears were clues, Tyler thought, to the price of tolerance.

Tyler saw Zach Turner and his wife approaching, as well. They were a nice couple from Virginia. He'd spent over an hour with them at the edge of the lazy river chatting about Zach's tours in Iraq and Afghanistan. Tyler had found the story of the IED explosion that took Zach's leg off below the knee particularly fascinating. Now he found it fascinating that the terrorists had allowed him to put on his prosthetic leg, but not a shirt. In this dim light, his burn scars seemed somehow more prominent than they had in the full light of day. Both of them looked shaken.

Annie gripped Tyler's hand ever more tightly as they scaled the shallow steps that led to the upper pool area. It was entirely possible that her fingernails were drawing blood from his palm, but he didn't want to complain.

"There are no children," Annie whispered.

Tyler didn't know what she meant at first, but then he saw it, too. The Turners had eleven-year-old twin boys, but they were nowhere to be seen. Ditto the two girls who belonged to the Severances.

Annie's grip tightened even more. "You don't think they—"

"No," Tyler said, cutting her off before she could say the unthinkable. "The parents aren't upset enough for that." He didn't know if that was true, but that was his story and he was sticking to it.

At the top of the steps now, on the upper pool deck, their conductor said, "You can let go of each other now. If you can find a seat, take it. If you try to leave, you will be shot."

Tyler was happy to be shed of the sweaty guy's hand, but he was happy to keep hold of Annie's. Even if he'd wanted to let go of it, he didn't think she'd let him. "Let's grab a chair at the back, near the bathroom," he said. He didn't know why, exactly, but that seemed like a good place to be. Certainly, he didn't want to be in the front, where they would be most visible. The chairs near the restrooms offered them the added benefit of being near the bar and the back gate.

He didn't wait for an answer from Annie. Rather, he guided her past the pool's wheelchair ramp and toward the rank of chairs that nobody wanted during the day because they offered nearly full shade—the very opposite of why most people came to a resort like the Crystal Sands. The chaises he selected were constructed of the same canvas and heavy wood as all the hundreds of others, but theirs lay against one of the elaborate white ceramic planters that defined the outer perimeter of the pool area. Immediately beyond, toward the rear, lay the descending pathway that ultimately led to the garbage Dumpsters and the maintenance sheds for the golf carts, which toted guests from one end of the compound to another.

The flood of guest hostages continued to swell as sleep-deprived rich people arrived in their clusters of various sizes, each of them guarded by a team of riflemen.

"There are so many of them," Annie whispered. Her tone sounded like equal parts fear and awe.

Tyler assumed she was talking about the terrorists, not the guests, and he had to agree. These were some badass dudes. He had a horrible feeling in his stomach that people weren't going to take them seriously enough, and that more of the resort's guests were going to die before this ended—whatever the hell *this* was.

CHAPTER 2

What the hell is that?

Jonathan Grave's eyes snapped open. He thought he'd heard gunshots, a quick burst of automatic-weapons fire, distant but distinctive. Perhaps he'd been dreaming, but—

There it was again, and it was definitely gunfire. A sustained burst this time, and accompanied by screams.

"Gail," he said. "Wake up. Something's wrong."

She lay with her head on his chest and was slow to respond.

"Come on, Gail. Wake up. Somebody's shooting." As he spoke, he slid out from under her, and she stirred.

At the third ripple of gunfire, she was wide-awake. As she sat up, the covers fell away from her breasts and she moved quickly to cover them. Jonathan shot to his feet and darted naked to the sliding glass door that served as their window onto the beach. Out beyond the glass and the low hedge that surrounded their patio, everything looked normal in the silver light of the moon. It cut a brilliant slice across the calm waters, only to be lost in the rolling luminescence of the waves breaking against the white sand.

"What do you see?" Gail asked. He could hear her rising and dressing behind him.

"Nothing, yet," he said. "But that was definitely gunfire." He unlocked the slider and pulled it open.

"Whatever it is, I think pants and shoes would be a good idea," Gail said. She'd pulled herself into the cream-colored shorts and pink blouse she'd worn to dinner.

Jonathan looked down at himself. She had a point. He locked the door again. "Come over here and keep an eye out," he said. As she moved into his place, he padded quickly across the bedroom into the massive walk-in closet, where he'd hung his khaki 5.11 pants and golf shirt. He wasn't much for shorts.

"Talk to me," Jonathan said as he felt his way along the hanging clothes in the dark. Under the circumstances, turning on a light was a nonstarter. He heard more gunfire in the distance. Single shots this time, but they sounded closer than before.

"I don't see anything," Gail said. "But it sounds like they're working up this way, one bungalow at a time."

The Crystal Sands Resort was as high-end as a beach getaway could be, and Jonathan had chosen the bungalow farthest from the noise and the light of the clubhouse. The surf rolled two hundred yards from their patio at low tide and about a hundred yards closer when the moon pulled it nearer to shore. On the opposite side of the building—officially the front, he supposed—their ornate wood and etched glass door was separated from the steep sloping jungle by only an access road and another twenty yards of well-groomed undergrowth.

Because their bungalow was last in line, he assumed they had some time, but it would be measured in seconds, not minutes. With every bungalow situated for maximum privacy, it was impossible to tell precisely what was going on beyond the row of trees that separated them from their nearest neighbors.

But the gunfire provided an important clue.

During his years of service for Uncle Sam, Jonathan had become an expert at dressing quickly in the dark. Leaning his back against the closet wall, he pulled on a pair of black athletic socks and then slipped his legs into his pants and his feet into a pair of Merrell hiking shoes. He anticipated a long night, and if there was a single important lesson to be learned about emergencies, it was that shoes are your most important assets. Other clothing was important, too, but you could run naked if you had to, so long as you had something on your feet.

He buttoned and zipped his pants and—

"Digger, they're here."

Jonathan swung back into the bedroom in time to see Gail backing away from the glass doors as two men dressed all in black glided through the moonlight. If they'd seen Gail, they made no indication of it.

"They move like they know what they're doing," Gail said. "And they have hostages." A former member of the FBI's Hostage Rescue Team, she knew training when she saw it. The leader of the two-man team moved with his weapon at low ready, while the other one guarded a young couple that they'd spent some time with at the pool. The second guy looked tough, but from the way he was holding his rifle—they both carried some form of AR 15 clone—he didn't look frightened. Both attackers wore tactical vests festooned with spare magazines.

"I don't see night vision," Jonathan observed. And why would they have it? Whatever they were up to, they had little reason to expect much resistance from a bunch of off-season beach vacationers. That one bit of complacency might provide Jonathan's best chance for victory.

The bad guys were still fifteen, twenty yards out when Jonathan's plan came together in his head. "Stay back and get behind something in case they get a shot off," he said.

"What are you doing?" Gail seemed simultaneously horrified and insulted. She'd never been much of a hider—had always been a hell of a fighter.

Jonathan didn't have time to explain. Hell, he barely had time to get into position. As he moved to the short wall where the sliding glass door met the lock, he wrapped his hand around the Benchmade Presidio Ultra that was always clipped to his pocket and opened the blade with a flourish. He pressed his back against the wall perpendicular to the door and brought his hands up into a fighting stance.

Gail hadn't moved. "Digger, what the hell—"

"We won't be taken," Jonathan said. "If I'm gonna die, it's gonna be on my—"

A brilliant white light split the darkness of the bedroom, catching Gail full-on.

"Don't move!" a voice yelled from beyond the door. Two seconds later, something struck the glass of the door and the panel disintegrated. "Get on the ground!"

the attacker shouted. "Get on the ground or I will shoot you!"

The tactical light from the lead attacker's rifle flared against the drapes as the muzzle crossed the threshold.

Jonathan struck like a scorpion. Grabbing the muzzle of the rifle just behind the brake, he lurched the weapon up to point at the ceiling. As the weapon shifted, the attacker's finger found the trigger and fired a round into the plaster. In the instant that the shooter's inner wrist was exposed, Jonathan slashed it with the razor edge of the blade, severing tendons and blood vessels, rendering the hand useless.

Continuing with the momentum he'd built, Jonathan pivoted to the shooter's other side. While forcing the attacker's arm even higher, he drove the point of his blade fist-deep into the attacker's armpit, severing the subclavian artery. He finished with a vicious slice into the blue meat of the man's neck, unleashing a fountain of gore. The guy was dead, but he didn't know it yet. He was done.

But Jonathan wasn't.

The fight wasn't yet five seconds old, and 50 percent of the threat was neutralized.

The guy who remained outside to keep track of the other couple was slow to react. He seemed startled. But then he got his shit together and pushed his hostages aside. As the bad guy's rifle swung up from low ready, Jonathan realized with more than a little irony that he had literally brought a knife to a gunfight.

Jonathan charged forward, using the dead attacker as a human battering ram. Driving his limp body forward, across the patio and past the margin of the surrounding grass, he shoved him into his partner to knock him off balance. In about two seconds, the bad guy with the gun would have all the advantage.

Jonathan slapped at the muzzle of that second rifle, too, pushing it out just the degree or two he needed not to be hit. With a fast and vicious horizontal swing of his blade, he slashed the attacker's eyes. The man had just begun to scream when Jonathan thrust the point of his blade through the soft tissue under the attacker's jaw and on into his brainstem.

The guy collapsed like an unstrung marionette.

Jonathan's heart hammered in his chest as he let the guy drop. He returned to his fighter's stance, ready for the next threat. The young couple embraced each other, seemingly ready to die at Jonathan's hand.

"Edwards, right?" Jonathan asked. "Lori and Hunter."

They nodded in unison. Or maybe it was a shiver.

"W-we met at the pool," Hunter stammered.

"Yeah," Jonathan said. The night had turned peaceful again. Sounds of distress continued to roll toward him from the direction of the clubhouse—some crying and an occasional gunshot—but the part of the world he could see was all moonlight and luminescent surf.

He turned back toward the room, toward the shattered glass and the bedroom beyond. "Gail, are you all right?" She had not moved. She stood in the middle of the room, her hands at her mouth. "Gail?"

She was still trying to process what she had just seen. She understood that she'd fallen in love with a crusader whose combat skills had been honed over nearly two decades of training and experience with the most respected elite Special Forces unit in the world.

Yes, she'd seen him kill before. Indeed, she'd killed right alongside him. But those incidents had all involved firearms and extraordinary marksmanship.

Killing with a knife seemed so personal, and Jonathan had wielded the blade with such expert precision that it took her breath away. Frightened her. The look on his face as he sliced and slashed the life out of those men was feral and furious. Some of it remained even now as he looked at her and asked if she'd been hurt. He seemed oblivious to the blood spatter on his naked chest and arms and even his face. He seemed . . . *focused*.

"Are you *hurt*?" he said.

Suddenly aware that she'd been frozen in place, she dropped her hands and straightened her posture. "I'm fine," she said. It was time for her to become part of the solution. "What the hell just happened?"

She'd meant her question to be rhetorical, but he answered it, anyway. "Beyond the obvious, I have no idea," he said. "It would appear that the resort is under attack." As he spoke, he stooped to the body closest to the door. He wrapped his left fist around the reinforced tab, which existed on most tactical vests for the very purpose of dragging wounded comrades, and started pulling him back into the room.

"Oh, my God, what are you doing?" This from Lori, who seemed to be rejoining the real world.

"They're sure to realize that they're missing a couple of operators," Jonathan said. "Makes no sense to leave them where people can trip over them." He shot a look back toward the frightened couple. "You're welcome to help."

The couple remained frozen in each other's arms.

As Jonathan dragged his guy across the tile floor of

the bedroom toward the big bathroom, Gail slid past him and went for the other one.

By the time she'd made it to the patio and taken a grip on the other corpse, she tossed a glance back inside. She saw that Jonathan was depositing his guy at the base of the ornate claw-foot tub, probably with the intent of closing the door and turning on a light. That's what she'd do.

"You okay with that?" Jonathan called back to her.

She found the tab between the dead guy's shoulder blades and grunted as she hefted his shoulders. In the moonlight, the massive wound under the attacker's jaw disgusted her and she looked away. "I'm fine," she said. "I can drag so long as I don't have to carry." She shot a look to Hunter. "No, really," she said. "I've got this." The irony missed him entirely.

Several years ago, things had gone terribly wrong for Gail during an op, and she'd spent altogether too long feeling sorry for herself. Under these circumstances, it felt good to know that the strength she'd been working so hard to rebuild had finally returned. She sure as hell had come a long way since throwing away her cane for the last time just a little while ago.

"Next time you suggest a romantic getaway," she said, "I believe I'll think twice." She looked up and hoped that Jonathan could see that she'd tried to manage a smile.

He stood over the man he'd killed, straddling him and staring down, his knife still gripped in his fist. "Hey, Dig?" she asked as she pulled.

He snapped out of wherever he'd been. "Oh, shit, Gail, I'm sorry. Let me help." He started toward her.

"No," she said. For some reason, it was important to

her to finish this business of dragging the body. She wasn't rejecting *Digger's* help. She was rejecting *anyone's* help. "I just wanted to know if you're okay."

"Not a scratch," he said.

"You're still holding your knife."

"These assholes tried to kill us."

She was crossing the foot of the bed now. "Technically, I think they were trying to take us hostage."

"They pointed a rifle at you."

Something in his tone struck an odd chord and she let the dead guy drop as she stood. From here, separated only by inches, she saw something else in Jonathan's expression that she'd never seen before. Fear.

"But you're still holding your knife."

Truth was, Jonathan knew that the blade and release mechanisms were fouled with gore, and he didn't want to put that nastiness into his pocket. But he did it, anyway. He thumbed the release button on the locking blade, folded it, and slid the clip back into its designated place.

When both corpses were in the bathroom, Jonathan closed the door and turned on the shower light. It was the dimmest of the options on the five-switch panel, but it allowed enough light to see what they were doing.

The dead guys were both nominally white—one might have had some Hispanic blood—and both were in pretty good shape. Too thin and soft to be SEALs or D-Boys, but toned enough to show that they were fit. They wore identical kit, all black, all 5.11 Tactical gear, but that didn't mean anything. These days, half the young men their age wore tactical pants and shirts as a fashion statement. And let's be honest. They looked cool and the many pockets came in handy.

In fact, the pants Jonathan wore at that very moment were the same SKU, but in khaki.

He also noted that the chest rigs they wore were not plate carriers. They were constructed of a mesh material instead of Kevlar, and he took that as yet more evidence that they did not expect to meet much resistance. They each carried identical M4s and both packed four spare thirty-round magazines of 5.56-millimeter ammo. Their Glock 19 nine-millimeter pistols resided in cross-draw holsters on their chest rigs, a configuration that Jonathan had never liked. He was particularly intrigued by the two-way radios they'd strapped behind their shoulders. He didn't relish inserting a dead guy's earpiece into his own ear, but you could learn a lot by eavesdropping on radio traffic.

"Who would do something like this?" Gail asked. "What could they possibly want?"

Jonathan didn't answer because he had no idea. "Here's what I need you to do," he said. "Gather up what you need to live in the jungle for a while. Be sure to grab your meds, and pull together anything that can identify us directly."

"We're not here under our real names," she said.

"Doesn't matter. These guys' friends are going to find them sooner or later, and we don't need to make it any easier than necessary to find us." As he spoke, he worked the Velcro tabs that would release the dead guys from their kit. "I'm going to relieve these guys of everything they've got, and I want to be clear of here in no more than five minutes. Three is even better."

"Where are we going?"

Jonathan stayed focused on what he was doing. "The first stop is anywhere but here. We'll refine it later."

Four minutes later, he'd transferred every phone, wallet, piece of paper, and bit of lint from the bad guys' pockets into his own for later examination. With that done, he started to shrug into the first victim's vest—it had the most blood on it, so he took it as a gesture of chivalry toward Gail—but she stopped him.

"Wait," she said.

"We don't have time to wait."

"We have time for this," she said. She handed him a wet towel and a dry one. "You're disgusting. And there's a golf shirt on the sink for you, too."

He looked down at himself, at the blood that had spattered and smeared his skin. Then he looked at himself in the mirror. He looked like a serial killer. Yeah, they had time for him to towel away some of the foulness.

As he did, Gail donned the other vest and rifle sling. "I put socks and underwear for both of us into my carry-on backpack. Ditto toothpaste and toothbrushes, meds for me and toilet paper. Phones and laptops, too. Can you think of anything else?" Their clothes and assorted sundries would have to stay behind.

"The toilet paper is an especially good touch," Jonathan said. He pulled the forest green golf shirt on over his head and reached for the other chest rig. Then he slung the leftover M4.

"Time to go," he said. They just didn't know where or why or for how long.

Details.

Jonathan led the way out of the bathroom and back into the bedroom. "We should go out the front door," he said. "Maybe the bad guys—"

"Wait!" a voice yelled from beyond the patio.

Jonathan brought his rifle up reflexively.

"No!" He recognized the voice as belonging to a woman now, and she made a praying gesture with her hands. "Please don't shoot and please don't leave. Hunter is getting some clothes for us."

"Jesus," Jonathan grumbled. "I forgot about them."

"Okay," Gail said. "We can wait for a minute or two." She drilled Jonathan with a glare. "Can't we?"

"Sure," he said. "Why would we want to hurry?" As soon as the words were out, he regretted them. Not because waiting wasn't a stupid thing to do, but rather that he hated to sound whiny. "It's Lori, right?"

She nodded. "He should be right here. Who were those men?"

"Bad guys," Jonathan said. It was an accurate description of how he divided much of his world. There were good guys and bad guys. The rest didn't matter.

Another burst of machine-gun fire rippled the night.

"That's shooting, right?" Lori asked.

"It's healthier to think of it as people dying," Jonathan said.

"Oh, my God," Lori said.

"Oh, come on," Gail admonished.

"There is no better time for the unvarnished truth than when you're under attack," Jonathan said. To Lori: "Where's your bungalow? Are you right next door?" He pointed out the shattered door to the left.

"Yes."

Jonathan headed off in that direction. "I'll see if I can move him along a little faster."

Lori moved to intervene. "Please don't hurt him."

He stopped and forced a smile. "I'm *not* a bad guy," he said. "I just want to hurry him along a little."

"No need to," said a voice from just beyond the aura of light that spilled through the ruined doors. It was Hunter, and he'd found a pair of shorts, running shoes, and a polo shirt. He held out some clothes and shoes for Lori. "Thanks for waiting."

"Thanks for hurrying," Jonathan countered.

While Lori pulled herself into an outfit that looked remarkably like the one her husband wore, Hunter said, "I have a question for you." He addressed it to Jonathan.

He waited for it.

"Where'd you get the mad knife skills?"

"I grew up in a bad neighborhood," Jonathan said.

"Bullshit."

"Okay." It was, in fact, bullshit. Jonathan had grown up in unparalleled wealth under the protection of a father who happened to be one of Virginia's most notorious criminals. This was not a discussion he intended to have.

"And how come you were Steve and Alicia at the pool this morning, but Gail and Dig under pressure?"

He'd done that, hadn't he? He'd used Gail's name and she'd used his.

"No bullshit answer for that one," Jonathan said. "Just no answer at all. Hey, Lori, how are we doing?"

Her trembling hands were having a hard time wrangling her shoelaces. "I'm trying," she said.

Jonathan pointed with his forehead. "Why don't you give her a hand. This is not a place we want to stay."

Hunter got her fixed up, and they stood together.

"Stay close to us," Jonathan said, "and if there's shooting, hit the ground fast."

CHAPTER 3

"Looks like we were lucky to get chairs," Tyler whispered. Weary, confused guests flooded the upper pool deck, and the chairs were being gobbled up. During the day, there was always ample seating for those who wanted to sun themselves on the pool deck—and there were pool boys to fetch more if they were needed. However, in the dozens of times that Tyler had visited the Crystal Sands, there'd never been a time when every guest was here at the pool. Typically, they were strewn throughout the resort, from the kayak launch point to the beach to the bar to the golf course. Chairs would soon become a scarce commodity.

And it was hot. Every night was warm at the Crystal Sands—that's why people came here in the first place—but the steady breezes gave relief. As the bodies packed in, each of those ninety-eight-point-six-degree heat generators raised the temps and blocked the breezes. It became apparent to Tyler after only a few minutes that it had been too long since too many had had a shower.

"I wish they'd tell what they were going to do to us," Annie said.

"We've already seen what they'll do if we don't co-operate," Tyler replied.

"Will you two please shut up?" hissed the woman to their right. Aged somewhere between fifty and seventy, the lady was clearly a sun worshipper, with skin that made a football look pretty. She'd taken the time to put diamond studs into her ears before being herded out of her room. Or, maybe she just slept with them in. Was that even possible?

Tyler looked at the woman, said nothing.

"They've told us to stay quiet," the lady pressed.

"So, why are you talking?" Annie asked. Tyler smiled and she seemed pleased with herself.

The captors all looked like soldiers who'd bought their gear from the same store. Black on black on black, from shoes all the way up through shirts and what Tyler presumed were bulletproof vests. They carried the same guns and they all had radios attached to their vests, just behind their right shoulders. The radios ran to square microphones that looked to be attached by Velcro to the front side of their right shoulders.

Tyler counted eleven of them, all men, but there could have been more. He might also have double counted, since they all looked alike. They didn't say much, but when they did, it was in English. Since the accents sounded Russian, he ruled out your standard ISIS nut bags, but he wasn't sure that made him feel any better.

Best he could tell from the little he'd overheard, they referred to each other not by name, but by phonetic alphabet letters. He'd heard references to a Bravo, an Echo, and a Golf. He recognized the handles as elements of the military alphabet, so he assumed that there must be an Alpha, Charlie, and Foxtrot out there someplace. Plus more, he imagined.

Several of the other guests had dared to ask what was going to happen to them, but none of them got answers. One did get a punch in the face, though.

Over at the blue mosaic-tiled bar, two of the soldiers sat on high stools, goosenecking over a stack of wallets and purses and their contents. From what Tyler could tell, they were less interested in the valuables than they were in the credit cards and such. In fact, after they pulled the cards from the wallets, they cast the wallets themselves off to the side. They also seemed interested in passports.

It wasn't until Tyler saw a familiar green-and-white accordion-folded striped stack of paper that he understood what they were up to. "They're matching IDs to the guest roster," he whispered.

"How do you know?" Annie asked, which startled him. He didn't know he'd spoken aloud.

"The paper," Tyler whispered. "My stepfather, Baker, won't hesitate to spend ten grand on a new chandelier in a guest room, but the hundred bucks to replace the antique dot-matrix printer at the reception desk is a step too far. That's the only place we use that paper."

Tyler's attention was drawn to an intense discussion between two of the guards, one of whom carried a megaphone that he hadn't yet used. The other man carried a manila folder that was stuffed with papers. They disagreed over whether or not it was time to start something. The objection had to do with some people who were missing.

The captor on the left cocked his head to the side

and said into his radio, "Hotel, this is Alpha. Is Foxtrot with you?" He waited maybe ten seconds and then repeated the question. "Their radios must not be working."

"Or something happened to them," the other one countered.

Alpha looked annoyed. "They were Sector Eight, is that correct?"

"Yes." Tyler noted the absence of "sir" at the end. Not military.

Alpha sighed deeply. "Take a team. Golf and India. See what you can find. Leave me the list, and send Echo over to take notes."

"You got it." As the other man walked away, Tyler heard him say, "Delta, this is Bravo." It seemed that Alpha was in charge and Bravo was his second. Tyler wondered if the alphabet was a rank system, with Zulu being on the bottom of the pile.

After fifteen seconds or so, a new captor arrived to take Bravo's place next to Alpha. Smart money said this was Echo. This one had removed his skullcap, revealing yellow hair as a sharp contrast to all the black. Alpha handed the newcomer the clipboard, saving the megaphone for himself. He keyed the microphone and launched a squeal of electronic feedback. Tyler couldn't tell if it was intentional, but it, for sure, got everyone's attention.

"Ladies and gentlemen, settle down and listen carefully. I know that you have many, many questions, but I am not in a position to answer any of them at this time. Those of you who survive your ordeal over the next forty-eight hours will be perfectly justified in contacting your travel agent and demanding a full refund."

The alphabet men laughed, but they were the only ones.

Alpha continued, "Consider yourselves to be our captives. Anyone who tries to escape will be shot." He paused for effect. "I assure those of you who have been separated from your children that they are being well taken care of." If those words were supposed to be soothing, they had the opposite effect. Murmurs rumbled through the assembled crowd.

"Pay attention!" Alpha shouted. "These are unsettling times, and during unsettling times, people are most apt to make terrible mistakes. As some of you have seen all too closely, terrible mistakes bear terrible consequences. The gift of being shot with a high-powered weapon is to die quickly. The curse is to die slowly. So listen very carefully."

In the silence of Alpha's next pause, the sounds of snuffling could not be masked. Tyler imagined that such was the point. These people were all terrified. Tyler was scared, too, but not to the level of the parents. He got that.

"If you are a parent and you try to escape, your children will be killed first—in your presence—and then you may or may not follow them into death."

"You're animals." The comment bloomed from the middle of the crowd, from an indeterminate source. The words ignited a rumble, and while Alpha seemed alerted, he did not seem to be angered.

"Animals, are we?" he said. "I won't ask who said that because I understand that you are all animals, too. An armadillo's response to danger is to roll into his shell. When threatened, a frightened chameleon changes color to become invisible. A frightened prisoner makes noise anonymously because—"

A man in his sixties arose from a group that was sitting on the concrete near the shallow end of the upper pool. Tyler recognized his face, but he hadn't met him. "That was me," the man said. "I'm sorry if you thought I was hiding, because—"

A gunshot thumped the night and the man's head erupted in a hideous spray. He dropped to the deck as if his central core had evaporated. An alphabet component who hadn't yet made his letter clear lowered his rifle from his shoulder. A sixtysomething woman— presumably the dead man's wife—pulled the man's head into her lap and howled a sound that was pure grief.

"Ask yourselves if that was a worthy sacrifice!" Alpha yelled. "A wife lost her husband, children lost their father, and grandchildren lost their legacy. All because of a proud man's need to look brave. Was that a worthwhile sacrifice?"

Alpha zoned in on the Turner couple, Zach and Becky. He was the one who'd left a leg in Afghanistan.

"You two," Alpha drilled. "You've suffered the penalties of war and patriotism. Was that man's sacrifice a noble one?"

Tyler watched as Zach's face turned red from the neck up. Becky's gentle touch on her husband's arm looked like a well-practiced move. Zach's shoulders relaxed a little.

"No," Becky said. "The sacrifice was not worth the penalty." She wiped a tear and blew a kiss to the sobbing woman. "I'm sorry."

"I want to hear from the cripple," Alpha said. "What say you, Mr. War Hero?"

Zach's jaw tightened under the skin of his slender face. Even in the dim, deflected glow of the swimming lights, the throbbing muscles in front of his ears stood out in high relief. He said nothing.

"I expect an answer, War Hero."

Becky cupped the line of his jaw with her hand. "Please," she said.

Zach gently pushed her hand away. "I'm not a war hero," he said.

"Excuse me?"

Zach started to stand, but Becky pulled him back down into his chair. "Think of the kids," she said. Tyler wasn't sure that he'd actually heard the words, but he easily read her lips.

"I said I'm no war hero," Zach repeated, this time loudly enough to be heard by everyone. "The heroes lost their whole souls over there. I'm just a guy who's missing a leg."

That didn't exactly jibe with what he'd told Tyler at the pool, but under the circumstances, who couldn't forgive being a little fast and loose with the facts?

"You haven't answered my question," Alpha pressed. "There's a dead man bleeding into the pool. His wife is covered in his blood. Was his a worthy sacrifice?"

The redness intensified in Zach's neck and cheeks. Becky clearly saw it and her posture telegraphed pure dread.

Zach stood, and weapons raised at every compass point. "I don't know who that murdered man was," he said, "but I know that he was killed for stating his mind."

"Please, Zach," Becky whined.

"Is stating an opinion ever worth summary execution?" Zach continued. "I would say, probably not." He eyeballed the potential shooters one at a time. "Certainly, that is not a line that I would dare to cross." He returned his glare to Alpha. "Is that enough?"

Tyler watched the assembled riflemen. They deeply wanted to shoot somebody.

Alpha smiled, but it was all mouth and cheeks. His eyes remained dead. "Your answer will keep you alive for tonight," he said. "For now."

The threat melted Becky, but seemed to bounce off Zach. Maybe it was absorbed by him. "I'll take whatever mercies come my way," he said, and he sat back down.

Anatoly Petrovich Ivanov thought there'd been far too much shooting this evening. Mercenaries the world over enjoyed violence far too much, and their thirst for it closed their minds to peaceful alternatives. He had seen it in career soldiers, as well, but that was back in the day when rank meant something, where disobedience was met with due process and prescribed punishment. Here, with this crew, his status as the leader was subject to the willingness of his men to grant him the title.

Tonight, and for the next two, maybe three days, he and his team of twenty-eight fighting specialists were no longer Russian. In fact, they had no citizenship at all. Moscow wanted it that way, so that if things did not go according to plan, his government could deny any knowledge of the operation. Unlike the clownish

politicians of the United States, Russian politicians
were very good at keeping secrets. In part because of
honor, but also because, again unlike the Americans,
betrayal carried real consequences.

The assault plan required swift, intense violence,
but he had hoped for a loss of fewer lives among the
hostages. With one or two, you got everyone's attention and focused fear, but with too many, you instilled
a sense of hopelessness—of inevitable death—that
might encourage rebellion. And while people were
sheep, even sheep will turn violent if they are pushed
too far. Though Anatoly's team numbered twenty-eight
and they were armed, the hostages numbered as many
as two hundred. If they found a strong leader who
could motivate them, twenty-eight wouldn't be nearly
enough. That's why Anatoly ordered the children to be
sequestered from their parents. Nothing weakened
even the toughest man quite like his love for his children.

As the prisoners settled into place—he couldn't
bring himself to think of them as hostages—Anatoly
watched over Stepan Vasechkin's shoulder as the other
man sifted through stolen wallets in search of identification papers. One never knew who might be a guest
of Baker Sinise. He owed it to his team and to Moscow
to take a full accounting.

"This will take time," Stepan said. Until this was
over, his name was Lima.

"Something that I believe we have plenty of," Anatoly replied. Only English would be spoken during
their time at Crystal Sands, and most of them exhibited
acceptable British pronunciation.

The radios near him all broke squelch. "Alpha, this is India," a voice said. Anatoly knew India to be Gerasim Arturovich Kuznetsov, one of the few operators on this mission with whom Anatoly had served while in the Russian Army. He knew Gerasim to be a good soldier and a loyal comrade.

Anatoly leaned his jaw into the microphone at his shoulder. "This is Alpha."

"Alpha, be advised that the prime package is not here."

Anatoly's stomach flipped. He met Stepan's gaze and asked off the air, "Did he just say—"

"That the prime package is not here, yeah," Stepan said.

Into the microphone: "Where is he?"

Hesitation. "Um, can you come up to his quarters?" India said. "Third floor of the main building."

"Is it urgent?" he asked.

A pause. "I suppose not urgent, but it's important."

"I copy," Anatoly said. "I'll be up when I can."

CHAPTER 4

Tyler couldn't hear the words that Alpha and the other man were speaking at the bar, but there was no missing the fact that something was wrong. He could see it in the faces of the other captors, as well, all of whom heard the same radio communication. Lots of silent glances and subtle shrugs.

Alpha brought the megaphone back to his lips and keyed the microphone, triggering another squeal of feedback. "Damn it," he said.

That answered the question whether the feedback was done on purpose.

"I want you all to listen carefully," Alpha said. "As I call your name, I want you to move into the restaurant area to my left." It was the least formal of the seven restaurants on the property—more about burgers and fish sandwiches than haute cuisine. It was currently occupied by three soldiers, who projected pure menace.

In the far reaches of the assembled crowd, a profoundly pregnant young woman stood and aggressively waved her hand for attention.

The nearest handlers swarmed toward her, but

Alpha intervened. "Stop!" he commanded. "What do you want?"

"I'm Barbie Burris," the lady said. "I really, *really* need to use the bathroom."

The resulting chuckle from the crowd—including Annie—surprised Tyler.

Alpha, likewise, seemed amused. He looked to Delta, who referred to the printout.

"Is your husband, Michael, there with you?" Alpha asked.

A man who was perhaps the skinniest adult Tyler had ever seen stood and raised his hand. Perhaps he was sick, but the guy was shirtless, and in this light, every rib cast its own shadow.

"Very well," Alpha said. He gestured to the area in shadow behind where Tyler and Annie were seated. "The bathrooms are right there. Michael, you go to the restaurant." Alpha cocked the bell of the megaphone up, indicating that he was now speaking to the entire crowd. "As I call your names, if you need to use the facilities, you are free to do so, but only one half of a couple at a time. You will have five minutes. Do not make us come looking for you. That will not be good for the partner left behind."

This is how Stockholm syndrome works, Tyler thought. Some asshole gives you permission to do something that you have no choice but to do, and you end up feeling gratitude. They didn't threaten the individual, but rather they leveraged the concern over loved ones. Compliance driven by guilt. He was going to have to run that by his psychology professor when he got back to school. *If.*

Alpha began with the *A*'s—Rob and Sarah Anderson—and proceeded to carve his way through the alphabet. It took a few iterations for the crowd to learn the choreography, but soon the pattern became clear. When a name was called, the couple would stand, and Delta would check what he saw against the photo IDs that they'd collected. It was not a fast process, and emotions were raw. Many moved as though they were walking to their execution. For all Tyler knew, that was exactly what they were doing.

"They skipped me," Annie whispered. "I'm Banks, and they just called Dufresne."

Tyler beckoned for Annie to join him on his chair.

Annie shook her head. "Somebody will take this one."

Tyler set his jaw and tried to flash anger with his eyes. "Please," he said.

She clearly didn't like it, but she complied with his request. "I guess we're going to have to move soon, anyway," she said.

"No, we won't," Tyler whispered. "We've got to get out of here."

Annie's jaw dropped and her eyes grew wide. "But you heard what they said."

"I did, but—"

"They'll *shoot* us."

Tyler squeezed her thigh, perhaps a little too hard. She slapped his hand away.

"Please keep your voice down," he whispered. For his plan to work—hell for *any* plan to work—he needed not to draw attention to himself or to Annie. You can't be invisible when you're making a lot of noise. "They don't have our names," he said. "Don't you see? I'm never on the guest list, and you're not even here. They can take roll all night and our names will never come up. They'll get to the end, and we're the only ones who will be sitting out here."

"That doesn't mean they'll shoot us, like they would if we ran."

"If they *caught* us running," Tyler corrected. "Remember, I'm the owner's stepson. These guys are here for a reason, and if they—" He gasped as the truth dawned on him. "Baker's not even here this weekend." He didn't have a clue what these guys wanted, or why they invaded the Crystal Sands, but it had to be something bigger than mere robbery. "Annie, I *need* to get out of here."

Annie did not seem pleased. "How?"

"I think I know a way. I know some places that these guys probably don't know about. At least not yet. You need to trust me and follow me."

"Tyler, I like you and everything, but I'm not going to get shot for you."

"You'd rather get shot for them?" That came out wrong, but he couldn't understand why she would resist a chance to get away. Would she rather be a victim?

"If you do what they say, they won't hurt you."

"I can't," he said. "I've got to get out of here before they find out who I am. You can come or you can stay, but I have to go."

Annie looked hurt. "You'd leave me?"

Tyler cast a glance at Alpha and Delta, the two soldiers closest to him. They seemed thoroughly absorbed in their paperwork and in watching the couples wander from poolside to the restaurant. His window of opportunity was closing.

Annie pulled on his sleeve. "You can't leave me here alone." Her comment drew a concerned look from a heavyset older woman, who was sitting on the deck near them.

Tyler fired a glare at Annie, then backed it down. It made zero sense to turn this into an argument. "Please keep your voice down," he whispered so softly that it was barely audible. "I know a way. Please come with me."

When Alpha called Hartwig—or something like that—the offended older woman raised her hand, and then struggled to rise to her bare feet and swollen ankles. Tyler got up from his seat to assist. "Here, ma'am, let me help."

He grasped her hand in a powerful thumb grip, and cupping her dimpled elbow with his other hand, he leveraged her to her feet. Ms. Hartwig leaned in as if to kiss Tyler's cheek and whispered, "Don't let a whiny girl get you killed. If you go, run for all of us. I'll give you the distraction you need." She ended it with a real kiss and turned to her captors. "I'm coming," she said. "Just takes me a little longer. . . ."

Did she say "distraction"? Tyler thought. What did that mean? And how did she know that—

Ms. Hartwig was winding her way through the others in her way when her knees wobbled and she toppled sideways into a crowd of others. They tried to catch her, but there was a lot to catch. As she fell, several of the other guests lost their balance. Two of them splashed into the pool.

In that instant, Tyler saw that every eye in the complex was staring at the older woman. This was his chance. This was her favor to him. He turned to Annie, who was also staring at the spectacle at the water's edge. "Annie!" he whisper-shouted.

She either didn't hear him or she chose to ignore him.

Either way, this was it. This was the unique moment when this would happen or it wouldn't. "Bye, Annie," he said.

Bending low at the waist, he scurried behind the backs of two of the guests and made his way to the waist-high locked gate that closed the pool's utility area off from the places where guests were allowed to go. He fought the urge to look behind him as he rolled his body across the top of the squatty fence and into the near-absolute darkness of the other side. A flight of six concrete steps was there, leading to a short subterranean sidewalk, which, in turn, led to a heavy steel door that was always locked.

Unless you knew where the key was hidden.

Tyler came down here frequently to smoke weed and hang with his buddy Jaime Bonilla. In fact, it was hard to think of a patch of real estate at the Crystal Sands where he *hadn't* smoked weed with somebody. Jaime was a leadman for the maintenance crew, and consequently was a keeper of all the keys. To facilitate those times when Tyler wanted to toke alone, Jaime'd had an extra key made, which he stored under a loose bit of concrete that rested under a triangular box of rat poison. Call it a poor man's security system.

Tyler had never done this by feel before, but he was counting on muscle memory to pull him through. Facing the door, he used the flat of his left hand to follow the contour of the steel door from left to right until his fingertips found the vertical seam where it met the hinge side of the jamb. That put him close to the inside corner where the walls met.

To his left and eight feet above his head, the decorative hedges and planters did nothing to mask the sounds of the continuing roll call. The commotion of Ms. Hartwig's fall had died down, but the fact that another one had not blossomed in its place told him that no one had noticed that he was missing.

Yet.

After he'd acquired both walls, he converged his hands into the corner and traced the seam straight down to the ground, where he found the container of rat poison, right where it was supposed to be.

He cringed as his fingers sifted through what could only be rat shit. He hated rats. And mice. And pretty much every other critter that didn't bark and wag its tail. As he lifted the box to get the key, his mind conjured images of rat turds being driven under his fingernails. He didn't realize that his hands were shaking until he heard them rattle against the hard plastic of the trap.

Keep it together, he told himself. If he could get through this door, he'd have a chance at getting away. If he couldn't get through . . . He *had* to get through.

He used both hands to lift the box and move it off to the side. As he did, something poured out of the holes in its side, launching a stench that made him gag, a combination of stale shit and dead things.

Jesus, when this was over, he was going to scrub his skin till he saw blood.

He pried up the chip of concrete and found the key just where it was supposed to be. His fingers fumbled it and it dropped with a *tink,* which sounded like a striking bell.

"Shit!" The word was out before he could stop it. For the first time, he dared a look back toward the top of the stairs. A guy in his thirties stood there, just on the other side of the gate, his face folded into a scowl. Tyler couldn't tell if the guy had seen him, or if he was just staring out into space.

Please don't say anything, he prayed. *And if you haven't seen me yet, move the hell out of the way.*

That thought did it. The man at the top of the stairs heard his name and he raised his hand. "Here," he said, and he pointed toward the restrooms. "I need to go," he said. Apparently, he got approval because he thanked somebody and turned his back on Tyler to head off to pee.

This time when Tyler got his fingers on the key, he held on tight. Using his left thumb to index the slot, he used his right hand to slide the key into place. It was always tricky to get this lock to turn. You had to jiggle things, but less tonight than on other nights, thank God. The knob turned and he pulled. He winced as he anticipated the metal-on-metal scraping sound that always accompanied this part.

It couldn't have been as loud as it sounded to him—otherwise, people would be shooting by now. He opened the door only exactly as much as he needed to slip through, and then pulled it closed behind him. Somehow, the scraping sound was less terrifying when he had a steel panel between him and the people with the guns.

With the door closed, he spun the button on the lock. And he found himself in total darkness.

CHAPTER 5

"So, what do we think the 'prime package' is?" Hunter Edwards asked as they navigated their way through the undergrowth in the dark. Jonathan and Gail had both kept their radios on, and that was the first bit of chatter that had come through.

Gail shifted her shoulder so that Jonathan could reach the radio, which was strapped to her vest behind her left shoulder. "Turn mine off," she said. "We might want these later, and it doesn't make sense to drain both batteries."

Jonathan's fingers found the correct button in the dark and twisted it to the OFF position. "Good idea," he said.

Lori said, "What does 'prime package' even mean?"

"Whatever they determine it to mean," Hunter said. He walked behind Jonathan, and Lori behind Gail. "Say, Digger, you never did elaborate on where you got those knife skills."

Jonathan ignored him. The use of real names was a big problem, and a rookie error on his part. His head had been in survival mode, he figured, not tactical mode. Having spent decades of his life training and living the role of the wolf, he'd let his guard down and transformed himself into a sheep. That moment was past, but the damage was done. And dickless back there kept using the slipup as a prod. How could Hunter think that was a good idea?

"What do you two do for a living?" Gail asked. Jonathan took it as her effort to change the subject and take him out of a homicidal frame of mind.

"I'm an investment banker," Hunter said. "We specialize in tech companies. The last deal we did was for seven hundred million dollars."

Such words did little to make Jonathan feel closer to the man. Bankers in general—and investment bankers in particular—ranked right up there with politicians and lawyers on his list of oxygen-wasters.

"Are you a banker, too?" Gail asked.

"Oh, no," Lori said. "I'm not that smart. I just run an art gallery in Phoenix."

"But she represents some really good up-and-coming artists," Hunter said. "Putting that community college associate's in art to good work."

"Tell me the truth, Hunter," Jonathan said without turning to make eye contact. "Do people often accuse you of being a dickhead?"

He stopped and turned.

"Because I've got to tell you, you have climbed up on my wrong side and taken residence there. I have no idea what lies ahead for us in the next hours or days, but we've got to find a way to make peace or go our separate ways."

Hunter's silhouette puffed up in the darkness. "You want to tell me what I've done to turn you into such an asshole?"

"Try showing a little respect," Jonathan replied. "We are, after all, saving your lives."

"Oh, is that what you're doing?" Hunter puffed up even bigger and took a half step closer. "So far, all I've seen you do is *take* lives." He looked like he might throw a punch. How entertaining would *that* be?

"Not here," Gail said. "And certainly not now. There's too much to do."

"Like what?" Hunter pressed. "We're walking through the dark after killing people whose friends are going to be *very* pissed off when they find out. What are we going to do? Hide?"

"Not a bad start," Jonathan said.

"Pretty goddamn cowardly for a guy with two guns," Hunter said.

Jonathan felt his control slipping. The *C*-word wasn't often slung at him, and it pulled the pin on his rage grenade.

"Definitely not the time or place," Gail repeated. To Hunter, she said, "Believe me when I say that. If you and Lori want to head off on your own, you're welcome to do that. But this bullshit dick-knocking has to stop. Now."

Jonathan's head whipped around to Gail. *Did you just include me in that dick-knocking comment?*

Yes.

They'd known each other long enough that they really could communicate without words. Even in the dark.

The radio broke squelch on Jonathan's shoulder, and

a panicked voice said, "Break, break, break, we have an emergency."

With a singsong tone, Jonathan said, "I bet I know what this is. . . ."

"Who *is* this?" a voice said. "And remember radio protocol."

"This is India, in Sector Eight. Hotel and Foxtrot are both dead. Their killers are missing. Bungalows Nine and Ten."

"That's us," Hunter said.

He's fast on his feet, that one, Jonathan didn't say.

"Are you sure they are missing?" the other voice asked. "Have you checked for bodies?"

"Alpha, you don't understand," Delta said. "Hotel and Foxtrot were killed by an expert. With a knife."

After a long pause, Alpha said, "Return to the Plantation House. Bring our men's equipment and weapons with you."

"That's a problem," Delta said. "Their equipment and weapons are all missing."

Tyler's friend Jaime Bonilla was nothing if not organized. Sometimes annoyingly so. But now, as Tyler fumbled through the darkness, he sent up a prayer of thanks to Jaime for being such an OCD pain in the ass. He moved in the dark with confidence that the center aisle would be clear. He knew without a doubt that the heavy black flashlight that Jaime used to illuminate his work would be right where it belonged, in its charger, mounted to the first rank of metal shelves on the right. And it was.

Tyler lifted the light out of its keeper, placed his palm over the lens, and pressed the switch. He didn't want a lot of light, but he wanted enough to be able to see what he was doing. At this point, he'd reached the end of his initial plan, which was simply to get out of the terrorists' view. He wanted to buy some time and some anonymity, but both of those would run out soon. How long could it possibly take before they realized that they had two more sets of identification than they had people signed into the hotel?

And how much hope should he hold out that Annie would keep his secrets? Especially after he'd dumped her. But hey, it's not like he didn't offer to bring her along. Still, he felt like a shit for leaving her.

Past was past. Now that he'd given the crazy guys with guns a reason to execute him on sight, he needed to focus on the business of staying *out* of sight.

He needed to put distance between himself and the attackers—and the sooner, the better. There was a section of old houses—shacks, really—on the back side of the island that the construction workers used while they were building the resort. He doubted that tonight's assholes would know anything about them. It wasn't like Baker Sinise put the shantytown in the brochures that sold accommodations for a gajillion bucks a night.

The original roads from the shantytown to the resort had mostly been converted to hiking trails. These now veered away from the old housing to take exploration-minded visitors through the rain forest to the bamboo forest, and finally to the gem in the Crystal Sands' crown: the ninety-foot waterfall. This was reached through a backdrop of spectacular flowers whose names

SCORPION STRIKE   49

Tyler could not have guessed on a multiple-choice quiz.

As he visualized the overgrown roadway in his mind, his gaze shifted to the other end of the maintenance room. He could almost see the Peg-Board to the right of the door, where he knew he would find the keys to every one of the golf carts—the bell staff called them "tycoon taxis." The carts conducted guests from the check-in desk to their rooms, and later to just about anywhere they wanted to go on the property. Two of them would be parked under the porte cochere in front of the Plantation House, but the other six or eight would be pulled into the squatty pole barn that was hidden from curious eyes. The keys were kept locked up because kids came to the island with their parents, and kids were born with the ability to sniff out joyrides that never ended well for the equipment involved.

Keeping his fingers across the flashlight's lens, he made his way to the door and scooped all of the keys from the board and into the front pocket of his khakis. You never knew which cart would be parked in front and which would be blocked in. Plus, why make it easy for the terrorists to get around?

Jaime had installed a heavy-duty dead bolt on the back door because it was so secluded from view, and he worried about vandalism. Tyler couldn't remember seeing Jaime use the door even once. Well, there's a first time for everything.

The bolt slid smoothly from its keeper, and the knob turned easily. Tyler pulled on the knob while pushing with his shoulder to keep the door from bursting open or squealing on rusty hinges. He sent up a silent prayer of thanks when the heavy steel panel pushed open with only the faintest whisper of a scraping sound.

He killed the flashlight as soon as the door was open, and peeked out with one eye through the tiniest crack he could manage. The wash of the pool lights provided enough illumination for him to see where he was going, which meant that there was enough illumination for others to see him going there.

He widened the opening just an inch or two at a time and scanned the full range of his vision over and over again. He could hear the movements and muffled conversations of the prisoners and their captors, but saw no faces. Back here, he was easily ten feet below the level of the pool deck, making the shield of the shrubbery even more effective. When he finally stepped clear of the doorway and still saw no one, he decided that his greatest enemy now was noise. He watched the placement of his feet as he moved down the sidewalk toward the pole barn with the tycoon taxis.

To his left, the pool filter equipment kicked on and damn near made him scream. With the cover of extra noise, he picked up his pace. He figured the farther he got from the assholes, the less critical was the need to be quiet.

Of course, that presumed that all the bad guys were clustered at the pool. For all he knew, the island was crawling with them.

Don't get cocky, dumbshit.

The sidewalk behind the pool dropped even lower down the hill. Immediately before the gate in the hedges, which would lead him back out to the common area of the resort, he took a sharp right into the blackness of the palm tree archway that ultimately led him to the pole barn. He wondered if the guests had any idea of how much effort and money it took to give the impression of a natural habitat. These were details on which Baker would make no compromise.

Again using his fingers to filter the light, Tyler dared quick flashes so he could see enough to navigate, and finally, there they were. The tycoon taxis reminded Tyler of World War II photos he'd seen of planes lined up on the deck of an aircraft carrier. They sat nose-to-tail in two perfect columns, each plugged into a charging station on the adjacent wall. The first cart in the closest column sported an inconspicuous *12* on its nose. Tyler dared a full blast of illumination from the flashlight as he hunkered down on the concrete floor between Cart 12 and its neighbor. He pulled the bundle of keys out of his pocket and sorted through them till he found the one with the corresponding number. He separated that one out, snuffed his light, then tossed the rest of the keys back into the darkness.

Tyler stood, slid behind the wheel, and slid the key into the ignition. The electric cart started silently, thank God. He reached down to the front of the seat, rocked the transmission lever into the forward position, and eased his foot onto the accelerator. The brake kicked out automatically, and he was on his way.

The tycoon taxis all came equipped with headlights, but Tyler didn't dare use them. Instead, he did the flashlight finger trick again until he was free of the overhanging foliage and into the open night. There, the cart path was illuminated by dim overhead floodlights that were hidden in the trees, so camouflaged that they were truly invisible during the day, and barely provided navigable light after dark. The point of the lights, Baker had explained, was to provide safe walkways, not safe streets.

"Do I go fast or do I go slow?" he asked himself aloud. The instant he heard it, he realized that there was only one reasonable answer. While moving quickly might attract more attention and increase the risk of a wreck, going slowly increased the time that he'd be in some asshole's gun sights.

Fast, it would be.

Anatoly Petrovich Ivanov climbed the stairs of the main house's magnificent sweeping staircase two risers at a time. The fine hardwoods and the grass paper wall-coverings were lost on him, as were the fine details of the cut crystal sconces and the bauble-coated crystal chandelier. Baker Sinise was a rich guy who catered to clients with rich tastes. Yeah, he got that, but none of the opulent flourishes contributed to Anatoly's mission, so they were all irrelevant. He didn't care about protecting the objects and the art, but he had no interest in destroying them, either. His mission was a simple one: to leverage Baker Sinise to perform the task that only he could perform.

It was a mission that would be rendered vastly more complicated if what India had told him was, in fact, the truth: Sinise was not here. How could that happen? How could their intelligence have been so wrong?

The stairway to the third floor of the Plantation House—to Sinise's living quarters—lay hidden from casual view behind a door that appeared to be a wall panel that was no different than all the other walnut paneling that adorned the Plantation House. It was already ajar, no doubt because members of his team had neglected to close it behind them. And what would have been the point?

These stairs were steeper, but only slightly narrower than those of the grand staircase, probably to allow for the passage of furniture and such. As he neared the top of the steps, he could hear the voices of his team churning through the events of the evening. The fact that they were speaking in Russian piqued his anger. Why did mercenaries have such a difficult time following the simplest of rules?

"English!" Anatoly yelled before he'd emerged from the stairwell. "For God's sake, how many times do I have to tell you?"

As Anatoly crossed the threshold into Baker Sinise's private quarters, he didn't even try to hide his admiration. If it was possible to be even more over-the-top opulent than the public spaces, then he'd managed to achieve it. Every polished surface gleamed, and every square inch of fabric-covered surfaces was spotless. "My goodness," he said. "It seems there is a lot of money to be made in the weapons trade."

"Tolya," said Gerasim Kuznetsov. "You need to see this." He stood next to Viktor Smirnov, who somehow had beaten Anatoly up to the third floor after discovering the bodies of their comrades. Together, they had gathered around a teak dining table that could easily have seated ten people comfortably, fourteen if they touched elbows.

"Damn it, India," Anatoly snapped at Kuznetsov.

"English and no names. These commands are not complicated."

"I'm sorry," India said. "You're right, I should have known better."

For his part, Viktor Smirnov—Delta—stood silently, apparently hoping to project an air of superiority. He held a smartphone in both hands, and from posture alone, Anatoly knew that they had been looking at pictures.

"Let me see," Anatoly said as he approached them. He held out his hand and wiggled his fingers for Delta to hand over the phone.

The other man hesitated, but ultimately complied. "Notice the skill of these wounds," he said.

Anatoly had probably seen more dead men in real life than he had in pictures, so he felt no emotional reaction as he took in the images of his dead operators. They lay on what appeared to be a bathroom floor, surrounded by halos of uncoagulated blood that had spilled from their gaping knife wounds.

"It appears that they were murdered as they entered through the back door of the bungalow," Viktor explained. Younger than most of the other operators, and therefore less experienced, he appeared somewhat shaken. "There was some blood spray on the drapes and walls of the bedroom, near the veranda doors, but the final slaughter took place out on the veranda itself."

"So, they dragged the bodies inside?" Anatoly said. He thought it was an obvious conclusion, but it was always best to be sure of these things.

"And stripped them of all their equipment and weapons," Viktor reminded. "These are not the actions or skills of your standard tourists."

Anatoly turned to Gerasim. "What do we know about these tourists, India?"

Gerasim Arturovich lifted the pad that normally resided in his shirt pocket and read from handwritten notes. "This comes from the registration sheet. They are Stephen Terrell and Alicia Crosby, unmarried. They are from Norman, Oklahoma, and have no food allergies."

Anatoly cocked his head. "Why do I care about food allergies?"

Gerasim smiled, acknowledgment that they had known each other a very long time. "You asked what we know about them. I just told you everything."

"Are there photos?"

"None that I have seen. And, of course, there is no photographic security to monitor."

"Why 'of course'?" Viktor asked.

Anatoly explained, "Baker Sinise touts the lack of cameras in his marketing materials as a way to lure celebrities and others who want to rest assured that their private moments are, in fact, private."

"No accidental paparazzi," Viktor translated.

"Exactly." Viktor had no need to know the deeper details of their mission yet, so Anatoly decided not to explain to him how given Baker Sinise's other business, the last thing the old man wanted was photographic evidence.

"Do what you can to find out who Mr. Terrell and Ms. Crosby are. I'd like their photographs at the very least. And something about their backgrounds. Let's find out how a couple from Norman, Oklahoma, become talented knife slingers. I give that to you, Vik—" He blushed. "I mean, Delta."

"We need to go out and find them," Viktor said. "Punish them."

"Not at night," Anatoly said. "We have too much else to do."

"But they killed—"

"They will pay for the killing," Anatoly snapped. "I promise you that. But first we need to get the prisoners secured. As long as they are gathered out in the open, it's too easy for them to wander off. I'm sure that we've lost a few already. Once the bulk of them are secured, we'll have the manpower to go searching. But not until daylight. It's not as though they can go far. This is an island, after all."

"How long until they are ready to segregate the prisoners?" Gerasim asked. He hadn't been down at the pool deck for quite some time.

"Within the hour," Anatoly replied.

"That's going to be a risky time," Viktor said. "It only takes one or two to panic, and we'll have a revolt. We'll have to shoot half of them."

"It's always a possibility," Anatoly said. "Surely, we have proven by now that we mean what we say, and that the price of disobedience is very high. I guess we will soon see."

"The chances of panic would drop significantly if we kept families together," Gerasim said. "You know that I've never believed in that part of the plan. Husbands and wives should remain together."

"This is the third time you've mentioned it since last night," Anatoly said. "Your objections are noted." He turned to Viktor. "You owe me information on Mr. Terrell and Ms. Crosby."

Anatoly turned back to Gerasim as Viktor left the room. "How did we miss that Sinise would not be here?"

Gerasim shook his head gravely. "I have no idea." Then he smiled and picked up another piece of paper from the table. "But we know where he is."

CHAPTER 6

"Wait. Stop," Jonathan said. he raised his hand to bring them to a halt. The moonlight lit their trek well enough to keep them from running into trees or falling off a cliff. "Is that a motor?" They'd been following a rough trail, and since their first steps on it, he'd been worried about encountering vehicles.

The others stopped. "Is what a motor?" Hunter asked.

"Shh." In the distance, beyond their field of view, Jonathan could make out the whine of an electric motor.

"I know that sound," Gail whispered. "It sounds like a golf cart."

"One of those golf cart taxis they used to take us to our room on the first day." It was nice to hear Lori speaking for the Edwards family now.

"They're coming to get us," Hunter said. He headed for the jungle to the left. "We need to get out of sight."

"Okay, Gunslinger, what say you?" Jonathan used the alias that Gail had disliked for years, but couldn't shake because it was such an apt description of her talents.

"I think it might be nice to have wheels," she said.

"See?" Jonathan said, flashing a smile. "I knew this trip would bring us closer together."

The sound of the motor was getting closer. From around the curve, a brief flash of white light illuminated the path, and then went out. Whoever the driver was, he didn't want to use his headlights.

"How do you want to do this?" Gail asked.

"We'll flank the road and hit him with white light as soon as we see him. Frankly, I think it's one of us—an escaping good guy."

"If you're wrong?"

"We'll have a shoot-out."

This was one of very few times that Jonathan had performed anything close to a hot operation without his lethal friend and fellow operator, Brian Van de Muelebroecke, aka Boxers. He would have liked the shoot-out line. As it was, Gail just took her place on the opposite side of the path without saying anything.

There was nothing special about the SureFire light clamped to the muzzle of his M4—just a white light with about a bajillion lumens. To get nailed in the eyes with bright white—

The cart turned the corner into view.

Jonathan brought his M4 to his shoulder and his thumb found the rubber button on the back end of the light. Both his and Gail's lights erupted at the same time, and night became day times two. In the initial two seconds, Jonathan noticed two things. One, the driver wasn't armed. Two, the driver was a kid. A teenager.

The driver let out a startled yelp and steered the golf cart into the ferns and bushes that lined the path. "Don't shoot!" he yelled. "Please don't shoot!"

Jonathan killed his light, and Gail redirected hers so it was no longer in the kid's eyes.

The driver hopped off the cart and started to run into the jungle when his feet tangled and he face-planted. "Please don't shoot. Please!"

"Hush!" Jonathan snapped. "We're good guys. We're escaping, too." He spoke more loudly than he wanted to, but he had to break through the kid's panic. He thought he actually recognized him. "Your name's Taylor, right?"

The kid rose to his feet, but he didn't approach. "Tyler," he said. "Stratton. Tyler Stratton."

"Your father works here, doesn't he?" Gail asked.

Tyler's head whipped around to Gail. Apparently, he hadn't realized she was standing there. "Works here? Yeah, sort of, I suppose."

"Owns the place, right?" Jonathan prompted.

Tyler cocked his head. "How did you know?"

"It's not like you keep it a secret," Jonathan said. "Is there any female between the ages of eighteen and thirty that you haven't hit on with that as your lead-in?"

A smile bloomed on the kid's face. "It works." He pointed at their weapons gear. "Where did those come from?"

"Their former owners," Jonathan said. "Where were you going in the cart?"

Tyler said nothing. He was gauging them.

"It's not a hard question," Jonathan said.

"Trust is hard to come by on a night like this," Gail said. "We understand."

Tyler still didn't want to answer.

"Where were you going in the cart, Tyler?" Jonathan pressed.

From behind: "I guess this means it's safe to come out?" Apparently, it had been too long since Hunter had heard the sound of his own voice.

Jonathan ignored the other man as he kept his eyes focused on Tyler.

"So, there are more of us?" Tyler said, noting the approach of the Edwardses. At least he said "us." Jonathan took that as a good sign.

"I imagine there will be a few more, too," Jonathan said. "People don't like to be caged."

"You don't understand," Tyler said. "They've separated kids from adults. If anyone tries to get away, not only will they shoot the one who's running, but they'll shoot the whole family."

"Oh, my God," Lori said.

Jonathan looked to Gail, who winced.

"That sounds like a bluff to me," Hunter said.

"And to me, it sounds like a damned clever strategy," Jonathan countered.

"We don't need a smart enemy," Gail said.

"Any clue what any of this is all about?" Jonathan asked Tyler.

"No. But if it has something to do with my stepfather, they're gonna be pretty pissed. He's not here."

Jonathan waited for the rest.

"He's over on the mainland. Some overnight business meeting that came up suddenly."

Jonathan's inner warning bell dinged. "What kind of business, and how suddenly?" As a rule, Jonathan didn't believe in coincidences. When said coincidences happened in concert with bad events, he presumed them to be intentional acts.

"I have no idea," Tyler said. "We don't talk about business very much. Actually, we don't talk about anything very much. We don't talk about business at all."

"You're the owner's kid!" Hunter exclaimed.

Welcome to the show, Jonathan didn't say.

"How did you get away?" Gail asked.

"I slipped out when they weren't looking," Tyler said. "I know stuff that regular guests don't know."

"Like how to slip out when people aren't looking," Jonathan said, drawing a smile.

"I figured that once they figured out who I was, and where my stepfather isn't, I'd wish I was somewhere else."

"Weren't you with a young lady?" Lori asked. Her voice was heavy with disdain.

"Annie," he said.

"But didn't I hear you say that if one part of a couple ran away—"

"The others would be killed, yeah."

Tyler's words sort of sucked the air out of the jungle for a second or two.

"Look," he said, "I'm not proud that I left, okay? I asked her to come with me. *Begged* her, but she wanted to stay."

Jonathan cleared his throat. He got where the kid was coming from, but he wondered how he was going to feel about the decision later if something bad happened to his girlfriend.

"And besides, it's not like we're an actual couple," Tyler pressed. "There's no record of her being here, either. And even if they connect us, my last name is different than my stepfather's. So, even if they puzzle out who I am, what are the chances they'll figure out my relationship with her?"

"All it would take is for one of the other hostages to want a favor at her expense," Hunter said.

"Moving along," Jonathan said. "What's done is done, and it's not our job to judge you or anyone else. Chances are, this whole thing will take care of itself quickly, and there'll be no more loss of life." That last part was total bullshit. In fact, Jonathan fully expected this to get much, much worse before it even began to turn the corner.

He changed the subject. "You were going to tell us where you were going."

When the kid talked about a shantytown, Jonathan had wondered if he knew what that meant. It was clear that he did. There were ten of them in all, constructed of tar paper and two-by-fours and arranged in parallel rows straddling the overgrown remains of what had once been a road. The structures had not aged well. Windows were mostly broken, and relentless water and humidity had inflicted brutal damage to the roofs and floors in particular.

"Are you sure it's safe to use a flashlight here?" Hunter asked. "Aren't we going to attract attention?"

"It's a big jungle," Jonathan said, "and we're on the other side of the mountain. There are no guarantees, but rest assured that if I thought it was a bad idea, I wouldn't do it."

"How long ago were these abandoned?" Gail asked.

"At least twelve, maybe fifteen years," Tyler said.

He pointed to the shack that was farthest down on the right. "That last one down there isn't in too bad shape. Me and a buddy sort of keep it up. We don't have glass for the windows, but there's that roll-up plastic stuff for the bad storms. We cover the windows when we're not here, and the roof is in pretty good shape."

Lori cleared her throat. "Are the outhouses . . ."

"They work, and we even have toilet paper," Tyler said, earning a smile from Lori. "But this is still the jungle. I wouldn't sit without checking first."

"Thanks for the safety tip," Gail said.

Jonathan held up his hand, a signal for all of them to stop. "Do you smell anything?" he asked Gail.

She sniffed the air. "Weed?"

"That's what I got." Jonathan thumbed the safety switch to FIRE and brought the M4 to his shoulder. "Y'all stay here," he said. Maybe the bright white light hadn't been a good idea, after all.

"Wait!" Tyler said, racing ahead. "Jaime, is that you?" he whisper-shouted.

"Who the hell is Jaime?" Hunter asked.

"Dude, if you're there hiding, step out. It's me. It's Ty."

"Hold where you are," Jonathan said. "I don't know who Jaime is, but if that's not—"

"It's him," Tyler insisted. "I know it is."

"Stop, goddammit!" Jonathan shouted. No whisper to it. "Jaime, if that's you and you're hiding, this is the only chance you will have to present yourself." He opened his muzzle light to its widest aperture and lit up nearly the whole structure.

From somewhere up ahead, a shaky voice said, "Don't shoot. Please don't shoot."

"We're getting that request a lot tonight," Jonathan said just loudly enough for Gail to hear.

Tyler turned to face Jonathan and waved both his hands. "That's his voice," he said. "That's Jaime Bonilla. He's the maintenance guy here." Then he turned and hurried to the door of the tar paper shanty and pulled it open.

A dark-skinned man dressed in flowered shorts and a wifebeater lunged from the opening and tackled Tyler to the ground.

Jonathan tracked them with his muzzle, but couldn't get a clear target through the tangle of flailing limbs.

"Jaime! Jaime!" Tyler yelled. "It's me. What are you doing?"

Jonathan let his rifle fall against its sling and he waded into the fight. It was really more of a schoolyard flail fest, the kind of struggle where both players were guaranteed to escape with only a few bruises. The kind of fight you saw among people who didn't know how to fight.

Jonathan found a shirt collar, closed his fist around it, and pulled. The fabric pulled then tore, but it held enough to peel Jaime out of the scrum and onto his feet. Barely older than Tyler, he weighed maybe 125 pounds, and he was still flailing. He spun to flail on Jonathan, but whatever he saw convinced him in an instant that throwing that punch would be a bad idea.

Jaime pulled away. "Who are you? What the hell is going on?"

"Settle down, son," Jonathan said. "We're in the same boat as you. No clue what's happening, and just trying to stay alive. Now, are you going to settle down, or are we going to have an issue?"

Jaime looked to Tyler. "Sorry, bro. I thought . . . oh, hell, I don't know what I thought. Did I hurt you?"

"No, I'm fine."

"What's going on down there?" Jaime asked. "I heard all this shooting, and then there was screaming. I mean, what the hell?"

"Terrorists." Tyler took the better part of a minute to catch his friend up.

As they chatted, Jonathan poked Gail's arm, and motioned for her to join him, away from the others. Together, they swept the structures in a search for bad guys, but neither was surprised that the shacks were empty.

"We can't win this fight," Gail said. "Not if it comes to shooting. Even if we got rifles for every one of them—"

"Yeah, I know," Jonathan agreed. "Whoever these terrorists are, they seem to have skills. That's concerning."

"Right," Gail said with a chuckle. "That's exactly the word I was going to use."

"You were able to snag our cell phones on the way out of the room, right?"

"They're in my backpack."

"Okay, it's time to wake some people up."

Gail unslung the backpack and was able to reach directly to the phones. "You calling Mother Hen?"

Jonathan took his phone and pushed the button to bring it to life. "Yup. We need reinforcements."

CHAPTER 7

Back when she was a teenager, Venice Alexander had decided in a pique of adolescent self-importance that her name was too boring. Her mother, now known to everyone in Fisherman's Cove simply as Mama, had been named Florence by her mother, Roma. When she had a daughter of her own, she insisted on perpetuating the generations-old tradition of humiliating children with names drawn from Italian tourist destinations. So, Venice decided to elevate her name with a more exotic pronunciation. From then on, her name was pronounced Ven-EE-chay. Everybody got it wrong on the first try, but that fact made for a great trap to filter out telemarketers.

The single mom of a thirteen-year-old boy—Roman, and yes, he hated his name, too—she'd been a part of Jonathan's life for as long as she could remember, back to the days when she was a little girl with a crush. She'd grown up in the mansion she now called home, on the grounds of what was now Resurrection House, a charitable home for the children of incarcerated parents. Back then, though, she lived in the basement with Mama, who was the full-time housekeeper for the Gravenow family, whose only child was the boy named Jonathan. Venice was never sure why Jonathan changed his name, but she suspected that it had much to do with the fact that his father was a notorious criminal.

Venice was thrilled that Jonathan and Gail had finally carved out time to be together. Their absence tripled the amount of work she had to balance at Security Solutions, but if it could bring happiness to Jonathan, and restore some of the confidence that had been beaten out of Gail in that terrible attack a while back, then the extra effort would be worth it.

Besides, it never hurt for the boss to feel as if he owed you a favor.

She'd had trouble sleeping tonight, and she couldn't determine why. The day hadn't been especially stressful, she'd had ample time to spend with Roman, and even the boy's adolescent angst seemed to be tamed for the moment.

It didn't help that JoeDog had chosen Venice's bed as her own this evening. The black Lab lay sprawled sideways, as she was wont to do, but Venice was something of a coffin sleeper and still had adequate room. She didn't even mind the dog's snoring, though the flatulence could be eye watering.

Because she'd been thinking so intently about Jonathan, it did not surprise her when her phone rang and it was him.

"It's awfully late there, isn't it?" she asked as she connected the call.

"The island has been invaded," Jonathan said.

Venice had been expecting a sharp retort, but she

didn't understand the humor in this one. "*Which* island is being invaded?"

"Ours. The Crystal Sands Resort."

"'Is being invaded.'" Saying it again did not make it more sensible. "What does that mean?"

"It means that a whole bunch of bad guys have invaded the resort and taken hostages."

Venice sat up in bed, causing JoeDog to open an eye and then close it again. "You're serious, aren't you?"

"As a heart attack."

Her head raced nearly as fast as her heart as she tried to make pieces fit. While she hadn't slept, she realized that she wasn't fully awake, either. "So, you and Gail are hostages?"

"Not in the active sense," Jonathan said. She could hear the irritation growing in his tone. He was tired of the warm-up conversation, and wanted to get to something meatier. "Some guys with guns came to our bungalow and tried to take us, but it didn't go well for them. We got away, but there's only so far to go when you're on a friggin' island."

"Well . . ." She had nothing. "Did you call the police?"

"It's an *island,* Mother Hen. And it's private. Shit, I don't even know what its nationality is. That's why I'm calling you."

His use of her code name told her that he was in the presence of others. "It's not just you and Gunslinger, is it?" Code name for code name.

"No, it's not. We picked up a few strays. Gunslinger and I have guns and we have access to the bad guys' coms, but these aren't your average terrorists. They appear to have training. And heart."

"Islamic?"

"Blond hair," Jonathan said. "Take from that what you wish. We got everything from the dead guys' pockets, but we haven't had a chance to go through it all yet. This whole incident isn't yet two hours old."

Venice felt the friction in her brain gears reduce. She was waking up, and a task list was beginning to take shape.

"Are you in a safe place?"

"For now, I think so, but they're gonna come searching for us. Certainly by daybreak, and it would be nice to have some kind of a plan by then. A shadow of a plan will do."

"I'll go to work on it," Venice said. As she rolled fully out of bed, JoeDog was wide-awake and looked uneasy. She seemed to know that her best friend was in trouble. "How do you want to stay in contact?"

"For now," Jonathan said, "wait for my calls. I don't know how long this will go on, and I don't know how much access we'll have to power. I'm going to keep the phones off when we're not talking."

Venice felt like she needed to say something encouraging, but she didn't know what that might be.

"I'm hanging up now," Jonathan said. "I know you won't let us down. You never do."

After the click, Venice stared at the phone until the dial tone returned, and for a while longer after she'd disconnected. Jonathan's voice carried a tone that she'd rarely heard in the past. He didn't sound scared, exactly, but something close to it. Rattled, maybe. He needed a plan. He needed resources.

He needed help. Quickly. At four in the morning.

She dressed quickly. No shower, no makeup. That

could all come later. She had to get to work. JoeDog, for her part, seemed delighted to have something to do, and walked circles around Venice's legs, threatening to trip her.

"Do you know this is about your friend Jonathan?" she asked. She'd heard that dogs had sixth senses about their masters, and it was rare to see this much agitation out of JoeDog.

Venice pulled on a sweater over her jeans and slipped her bare feet into a pair of black flats. It was an outfit that she'd never wear to the office, but that was exactly where she was going, and this was an emergency.

She opened her bedroom door onto the sitting area of the master suite, padded across the inlaid hardwoods and Persian rug, and opened the massive double doors into the expansive second-floor hallway. Every time she walked these halls, she couldn't shake a sense of guilt that this was where she and Mama had ended up, given where they'd started. But Jonathan wouldn't have it any other way. When he'd deeded the family manse to Saint Katherine's Catholic Church for a dollar, his one condition was that Mama and Venice would always have a home there, and that the structure would be used as the headquarters for Rez House.

Early on, the mansion was the entire school, from classrooms to dormitories. Over the years, it had expanded to separate classroom and dorm buildings, leaving the mansion primarily as an administrative building.

JoeDog led the way down the stairs and across the foyer, drawing the attention of Oscar Thompkins, the head of the nighttime security team. After some violence a while back, a permanent security presence had become a necessity. He had one counterpart patrolling the dormitory building and another patrolling the grounds.

"Evening, Ms. Alexander," Oscar said. "A little late for a stroll, ain't it?"

"Something came up," Venice replied, forcing a smile. "Gotta go into the office."

"Ain't you gonna take a jacket or nothin'? It's cold out there." A native of the Tennessee mountains, Oscar had a good heart and a drawl so thick it sounded fake.

"It's only a short walk," Venice said. She never broke stride as she beelined to the massive panels of the double doors. She was still crossing the porch when she made her first phone call.

A familiar but gravelly voice answered after four rings. "Um . . ." He cleared his throat. "Hello?"

"Good Morning, Father," Venice said. "Sorry to wake you, but this is important."

"Venice? What time is it?" Father Dom D'Angelo was one of Jonathan's closest friends, and had been since they'd been roommates all through college at William & Mary.

"A little after four, but this is an emergency. Digger is in trouble."

"I thought he's on vacation."

"Can you think of anyone more apt to find violence in paradise?" She cringed at the callous sound of her words. "I don't have time to explain now, but can you please place a call to Wolverine and arrange a meeting between her and me ASAP? Then, come to the office?" Wolverine was the moniker for Irene Rivers, director of the FBI, a longtime friend of the Security Solutions team.

"Of course. Does Boxers know?"

"He's my next call."

Dom gave a wry chuckle. "Better you than me," he said. "I'll be over as soon as I can." They hung up.

As Venice let JoeDog lead the way down the stairs from the lawn to the sidewalk, she realized that maybe she could have listened to Oscar. There was a definite bite in the air. She moved a little faster to keep warm during the three-block walk to the end of the street to the converted firehouse that doubled as Jonathan Grave's home and tripled as the headquarters for Security Solutions, the high-end private investigation firm he ran largely as a means to provide cover to the covert side of the company. It was that very covert side that commanded the bulk of Jonathan's time and attention.

Her ID card and six-digit PIN gained her access to the outside door to the office—a separate entrance from that which led to Jonathan's home. As she stepped inside and climbed the stairs to the third floor, she waved at the security cameras. When she came to the interior door to the bull pen—the overt office space where nearly a dozen investigators and support people worked every day—it buzzed and she pulled it open.

She turned left, and approached the interior door that led to the Cave.

"Good evening, Ms. Alexander," said the guard at this interior security point. "Or, good morning, I guess."

"Good morning," she replied. In no mood for small talk, she nonetheless could not bring herself to be rude. She felt bad enough that she couldn't remember the man's name. Typically, if she was working at this hour, it would be from the other side of the security door.

"Father D'Angelo and Mr. Van de Muelebroecke will be joining me soon."

She touched her card key to the pad and the guard opened the door for her.

Venice headed directly for the War Room, the rectangular teak conference room that housed every techie gadget that a girl could want. She settled into her seat at the end of the table opposite the massive projection screen. As the systems booted up, she lifted the landline receiver and dialed Boxers' number from memory.

"Mother Hen's on it," Jonathan said to Gail. "She's rallying the troops, so maybe we'll have some useful intel within a couple of hours."

"Who did you call?" Hunter asked.

Jonathan hadn't seen him coming, and the voice startled him. "It's a universally bad decision to sneak up on me."

"Noted. And nonresponsive. So, what, are you like military or something?"

"Something like that, yeah."

"Look, Digger—"

"Don't call me that," Jonathan snapped.

"What, then?"

Jonathan knew what would follow, but he answered, anyway. "Call me Scorpion."

"Bullshit."

Jonathan settled himself with a deep breath. "Please don't push me. Truth is, I'm in a line of work where real names are never used. In fact, they're liabilities. I'd consider it a personal favor if you would forget any other names you've heard."

"If they're such liabilities, why were you using them in the first place?"

"We didn't expect to be working on this trip," Gail said.

"So, do you have a super cool code name, too?"

She clammed up. Gail hated her handle.

"It's Gunslinger," Jonathan said.

Hunter recoiled. "Holy crap. That's a little on the nose, isn't it?"

"Don't cross her," Jonathan said. "Trust me. It's a handle well-earned." He chuckled when he said it.

"So, you do security work for the government," Hunter concluded.

"Just don't ask me to confirm or deny," Jonathan said. The guy clearly liked the conclusion he'd drawn for himself, so he let it go. Besides, it was more true than it was false.

"If you'll excuse us," Jonathan continued, "we need to do some work here."

"Go ahead," Hunter said.

Jonathan wanted privacy. He wanted to roll back the clock and avoid the Edwardses altogether, but he realized he had to resign himself to the fact that neither was more likely to happen than the other. And why not? Everybody was as deeply into whatever this was as everyone else.

"Hey, Jaime," Jonathan called.

The kid perked up. "Yes, sir?"

Jonathan beckoned him over. "Have a seat with us. Everybody can gather around if you want. Tell me everything you know about what you think might be happening here."

Jaime gave an exaggerated shrug. "I have no idea.

Like I said, I was up here when the shooting started. I don't even know—"

"What goes on here at the Crystal Sands that might attract the attention of terrorists?" Jonathan asked.

"Many rich people come here," Jaime said. "That's a lot of ransom taking, no?"

It was a possibility. Hell, at this point, *everything* was a possibility.

"Wait a minute," Jonathan said, snapping his fingers. He looked to Gail. "Whoever these guys are, they had to get here by boat, right?" He turned to Jaime. "There are no airstrips here, correct?"

Jaime nodded. "That is correct. Mr. Sinise does not like the sound of aircraft. Plus, he thinks that the long boat ride calms people."

"Maybe they came in on helicopters," Tyler suggested.

"No." Jaime was emphatic. "We never hear helicopters out here. If there'd been one, I would have known it. I hear everything."

"By boat, then," Jonathan said. "Given their numbers, it would have had to have been a big one."

"And it should still be parked at the dock, right?" Gail said.

"They've got to have an exfil plan," Jonathan said. Back to Jaime: "I'm turned around. Where do the ships come in?"

Jaime pointed to the jungle. "About a mile, mile and a quarter that way."

"Along this trail?"

"No. Well, for a while, but then this trail joins the main roadway. The one you came up on."

"I imagine they'll have left guards," Jonathan mused aloud.

"What are you thinking of doing?" Lori asked. The dread was heavy in her voice.

"We need to get an idea of what we're involved in," Gail said.

"It's dark," Hunter said. "I think that's too dangerous. Why don't we just hold out until daylight?"

"Because we're more detectable when we can be seen," Jonathan said. He delivered the line laden with irony, but it seemed to have missed its target. "Once the sun comes up, we'll need to go to ground. That's when the serious hiding starts."

"Do you think they're going to come looking for us?" Tyler asked.

"Most definitely," Jonathan replied. "I killed two of their men and they know we have guns."

"Then what will we do?" Lori asked.

"Hide until and unless they find us."

"And after that?" Jaime asked.

Jonathan thought the answer to be so obvious that he just let it hang unanswered. He checked his watch and said to Gail, "It's zero one-fifteen now. That gives us six hours to explore and gather whatever intel we can."

He turned to the others. "Tyler, we're taking your golf cart. Jaime, is it easy to navigate our way to the boat dock?"

"Just follow this old trail till you get to the roadblock. Drive around that and turn left. That road will take you all the way—"

"Wait," Hunter said. "You're going to just leave us here?"

"Sure, why not? It's out of the way and it looks reasonably safe. We'll be back before daylight."

"Then leave us with a gun."

"That's not happening," Gail said.

"Suppose they come for us?"

"Hide. And if they find you, hope they play nice with you. If you see a third option, I'd be happy to listen to it."

"We can go with you," Tyler suggested.

"No, you can't," Jonathan said. "I don't know what we're getting into. I don't know if there'll be guards, and I don't know if there'll be shooting. Gunslinger and I have done this stuff before. I don't want to have to worry about you if things go south."

"I promise I'll give you a full accounting when we get back," Gail said.

With that, they turned and headed to the big golf cart. Jonathan half expected to have to fight the others from climbing aboard, but was relieved when they decided to stay in place. Gail slid into the driver's seat and grinned up at him. "You can ride up front with me, if you want," she said, and she stuck out her tongue.

"Oh, so it's going to be *that* way, is it?" He walked to the shotgun seat and they took off.

The path was every bit as rough on the back half as it was on the first half. Jonathan hung on to the roof post to keep from getting bounced out.

"I'm not used to these kinds of bumps," he said. "Normally, Boxers drives, and his mass smooths it all out."

He got the laugh he was trolling for. Boxers was Jonathan's longtime friend and battle buddy from back in the days when they were both in the Army. Nearly seven feet tall and built like a tree, he was the most lethal human being Jonathan had ever known. As much as Big Guy had no place on a romantic retreat to an exotic island, it would have been great to have him on board now.

They drove with the headlights off, but there was enough ambient light to make out important things, like shifts in the road and obstructions. Holes were a little tougher to spot, explaining some of the bigger bumps.

Gail pointed ahead. "Think that's our roadblock?" The berm appeared as a horizontal black stripe across the path, maybe twenty-five yards ahead.

"It's clearly man-made," Jonathan said. He whispered very softly now, his words barely audible. "Stop here and kill the motor."

They sat in silence in the cacophony of jungle night sounds while Jonathan listened for anything out of the ordinary. Mechanical sounds, battle rattle, voices, anything.

"I think we're alone," Gail said.

"I think you're right. You know, we've never done it in a golf cart." He got the glare he expected. "I'm going to walk up to the berm and make sure things are clear."

"Find a route for me to get around that thing in this thing," Gail said.

"Yep." He slid out of his seat and walked down the path, using deliberate steps, heel-toe, heel-toe, in a fluid rotation that looked odd as hell to those whose survival had never depended on stealth.

The berm was taller than he thought it was going to be, every bit of eight feet. Because this was the goddamn jungle, where if you dropped a seed today you'd have a tree tomorrow, it was thick with vegetation. It was hard to make out detail on this side of the berm because of its moon shadow, but the darkness moved as the flora moved with the breeze. He considered climbing over to peer at his surroundings from the top, but opted to walk around the side, instead. He had to blaze a trail for the cart, anyway.

He followed the base of the berm around to the left. If Tyler and Jaime had passed this way in their carts, you couldn't tell from the foliage, at least not in the dark. But the plant life near the base was of the fern variety—as opposed to the tree variety, which was the total limit of Jonathan's spectrum of horticultural knowledge—so with a little momentum, the cart shouldn't have any trouble navigating around it.

Jonathan brought his rifle to his shoulder as he rounded the berm to the front side. Old habits died hard, and he'd never seen a downside to being ready to shoot, just in case. He moved slowly, as ever aware of his footfalls. Over the centuries, while human eyesight hadn't adapted its acuity to the dark, it had evolved to sense motion perhaps more readily in darkness than in light. He couldn't remember the last time he'd wandered at night with a rifle, yet without NVGs—night-vision goggles. Without that kind of force multiplier, he was just another guy with ammunition and a bang stick.

The far side of the berm—the front side—looked pretty much like the back, with more crumbling pavement at his feet.

He scanned continuously for targets as he advanced forward, but saw nothing but night. Finally, about twenty yards out, he found the fresh pavement of the main road. It intersected the old path at a right angle. He looked left and then right, but saw nothing worrisome. He closed his eyes and stood unmoving for the better part of a minute, letting his ears earn their keep. Nothing there, either. That was good.

He walked back and summoned Gail to come on through.

Twenty minutes later, the grade of the road shifted steeply downhill, and the darkness ahead brightened. "I remember this from the day we arrived," Gail said. "The docks are just down at the bottom on the right."

"Look at the way they've got the place lit up," Jonathan said. "They're clearly not worried about being spotted or getting caught."

"Caught doing what?"

"Well, that's the million-dollar question, isn't it? Can you find a spot to pull this off the road and behind some bushes? I want to approach on foot."

The perfect spot lay about thirty yards closer to the light, where a tree had fallen, but never quite made it to the ground because of interference from nearby foliage. The effect was to create a leafy cave that was just about the width and height of the cart. Gail pulled it in until it could go no farther, and they set off down the hill on foot.

They walked on the pavement as close as they could to the edge. If someone approached, they could jump out of sight. That assumed that their opposing forces continued to disregard light and noise discipline.

"Has there been much radio traffic about us?" Gail whispered.

"They know our names—well, the names we gave

them—and they're trying to find likenesses of us. They're not pleased to be missing rifles and ammunition."

"And tell me why, exactly, you think it's important to check out this boat."

"To gather intel," Jonathan said. He didn't know how to state it more clearly, because he didn't understand how it wasn't obvious. "As they say at Faber College, knowledge is good."

"You know there's only two of us. We can't possibly fight them all."

"I don't see that we have a choice. These people are terrorists. They've already killed. If we surrender, we're sure to die. If we fight, we've got a chance."

"Just remember that I'm not Big Guy."

Jonathan scowled at her. "Surely, that was not an apology," he said.

"No, just an observation. I'm not a 'fight first, ask questions later' kind of girl."

"Got it," Jonathan said. It was a quirk of Gail's personality that he could not understand. He got that she was a lawyer, and that she'd cut her teeth in law enforcement and not the military, but she had trouble adjusting to the significance of her skills and abilities in the world of door-kickers. They'd talked about this many times before.

If he had his way, they would not talk about it again tonight. They had way too much work to do.

CHAPTER 8

The invaders' boat, it turned out, was more properly classified a ship. Jonathan wasn't much of an expert on things that floated, but to his eye, this vessel looked like a retired minesweeper. He couldn't see the flag on the fantail from this angle, but under the circumstances, he wouldn't trust the declared registry, anyway. As far as he was concerned, they might as well be flying the Jolly Roger.

"Wow," Gail whispered. "That's a lot bigger than I thought it would be."

High at the bow and low at the stern, this vessel was capable of carrying significant cargo. "Me too," Jonathan agreed. "That thing is designed to float more than just troops."

"Like what, do you think?"

"Let's think about that. How many commodities are worth the expense of transporting a small army?"

"Drugs?" Gail guessed.

"It'd take a shit ton of drugs to fill the hold on that ship."

"Gold, then?"

"I vote weapons," Jonathan said.

Gail looked at him, clearly waiting for more. "Because high-end resorts are famous for attracting gunrunners?"

"I just can't think of any other terrorist-worthy cargo that would require that much boat."

A long silence followed in which Jonathan could feel Gail's glare. "You're staring at me," he said.

"Are we going to board that ship?" she asked.

"Can you think of a better way to gather intel?"

Gail sighed. "Unfortunately, no. Doing nothing really isn't a viable plan, is it?"

"Die hiding or win fighting," Jonathan said.

Gail knew better than to offer up the obvious third option—*die* fighting. First, it was head space where Jonathan was famously reticent to go. Second, there was no denying that dying while fighting was demonstrably better than dying while curled up in a ball, begging for your life.

"Have you ever taken down a ship before?" she asked.

"I've trained for it."

"Dare I ask how big the assault force was?"

"Are you sure you want to know?"

She waited.

"Twenty-three," he said with a chuckle. "But the scenarios were all about a vessel at sea with a full complement of bad guys. This ship is, like, parked."

"I believe the term is *moored*. Or maybe *berthed*."

Jonathan gave her a long look, and then reached out for her hand. "We joke about this, but it's serious shit. Are you really up for it?"

"Is there a choice?"

"Don't do that," Jonathan said. "I'm not in charge. I don't want to push you beyond—"

"Whoa, cowboy," Gail said, covering his hand with her own. "I wasn't being passive-aggressive. I really don't think we have a choice. 'Win fighting,' right?"

He covered her hand, too. Hands all in. "You know, this is not the trip I planned."

"Glad to hear that," she said. "Otherwise, there'd be some serious counseling in your future."

"This Scorpion guy," Hunter said. "You know that's not his real name, right? His real name is Digger. Who said he was in charge?"

Tyler had spent countless days and nights dealing with boundless egos and senses of entitlement, but Hunter and Lori were of a class all their own. "They seem to know what they're doing," he said.

"Having guns doesn't make you an expert in anything," Lori said.

"How'd they get their guns?" Jaime asked.

"By killing their previous owners," Tyler said. "With knives, right?"

"Suppose they find the terrorists' boat and sail away without us?" Hunter said. "The only way to be sure that doesn't happen is to be there with them."

"They're gonna pick a fight with the people on the boat," Tyler said, "and the people on the boat are going to fight back. I don't want anything to do with that."

"They left us defenseless," Lori said. "Suppose the terrorists come here and find us—"

"They won't," Jaime said. "No one knows of this place."

"No one knows of this *island,*" Hunter said. "Yet here we are being invaded. Whoever these people are, they seem to know a lot, whether you think they should know it or not. If they *do* figure out that this shanty-town is here, and they *do* come to clear it out, we'll be doomed. Scorpion and Gunslinger—and what stupid names those are—care more about themselves than about us. Why else would they leave us unprotected and insist on going ahead without us?"

"Maybe when you kill your own terrorist, you can keep the gun," Tyler said.

Hunter didn't seem to hear. "I think we need to catch up with them," he said. "I don't want to get left behind."

Tyler evaluated everyone's reaction to be within the same sleeve as his own: "Are you out of your mind?"

"What?" Hunter said. "Why are you looking at me like that? Do you *want* to be abandoned? If we follow them, we have a chance to get off this island. We have a chance to save our lives."

"I'm staying here," Tyler said, and he wanted there to be no doubt about his commitment. "Rattlesnake and Straight Shooter—whatever the hell their names are—are out looking for a fight. I am the very opposite of that. I am proud to declare myself a devout coward."

"That's not true," Jaime said. "You dared to escape."

Tyler accepted the kind words with a nod. The fact that he left Annie behind was a big asterisk on that particular act of bravery.

"You," Hunter said. "Jamie, is it?"

"Jaime."

"Right. Jaime. How did you get up here? Do you have a golf cart, too?"

Jaime looked to Tyler, who said nothing. He knew that Jaime had his own personal transportation, but that was not for him to reveal or conceal.

"I do," Jaime said. Tyler didn't think his friend was capable of telling a lie, but this seemed like a good time to start.

"Let me borrow it," Hunter said.

Jaime pointed to a spot beyond and behind the restored hut. "It's back there," he said. "But I think you're making a huge mistake."

"And why is that?"

"Because we're safe here, at least for now. People with guns are already looking for us. Why would you deliberately piss off the only armed friends we have on the island?"

"Listen to them," Lori said. "I think they may be right."

Hunter's mouth set in a thin line. "Look, I don't like this guy. I don't trust him. We've already caught him in lie after lie. Why should we trust him now?"

"Because he saved your life?" Tyler offered.

"No," Hunter said. "Even that's a lie. He saved his own life. We were just there. And he wasn't happy about it."

"So, what is your plan?" Jaime pressed. "You follow them and find them without getting caught or getting shot. Then what? It seems to me that you'll only get in the way of whatever they're trying to do."

"*That's* the part I want to know," Hunter said. "That's the part I don't trust." He turned to Lori. "Are you coming with me or staying with them?"

Tyler felt sorry for her. She looked like she wanted to stay, but she stepped off with Hunter.

"What about you two?" Hunter said.

"I think I will stay here," Jaime said.

"Yeah, I'm good," Tyler replied.

"We won't wait for you, you know," Hunter warned. "If we get the opportunity to sail away, we're gone. No looking back." He didn't wait for an answer. He turned on his heel and led Lori into the darkness behind the shed.

"Not a lovable guy," Jaime said.

Tyler coughed out a laugh. "Yeah, no shit."

Venice's computer dinged with an incoming message at the precise moment Boxers slammed his way into the Cave and strode into the War Room. "What do we know?" he said. If he saw Dom sitting in the chair nearest the door, he made no indication.

"And good morning to you, too," Venice said. After one look at Big Guy, she abandoned her effort to lighten the moment. He was amped and in no mood for small talk. "We know they're healthy, and we know that their island resort is under assault."

Her telephone rang. She looked at the caller ID. "And we know he's on the phone." She pressed the speaker button. "Hello, Scorpion. I'm here with our Special Friend and Big Guy." It was a long-standing tradition to avoid the use of real names when dealing with any aspect of the business that might involve shooting. Special Friend was the unofficial covert handle for Father Dom.

"The hell's goin' on down there, Boss?" Boxers said.

"Still trying to figure that out, Big Guy. I apologize

to the entire world for interrupting your ever-critical beauty sleep."

"At least you've got a few thousand miles of separation," Dom quipped.

"Yeah, ha, ha," Boxers said. "But seriously."

"Mother Hen, I just sent you a picture of the ship that transported our bad guys to the island. I'll take whatever you can figure out, as quickly as you can figure it out."

"You got a plan?" Boxers asked. His body language screamed that he was ready for a fight.

"Sort of," Jonathan said. "Gunslinger and I are going to board the vessel and see what we can see."

The big screen at the end of the conference table lit up with the picture Jonathan had sent. According to the bow markings, they were looking at the *Olympia 3,* and the flag of registry was from Denmark.

"You're being invaded by Danes?" Boxers said with a chuckle.

"I wouldn't trust any of the official markings," Jonathan said. "We want to get on board and out in as little time as possible, so if you can somehow give me an idea of the layout, that would make things a lot simpler. Personally, I think it's some kind of old minesweeping ship."

"Got it," Venice said. The big screen danced again, and now the display showed a black-and-white twin of the ship in Jonathan's message. "It appears to be a YMS Class minesweeper, circa early 1950s."

"How did you do that?" Jonathan asked. Off-mic, they could hear him relaying to Gail that Venice had already identified the type of boat.

"There's a thing called the Internet," Venice said as she continued to type. "It's searchable and they've got pictures and everything."

"What are you going to be looking for?" Boxers asked.

"Whatever we can find. I want to know who we're up against."

"Pretty high-risk fishing trip," Boxers said.

"I don't know that it is," Jonathan said. "There doesn't seem to be a security contingent around the ship. I can't imagine that to be the case, but whatever they've left behind is a small crew. The bulk of their forces are deployed guarding guests and whatever else they're doing back at the resort."

"That sound like there's some distance between you and them," Dom said.

The screen at the end of the table changed again, and there was an annotated aerial photo of the Crystal Sands Resort, courtesy of the island's publicity department. "I just pulled up a map of your resort," Venice said. "I presume you're down at the piers?"

"Exactly."

The island was roughly the shape of the letter *C*, oriented with the open part facing south. Beaches surrounded the entire landmass, with lowlands at the east and western ends, and hills in the middle. The piers were located on the easternmost side, with the resort structures on the western side.

"Boss, I gotta tell you that I think it's a mistake to try to take down a vessel that size by yourself."

"First of all, I've got Gunslinger with me, and second, I'm not going to *take it down*. We're going to get in and out and gather some intel."

"How about you just hunker down and wait for the cavalry?" Boxers suggested.

"Easier said than done," Venice said. That drew the attention of everyone in the room. "Our Special Friend arranged for me to have a chat with Wolverine a little while ago. The Crystal Sands Island is privately held, but it is loosely a possession of Costa Rica."

"So, the FBI has no jurisdiction," Jonathan said, jumping ahead.

"It's even more complicated than that," Venice said. "Costa Rica is one of just a handful of countries on the planet without a military. Even if they wanted to come and get you, they'd have no forces to do it with."

When she was done, Boxers and Dom both stared with expressions of disbelief. "Tell me that was a joke," Big Guy said.

"Wish I could," Venice said.

"That sort of sucks," Jonathan said.

"Baker Sinise's brochures brag about an anything-goes resort," Dom said. "I guess that helps explain how he gets away with it. There's no one around to enforce whatever laws they might have."

"How big is your OpFor, Boss?" Opposition force.

"I estimate something north of two dozen."

"You can't win that fight. Not without force multipliers."

"It won't be pleasant," Jonathan agreed, "but we don't have a whole lot of choice. For now, we're just gathering intel. We've found a place to hole up and stay out of the way during daylight hours."

"Then just stay there," Venice said.

"I don't think we can," Jonathan said. "We killed two of their guys. They know they have armed resistance on the island, and they're going to have to come looking for us."

"Are there more than just you and Gunslinger?" Dom asked.

"Affirmative. We've joined up with two other guests and two guys who work here."

"That makes six," Boxers said softly. Venice thought maybe he was thinking out loud. "Better than only two."

"That's another reason to board the ship," Jonathan said. "Between the two of us, we've got two rifles, two handguns, and barely a hundred rounds of ammo. I'm hoping they'll have a weapons locker on board."

"If they do, I believe that's where you'll find their security contingent," Boxers said.

"I believe you're right. Mother Hen, how are you coming on those deck plans?"

A set of drawings appeared on the screen. "I have some," Venice said, "but I have to tell you that there seems to be a lot of variation on what's where. That model ship is old enough that it's likely been reconfigured."

"It'll be what it is," Jonathan said.

An idea smacked Venice out of nowhere. "I think I might have a plan. Does Gunslinger have a phone, too?"

"Yes, but we've turned it off to conserve on battery."

"Okay, turn her phone on and hang up."

"That's a plan?" Jonathan said.

"Yes, it is," Venice said. "I'll call you back as a conference call. We'll all come along as you board the ship. If you end up at a dead end or something, maybe I'll be able to talk you out of it or around it."

The line went dead.

"You really think that will work?" Dom asked as Venice waited to redial.

"Sure. I mean, I don't see how—"

"This is bullshit," Boxers proclaimed, and he shot out of his chair. He headed for the door.

"Where are you going?" Venice asked, startled.

"I'm going to rescue them myself," he said.

"How?" Dom asked.

"I'll raise my own goddamn army," he said.

CHAPTER 9

Gail settled her bluetooth receiver into her ear and powered up her phone. "This is bizarre," she said as she waited for the phone to boot up. "Surreal." They'd discussed the rules of engagement, such as they were, and they could not have been simpler. If challenged, shoot. If spotted by a stranger with a gun, shoot. Then, gather weapons and ammo as you go along. When she'd agreed to rejoin the covert side of Security Solutions, with many months of physical and psychological therapy in her rearview mirror, she hadn't imagined that she'd be knee-deep in a tactical situation so soon. She'd certainly never considered that it would be run by conference call with not nearly enough equipment.

Gail and Jonathan had been watching the ship for over ten minutes, and had yet to see any activity. A gangplank led from the pier to a spot amidships, and in the glaring lights, she could see the markings and logo of the Crystal Sands Resort on the canvas strips under the gangplank's handrails. It appeared to be the very one by which they had disembarked from the resort ship barley thirty-six hours before.

"I don't believe for a minute that they left this un-guarded," Gail said.

"That's what we have to assume," Jonathan agreed. "Maybe they figured that by focusing their manpower on wrangling guests, they wouldn't have to worry about guarding the ship."

Gail's phone buzzed first. She answered, and then ten seconds later, Jonathan's buzzed.

"Are we all on?" Venice's voice asked.

Jonathan and Gail confirmed in unison. "Are you up for a run?" he asked her.

The truthful answer was that she had her doubts, but this was not a time to express them. This was the time to take her physical therapy final exam. "We'll all find out together," she said. "I'll do my best to keep up."

"All right, then, let's do this. Remember to zigzag." It was at once one of Jonathan's most annoying and en-dearing traits that he always felt the need to explain the obvious.

With this much ambient light, thanks to the massive floods that illuminated the pier, speed meant more than stealth. Even for an experienced shooter, a running person was a hard target to hit, especially when the person ran an unpredictable course. Throw in the fact that whoever the sentries might be, they would be star-tled to see that they had company, and a snap shot was even harder to make.

Of course, there was always the dumb-luck factor that made Jonathan's world more interesting than he often preferred it to be.

"Okay," Jonathan said. "Three, two, one . . ."

Jonathan bolted out into the open, digging in hard as he sprinted down the pier and slid to a stop at the base of the gangplank. Gail took off a second later. The legs felt strong, even though the hips were stiff. Nothing too bad. She could do this. With her M4 pressed into her shoulder and the safety off, she scanned mostly behind as they ran. She trusted Digger to take out the targets along the rails of the ship and what they could see of the superstructure, while she looked for targets that might sneak up from the rear. Nothing yet.

She slid into place at the base of the gangway only three or four seconds behind Digger. Good lord, she wanted some form of cover. She felt so open out here in the bright light.

"Howya doin', kid?" Jonathan asked. "I'm clear."

"I'm clear, too. So far, so good."

Jonathan said, "We're going up the gangplank now," and then she heard the electronic version through her earpiece half a second later. She knew this information to be for Venice back in Virginia.

"Three, two . . ."

Jonathan moved first. His footfalls sounded like drumbeats on the stainless-steel and aluminum gangplank, but there was no avoiding the characteristic clanking sound, and her strides were nearly as loud. By the time Gail arrived on the covered deck—promenade?—Jonathan had taken a knee and was sweeping the length of the ship with his muzzle, both forward and aft.

"I've got the rear," Gail said as she squatted behind him. She never felt comfortable using many nautical or military terms, not in the least because she felt that there was a high likelihood that she would screw them up. "And I'm clear." Now that they were aboard the vessel, she couldn't keep herself from whispering.

"Also clear," Jonathan said.

And for both of them, that was something of a lie. Their views were limited, at best. While they had a clear view of the starboard side, a roof overhead masked whatever may lie above, and a heavy bulkhead obscured everything else.

"Okay, Mother Hen," Jonathan said. "We are on the covered exterior passageway on the starboard side. There's a door roughly amidships."

"Take it," Venice said. "If that design mirrors the one I pulled up from the Internet, you'll be in the dining area."

Jonathan turned to Gail. "I'll go in first and swing right. You follow and swing left."

She nodded.

"Now." Staying in a low crouch, she watched Digger shift to a left-handed grip on his M4, tilting it to the right to keep the red dot's reticle in line with his dominant right eye. He led with his muzzle, swung the corner, and squirted through the open door into the relative darkness beyond. Gail wondered if the reason he chose to take the right was specifically so that she would not be put into a position to shoot left-handed.

She was right on his ass as she cleared the opening and spun left.

They were in a twelve-by-twelve-foot room that had been outfitted with four picnic tables, complete with attached bench seating. The lingering stink of greasy food and greasy men—and could that be urine?—combined to form a stomach-churning cloud of offensiveness.

At the rear of the space, in Gail's sector of the room, a dark shadow concealed a corner that may have been a pantry. She advanced on it with her M4 ready.

And after three steps, she was face-to-face with a crewman, no more than five feet away. "Get down!" she yelled as she aimed her rifle at his face. "On your knees, now!"

The guy looked terrified. Not yet twenty-five, he wore only a pair of boxer shorts, and his hair was a mess. Clearly, he'd recently been in bed. He froze at the sound of her commands, dropped his empty coffee cup.

"Don't make me shoot you!" she said. "Down! Now! On the floor!" She motioned with the muzzle of her rifle, in case he didn't speak English. Automatic weapons were universal translators.

He dropped to his knees and laced his fingers behind his head. "I-I am no gun," he stammered in very broken English. "I am no weapons." It sounded like *weepons*.

Jonathan darted over to be next to her. "Why are you here?" he said.

Behind him, on the opposite side of the space, they heard the clear sounds of frantic movement from the other side of a closed door.

"Ah, shit. People are home," he said. He smashed the crewman in the cheek with the butt of his rifle and dropped him. He pivoted and said to Gail, "Stay close."

Mother Hen said, "Are you still in the mess area?"

"Affirmative," Jonathan said.

"The bunk room is directly across the hall."

"That explains the commotion," Gail said.

"Fast and hard," Jonathan said.

Stealth was no longer important. From here, containment was key.

"Remember, they're not armed," Gail said.

"They don't shoot at me, I won't shoot at them." Jonathan threw open the door to the passageway. Gail was surprised that the door was a standard hollow-core door panel with standard hardware, no different than what you'd find in an office building.

Jonathan pivoted right, while Gail pivoted left. Her view of the passageway was clear, but Jonathan yelled, "Down! Hands, hands, hands! Let me see your hands! I've got crew, Gunslinger."

She never turned her back on her sector as she moved to lend aid to Jonathan as he stormed the bunk room. Gail counted six crewmen on the first glance, all in various stages of panic. Caught in midsleep by the noise and excitement, they mostly just seemed confused.

"We won't hurt you if you cooperate," Jonathan said. To Gail's ear, he'd moderated his tone, moved to soothing mode. "No weapons, no fists, and we'll be out of here in no time. Gunslinger, hold the hallway."

Gail stood in the doorway to the bunk room, her back turned to the activity in there. If Digger needed help, he'd ask for it. She scanned the passageway from one end to the other, left to right and back again, in a continuous motion.

Behind her, Jonathan ordered his captives under their bunks, facedown, while he rummaged through their things. Gail wasn't happy that they'd made their presence known in such an obvious way. She stipulated that they needed as much intel as they could gather, but this was a level of risk—

She saw movement to her left, toward the front of the ship. A shadow moved along the intersecting hallway, advancing right to left.

"Scorpion, I've got movement out here."

"Need help?"

The shadow froze. Then it backed off. Slowly at first, then quickly.

"Shit," Gail said. "We've got a runner. I'm going after him." Jonathan said something discouraging in her ear, and she responded, "You do what you need to do so we can get out of here. I'm going after him." It was the right thing to do. The *only* thing to do. She pushed off and ran to the end of the passageway, where she pulled to a stop, pivoted to a leftie grip, and scanned to the right for her target.

She caught a glimpse just as an underwear-clad male disappeared out of the far door on the starboard side and headed left. There was no time to snap a shot. She pivoted back to the left, just to make sure that she hadn't been drawn into the trap of a cross fire—in which case, she'd already have died—then took off after her quarry. By her estimation, he had maybe a five-second head start.

"Stop!" she shouted.

The fact of his running was the problem. Was he getting a weapon? Was he calling for help? They couldn't afford to let him do either of those things.

Gail sprinted to the end of the cross passageway, took a second to calm herself, and then dared a peek to the left, and then another to the right. No guns. Not that she could see, anyway.

The doorway led her to a spot beyond the covered passageway where they'd boarded. Immediately to her left, a set of steep open stairs—she recalled being told that stairs were ladders in the Navy—led to the deck above.

Suddenly aware of a potential threat from above, she stepped away from the door opening and scanned for shooters who might be looking down on her. Nothing. That was the second time in thirty seconds when she'd survived despite her mistakes. This was exactly why SWAT and other assault forces worked as *teams*. As a solo, there are simply too many angles to cover.

All that lay ahead of her was more open deck, much of it stacked with stuff she didn't recognize. Boxes, canisters, that sort of thing. Her instincts told her that her prey had fled up to the next deck.

"Status report, Gunslinger." That was Venice.

"I think I've tracked our guy to the deck above us," she said. "I'm heading up there now."

"Be advised that's where you'll find the wheelhouse. The control room. Whatever the heck you call it."

"Got it," Gail said. She climbed the ladder as quickly and as quietly as she could, yet again keenly aware that she was exposing herself in a progression from the head down.

There he was! "I've got him," Gail said.

The man she'd spotted was just a few feet away from the door to the wheelhouse and sprinting toward it.

"Stop! Don't make me shoot." If he got to the wheelhouse—if he got anywhere—he could gain an advantage. She couldn't allow that to happen.

Gail brought her rifle to her shoulder and gave the runner one last chance. "Stop!"

If anything, he sped up.

Gail settled her front sight on a spot between the man's shoulder blades and fired. Fired again.

The man faltered with the impact of the first bullet, and the impact of the second appeared to propel him through the opening and out of sight.

"I hit him," she said.

"Is he dead?" Jonathan asked.

"I don't know yet."

"Approach cautiously."

Gail didn't bother to respond to that. Again, the biggest threat at this second—especially since shots had been fired—was the approach of previously unknown and uninvolved crewmen who had just been alerted.

She kept low and advanced in a scissor-step as she crossed the deck toward the open door to the wheelhouse, scanning in a continuous arc for additional targets.

"He's on the radio!" Jonathan announced in her ear. "Goddammit, he's on the radio. Kill him."

Gail picked up her pace. Still with no targets to shoot, she closed the distance to the wheelhouse door and swung inside.

There he was, on the floor, bleeding from a hole in his belly, a bloody microphone clutched in his fist. No more than twenty years old, and maybe 130 pounds soaking wet, he jumped when he saw her, and threw the crimson-streaked mic onto the deck.

"Don't shoot!" he said in heavily-accented English. "Please don't kill me."

Gail's finger caressed her trigger, but she hesitated. "Who are you?"

"My name is Harm," he said. He winced against a wave of pain. "Harm Mohren. I am Dutch. I am not with them."

"Why are you here?"

"Please help me. I have been shot."

"I know," Gail said. "I'm the one who shot you."

"For God's sake, Gail, what are you doing?" Jonathan said. She could tell from the effort in his voice that he was running.

She pulled her Bluetooth from her ear and slipped it into her pocket. "Answer me," she pressed, moving closer. "Keep your hands where I can see them."

"But it hurts." Harm started to cry.

"Keep it together, Harm. Answer my questions and we'll get some help for you. You tell me you're not with the terrorists, yet here you are. Why?"

"I am, em, how do you say it? Ship's company. Not a terrorist. I am with the ship. Now, please help me."

"Who are the terrorists?" Gail asked. "Why are they here? What do they want?"

"They don't tell me," the young man said. "They pay me a lot of money to bring them. I did not know where they wanted to go until after we were under way."

"Under way from where?"

"Rosarito."

"Where is that?"

"Mexico. On west coast. Now, please. It hurts so much."

Gail fought the temptation to move in closer, fought

the urge to offer aid. She needed to know what this guy knew, and this was her only opportunity. Relief from pain had long been one of the most effective means by which to leverage information.

"What are the terrorists here to do?"

"I told you. I don't know."

Gail moved to back away. "Then I'm sorry we can't help you."

Behind her, she heard footsteps quickly approaching, and she turned to see Jonathan on his way to join her. She held out a hand to stop him, then turned back to Harm. "I'm sorry that you have to die."

"Wait," he said. "They have explosives. And guns."

"More than what they took with them?"

Harm nodded. He coughed once and sent a mist of blood into the air. Some of it dribbled down his chin. "Oh, God," he said. *"Ik ben stervende."* He took a deep breath and seemed to lose focus.

"Where are the guns and explosives?" Gail pressed. "In the hold?"

He shook his head. "No, the holds are empty. That is why we are here. To fill them."

"To fill them with what?"

Harm lifted his hands and looked at the blood. "Nothing that is worth this."

"But *what*?" Gail said. She heard the urgency in her voice causing it to rise half an octave.

He looked at her. And he died.

"I think this is may be a bad idea," Lori said. They were navigating through the dark, going far too fast for her liking. "Maybe we need to go back."

"We are *not* going back," Hunter said. "That boat or ship, or whatever the hell it is, is our way out of here. I'm not going to let you get left behind while Scorpion Digger, or whatever his name is, takes off."

"I don't think he would do such a thing," Lori said. "He seems like a saver and not an . . . abandoner."

"So, you're siding with the others," Hunter said.

She started to reply, but swallowed her words. This was Hunter in a nutshell. All competition, all the time, and never wrong, even when he was. The argument always went the same way from this point, and now was not the time to have it.

"You had the choice to stay behind," Hunter went on. "I don't need you piling a bunch of shit on our situation."

Lori sat quietly.

"Am I making myself clear?"

"As crystal," she said. At the height of any battle, one of Hunter's most wielded attack weapons was condescension and demanding language. Lori was sick of it. This vacation was a mistake—Hunter's vision of retaliating against her request for a divorce by throwing lots of money at it. "Can you at least slow down a little?"

His foot got heavier on the accelerator pedal. He could be such an asshole. Thank God there were no kids in the marriage, or else—

"What's that?" she asked. It sounded like an engine and it was coming up from behind them. "Is that a truck?"

"Oh, shit," Hunter said. He leaned onto the accelerator even more.

"We need to get off the trail," Lori said. "This golf cart can't outrun—"

"Shut up, Lori. Can you just do that one thing for me?"

At this speed, Lori could no longer distinguish between the center of the road and its shoulders. It was pointless to argue, so she wrapped her fist around the roof support and hung on.

Within five seconds, headlights swept the trees on the curve behind them, and a few seconds after that, they were overtaken.

"Stop that train!" someone with a heavy accent yelled in English. "Stop or we will shoot."

"Jesus, Hunter, what are you going to do?" Lori said. "They're going to shoot!"

He let up off the accelerator. "Okay, fine," he said. "Is this what you wanted? You wanted to get caught?"

The question was so absurd that she couldn't form an answer before the soldiers were on them. At first, there were only four of them, but within another few seconds, a second vehicle arrived—both were pickup trucks bearing the logo of the Crystal Sands Resort—and disgorged four more soldiers.

"Hands up!" someone called. "Hands up right now. Hands!"

Lori raised her arms to the point where her hands hit the roof of the cart and could go no farther. She didn't look to see what Hunter was doing. Whether he was being an ass or a pussy, she just didn't want to know.

"Get out of the train," the soldier said. To call the cart a "train" made sense, she supposed, considering that the cart could comfortably transport as many as twenty-four people at a time. Throw in the fact that

English was clearly not this soldier's first language, and it made even more sense.

"Do not put your hands down." It was a chore to butt-walk to the edge of the bench seat and swing her feet to the ground without using her hands.

"Who are you?" another soldier asked.

"We're guests of the resort," Hunter said.

"We're the Edwardses," Lori elaborated. "Lori and Hunter Edwards."

In the wash of the headlights, she could see that her words triggered some form of recognition. Three of the soldiers exchanged glances, and one of them stepped away from the others to speak into his radio. While he was away, the soldier closest to Lori pulled her hands down one at a time and bound them behind her back with zip ties.

"What are you going to do with us?" Hunter asked. His voice shook as he spoke.

If the soldiers heard him, they made no indication.

Lori kept her eyes averted. If she looked at Hunter, she didn't think that she could stifle the words that boiled in her throat. If he'd just stayed put—if he'd just done what they were asked to do—her hands wouldn't be bound behind her back, and they wouldn't be in a position of begging for their lives. This was no time for a lecture.

"Hunter and Lorelai Edwards." It was the voice of one of the soldiers, and from his bearing, she assumed him to be the leader of this group. He approached as he spoke, closing the distance between himself and Hunter to less than three feet.

Hunter nodded. For the first time, Lori saw that Hunter's hands had been bound, as well.

"You are from Bungalow Nine, are you not?"

"Yes, sir, we are. Were, I mean."

The soldier threw a vicious punch into Hunter's midsection, collapsing him in a heap. He disappeared from Lori's view, so she could not see where the two brutal kicks that followed landed on his body. But she could hear Hunter retching and gasping for breath.

"That is what you get for killing my compatriots," the soldier said.

Hunter said something through his pain, but it got lost in the impact of a third kick.

"Say nothing," the soldier said. Then he turned to Lori. "And what about you, pretty lady?"

The soldiers all closed in around her, as if to block her way if she decided to run. None of them touched her, but the soldier who'd beaten her husband looked wired for murder. Details were hard to discern in the glare and harsh shadows of the headlights, but she caught the very pale complexion and the red beard stubble. More than that, she caught the thick, muscular neck and the hard set of his mouth. All of that was terrifying, but the rest paled in comparison with the vivid heat of his glare.

"What is the correct penalty for executing my soldiers?"

CHAPTER 10

Jonathan arrived on the deck pissed, ready to do harm.
but when he saw what Gail was doing, the information she was gathering, he pushed the anger down. They
needed intel, and if there was one person who could
give it, it was the ship's captain. If, indeed, that's truly
who he was.

He'd heard most of what had been said, even though
much of the electronic conversation was muffled after
Gail stuffed her earpiece into her pocket. And Venice
had already told him that he deserved that bit of rude-
ness, that Gail was doing exactly what needed to be
done.

What neither of the ladies knew, however, was the
volume and pace of the radio traffic surrounding the
captain's alert that "Home Base" was under assault.
Most definitely the sort of message that would bring
large numbers of bad guys storming their way. He
came up to tell Gail that they needed to get the hell out
of here, but when he heard about the guns and explosives, he got an idea.

What were the two data points they had on that?

One, that they were not in the hold, and two, by definition they had to be someplace else. Belowdecks, he'd
found all kinds of documents and identifications—
he'd scooped up as many of them as he could and filled
the pockets of his pants and his vest with as many as
they would hold—but he saw nothing in the way of
weapons. Now, granted, there was a lot of ship that
they hadn't yet seen, but—

The crates on the deck.

"He's dead," Gail said. She'd returned to the door of
the wheelhouse, her body framed in the opening.
"How much of that did you hear?"

"Pretty much all of it," Jonathan said, but he'd already moved on. "Here, come help me. I think I know
where they keep their ammo and explosives and your
guy's friends are on the way."

"If we've got any time, I want to search the wheelhouse for intel, instead."

Actually, that was a damned good idea. "Two minutes max," he said.

They separated. Jonathan advanced to the forward
part of the deck, where cube-shaped objects of various
sizes had been draped with tarps. They stood six to
eight feet high and had been sealed with shrink-wrap.
Jonathan pulled the knife from his pocket and slit the
plastic on the nearest crate. As he pulled that away, he
slit the tarp, as well, revealing that the big containers
were, in fact, stacked smaller containers. All of them
displayed explosives labels of varying scariness. The
ones marked *Class 1.4* were undoubtedly small-arms
ammunition, and the ones marked *Class 1.1* meant some
form of high explosives. *Class 1.1A* was the really good

stuff, but *Class 1.1B* were likely the detonators needed to make the really good stuff go boom.

"Mother Hen, next time you see Big Guy, tell him that I have just discovered the weapons cache of his dreams."

"Take a picture and send it to me," she said.

Jonathan didn't have time for that. He let his rifle fall against its sling as he strode to the outer bulkhead of the wheelhouse to pull a fire axe from its mount, and then moved back again to the stacked crates. With two full swings on the crate marked *Class 1.1D,* the wooden case broke open to reveal a collection of M67 hand grenades. Normally, those types of grenades were shipped in their own squatty cardboard tubes, but these looked like they'd been tossed into the crate, maybe twenty of them in all. Yeah, these were coming with him.

The radio receiver in his left ear popped to life. In heavy-accented English, he heard, "Alpha, Alpha, Alpha. Emergency message."

"Hey, Gunslinger," Jonathan said for the benefit of his Bluetooth, "if I'm back in your ear, step it up. Something's happening."

"Who is this?" a second voice asked on the radio.

"This is X-ray. We have found the killers from Bungalow Nine. They are on their way to Home Base."

Jonathan relayed what he'd just heard. This wasn't good.

"Verify their names," said Alpha.

"Stand by."

During the short break, Jonathan said, "We might have hung around too long already."

"Then let's get going," Gail said from very close by.

He whirled to see her crouched maybe four feet away, her posture matching his. Papers were erupting out of the pockets of her vest.

"Got room for a couple of hand grenades?" Jonathan asked, handing her three of them.

"You do know how to sweet-talk a girl, don't you?" She hung them by their safety spoons from the PALS loops in her vest—Pouch Attachment Ladder System. Gotta love Uncle and his acronyms. "Time to move?"

Jonathan stuffed five grenades in the loops of his own vest. "One more minute. I want to grab some more ammo."

"Suppose we don't have another minute?"

"All the more reason to grab more ammo." Jonathan slammed the axe blade down onto the crate marked with the *Class 1.4* label. The wood crunched, and with two more whacks, the contents lay exposed. "Bingo," Jonathan said. It took some pulling and maneuvering, but he was able to lift a green ammo can free of the container. A painted stencil on the side read: *Ball Ammo 5.56 mm NATO.* From the weight, there had to be four or five hundred rounds inside.

"Alpha, this is X-ray," the voice said in Jonathan's ear.

He held up a finger. "They're talking again." But this time, he walked as he talked.

X-ray continued, "Their names are Hunter and Lorelai Edwards."

"Oh, shit," Jonathan said. "Mr. and Mrs. Asshole just got themselves snatched." He led the way back toward the gangplank.

"Are you sure they are the ones who killed our men?" Alpha asked.

"They say no, but who else can they be? They were in Sector Eight, and Hotel and Foxtrot are dead. If they are not the killers, then they must be . . . *assotsiirovan-nykh*."

"English," Alpha instructed. "The word is *associates*. Do nothing with them where you are. Bring them back to the Plantation House for questioning."

"What about the call for help from Home Base?"

"You are in two vehicles, are you not? Put your prisoners in one and send them back here. Send the other truck to investigate the ship."

Jonathan stopped at the top of the gangplank and turned to let Gail go ahead of him. "They're on the way right now," he said. "We need to pick up the pace and get under cover."

"We're not going to engage." She said it as a declaration.

"Not unless we have to," Jonathan said. "God grant me the serenity to walk away from the fights I cannot win, win the fights I can, and the wisdom to know the difference."

Once on the pier, they had no option but to sprint back the way they'd come—back toward the road. If they got caught out here, they'd be without cover, totally exposed.

"You go first," Jonathan said. "I'll cover you from here. Duck into the darkest shadow you can find on the far side. When you're in place, cover me."

"We should go together."

"Gail, if I see a vehicle, they'll all be dead before

they know they've been shot. Can't do that and run at the same time. Go."

He dropped to a knee. He brought his M4 to his shoulder and leveled the muzzle at the mouth of the road, where it met the ramp of the pier. With both eyes open, he could simultaneously aim and watch Gail dash down the length of the wooden structure. He was genuinely impressed with her recovery, though he noticed the beginnings of a limp that he had not seen earlier. They needed to rest.

As soon as Gail was within a couple of strides of shadow, Jonathan took off. There was nothing tactical about this sprint. He just wanted to get the hell off the X and get under cover. All this bright light and high exposure left him feeling jumpy. His feet pounded on the wooden decking and his gear bounced awkwardly against his body as he closed the distance and slid to a stop in the leading edge of the shadow. From here, he worried about colliding with Gail.

"Are you there?" he whispered.

"Twenty feet ahead and a little to your right."

He followed the sound and took a knee beside her. "Holding up okay?" he asked.

"I'd consider it a personal favor if you stopped asking me that question."

"Y'all know I'm still here, right?" Venice asked.

Jonathan smiled. "Thanks for the help and the attention, Mother Hen," he said. "We're going to turn you off and preserve battery power."

"Not yet," Venice said. "We need to set a time for you to call back."

Jonathan looked at his watch. "It's zero two forty-seven local time. We're going to need to get some rest. How about I call you at zero six hundred my time?"

"That works for me," Venice said. "Talk to you in a little over three hours."

They clicked off. Jonathan kept his phone in his pocket as he pressed the button to power it down. He didn't want to risk an inadvertent flash of light.

"What now?" Gail asked.

Two seconds later, the glow of headlights painted the jungle around them. Jonathan put his hand on Gail's shoulder and pressed her closer to the mulchy ground. He lay on his belly next to her. "From here, I think we just wait to see what happens," he said.

There's something terrifying about a telephone call at zero dark early. Beyond shattering the peaceful silence of the sleeping hours, a ringing phone portended bad news 100 percent of the time. People simply did not wake you up to share the news of a job offer or a funny story they heard at work.

So, when that goddamn bell ripped through the Wests' bedroom, Henry was wide-awake and bolt upright with the receiver in his hand before the first ring had stopped. He had to reach over Sarah to do it. She barely moved. Perhaps it was his past or his current line of work that made him so allergic to the late-night interruptions.

"Yeah," he said. Or at least he tried to. He cleared his throat and tried a second time.

The voice on the other end said, "Conan, we have a problem."

His stomach flipped. He hadn't been called Conan in a very long time, a whole life ago. He recognized the voice, but couldn't place it.

"It's Boxers," the voice said. The timbre of the voice was equal parts Darth Vader and earthquake.

Definitely not someone he'd expected to hear from. "Big Guy. Jesus, what time is it?"

"You don't want to know. We need to talk."

"Now?"

"I wouldn't have called you if it wasn't important."

Fair enough. Henry hadn't seen Box in quite a while, but there's no way he could have evolved into a chatty guy.

Henry looked at his sleeping bride. Whatever was coming, he was certain that she neither needed nor wanted to hear it. "Call me back in five minutes," he said. "Let me splash some water and wake up."

"Five minutes," Boxers said. "No more."

"Yup." Henry laid the receiver back on its cradle, then reached behind to unplug it. Sarah was asleep now, and given his suspicions, he didn't want her waking up for the next call, either. He went to the bathroom, washed his face, gave his teeth a quick brushing, and was just crossing the threshold of his home office when the phone rang exactly four minutes and sixty seconds later.

"Hey, Box. What's going on?"

"Digger and Gail have been taken hostage. It's a resort island off the coast of Mexico and we need to go get him."

"Whoa, whoa, whoa," Henry said. "Slow down. First of all, who's Gail?"

"Gail Bonneville," Boxers explained. "Gunslinger.

She's part of our team and she's Digger's on-again, off-again squeeze."

"Is that the same as a girlfriend?"

"We don't have time for the usual shit, Conan. This is serious."

Henry had never heard Big Guy so agitated. He was famous throughout the teams as the stout rock in the middle of the howling sea. "Okay, sorry. What happened?"

"We don't know, exactly. We got an alert from Dig that bad guys had stormed the island—it's called the Crystal Sands Resort—and they took everyone hostage."

"How did he contact you if he was a hostage?"

A beat. "Well, okay, *they're* not hostages exactly, but everyone else is. They tried to grab Digger, but it didn't go well for the bad guys." For the first time, there was a trace of a smile in his voice.

"Have you called the Mexican police?" Henry asked.

"I haven't called anyone. But the lady in my office—"

"That would be Mother Hen?"

"Yeah. She said—"

"Does she have any idea that you refer to her as 'the lady in my office'?"

"God damn it, Conan, I don't have time for that shit."

"Because she'd kick your ass."

The phone went dead.

"Oh, shit." Maybe he'd pushed too hard. Henry understood that Big Guy and Scorpion were close, and maybe he should have cut him more slack. But if—

The phone rang again, and Henry picked it up.

"Sorry, Conan. I was out of line."

Holy shit on a shingle. Did Big Guy just apologize? Jesus, this really was serious.

"The island is off the coast of Mexico," Boxers explained, picking up where they'd left off. "But it's not a part of Mexico. It's a part of Costa Rica, which has no military."

"But you said it was a resort," Henry said. "Surely, some of the guests—Digger and Gail included—come from a nation that has a military."

"You know how long that would take," Boxers said. "These assholes are killing people now."

For the first time, it dawned on Henry what this call was really about. "Where is this going?" He needed to hear it articulated.

"I'm putting together a team to go out there and get them."

"And I'm on your list."

"Wow. And to think you're not related to Sherlock Holmes."

Henry fell silent, and Boxers had the good sense not to interrupt it. "This is a big ask, Box. I haven't kicked a door or shot a gun in over seven years."

"But you're still in the Community," Boxers said. "The rest is like riding a bike."

"Give me a day to think about it," Henry hedged. Jesus, if Sarah found out . . . He'd made a promise and—

"Digger doesn't have a day. For all I know, he's already dead. We have to move now."

"Now?" Henry thought maybe his sleep-addled brain wasn't processing things correctly. "As in, right *now*?"

"As in within the next few hours," Boxers said. "I'll be in touch with the details. I have your cell number."

Henry shifted the phone to his other ear. "Jesus, Big Guy, this is so out of left field. I've got work obligations—"

"You've got vacation and sick leave. The good works of the NSA can churn on for a few days without you."

"What about my family?"

"They can churn without you, too. How many unexpected work trips do you take as it is?"

"But this is one I might not come back from."

A long beat. "And Digger had nothing else to live for when the Taliban had triangulated your hidey-hole? Do you remember that day?"

"Don't go there," Henry said. "You don't need to. Who else is on the team?"

"So far, it's you and me. Meet me at the Manassas Airport at eleven. I'll have a better idea by then."

CHAPTER 11

Hunter was hurt worse than Lori had thought. she could tell by the way he listed to one side and the way he gripped his belly. His nose had clearly been broken, the bridge swollen to three times its normal size. The flow of blood had slowed to a trickle, but a deep purple hue had begun to set in around his eyes. The bumpy ride in the bed of the pickup clearly erupted a new jolt of pain with every root or pothole.

"How bad is it?" she asked.

He shook his head.

"Hunter?"

"I think they might have ruptured something in my gut." As he spoke the words, he turned his head to the side and vomited.

"Both of you shut up," ordered the soldier who'd been assigned to guard them. "There will be enough time later for you to say whatever you want."

"He's my husband," Lori said.

The soldier hit her hard with an open hand, whipping her head to the side and filling her sinuses with the smell of copper. "Silence."

A few seconds later, she felt a trickle of blood tracing its way through her left nostril, and she was powerless to stop it as it dripped onto her crossed legs. She looked over to Hunter, but he'd gone somewhere else, mentally.

Their route took them past the backyard of their bungalow, and around to the rear of the swimming-pool complex. Even through the metallic stench of blood, Lori could make out the smell of chlorine. She could also hear voices, but could not make out the words.

Their pickup truck plowed past all of that, into alternating darkness and lit confusion that looked entirely unfamiliar. She figured that they must now be in a part of the resort where guests never went—the servants' quarters, if you will, where the man behind the curtain made hospitality look easy. This was where the maintenance teams were headquartered, where the trash was disposed of, and, she imagined, where vermin were incinerated before they could make an appearance and raise the blood pressure of a visitor.

Only a minute or two later, they emerged into more familiar territory. She recognized the elaborate porte cochere of the main entrance of the Plantation House. In this spot, just two days before, they had been greeted by uniformed bellmen who made sure they had a mimosa in hand before they crossed the threshold into what was to be the vacation of a lifetime.

As the pickup pulled to a stop, other soldiers filed out of the front door to surround it. One of them dropped the tailgate and motioned for them to get out. "You will follow me."

Lori struggled to find her feet with her hands bound. The soldier helped her by steadying her shoulder as she scooted on her butt to the edge of the tailgate, where she got her feet over the side. He steadied her shoulder again as she slid to the ground. Then he took her by her arm and guided her toward the giant wooden and cut glass doors.

"What about my husband?" she asked, craning her head to look around to him. He still listed to the side. In the bright light of the porte cochere, he looked terribly pale.

"Worry about yourself," the soldier said. "He will come along."

Lori allowed herself to be escorted across the sparkling tile of the entryway and up the grand staircase. From there, she went through the doors that led to a hidden staircase that ultimately took her to the third floor. Her heart hammered and her knees felt weak as her escort changed his grip from a gentle force on her biceps to a broad hand flat against her shoulder blades. He pushed her toward a set of interior double doors. They opened as she approached, which frightened her even more. It meant that someone had been watching her.

More soldiers. To her, they all looked alike. Actually, that wasn't true. She had no idea what they looked like. All she saw were the guns. Many, many guns. Rifles and pistols. The room smelled of sweat and oil and solvent.

One of the soldiers stepped forward. "Mrs. Edwards," he said. "How nice of you to join us."

Lori detected the trace of an accent, but she couldn't place it. "Could you untie my hands, please?"

"Absolutely not." He smiled after he said the words. Not in a mocking way, she didn't think. Commiseration, maybe? "You are a prisoner, and will be treated as such."

Another soldier said, "We told you what would happen to people who tried to run."

"Shut up," the lead soldier barked.

"What?" Lori said. "What would happen?"

"You will be shot."

"I said, *shut up!*" the commander yelled. "Get out of this room. This instant." Then he said something in a language Lori didn't understand. It sounded Eastern European.

The other soldier hesitated, and then stormed out the door through which Lori had just entered.

"Who are you?" she asked.

"That is none of your concern. You killed two of my men."

"Are you going to shoot me?"

The man's eyes narrowed, and the smile returned. "My name is Anatoly," he said. "I am the man in charge of this little army. I make every decision. When we are done with our discussion here, we will both know whether or not you will be shot."

Lori felt the panic swelling inside, growing like an inflating balloon in her belly. "But I never heard your warning about leaving."

"That's right. I understand that. How could you possibly have heard when you'd already killed my men and run away?"

The room shimmered and moved in her clouding vision. "May I sit down, please?"

"No, you may not."

She sat, anyway, landing heavily on an overstuffed

cushion on the sofa. It was that or fall. Anatoly seemed to understand.

"I didn't kill anyone," Lori said.

"This does not surprise me," Anatoly said. He took a step closer. "You do not look like the type of lady who knows how to fight. But you were with those who did kill my men, were you not?"

"It wasn't Hunter, either. My husband. He doesn't know how to fight, either."

Outside, beyond the windows, commotion rose in the night. People were upset. A few screams, and then a gunshot. The noise peaked, and then after more gunshots, it settled down to a murmur. From where she sat, Lori could see only the back of a soldier who blocked her view with his body. When the soldier turned, he jerked a nod at Anatoly.

"He certainly will not fight now," Anatoly said.

Lori cocked her head. Anatoly's expression told her that she should be reading something dire in his words, but she didn't understand the message. And then she did. "Oh, my God."

"You are a widow now, Mrs. Edwards. I am sorry for your loss, but you must realize that I had no choice."

It was too much. Pain and sadness and shock all flooded over her at once and she couldn't process it. She should be crying. She should be upset. But all she was, was scared.

"Tell me who killed my men," Anatoly said. He took another step forward, where he towered over her, looking down. "That is your one hope to avoid a bullet."

Lori thought of all the terrible thoughts she'd had

about Hunter earlier tonight. The stupid arguments. There was no taking those back now. She'd—

"Mrs. Edwards."

She looked up. She didn't try for eye contact at this distance. It would have hurt her neck to crank it back that far. She settled for looking at his belt buckle, instead. "I'm right here."

"I do not like repeating myself."

Jesus, what had he just asked? Oh, yeah. "I don't know their names," she said. "They call themselves by code names. They were in the bungalow next to ours. The bungalow where they put the bodies."

"So, you *were* there."

"You already knew that." A hard slap to the left side of her face retriggered her nosebleed.

"Do not be flippant."

Lori said nothing. She couldn't think of anything to say that would not earn her another slap.

"Their names are Stephen Terrell and Alicia Crosby," Anatoly said. "And at least one of them is a skilled fighter."

"You have to understand that there was not a lot of time for conversation. We—"

Fast-approaching footsteps from outside the double doors drew everyone's attention. After a rapid three knocks, the man who'd been thrown out only moments ago rushed back in. He spewed out an urgent message in the language that was sounding more and more like Russian to Lori's ear.

As Anatoly listened, color rose from his neck into his cheeks. He trembled. When he returned his gaze to Lori, she knew she was going to die.

* * *

"Jesus, they shot the husband," Jonathan whispered. They hadn't moved from their concealment, watching as the team of four soldiers filed up the gangplank to investigate the crewman's distress call. The news broke over the monitored radio channel.

"Oh, my God," Gail breathed. "The bastards. What about Lori?"

"No word."

"They're animals."

Jonathan didn't respond. What was there to say? They were posed almost identically, side by side, three feet apart on their left knees, rifles at the ready.

"Murder doesn't come for free," Jonathan said finally.

Gail pivoted her head toward him, waiting for more.

"Hunter didn't kill anyone. He was just a pussy who was in the wrong place at the right time." He returned Gail's gaze.

"Tell me," she said.

"We're going to kill these guys when they're coming back down. We need to start culling their herd."

Gail said nothing as she turned back to her rifle and its sight picture.

"We have to get them all," Jonathan continued, "and we have to drop them fast, before they can radio for help."

Gail still did not move, did not respond.

"Are you hearing me?"

"Yes, I am."

"Are you in?"

"Would it matter?"

Jonathan felt anger swelling. He got that she was

tired, and that this was stressful, but this was hardly the time for passive-aggressive bullshit.

And that's exactly what I'm engaging in.

His ear lit up with the announcement that the boarding team had found the ship's captain dead.

"They found our surprise," Jonathan relayed.

"*My* surprise," Gail corrected. "What's our next move?"

Jonathan held up a finger as he listened to the radio. "There's some discussion about whether or not they should search the ship," he said. He listened some more. "Nope, they've been recalled to the plantation, where they'll figure their next move. That's smart. Four people isn't enough manpower to track down a shooter on a ship."

Gail gave him a wild-eyed look. "We did it with two."

"We were looking for people, not shooters," Jonathan corrected. Then he flashed the smile that had melted so many hearts over the years. "And people rarely accuse me of being smart." He shifted his tone to a more serious one. "When they come down the gangplank, if they come as a cluster, that will be our best chance to nail them. If they play out in a longer string, we might have to divide our shots between the gangplank and the pier. No matter what, no one gets closer than the spot where the pier meets the paved apron. Does that make sense?"

"No closer than the apron."

"Wait for my command. Your targets will be the closest ones, I'll take the two in the back."

"Got it."

And they waited. It seemed like a very long time,

longer than it should. And then he saw why. They were carrying the captain's body down the gangplank. Other crewmen gathered along the rail, watching.

"Why would they do that?" Jonathan whispered.

"It would be hard to leave a friend to rot in the heat," Gail said.

"Yeah," Jonathan agreed. "If they're expecting to go home on that rust bucket, they probably don't want it to smell of rancid corpse."

"Jesus, Dig." Gail shifted her position. "We've got 'em all on the gangplank."

All four of the soldiers were lined up on the gang-plank, with the two in the rear jammed up behind the body bearers. The two who were not on the body bag were on point, squared away in their stances as they advanced sideways, their rifles to their shoulders. These guys clearly knew that they presented tempting targets.

"Not yet," Jonathan whispered. "They're too amped. They're scanning for shooters and their weapons are at the ready." The trick to winning a gunfight was to do it with as few bullets as possible, and with something close to zero return fire. "The body bearers will be your targets. I'll take the shooters. Wait till I fire, and then take aimed shots." He knew that this level of coaching was going to piss Gail off, but it had to be said.

Jonathan watched through his three-power scope, tracking the movements of his chosen targets. He waited until the soldiers with the body were on the level surface of the pier and the shooters were about to make the transition. Instinctively, they shifted their eyes from the target horizon to where they were placing their feet. That presented a perfect profile picture. Jonathan settled his reticle on the first shooter's ear and squeezed the trigger.

The second soldier clutched his shoulder and fell.

"Shit, they didn't zero their weapons!" he said, but his words were lost in the sound of Gail's barking rifle. As the lead shooter reacted and started to bring his rifle to bear, Jonathan shifted his sight picture to the right, guessed at the Kentucky windage, and pressed the trigger. The guy dropped, but Jonathan didn't see where the bullet hit—or if it hit him at all.

Meanwhile, in the foreground, Gail's first target dropped under a cloud of brain spray, and the second pirouetted like a top and spun face-first onto the planks of the pier.

"I'm moving up," Jonathan said. "Stay put and watch for reinforcements." He didn't wait for a response as he left his cover and advanced toward the ship with his rifle to his shoulder. As he passed the first body, he fired another shot into his head, just to make sure. There was a message to be delivered to the assholes who found the bodies, and he wanted to make sure it was crystal clear.

He skipped the captain's body, but tapped the second guy Gail had dropped. From the way the body jerked, it was clear that he hadn't been dead yet. The fact that he hadn't heard any more radio traffic encouraged him that the two on the gangplank might be dead already. He couldn't trust that, of course—no one was dead until they were by-God dead—so he kept his focus on the side panel that masked the men he'd shot.

When he was within fifteen feet, he stitched a seven-round string of holes through the fabric into the deck of the gangplank beyond, where he calculated his targets to be. No one shot back.

Before advancing farther, he replaced the partially-expended magazine with a fresh one and switched to a left-handed stance as he swung the turn to the right. The lead shooter couldn't possibly be any more dead. The shot to his left ear had avulsed most of the right side of his face. Blood-tinged white brain matter lay gathered in a lump on the aluminum surface of the deck.

The second gunman was more of a problem. Still alive, he was working hard to pull himself up the incline to the deck of the ship. From the way he moved, dragging his lower body, Jonathan figured that he'd maybe clipped his spine. He drew a bead on the guy, but then lifted his finger from the trigger.

"Hey, you," Jonathan called.

Startled, the wounded man fumbled with his rifle to get it into play.

"You don't want to do that," Jonathan said. As he approached, he held his aim. "I'll kill you if you go near that weapon."

The soldier wasn't convinced. Jonathan could sense him weighing his options. Two seconds later, he ostentatiously lifted his hands from his M4 and did his best to raise them. Jonathan approached no closer than six feet, then stooped down. This man couldn't have been more than twenty-two years old.

"What's your name, son?" Jonathan asked.

The kid eyed the muzzle that was staring at him and trembled.

"Not a lot to lose for you right now," Jonathan said. "Your friends are all dead, and you soon will be, without medical attention. I don't see a downside to answering a few questions. Now, what's your name?"

More silence.

"You don't want to die anonymously, do you?"

The trembling worsened. "Sergei."

"What's the mission here, Sergei? Why did you invade a vacation spot and bring an army with you?"

"Please help me."

"In due time. Answers first."

"I am doing job."

Jonathan noted the dropped article. "Are you Russian?"

Sergei hesitated, and then he nodded.

"Are all of you Russians?"

Another nod. "Yes."

"Are you Russian military?"

"Once. I used to be."

"Is that true of all of you? Are you all mercenaries?"

The word seemed to confuse him.

"Soldiers for money," Jonathan clarified.

"I do not know. Commander does not like us talking to each other about other days."

This made sense to Jonathan. The simultaneous strength and weakness of mercenary forces the world over was that they owed allegiance to nothing but their own bank accounts. The less they knew about each other individually, the less downstream liability for all of them if something went wrong. On the flip side, it's hard to depend on your buddy dying for you when he's not actually a buddy.

"Were you recruited in Russia?"

Sergei shook his head. "No. In Kiev. Ukraine."

"Who recruited you?"

"A man. I do not know his name. I went to a place and the man gave me money and told me to be in Mexico City by last Saturday."

This also rang true under the circumstances. Whoever was in charge, they were hiring guns, not strategists. Guns and the people who carried them needed to know when and whom to shoot. They did not need to know why.

They stared at each other for a long few seconds. "You kill me now," Sergei said.

"I haven't made up my mind yet," Jonathan said. It was a statement of fact. The kid had been cooperative. He'd been—

"That was a request, not a question," Sergei clarified. "I am paralyzed. I am bleeding. Better to die fast by a bullet than die slow from infection."

Jonathan narrowed his gaze. These were the decisions that woke him up years after the fact. Killing in the frenzy of battle weighed on his conscience—how could it not? But selective killing was hard.

"Please," Sergei repeated.

Jonathan settled himself with a deep breath. "Sleep well," he said. And he pulled the trigger.

CHAPTER 12

"Wait. What? What time is it?" Jesse Montgomery wasn't sure he was awake yet, let alone that he was hearing correctly.

"Zero dark early, kid, and it's time to rise and shine. I'll be by to pick you up in thirty minutes."

"And where are we going again?"

"Zihuatanejo."

"Gesundheit. Is that a place?"

"We're going back to Mexico, sonny boy."

Something hitched in Jesse's stomach. "I thought we were supposed to stay away from Mexico." The man on the other end of the phone was Davey Montgomery, Jesse's father. Less than a year ago, they'd helped take a healthy divot out of Mexico's northern coastline. He didn't know how to say *persona non grata* in Spanish.

"As I understand it, we'll just be passing through."

"As you *understand* it? What the hell is going on, Davey?"

"See you in a half hour." The phone went dead.

"Well, shit." Jesse swung his feet to the carpeted

floor of his brand-spanking-new apartment and turned the switch on the nightstand lamp. Squinting against the assault to his retinas, he padded to the en suite bathroom and set about the chores that needed to be done. Every time he looked at his new digs, he smiled. All too recently, his accommodations had ranked at the bottom of the shithole scale. Only slightly before that, they had consisted of concrete walls and steel bars.

Then he met a priest who introduced him to a voice on the phone who called herself Mother Hen, and everything changed. Whoever she was in real life, she had some pretty strong contacts that were able to get his probation canceled, on the single condition that he could steal a big-ass boat and get it to Mexico to rescue a guy named Scorpion and a truly terrifying creature who called himself Big Guy (because Gigantor was already taken).

That job led to others, all of which bore the common thread of stealing stuff for the good guys. Of course, none of what he did was *official*. That meant if things went badly, he'd be on his own, without official cover. On the flip side, it also meant that payment came in the form of cash, with no IRS 1099s attached. If people asked him where he got his money—and they never did—he'd just tell them that he inherited it.

The worst part of his new line of work was the frequent proximity of violence, and he was not a violent man. Never did have the stomach for it. His father, Davey, on the other hand, was a retired violence specialist. All he'd tell Jesse was that he worked for the Navy, but he'd never elaborate. Jesse took him at his word, never questioned it. Though he often wondered where Davey *really* learned his excellent killing skills.

As he pulled on a pair of jeans and slipped into a T-shirt, it occurred to him that he didn't know how long they were going to be gone. But he knew all too well that Mexico was hot as hell, so he grabbed a backpack and threw in a pair of shorts, some swim trunks, underwear, and flip-flops. He added a toothbrush and some deodorant and declared himself ready.

As was typical for Davey, thirty minutes meant thirty minutes exactly. As his old man pulled up in his 'Vette, Jesse stepped out of his front door and into the lightening darkness and Nashville chill. Davey had the top down, despite the cool temperature. It was a Davey thing. If you paid for a rag top, then you by-God drove with the top down. He made exceptions for rain and severe cold, but not until there was a deluge or the mercury had dropped below forty.

If there was one takeaway for Jesse from prison, it was that being a little too cool was orders of magnitude better than being a lot too hot.

"Mornin', Jesse boy," Davey said. He was dressed like a hood from the 1960s. Long black coat, T-shirt, black jeans, and motorcycle boots.

Jesse dropped his backpack into the backseat, opened the door, and dropped himself into the front bucket. "You gonna fill me in on the details?" he asked.

The Corvette made a throaty growl as it pulled away from the curb.

"We got another job," Davey said.

"Which agency?"

"This one's private sector, but the pay's the same."

"In a city whose name sounds like a sneeze."

"Nope," Davey said. He looked over his left shoulder

as he signaled a lane change. "It's on an island off the coast of the city whose name sounds like a sneeze."

"Another boat job?"

"Exactly."

"What do we need to do?"

Davey cast him a sideward glance. "Remember the guys we rescued from Mexico?"

Jesse felt himself scowling. "Big Guy?"

"The other one."

"Scorpion."

Davey grinned. "Yeah. Well, he needs to be rescued again."

"From who?"

"We're not sure yet."

"We?"

Davey returned his eyes to the road. "Me and Big Guy."

The more they discussed this, the less sense it made. "Big Guy is not with Scorpion?"

"No, Gunslinger is with Scorpion."

"Jesus. Who's 'Gunslinger'?"

"Scorpion's girlfriend. She's an operator, too."

Realization was beginning to dawn. "Wait, do you know these people?"

"We've gotten together a few times."

"Since the Mexico thing?"

Davey gave a shrug. "I used to be part of a fairly small community," he said. "After Mexico, Big Guy and I kept in touch. We've had dinner a couple of times. He called me for help on this."

Jesse listened as his father told him all that had been relayed to him by Big Guy.

Jesse summarized, "So, let me get this straight. Big

Guy is assembling a little army to do battle with a big army to rescue two people."

"Or maybe we'll be rescuing dozens of people," Davey said. "A hundred or more. All of the guests at the resort."

"Isn't that a suicide mission?"

Davey gave him a look. "Not if you know what you're doing."

Jesse watched his father drive in silence for the better part of a minute, weighing the difference between rational confidence and bullshit braggadocio. Then he got hit with a thought: "Wait. Why am I going along? I don't know how to shoot people."

Davey's grin turned huge. "Somebody's got to stay with the boat," he said.

Tyler and Jaime shared a joint and did their best to remain calm as they waited. The "clubhouse," as they called their restored shanty, which normally felt roomy and amply proportioned, seemed small and claustrophobic tonight. The weed helped a little, but in the way that a garden hose helps with a forest fire.

"Suppose that shooting was them?" Jaime asked.

"Thinking the same thing," Tyler said. "What's the worst that could happen?"

"To us or to them?"

"Is there a difference?"

"Well, yeah," Jaime said. "Me dying is a hell of a lot different than them dying."

Tyler found that funny. Or maybe the weed found it funny. "We need to *not* get caught," he said. "That's the main thing."

"How do we do that?"

Tyler shrugged. "By being smarter than them. By staying out of the way. Out of sight, out of—"

"You know you can smell that shit from fifty yards away, right?" It was Scorpion's voice, and it startled the crap out of Tyler. Almost literally. Then Scorpion appeared in the doorway. "And I think you should use your inside voices, not your playground voices, when people want to kill you."

Gunslinger came in behind him. Each of them carried an extra rifle and extra vest with stuff in them. "Let me have your seat," Scorpion said. "I'm a working man. Each of you two put on a vest."

He tossed one onto Tyler's lap, making him jump.

Tyler stood and turned the vest over in his hands, trying to figure it out. "You don't put it on like a coat," Scorpion said. "It slips over your head. Here." He took the vest from him. "Put your arms up, like your mommy's putting a sweater on for you." Tyler did just that while Mr. Macho settled the vest onto his shoulders. It felt lighter than it did when he was holding it.

"Did the others find you?" Jaime asked.

"Nope, they were shot and killed," Scorpion said. He didn't drop a beat. "Why'd you let them leave?"

"How was I going to stop them?" Tyler asked.

"If you knew then, what you know now, you'd have found a way."

"Come on, Scorpion," Gunslinger said. "That's not fair."

"Reality so rarely is." Scorpion sat heavily in the overstuffed chair. "So, here's where we stand. Apparently, the bad guys made a promise early on that anyone caught off campus, so to speak, would be summarily shot."

"And their whole families," Tyler added.

"Then here's hoping that Dipshit and his bride didn't have children."

"That's pretty harsh," Jaime said.

Scorpion started to say something, but then settled himself and tried again. "I don't know how to do what needs to be done without being harsh," he said. "So far tonight, by my count, Gunslinger and I have killed seven men, all of whom were doing their level best to kill us first. That makes me testy. Then, when I try to save a yuppie couple's ass, they piss on my shoes and get themselves killed, anyway. So, from here on out—from now until this thing is over—when I say something, mentally insert a *please* or a *thank you* or a *by your leave* wherever you think it's appropriate. Meanwhile, follow my orders or leave us the hell alone. Do any of those words or concepts confuse you?"

Tyler gaped. He wasn't sure anyone had ever spoken to him like that. The tone pissed him off, but the words made perfect sense.

Scorpion wasn't finished. "You're both going to have to pull your weight, though. We brought rifles for you, along with ammunition."

"Where did—" Jaime cut himself off before he could finish the stupid question.

"Yeah, that's exactly where," Scorpion said with a smile. "Have either of you ever shot before?"

"I had a BB gun when I was little," Tyler offered.

"The most important thing to remember is to keep your booger hook off the bang switch," Scorpion said.

Tyler didn't get it.

"Keep your finger off the trigger," Gunslinger translated with a roll of her eyes.

"And keep the safety on till it's time to shoot. I'll give you a tour of your weapons when we have more light. I'll also want you to carry stuff when we move."

"Are we going someplace now?"

"I don't want to move tonight if we can avoid it," Scorpion replied, "but the thing about enemies is they get a vote in any plan you make."

"There's a concern that the Edwardses might have told them about this place," Gunslinger explained.

"Oh, shit," Tyler said.

"So here's what I need you two to do," Scorpion said. "Go outside and sit and watch while Gunslinger and I get some work done."

That piqued Tyler's interest. "What kind of work?"

He watched as Scorpion and Gunslinger dumped dozens of bits of paper from their pockets onto the floor at the base of the chairs.

"We need to find out who our enemy is, and what they're trying to accomplish."

"Aren't they just terrorists?"

"Terrorists kill and run," Gunslinger said.

"These guys brought a big-ass ship with them," Scorpion went on. "That tells me that they're here for more than just mayhem. They're here to get something and take it home with them."

Jaime stood a little taller and cocked his head. Tyler caught it, and so did Scorpion.

"All input is welcome," Scorpion said. "If you've got a theory, I'm all ears."

"I wonder if it has anything to do with the storage caves," Jaime said.

CHAPTER 13

Baker Sinise chose to ignore the ringing phone on the bed stand. Whoever it was at this ridiculous hour, they would give up sooner or later. Or so one would think. After eleven rings, however, it became clear to him that the caller was determined. He snatched the receiver off the cradle and brought it to his ear. "What!"

"Good morning, Mr. Sinise. This is Rosaria at the front desk. There are some gentlemen here from *la Policía*. Shall I send them up, or should they wait for you here? They say it is a very urgent matter."

"What kind of urgent matter?"

"Yo no se," she said. "But they tell me, and I quote, 'One way or another, we need to talk to Mr. Sinise now.'"

Baker sighed. What had Tyler done this time? "Yeah, okay. Give me five minutes. *Cinco minutos.*"

Tyler knew that this getaway was important to Baker, knew that he needed time away from the resort to get his head together. It had been a stressful couple of months, and these five days seaside in Zihuatanejo—

being served by others, rather than being responsible for providing service—were just what he needed. That boy was impossible.

"Boy, my ass," he said aloud. Tyler was nineteen, a man by any definition. The world was full of wounded veterans who were younger than he was. Sooner or later, he was going to have to start acting the part.

Right after I stop enabling him. He heard his ex-wife's voice in that last thought, in the same tone as she phoned in all of her tidbits of advice from wherever in the world she and her sugar daddy were traveling.

Baker decided to take the time to brush his teeth and run a dry razor over his face before going downstairs. While he had done nothing wrong, and the police were here reportedly just to talk, this was Mexico. When people of means were in this part of the world, excuses to detain and extort money were often created on the fly. Always best to approach such times with personal hygiene chores all taken care of.

He'd chosen to stay in the Hotel Del Mar for its old-world charm and very generous bartender, but the trade-off for charm was iffy climate control. Thus, his room was only on the second floor—all the better to stagger back from Pedro's pours. He donned the beige suit and pink shirt he'd worn all day yesterday. Then Baker walked out of his suite to the center of the hallway and turned left to head down the grand staircase to the lobby, where the registration desk was located on the far end, on the right.

As he swung the turn, his first thought was that the cops must be working on some kind of undercover deal. They had a rigid posture about them, almost a military bearing. It's not at all what he'd come to expect from the local constabulary, particularly not in this little corner of Zihuatanejo. The unexpected appearance gave Baker an uneasy feeling, which spiked off the charts when the pretty young thing behind the desk made eye contact with him, then hurried around the corner and disappeared into the office.

The rest of what happened, happened with startling speed. The cop on the right raised his hand, as if it were holding a pistol. Baker heard a *pop* and then he seized and fell. He tasted and smelled blood and was fully aware that he'd just been Tasered. He had no idea why or by whom, but those details seemed of little importance as his body jerked on the tile floor. He was still flopping when the other cop approached him, leaned over, and cocked back a fist.

Then . . . nothing.

Jonathan gaped at Jaime. "What kind of 'storage caves'?"

Jaime shrugged. "I don't even know if that's really what they are. But I can't think of anything else they might be."

"Where are they?"

Jaime pointed to a spot that might have been through the roof. "Over there. On the other side of the island."

"Are they used?" Gail asked. "And if so, what's in them?"

"Only a few are used. These are massive man-made caves made of reinforced concrete. The ones that are used have big locks on them. I've only seen them once or twice, and I've never spent any serious time around them. It's a firing offense to be anywhere near them."

"Even for the maintenance guy?" Tyler asked. "And how come I don't know anything about them?"

Jaime laughed. "Because your father would tear me a new asshole if I told you." He seemed to have hurt Tyler's feelings. "Sorry, dude. I didn't mean any harm."

"Tell me what you do know about these . . . caves," Jonathan pressed. In his experience, large reinforced concrete "caves" meant only one thing, and it had nothing to do with geology. He didn't want to test-drive his theory, though, until he had more to go on.

"That's really about all of it," Jaime said.

"'About all' means there's more." Gail was losing patience, too.

"Every now and then, the marina gets active at odd hours," Jaime explained. "Always at night. Late. That's why I didn't think much about the ship with the terrorists on it. You know, until I saw that it had terrorists on it."

Jonathan's mood darkened even more. "You weren't startled even by the size of the ship?"

Jaime did a bobblehead thing as he thought about that. "I guess tonight's ship is bigger than most. But about the same as some."

Jonathan asked, "What typically follows the arrival of these vessels?"

"What 'follows'?"

"Yeah, what do they do? Do the crews stay here at the resort? Do they—"

"Oh, God no," Jaime said. "Mr. Sinise would never stand for that. They come, they get their work done, and then they're out of here. Often before dawn, but always before noon. Well before the guest ship arrives at two."

"Are they off-loading cargo?" Gail asked.

"I believe so. I've never actually watched them working. Again, I would lose my job if I got caught watching that."

"Surely, there must be some signs of something," Jonathan said. "When you go down to meet the incoming passengers, you must see some kind of evidence of what these mystery ships do."

"I think you're really asking me if I think that these ships bring things for the cave. And yes, I do think that. But I can't swear to that."

"Why do you think it?" Gail asked.

"The forklifts will be low on battery power or gas, depending on which machine. We'll find pallet nails and bits of wood and debris. All of that has to be cleaned up before the guests arrive. There can be no mess for the guests."

Jonathan remembered how impressed he was with the pristine cleanliness of the place when he and Gail first arrived. "Do you see military items?" he asked.

"You mean, like bullets and things?"

"Yeah, but also other things. Do you see torn labels with pictograms on them? Drawings of little explosions?"

"Excuse me, Scorpion," Tyler said. "You seem to be going someplace with this. What are you thinking?"

Jonathan shared a glance with Gail, who clearly had gone to the same place as he. "The kind of structures you just described are typical of explosives-storage facilities," he explained. "Bombs and rockets and bullets, and what have you, all need to be stored somewhere before they're deployed. That's where storage magazines come in. They're stupid-expensive to build because they have to be engineered in such a way as to contain any accidental explosion if one were to occur. You've seen the insides?"

Jaime nodded. "When they're unlocked, they're just there."

"Describe the doors," Gail said.

"Huge," Jaime said. "Made of steel, I think. Like bank vault doors, but ten times the size."

"Does my father ever go down there when they're moving things from the ship?" Tyler asked.

"I don't know, Ty. I've never seen him down there, but like I said, I'm never down there when they're off-loading."

Jonathan stood. "Well, I think we've hit upon a corner of the *why* of the evening. This has something to do with weapons. The Russians, or whoever they are, want what your daddy's got."

"And he's not here to give it to them," Jaime said, completing the logic.

"Wait," Tyler said. "My father does not have a bunch of weapons on this island. He wouldn't do that."

"Evidence to the contrary," Jonathan said. Nothing could be less relevant to him right now than a son's loyalty to his father.

"That's not much to go on," Gail said. "Even if you're spot-on, there's a lot more to know."

Jonathan checked his watch. "And it's six-thirty," he said. "Time for our check-in call. Excuse us, gentlemen." He pointed with his forehead to the shanty's door. "Remember to stay quiet and keep an eye out for movement."

Gail lowered the pitch of her voice to as low as her alto vocal cords would allow, and said, "And keep your damn fingers off the triggers." She winked at Jonathan. "I figured you were missing Big Guy."

Henry West felt his bride's glare burning blisters into his back as he threw clothes into his suitcase and tried mentally to inventory what he was missing versus what he had.

"I don't understand why you can't tell me where you're going," Sarah said. "I don't need to know why, but you always tell me the *where.*"

Henry avoided eye contact and the delay that would bring. "I don't understand why you have to keep pressing when I already told you that I can't tell you."

"Can't or *won't?*"

"One leads to the other," Henry said. *Jesus, how does she see through me so easily?* "You know the kind of work I've always done. Part and parcel, babe. Part and parcel."

"Are you telling me that this is for work, then?" Sarah asked.

He wasn't going to lie to her. They'd been through too much over too many years for him to insult her that way, so he said nothing. He crossed in front of his bed and pulled a baseball cap off the top shelf of his closet.

"Oh, my God," Sarah said. She brought her hand to her mouth. "They pulled you back in. You're back with the teams."

Henry didn't think for a second that his poker face was solid enough to pull off a lie, even if he'd been inclined to try. "I am *not* back with the teams," he said. "I'm still with No Such Agency, just as I've been since I left the team."

"Please don't lie to me, Henry. That's your Conan hat, and you haven't worn it in years."

Henry felt deflated. "I wasn't lying," he said. "Not really. I haven't rejoined the teams."

"But?"

"But I have to help a friend." He could feel the heat of her anger.

"Henry, you promised. And not just me. The kids too."

He turned away from his packing and squared up to her. He reached out for her hands, but she didn't respond. He didn't move until she finally gave in and took his palms in hers. "I am not lying. I have not joined with any official team, but yes, I have joined with an unofficial one, and this is a one-off. One in a row is not a trend."

"Who are the others you'll be with?"

"I don't know them all, but I can't tell you about any of them. That's just not the way it works."

"Will it be dangerous?"

"Isn't everything these days?"

"Don't," Sarah said, and she tried to pull back. But she didn't try very hard. He wouldn't let her. "You know what I'm asking. Will there be shooting?"

"Probably," he said.

"Is this official government business?"

"The government can't do what we're going to do. More precisely, there is no government where we're going." He saw her face darken and he tried to put a new spin on it. "I'm making this sound worse than it is. A friend of mine—a man I owe my life to, literally—has been taken hostage in a place where there is no hope of government intervention."

"In this country?"

"I can't tell you that."

Her exasperation was growing. "Can you at least re-assure me that what you're about to do is legal?"

He just looked at her, letting his silence serve as the answer she didn't want to hear.

"Jesus, Henry. How can you do this? How can you risk everything—your life, our kids' futures, *my* future—for a stranger?"

"He's not a stranger," Henry said. This time, he let her hands go. "He's the very opposite of a stranger."

"He's a stranger to me!"

"Sarah, what do you want me to say?"

"I want you to say no!"

"I can't."

"You mean, you won't."

"Fine, then. If that makes you feel better, then I *won't*. But because I can't. This guy would move heaven and earth to do the same for me." He felt his throat thickening, a total surprise. "And that's after he already damn near died to save my life. You want to talk about your future and the kids' futures? We have a present day because of him. In my world, you don't turn your back on that. Can't, don't, won't, whatever the hell you want to call it—it's who I am. It's who I hope you want me to be, and who I hope the kids grow up to be."

Sarah stared, tears in her eyes, but she wasn't cry-ing. She looked less angry.

Henry moved in and took her hands again. "You knew

what you were getting, even way back then. There's a code, and the code is good. Sometimes we risk everything because the goal is that important. I love you. I love you all. But if I expect Kenny and Lindsay to respect me, I need to respect myself first." He pulled her into a hug.

Sarah pressed her face into his chest, wiping her tears on his shirt. Her hand wandered to his crotch. "Speaking of Kenny and Lindsay, did you know they won't be home for, like, hours?" She pushed him toward the bed and Henry fell backward onto the mattress. He closed his eyes and cupped her face as she fondled him through his trousers.

Then she stopped.

He opened his eyes to see her staring down at him, a curious expression on her face. "What?" he asked.

"Are you even any good at the Conan stuff anymore?"

CHAPTER 14

Venice Alexander carried the burden of many secrets. The business of Security Solutions thrived on them, and in most cases, revelation of the secrets she kept would cost people their lives. Early on, she found the burden to be crushing. However, as time moved on and she saw the long-term benefits of what Digger and his team were able to pull off in the field, she realized that the benefits outweighed the liabilities. It was all a matter of trust.

But there were other secrets, too—secrets that she'd never shared with anyone—and those were the ones that allowed her to do her job so well.

In the dark world of covert shooters, Mother Hen was a handle recognized by everyone. Admired as a force of nature, she was an unstoppable, unstumpable solver of critical riddles and problems. But no one outside of Security Solutions—and the executive suite of the FBI—had any idea of her true identity. And it wasn't for lack of trying. You don't tap into the resources that Venice tapped into without inviting retaliatory hacks. Thankfully, Digger never said no when she asked for resources, and those resources, combined with her skills, kept attackers at bay.

In the dark world of computer hackers, she was a nobody. Mother Hen might as well have been Mother Goose. But FreakFace666 was beyond famous. He was a key player—the leader, if there was such a thing—of Gloomity, a hacker army that most recently revealed to the world the sealed juvenile court records of a child molester campaigning to be mayor of San Francisco. That hack was actually a commission from the candidate's opponent, who'd paid a hefty sum in bitcoin. FreakFace666 didn't want the money—in fact, Gloomity donated it all to a child-protection charity—but the whole point of creating chaos was to make people pay in as many ways and on as many planes as possible.

FreakFace666 had no idea who the other players in Gloomity were, and that was exactly how he liked it. For all he knew, one of those other electron teasers was an FBI agent or a Scotland Yard inspector. He didn't care. These major hacks could go on with impunity, with a nearly zero chance of backlash or repercussion, so long as anonymity was the rule of everything.

FreakFace666 knew who Mother Hen was, though. Because they were the same person.

FreakFace666's pronoun was *he* because that's what the hacker world expected. And that was Venice's one secret that no one else in the world knew about. It helped that Jonathan was a confessed and proud Luddite who would have difficulty even conceiving of the right questions to connect the dots to her alt-identity. He also didn't care. She got him the information he wanted, more or less when he needed it, and that appeared to be the beginning and the end of it for him. He had to know that she was making special things happen, but he never asked the questions, and she never presumed to give him what he clearly didn't want to know.

It was the nature of FreakFace666 that he had to break laws in order to have the street cred with others in the hackersphere. It was the part of his identity that Venice disliked, but it was necessary if she was going to get the help she needed from the people from whom she needed it.

There was nothing especially exotic about the current task at hand—finding out why there was a complex of explosives-storage facilities on Crystal Sands Island and who put them there—but it was vexing, nonetheless. Truth be told, she wasn't sure where to start. The commercial Internet search sites were useless, but was that because the information was buried, or because she didn't enter the right search parameters? This was the kind of intellectual spelunking that could inspire her to kill hours without a bathroom break, but she didn't have that kind of time.

Digger and Gail didn't have that kind of time.

FreakFace666 rarely worked from Security Solutions' office at all, but he never worked out of the War Room. Venice knew of no vulnerabilities with the equipment there, but the consequences of a breach from within were too devastating even to consider. She rose from her command chair in the War Room and buttonhooked a right to turn into her office. She closed the door and spun the blinds shut. Whereas Jonathan had furnished his office on the model of a rich man's city club, Venice preferred efficiency of function. Digger called her decorating aesthetic "chrome and glass," but the reality of it was closer to Scandinavian mini-malist. She liked light-colored woods and polished metallic finishes.

FreakFace666 kept his laptop computer in a wall safe that was controlled by both a fingerprint scanner and an eight-digit combination. The fact of the safe was no secret, but the contents thereof were. And Digger had never asked about it.

Venice took her time establishing her online presence, routing her way through multiple servers before finally projecting herself to be on a server in Sri Lanka. It was part of FreakFace666's persona that he always appeared from a different part of the world. For this visit, though, the research to be done was so on-the-nose that FreakFace666 masked his identity with the moniker BadThings, an identity that had never been used, and likely never would be used again. If Freak-Face666 had appeared as himself, he'd have been swamped with greetings from admirers and hangers-on. BadThings, on the other hand, could wander the dark corridors unmolested.

Venice was hunting for one particular individual. His real name was Derek Halstrom, and he worked for the National Security Agency. He thought his avatar of TickTock2 was unbreakable, and it would have been if he hadn't let his guard down for just a few seconds, about three years ago, and allowed Venice to slip in behind his invisibility cloak. Once in and undetected, she could own him for as long as she wanted. As was so often the case, the hackers who thought they were the best let their egos blind them to the fact that there were millions just like them, trying to take them down.

Derek Halstrom got mediocre performance appraisals

at NSA, and was twice disciplined in the past year for taking improper precautions with classified materials. Something about not putting them back in the safe within the allotted time period. He clearly was not happy in his work.

But TickTock2 loved the fact that he knew stuff. He loved that when the Interwebs were all abuzz with rumors and innuendos he could be the definitive source to set the record straight. Venice knew this not by conjecture or through social engineering, but because TickTock2 kept a journal on the same computer from which he ran his hacking empire. The only way Venice could make sense out of such a stupid decision—okay, the journal itself was an unthinkable idea—was that maybe if the balloon went up on a bad hack, he'd be able to trash all the evidence with one destruct button.

TickTock2 also enjoyed something of a bromance with FreakFace666. If you're going to preen, after all, you want to preen for the best.

Venice had to ping for only about twenty minutes before she found him. Then it was a matter of getting his attention. At this hour of the morning, she assumed that he hadn't yet left for work.

Good morning, TickTock2, she wrote. **Gotta minit?** This was the Internet. Dumbing down the language was an important part of her cover.

Wattup?

Ur the guy who knows secret shit, right?

Idk u—I don't know you.

Venice took a deep breath. There was no time for subtlety. **But I know you, Derek.**

In her mind, she pictured the panic, the feeling of the world coming apart. TickTock2's instinct would be to shut down the computer, but if he did that, she'd just text him on his phone. Working as he did for the NSA, he had to know that once a hacker had your personals, the hook was sunk too deeply ever to be retrieved.

She wrote, RU there?

What do you want?

Just information. Nothing that will send you to jail. Except, of course, everything TickTock2 has ever done could send Derek Halstrom to jail. Just in case, there was any remaining doubt in his mind, she had to drop the last name.

Venice typed in a detailed longitude-and-latitude string. I need to know what used to go on here.

Where is it?

Off the west coast of Mexico. Get back to me in two hours.

That's not enough time. It was not lost on Venice that the more stressed Derek became, the better his English.

It's all I have, so it's all you have. Then, just for good measure, she typed in his boss's phone number. That's even his private line.

He went silent. She saw him trying to cope with it all as he felt the walls coming in at him.

Ur wasting time, Venice typed. And she felt she owed him a slice of bitter truth: This is not a bluff, Derek. A lot is at stake. You don't want to cross me.

How do I get back in touch with you?

I'll be here. One hr 59 mins.

TickTock2's avatar disappeared from her screen. She hoped it was because he was in a hurry, and not because he was going to do anything stupid. She'd never deliberately hurt anyone before, but if he crossed her on this, she would nail his hide to the prison wall.

Thirty-seven minutes later, her laptop dinged, and Derek had returned. **I have what you want, but then it's over, right?**

Venice thought it best to be honest. **It's over till I need you again. There's no statute of limitations on treason. I'm not all that demanding, but I'm impatient as hell.**

TickTock2 fell silent for the better part of a minute, making her wonder if maybe she'd pushed him too far or too hard.

Then he spoke up again and totally ruined her day. Jonathan and Gail were in worse trouble than she thought.

As soon as the sun cleared the horizon, the heat and humidity both blossomed, and it became clear why Baker Sinise had positioned the resort on the part of the island he'd chosen. On this side—the unglamorous side—the air didn't move, allowing the flies and mosquitos to feast on invaders. Now that they could see where they were going—and others could see them going there—Jonathan decided to leave the roads and trails to hike through the belly of the jungle. Now that he was aware of what he was increasingly certain were explosives-storage magazines, he wanted to get a look at them. He wasn't sure what he was looking for, but more information was better than less. Maybe the size and configuration would tell him something.

Storing energetic materials—explosives—was itself a science. On military facilities, and those of their contractors, storage magazines, as they were called, were designed and arranged with the specific purpose of preventing a catastrophic explosion in one bunker from propagating to other bunkers. This was particularly critical for the storage of Class 1.1 mass-detonating materials. Say there were three adjacent storage magazines, each storing thirty thousand pounds of explosives. With improper bunker design or management, a thirty-thousand-pound incident could become a ninety-thousand-pound Armageddon. That was always bad.

Size mattered. From the physical volume of the structures—which Jaime had already professed to be huge—to the thickness of the walls, there was much information to be gleaned from a physical inspection.

During his scheduled six-thirty phone call back to the office, he'd relayed to Venice what they knew so far. She, in turn, seemed to be confident that she'd be able to cobble together the rest of what they needed—or at least some of it. He was scheduled for another phone call in twenty-five minutes.

As jungles went, this one was less dense than most. Jonathan wondered if that was Mother Nature's work, or the result of culling and trimming at the hands of the resort management team. The stench of rot and wetness that had come to define such places in his mind was less pervasive, and it was a relief to be able to see ten yards ahead rather than the two or three feet afforded by less friendly rain forests. The net effect was to make him feel less like he'd entered the wrong end of the food chain.

"I always liked the view from up here," Tyler said as they reached what Jonathan figured to be the highest point on the island. "It feels like you can see forever."

And forever, it seemed, consisted of nothing but water.

"How much farther to the magazines?" Gail asked. She was soaked through with sweat, and she'd used a length of paracord she'd found in her vest to tie her auburn hair back into a ponytail. It probably wasn't a look for everyone, but Jonathan thought she looked sexy.

"Not far," Jaime said. "Another ten, maybe twelve minutes." He looked back to Jonathan. "It is much closer when you use the trails."

"Couldn't be," Jonathan said through a smile. "What we're walking is a straight line. The roads meander."

"But they're much faster."

"Faster and closer are different things, Jaime. And getting shot and having to be carried—a likely result if we'd used the trails—makes the trip longer still."

Gail's posture straightened, as if on alert, and Jonathan held up his hand for silence. Something out there had attracted her attention. Jonathan didn't see anything.

"What've you got?" he asked.

Gail shaded her eyes with both hands, then extended one arm to point to the east. "A boat," she said. "Hard to see against the sun, but I know it's a boat."

Jonathan mimicked her posture, shading his eyes, and so did the other two.

"I see it," Tyler said, and he leveled his pointer to the same spot on the horizon. "Is that the *Express*?"

This was getting frustrating. "What the hell—" And then he saw it. Bravo to Gail for being the first to pick it out. In the distance, all but lost in the reflective glare of the rising sun, he could just discern the outline of a speck. If others were certain, he'd stipulate that it was a boat. "What is the *Express*?"

"It can't be," Jaime said. "It's not due for another two days."

"I'm guessing it's the ship that brought us out," Gail said.

Tyler said, "Exactly. Maybe they're the rescue team."

Jonathan rejected that out of hand. "Absolutely not. It's daytime and it's too slow. Could they be bringing more guests?"

"You know what you have to do to come here," Jaime said. "It's a minimum four-night stay because the boat only comes out here every four days."

"Suppose somebody gets sick?" Gail asked.

"And why didn't we talk about that before we settled on this island as a vacation spot?" Jonathan quipped.

"We have an infirmary here," Jaime said. "With a staff doctor. If it was something serious, we'd call for a helicopter."

"Anybody have a theory?" Jonathan asked.

"Could always be more soldiers," Tyler said.

"Somebody else come up with a theory," Jonathan said. "I don't like Tyler's."

"Supplies, maybe?" Gail offered.

"I don't know what supplies they could need that they don't already have," Jaime said.

Tyler doubled down. "I think it's more soldiers."

"I think you're right," Jonathan said. "But why use the company shuttle? Or, alternatively, why did they use the other ship if the shuttle was available?"

"I think we're getting ahead of ourselves," Gail said. "First of all, it's too far out to tell for sure if it's the *Express*. It's also too far out to tell for sure that it's even coming here."

"You're right," Jonathan said, and he helped himself to a deadfall, which he straddled like a horse. "Take a seat, everybody. Let's see what happens."

"What about the caves?" Jaime asked.

"Caves are stationary," Jonathan said. He pointed out to the horizon. "That, however, is moving. Let's see what it does. Besides, I've got to make a phone call, anyway. Tyler and Jaime, spread out to our flanks and make sure no one sneaks up on us."

"How far out?"

"Not far," Jonathan said. "Fifteen, twenty yards. Don't shoot anybody who doesn't shoot at you first."

"That sounds like a way to get killed," Jaime said. "Doesn't the second shooter in a gunfight usually have the worst day?"

Jonathan conceded the point with a smile. "Okay, then. You can shoot them when they start to point a gun at you. I just don't want you shooting a wayward resort guest if some of them were able to get away."

Tyler objected, "But if—"

"Read the tea leaves, Tyler," Gail said. "We need to make a phone call, and we want it to be private."

The two youngsters looked at each other and split.

"I didn't want to hurt their feelings," Jonathan said.

Gail laughed. "Yeah, right."

Jonathan pulled his phone from its pocket and powered it up. When it was fully booted, he called the office on speakerphone. Venice answered on the first ring.

"Thank God," she said. "I was going to explode soon if I didn't get to tell somebody what I found out."

She and Jonathan had known each other a long time. He understood that there was more fact than hyperbole in her words. "Sounds exciting."

"You're vacationing on the storage location for Soviet nuclear weapons," Venice said.

CHAPTER 15

"Come again?" Jonathan said.

"You heard correctly," Venice said. "A storage place for Soviet nukes."

"The Soviet Union no longer exists," Gail said.

Jonathan made a rocking motion with his hand. "Well . . . a rose by any other name, right?"

"I don't mean that it stores nukes now," Venice said. "That's what it used to be."

"How did you find this out?" Jonathan asked.

"I can't tell you. But I can give you some background if you'd like."

Jonathan stifled a laugh. As if there was a way to stop her. Venice loved her dramatic reveals, and because they were so frequently earth-shattering, he loved them, too. Okay, he *tolerated* them. And for the first time, he was grateful that Boxers was not there with him. Because Big Guy *hated* the dramatic reveals.

"Remember you told me that Crystal Sands Island is privately owned, and it has no real allegiance to any nation?"

"I told you that it is a protectorate of Costa Rica," Jonathan corrected.

"Which is almost the same thing," Venice said, "but even that was not the case until a relatively few years ago. Certainly, not until after the fall of the Soviet Union."

Jonathan placed the phone down onto the fallen tree that served as his seat, and shifted his position until he was sidesaddle. "Okay, what allegiance did it have before that?"

"It didn't have any! It literally was privately held, without any claim by any nation. The world thought it was part of Mexico—I mean, why not, right? Given its location."

"I'm not following," Jonathan admitted. "What does this have to do with storing nuclear weapons?" He looked to Gail, and she didn't seem to get it, either. Obviously expecting a long phone call, she was lowering herself to the ground at the base of a tree.

"It turns out that the Soviets were smarter than the rest of the world. They reached out to the previous owner of the island—a Russian name I couldn't begin to pronounce, so we'll call him Boris—and they worked out a deal. For an amount of money nobody's been able to figure out, he allowed the Russians to build storage facilities there."

"For nukes?" Jonathan had never heard of this, and he was better dialed into such things than most.

"That's what my source tells me, and he's in a position to know. As I understand it, the Soviets wanted to have a cache in their back pocket within range of the United States. This way, when things went bad, they'd have supplies that we never knew about."

Gail had lain back against the tree and pulled her

cap over her eyes. She could have been sleeping, or she could have been listening passively.

"Did they have launch mechanisms, too, or just the storage?" Jonathan asked.

"I didn't have that vocabulary in my head to ask the question," Venice confessed.

"Can you find out?"

"I suppose, but you need to understand that this particular source is one of my least cooperative ones. If it's a data point you need to know, then I can press. But if it's just curiosity, I'd prefer to leave it alone."

"Nah, leave it," Jonathan said. The significance of such a cache—and the fact that Uncle Sam didn't know about it—could have been catastrophic if there'd been a war with the Soviets. While Uncle was focused on all the known targets, the vast majority of which were in the Northern Hemisphere, Ivan could have been quietly planning a hit from the south. He questioned whether such a thing was possible without the cooperation of the Mexican government, but those were questions for diplomats, not retired soldiers.

"So, how did Costa Rica get control of the place?"

Venice chuckled on the other end of the connection. "That's pure politics. I don't know who found out about the island first, but it happened when someone was rummaging through Kremlin records after the fall."

"Somebody must have shit pickles," Jonathan said. The comment elicited a smile from Gail, so he knew she was still on board with the conversation.

"I imagine they did," Venice said. "But ultimately our guys found out about it, and the United States made claim to it all."

Jonathan's turn to laugh. "How'd that work for them?"

"Less well than they'd probably hoped," Venice said. "Central and South America all accused the U.S. of a landgrab, and the Organization of American States got involved. Lots of discussions and dealings, and finally, specifically because Costa Rica has no real military, all parties agreed that the island should go under their control. The gringos were kept out of the backyard, but no other country got a leg up militarily."

Jonathan thought it was a pretty fair compromise, actually. Much better than much of the quirky shit the OAS had tried to pull off over the years. "How did it become a resort?"

"That's less clear," Venice confessed. "My guy's interests in all this are fairly narrow. What we do know is that the Costa Ricans sold the property for a great deal of money about twenty years ago."

"To Baker Sinise?"

"To Crystal Sands Properties, LLC," Venice said. "Which is owned by Baker Sinise."

Jonathan fell silent as he weighed what he'd just learned. It was all very interesting, but it fell a mile short of explaining why the island would be invaded.

"Wait a second," Jonathan said. "The nukes aren't still here, are they?"

"Oh, God no," Venice said. "They were returned to Russia as part of the deal. Now ask me where Crystal Sands Properties, LLC, got the money to buy the island. The price tag was eighteen million and change."

"Where?" He knew she wanted nothing more than for him to ask the entire question just as she'd presented it, but there was no way.

"He didn't," she said.

Jonathan scowled. "Wait. What?"

"From what I can tell—and remember I've only been at this research since we last spoke—I don't see how he could afford to buy the island or where the money came from."

Jonathan felt his fatigue showing through. "I'm fuzzy here, Mother Hen. Are you suggesting something?"

"Didn't you tell me that there are nighttime shipments and that some of the magazines are locked?"

Then he got it. "Running a resort isn't his only business, is it?"

Gail lifted the hat off her face and sat up. "Gunrunning?"

"There's a new voice!" Venice declared. "I was wondering where you'd gone, Gunslinger."

"It doesn't have to be just gunrunning," Jonathan said. He sat taller on his log, totally engaged.

"I'm not the expert in these things," Venice said, "but it seems to me; that which can hold megatons of explosives can hold a lot of other stuff, too."

Jonathan refused the urge to explain that nuclear yield and explosive weight had precious little to do with each other because he agreed with her larger point.

"This makes perfect sense," he thought aloud. "The late-night shipments, the enforced secrecy, the obsessive cleanup after the fact."

"But why tonight?" Gail asked. "Okay, last night? What was different?"

"And why the hostages?" Jonathan added. "You want

to steal munitions, you steal them. In and out. The only reason you'd have to kill is if someone fought back, and they weren't anticipating a fight."

"I'm not there," Venice said, "but from what you've told me so far, it sure sounds like they were expecting a fight."

Jonathan shook his head. "Fighting and intimidation are different skill sets requiring different weapons. These guys brought no body armor, I haven't seen any night vision, and they didn't set up defensive positions. At least not at first. Bet you bucks to buttons they have by now. Theirs was not a tactical takedown of the island. It was just thuggery."

"Sounds to me like you've figured something out, Scorpion," Venice said.

"Nothing definitive," he replied. "We don't know enough about squat to be definitive on anything. But there are only three reasons to take hostages. You've got pure terror—just kill people and break things—you've got ransom for money, and you've got bargaining, whether for policy or something else."

Jonathan stood tall and shielded his eyes to look at the horizon. The ship was much closer now, and it clearly was the *Express*.

"Hey, Slinger," Jonathan said to Gail. She, likewise, rose to her feet. "Do you suppose they made a phone call of their own and are coming out here with a boatload of money? Literally?"

"It's possible," she allowed.

"But?"

"But we'll see soon enough. This just seems like a lot of effort for a kidnapping."

"Hey, guys," Venice said from the phone. "Can you talk a little closer to the phone? I can't hear you."

They wandered back closer to the phone. "Mother Hen, I'm still paranoid about battery life. Thanks for this information. Press on, please, and find out what you can about the shipments that come in and out of here. And take a look at the identity papers we sent to you. Just find me some answers, please. And if you can't find answers, find some more relevant questions."

"Talk in another two hours?" Venice asked. She clearly was peeved that she was being shut out, but there you go. "Oh, and so you know, you should have cavalry at your side sometime tonight."

Then she was gone.

Jonathan was still dialed into his ongoing speculation with Gail. "There's no such thing as coincidence," he said. It was a long-standing adage in Jonathan's world that when two bad events occurred in close proximity, they were always related.

"The magazines," she said.

"Exactly. They are the key. Something's in there, or something's coming that's worth a whole lot of effort and violence."

"And it's not coming on the *Express,* is it?"

"I guess we'll see," Jonathan said. "Hey, Jaime! Tyler!"

They both reappeared. "Lead me to a place where I get a better view of what comes on or off that *Express* boat."

CHAPTER 16

As the sun rose, and the various scenes around the pool resolved into better focus, Zach Turner's sense of dread deepened. The terrorists—the alphabet men, as he'd come to think of them—had employed the aid of hostages to fish the one body out of the pool, and then to hoist the bodies of the husband and wife by their necks to decorate the fancy carved archway that marked the entry to the pool deck. They'd chosen their helpers, it seemed, by their inability—their perceived disinclination—to refuse or to fight back.

Zach's dustup with the lead bad guy early on had led to continual scrutiny, both by the terrorists and by Becky, who still seemed angered by his initial showdown. He'd hoped to inspire others around the pool deck to push back, to at least show a little resistance, but he realized now that he'd misplayed his hand. They hadn't yet been miserable enough to rally to his side, and now they were too frightened.

They'd talked themselves into believing that there was mercy to be found in these animals if only they just cooperated. The hanging corpses, notwithstanding.

The assembled hostages feared for their children, and they feared for themselves. They were palsied by fear. And that was exactly where the terrorists wanted them.

Now they'd lost any advantage they might have had, at least until darkness fell again, and that would be a long, long time. As the sun climbed higher in the crystal sky, the thermometer rose along with it. The stench of sweat had only begun to bloom, and along with it—inexplicably, he thought, given that they were all adults—the stench of excrement. They were permitted to use the facilities, for God's sake. How would grown men or women have so little self-respect that they would soil themselves?

Zach was not going to allow himself to die this way, and he wasn't going to allow it for Becky, either. He didn't yet have even the beginning of a plan, but the only way these assholes would get a chance to display his corpse would be if there were three or four corpses from their team to display next to it.

He surveyed his fellow hostages in search of faces or physiques that might indicate a familiarity with fighting, and perhaps the willingness to do so now. It was the nature of hostages to underestimate their ability to conquer their captors. In terms of sheer numbers, Zach's team had at least a three-to-one advantage. Yes, the bad guys had guns, and that meant that some good guys would die, but with enough manpower behind the attack, the majority would prevail. Then the good guys would have guns, too, and the bad guys' advantage would soon evaporate.

With the recent spike in active shooter situations around the world, Zach had given this a lot of thought.

One guy walks into a bar or into a school with a gun and starts blasting away. Everyone runs, most often to exactly the wrong place—to the emergency exits, which are choke points and therefore killing fields, or to some restroom or far corner from which there is no escape. Then they await their turn to die.

This made no sense to Zach. Why weren't leaders training people to fight back? The most powerful rifle in the world was useless to the shooter whose arms were broken and whose head was smashed.

When he thought about the violence that high schoolers brought to the football field on a Friday night, why not train those massive athletes to employ the same violence against bad guys? Sure, some would likely die in the process, but think about how many lives might be saved.

"How'd you lose the leg?"

The voice startled him. It belonged to a man in his sixties who'd spent enough time in the sun over the years to convert his skin to parchment. A shock of white hair adorned his head, and a matching pornstache framed his mouth. He offered his hand. "Dan Crawley. From Des Moines."

Zach accepted the offer. "Zach Turner. Virginia Beach."

Dan's eyebrows arched up. "There's some interesting work goes on in Virginia Beach," he said. "Your shoulder-to-waist ratio tells me that you might have something to do with that."

Zach smiled. "Not so much anymore," he said. "A Hadji with a shovel and an artillery round sort of limited my usefulness." Zach saw no need to tell this stranger that in his current civilian billet, he was the lead firearms instructor for the Naval Special Warfare Development Group—DEVGRU—known to most of the world as SEAL Team Six.

"I was with Team One," Dan said. "A long time ago."

"Vietnam?"

"And others," he said. "So, what are we going to do about these shit eaters?"

"Stop it," Becky whispered. "You don't have to be the hero all the time."

An older woman leaned forward to make herself visible from behind Dan. "Millie," she said. "I'm with him. And, honey, save your breath. It's a waste of time to try to keep a sheepdog from protecting his flock. I've tried for years, and it's the road to frustration."

Zach suppressed his smirk. "I think we have to wait for an opening," he said.

"What do you think of the crowd?"

Zach surveyed them again. Lots of cowering and sweating. Some crying. But some eye contact, too. One couple in particular, on the far side of the pool—a man and a woman—looked like they might have been cops or firefighters. They seemed to be dialed into the burgeoning conspiracy. Zach nodded to them, and they nodded back.

"I think we can probably pick up some help," Zach said. "But I worry that the others might have tipped to the other side."

"I don't follow," Dan said.

Zach explained, "In my experience, if you push hostages far enough, not only does Stockholm syndrome kick in, but they'll be so frightened of dying that they'll get into the way of rescuers."

"Well, I'll tell you this," Dan said. "I spent way too many years keeping Russian asshats from hurting my family. I sure as shit am not rolling over now."

Anatoly had put off the terrible chore for as long as he could. These men had died in service to his team, and if for no other reason than that, they deserved a respectful viewing. Two hours ago, he'd ordered that the seven corpses be arranged in the freezer that served the restaurants of the Crystal Sands Resort. As much as he hated the hint that these noble soldiers should be treated as slabs of meat, the realities of biology and chemistry could not be denied. There was no honor in putrefaction, the single most reliable force of nature in this part of the world.

They'd been stripped naked and draped as modesty required, arranged shoulder-to-shoulder on the tile floor. Anatoly recognized every face, and felt shame that he did not remember every name. While not a religious man, he felt a moment of silence was appropriate under the circumstances. As he toured the bodies, he paused at the feet of each corpse and bowed his head, as if in prayer. The sentiment was less important, after all, than the display.

As he finished with the sixth body in the line, he looked up to engage the eyes of Viktor Smirnov and Gerasim Kuznetsov (Delta and India), his closest lieutenants. "How could this happen?" he asked. He kept his voice calm, even as his guts churned a toxic stew of bile and adrenaline.

"The couple in Bungalow Ten," Viktor said. "After

they killed the initial invader force, they had guns and from there—"

"I know what happened," Anatoly snapped. "We all know what happened. These guests—these *sheep*—killed seven highly trained operators. What I want to know is how that was able to happen."

"We didn't adequately anticipate," Gerasim said.

Anatoly glared at him. "More obvious words were never spoken," he said. "What do we know about Stephen Terrell and Alicia Crosby?"

"Very little," Viktor said.

"Except we have reason to suspect that those are not their real names," Gerasim said.

"And what reason is that?"

Gerasim shifted his stance, grasping his hands behind his back, and looking to the floor. "The names and passport numbers seem to trace back to a couple who has been dead for the last three years."

Anatoly felt his ears growing hot. "I see," he said. "Do we have any idea who these people truly are?"

"No, sir," Gerasim said.

Viktor made a slashing motion in the air. "I disagree," he said. "Look at the bodies. Deep, expertly delivered knife wounds, precision gunshots. While we might not know their names or their passport numbers, we can conclude that they are part of the Community that trains its members in the art of killing."

"This does not make me feel better," Anatoly said.

"I did not understand that to be my mission," Viktor replied. "To feel better in this line of work is to be unemployed, Anatoly. You know this. What is important is that we know the capabilities of our enemy. Any information beyond that is an unearned gift."

Anatoly knew that Viktor was right. The fact that the existence of these talented killers had escaped their detection, and that they had been able to inflict such penalties on Anatoly's team, was entirely irrelevant. What was, was. What existed, existed.

"The job now," Anatoly said, "is to neutralize the threat."

"Absolutely," Gerasim agreed.

Again, Viktor held up his hand. "Why?"

Anatoly scowled. How could this not be obvious? "I don't understand."

"Why is neutralization important?"

Surely, Viktor was just playing the role of devil's advocate. "They killed our teammates, Viktor. That cannot go unpunished."

"Because punishment will bring our teammates back to life?"

"Whose side are you on?" Gerasim asked.

"I am exclusively on the side of victory," Viktor replied. "These covert killers have gotten the upper hand at least twice now, and we have paid a heavy price. Nothing can change that. We have to think strategically, and revenge is a luxury that we cannot afford. To focus on capturing that couple or on wreaking vengeance weakens every aspect of what we're here to do. As it is, we have barely enough people to guard the prisoners while the others of us are sleeping or eating. If we send out patrols to find these two killers, that will draw against our strategic forces. It will string them out and tire them. We simply do not have the manpower."

Anatoly used both hands to make a sweeping gesture at the dead men on the floor. "These men were your colleagues, Viktor."

"And they will live on forever as such in my memory," Viktor said. "But that doesn't change the larger point. They are already dead. If we resist our urge to chase after the killers, perhaps we can limit the number of other colleagues who join them in the Great Beyond."

"What will the rest of our team think if we let this atrocity go unavenged?" Gerasim asked. He seemed equally aghast. "Soldiers in harm's way need to know that their commanders are behind them."

"These are not soldiers," Viktor said with a dismissive grimace. "None of us are soldiers. Not anymore. We are mercenaries, and we all fight for the same thing—the money. Do not try to raise this to the level of a cause for the Motherland."

"We still must maintain an effective command structure," Anatoly said. "Which means we must demonstrate strong leadership. Teamwork is still important, and we need our team to be prepared to follow where we lead them."

"Then we need to lessen the guard on the hostages," Viktor said. "Let the children rejoin their parents. That alone will give us back six people. Use them to patrol for the shooters."

"No," Anatoly said. "I understand your point, Viktor, but the children are the leverage we need to keep the adults from rebelling against us."

"And to keep them from getting away," Gerasim said.

"Why do we care so much if a few get away?" Viktor said. His voice rose an octave with his frustration. "We have their cell phones and there no longer is any Internet connection. They can't get off the island, and even if they tried, they would drown. I do not see—"

"They will *conspire*," Anatoly said. "Stephen Terrell and Alicia Crosby, or whoever they are, will find them and arm them, and now we have a guerilla force in the jungle. The last thing we need is an armed, organized enemy." How could this not be clear to everyone?

"To do what?" Viktor asked.

"To shoot their captors," Gerasim answered.

"You yourself, Anatoly, said that keeping the children separate would prevent that from happening."

"Suppose they want to rescue their children?" Anatoly asked.

"They wouldn't be that foolish," Viktor said, though his shifting eyes told Anatoly that his resolve was weakening.

"But if they were that foolish," Anatoly explained, "we would have to respond by killing them all, and then this entire episode would make us all the target of a worldwide manhunt that we could not possibly survive."

"As if the world community will forget what we do here with the current plan," Viktor said. His mood had soured. "Remember Leon Klinghoffer?"

Anatoly felt the first flash of anger at the mention of that name.

"Who?" Gerasim asked.

"An American Jew," Anatoly explained. "In the mid-eighties, the Palestinian Liberation Front—something like that—hijacked a cruise ship. When their terms were refused—"

"The man in the wheelchair," Gerasim remembered.

"Exactly. Those terrorists shot him and threw his body overboard, wheelchair and all."

"They told his wife that he was in the ship's infirmary," Viktor said. "Ultimately the United States captured the terrorists by forcing their plane down in Italy."

"Where the Italians let them go," Anatoly said.

"The Americans recaptured the leader," Viktor said. "I believe he died in prison."

"They recaptured him, what, thirty years after the fact?" Anatoly made a noise that sounded like *piff*. He didn't see the relevance.

"The point," Viktor pressed, "is that the Americans never forget. We have killed at least three of them. I don't know the nationality of the first man you killed, but I suspect he was American, too. We're all fools if we believe that America will rest until we are . . . What do they like to say? Until we are brought to justice."

"That was previous governments," Anatoly said, hoping to shut the argument down. "The Darmond administration only makes noise. They deliver ultimatums, and then they walk away from them. They will stay focused on us only until something else attracts the news cycle."

"Until a man is kept out of a ladies' room," Gerasim said with a laugh. "That will be their crisis."

"While the rest of the world starves," Anatoly said.

The discussion had run its course.

"Gerasim," Anatoly said, "I would like you to take

charge of finding the murderers. Kill them if you must, but I would rather you bring them to me. The others should see."

Viktor looked as if he wanted to say something, but after opening his mouth to speak, he closed it again.

Anatoly worried that he might become a problem.

Fourteen-year-old Erin Talley wanted to cry. She wanted to run, she wanted to scream. But she sensed— no, she *knew*—that if she did, everything here in the overcrowded cabin—they called it a bungalow—would fall apart. With no parents around to protect them, the other children, the younger ones in particular, looked to her to be strong.

And by staying strong, she allowed them to be weak. Allowed them to be the children that they were. That *she* was, too, but she'd been through more shit in her decade-and-a-half than most adults went through in a lifetime.

Erin's thoughts wandered to her sister. Mandy would have been twelve this week if the brain cancer hadn't stolen her, and this trip was all about celebrating her life and wishing her a blissful, pain-free afterlife. She would have torn these guys a new one if she'd been around and having a good day. Mandy didn't take crap from anyone, and with a terminal disease eating her from the inside out for over half her life, even the guns wouldn't have scared her.

Erin couldn't pretend to be anywhere near that strong—either physically or mentally—but being the healthy sister in a family of four had taught her a lot about the intricacies of personal interaction in the midst of a crisis.

She'd lost track of time, but in her mind it couldn't have been more than six, maybe eight hours since they'd all been pulled from their beds and dragged to this place. She'd been sleeping in her own room in their suite in the main building when the terrorists hit, and she'd never gotten a chance to see her parents before she was hustled to this place. She'd been one of the first eight or ten kids who'd been brought here. She now counted thirty-four, and it was crowded. Kids who were lucky enough to snag furniture to sit on were paranoid about leaving their spot for even an instant— even to go to the bathroom—and that turned out to be Erin's first negotiation of the night.

A bigger kid—a boy named Nicholas, probably her age—had not only claimed the sofa in the bungalow's living room, but he'd reserved all three cushions, allowing him to lie flat. When another boy—Ahmed, eight years old—hopped into Nicholas's place when the older one got up to pee, Nicholas, upon his return, lifted the little boy by an arm and a leg and deposited him on the floor, on top of two other children who'd fallen asleep. The result was a lot of wailing and crying, which put their guards on edge. The men with the guns didn't seem to like children in the first place. There was no doubt in Erin's mind that they didn't like children who made noise.

Erin stepped in as peacemaker. With a little flirting and by standing in a way that might have emphasized a certain anatomical outline beneath the T-shirt she'd worn to bed, she convinced Nicholas not to be an asshole, and to share his space with others. Being the biggest didn't equate to special privileges, especially in the presence of others who were so small. She wasn't sure that Nicholas understood the larger altruistic point, but he pulled in his landing gear and made room for other kids. Ultimately he'd abandoned the sofa altogether and claimed a patch of real estate on the floor under the dining-room table.

Now that the sun was back up, Erin had been trying to meet as many of the other kids as she could—even the ones who spoke no English, and whose origins she didn't know because she spoke no other languages. She'd determined that the youngest among them was five—a little girl from who-knows-where—and was thankful that the girl's older brother, eight, was there to help her. He didn't speak English, either, but he seemed to be a good big brother, and that kept his sister calm.

Erin had also determined that she and Nicholas were the oldest at fourteen. The sixteen-year-olds and older, she figured, were being kept with the adults. None of them had any idea what was going on, and the guards refused to say anything that did not deal directly with staying inside and keeping quiet.

Erin had chosen a spot against the dining-room wall, at the base of an elaborate breakfront hutch. She'd tried to sleep, and thought she'd been able to grab an hour or two, cumulatively, since they'd been captured, but real sleep—the kind that left you feeling rested—was well out of reach. She assumed it would remain that way till this was over.

As she sat, her knees pulled up to her chest, she tried to ignore the way the one guard looked at her. She figured if they were going to assault her, they would have done it under the anonymity of darkness, just as her uncle had done during his Christmastime visit. She'd never shared that incident with anyone. Telling your mom that her brother was a pedophile seemed too big a bomb to drop while she was nursing a dying child.

As Erin sat, she recounted the number of kids who were crowded into the space. Yet again, it came up at thirty-four. Her attention was drawn to a boy, eleven-year-old Isaac, if she recalled properly, who was winding his way over and around sleeping and chatting kids. Clearly, he was on his way to speak to Erin. He wore only a pair of briefs, and while clearly embarrassed to be nearly naked among others last night, he seemed not to care anymore. His face was dirty, a dark smear under his eye, and Erin wondered how that was possible.

"Boys piss outside now," a guard said.

"I don't have to piss," Isaac said. This was a new development in the captors' crowd control strategy. With so many kids and only two bathrooms, the boys were told they had to pee outdoors to relieve some of the pressure on the plumbing.

Isaac approached and sat on the floor next to her.

Erin said, "Hi."

"Hi."

"You're Isaac, right?"

"Yeah." His posture mimicked hers, his legs drawn up to his chest, arms hugging his knees. He stared at his feet as he wiggled his toes.

Erin wanted to ask if she could help him somehow, but decided that maybe he just wanted some company. If he wanted to talk, he'd figure out a way.

"You're Erin, right?"

That was her in. "That's right. Do you need something?"

"Are they going to kill us?" He asked the question still without eye contact, and with surprisingly little emotion.

"I don't think so," Erin said. If nothing else, those were the right words. "I certainly hope not."

"What about our parents?"

Erin was about to repeat her previous answer, but couldn't bring herself to do it.

The silence drew Isaac's eyes to hers. They were red. "There was a lot of shooting last night," he said.

Erin felt pressure behind her own eyes. "Yes," she said.

"Doesn't that mean that they were shooting people?" His voice caught on the question, and he used his palm to wipe snot from his nose.

"You need to be careful about drawing conclusions like that," Erin warned. "When you don't know something, that's all there is to know. Just that you don't know."

Isaac's features twisted into a scowl.

"Okay, maybe that didn't make a lot of sense."

Isaac smiled. "No, it didn't."

"What I meant to say is that you can't jump to conclusions. We don't know what that shooting was. Guessing what it might have been doesn't help anybody."

"I don't want to be an orphan," Isaac said. He used both palms to wipe his eyes.

"None of us do," she said. *But I bet some of us are going to be.*

CHAPTER 17

It was the phone call that Jolaine Cage never in a million years thought that she would receive, and from a man she thought she'd never hear from again.

To hear Boxers' voice on the other end of the line at such a punishing hour was beyond startling. Now, nearly four hours later, as she sat in a little coffee shop on the grounds of the Manassas Regional Airport in Manassas, Virginia, she replayed the conversation in her head.

"I guess you thought you'd never hear this voice again," Boxers said. Small talk had never been his strong suit.

"Because that's what you told me," she replied. "After you called me a *psycho*."

"Yeah, well, you took pleasure in seeing people burn alive, so . . ."

"Why are you calling me?"

"I need your help."

"No."

"Digger's in trouble. We need to get him out of it."

"Unless there's another Digger Grave, then I change my answer to *hell* no. To the twelfth power."

"He saved your life, Jolaine."

"He fired me."

"That circles back to the whole thing about people burning alive."

"He said I didn't belong on a team."

"No, he said that you didn't belong on *our* team. And he was right. What we do requires nuance and balance. You demonstrate neither."

"So, why are you calling me?"

"Because the last thing I want in the team I'm assembling is nuance and balance. I want violence and fortitude."

From there, she listened to the story about terrorists who had taken over a vacation resort and killed a bunch of innocents. "Digger and his friend Gail—a team member before you came aboard—"

"She was injured," Jolaine remembered. "I heard the story from Mother Hen."

"Yeah, well, they're back as an item, and they've both been taken hostage."

Jolaine's bullshit bell rang. "Jonathan Grave allowed himself to be taken hostage? I don't see that happening."

"Okay, not *him* exactly, and not Gail, but everybody else, and they need help."

"There are no police?"

Boxers told her about the lack of an army or police force because something, something, Costa Rica.

Jolaine tried to make the equation work. "You want me to become part of a two-person rescue crew?"

"There'll be more than two," Boxers said. "I don't

know how many, exactly, but there'll be more than two."

"You're cashing in on favors," Jolaine deduced.

"Every one I can."

In the end, she couldn't say no to Big Guy. They'd tried the girlfriend-boyfriend thing for a while, back in the day, and while it never really took, there was really a very sweet side to Boxers that he didn't want anyone to know about. It wasn't till after she hung up that she realized she hadn't asked how much this gig paid. Given the fact that the precious cargo was a billionaire, she imagined it would fatten her bank account at least a little.

Since leaving Security Solutions, she'd been doing office work for a trade association headquartered in D.C., and hating every minute of it. Digger had given her a nice recommendation letter, citing her previous duties as being "in support of multiple high-level corporate investigative efforts." Even she didn't know what those words meant, but as Digger had assured, they were just gobbledygook enough to attract notice from lobbyists. Her biggest challenge after being hired at the association was dancing around the questions of what, specifically, she had done for Security Solutions. She'd wing it with various iterations of coyness and evasion, and usually, that was enough. When it became necessary for her to make something up out of whole cloth, she'd call Venice, and Mother Hen would vouch for her.

The job paid the bills, but Jolaine hated every moment of it. Trade associations didn't produce anything. Rather, they thought lofty thoughts, sucked up to their members, and gave money to politicians for them to pretend to care about their cause. Influence peddling was the business of Washington, just as surely as steel used to be the business of Bethlehem, Pennsylvania, but unlike the denizens of the Rust Belt, the business of Washington was, first and foremost, self-perpetuation.

Boxers' only instruction to Jolaine was to arrive here in Manassas and wait for him. She got the strong sense that the presence of the team would precede the presence of a plan. And why should this operation be any different than others she'd been on?

Her phone buzzed in her pocket and she checked the screen. A text message read, **Hangar E4. ASAP.**

She wasted no time rising from the hard wooden seat and strolling back out into the chilly breeze. She slipped into her well-worn Nissan Sentra, turned the ignition, dropped the transmission into gear, and made the short drive to the designated building. Call it half a mile.

The aircraft hangars at Manassas were squatter than you'd find at larger airports because this was a place that catered almost exclusively to the community of executive aircraft. In her previous time with Digger's team, they'd had an arrangement with a client to have pretty much unfettered access to the client's jet. A Lear, she thought. Boxers had hated the small size—he called it a sardine can—so she was anxious to see if they'd found another set of wings.

The front of Hangar E4 looked like a standard office, accessible through a glass door that dumped you into an empty reception area. She could hear voices from deeper inside the space, and one of them was unmistakably Boxers'. She followed the sound, anxious to meet the team with whom she would soon be risking her life.

The center hallway dead-ended at the door to the hangar itself, but immediately before that door, to the right, another door opened to a conference room, where the others had gathered, Boxers and two other men. All of them had the thick necks and heavy-shouldered look of operators. A projector had thrown a computer image of an island onto the wall.

Their conversation stopped as Jolaine appeared at the threshold. "Good morning," she said. She worried that her smile looked as awkward as it felt.

The men's heads turned in unison, and Boxers unfolded himself from the chair he was sitting in to approach her with an extended hand. There would never be anything close to a hug from Big Guy. Not in front of the others. "Glad you could make it," he said. His handshake was much lighter than she'd feared. He turned to the others. "Gentlemen, meet She Devil."

They stood. She recognized Madman, aka Stanley Rollins, from her career-ending operation in West Virginia. "Nice to see you again," he said. His expression and body language said otherwise. But he shook her hand.

"Madman," she said. "It's been a while."

"Not long enough," he replied. Stanley Rollins had always been a cranky SOB, and for a while was deeply disliked by the Security Solutions team. As Jolaine understood things, he'd once been Digger and Boxers' commanding officer, and he'd done something that deeply pissed them off. She didn't understand the details, but apparently they didn't matter anymore because Madman had redeemed himself by doing a couple of favors for the boys.

"I'm Conan," said the younger man, and he offered a genuine smile. "Henry West. Not sure what that was about, but it's a pleasure to meet you."

"Stanley always has a stick up his ass about something," Boxers said. "But we let him play with the cool kids, anyway."

"So," Jolaine said. "What's the plan?"

"Infil by air is out," Conan said as a smile bloomed. "Unless we've got a cargo chute for Big Guy."

The comment caused a chuckle to ripple through the group, but Jolaine wanted an answer.

"We're going in by boat," Boxers said. "I've got assets picking up an HSB from a dealer in Zihuatanejo. They flew directly there, and we'll join forces with them."

Jolaine recognized HSB to be high-speed boat.

Madman said, "Tell me you're not planning to motor up to the dock under fire."

"I'm still not suicidal," Boxers said.

"But still a little scary?" Conan asked. "I always found you kinda sexy when you were a little scary."

Boxers blew him an air kiss with his middle finger, then turned to the projected map. "Here's our little slice of hell," he said. "The northwest part of the island is where all the touristy stuff happens. Down there in the southeast section in our infil site."

"That's the dock," Madman said.

"Yeah, well, the docks only take up about half an inch on the map there," Boxers said. "We'll come in at one of the other seven inches." His dislike for Rollins was palpable. "We'll motor out from the west coast of Mexico shortly after dark tonight, and we should be within swimming distance by midnight. Then it's *boom-boom* time."

"Wait," Jolaine said. "Swimming distance?"

"We'll have flippers and floatation gear," Boxers assured. "It'll be about a mile."

"Inflatable dry bags," Boxers said. "We'll seal our stuff inside the bags, fill them with air, and then tow the bags behind us."

"Standard stuff for MAROPS," Conan said. Maritime operations. He eyed Boxers with another smile. "And meaning no offense, Big Guy, when was the last time you tried an OTB insertion?"

"Okay, guys," Jolaine said. "Try to keep the acronyms to a minimum, okay? I'm the nonmilitary shooter."

"OTB is over-the-beach," Boxers said, "and I swim twelve miles a week at the gym, thank you very much. And if I had a pasta belly like you've grown, I'd be careful of throwing stones."

Henry West was in ridiculously good shape by mortal standards, but Jolaine imagined that there was probably a little extra skin over his six-pack than there used to be.

Boxers continued, "And before you say it, I've always had something of a pasta belly. Us D-boys had more important things to do than pose in front of mirrors like you SEALs." That got a high five from Madman.

Jesus, Jolaine thought. *I'm going into war with thirteen-year-olds.* "You say we launch tonight?" she said. "Where are we going to get the gear we need by then?"

"I've got a better question," Madman said. "We

haven't talked about mission needs. What's our load-out going to be?"

Boxers clicked a button on his laptop, causing the map to disappear and a list to take its place. "This is it, roughly," he said. "Lots of five-five-six and seven-six-two ammo. Three thousand rounds of both. M27s for you guys and four-seventeens for the Chief and me."

The M27 was a Marine Corps modification of the Heckler & Koch Model 416, which itself was a modification of the M4, which, in turn, was a modification of the Vietnam-era M16. Boxers preferred the larger variant of the M27, the Heckler & Koch 417, which was essentially a man-portable cannon.

Conan raised his hand. "Wait. The Chief?"

"Yeah. He and his son, Torpedo, are my assets for the boat."

"What are their backgrounds?"

"The Chief is a squid like you. Torpedo is a Millennial with big balls. I've run an op with both of them before."

Madman said, "What do you mean, he's a Millennial? No team experience?"

"I'm telling you he's a good kid," Boxers insisted. "Look, I want as much firepower as possible up there on the beach, and that means somebody has to stay with the boat. That's Torpedo's job. His real name is Jesse."

The rest of the list was a fairly standard load-out of armor and gear, with the very Boxers-centric additions of five claymore mines and five pounds of C4 explosives.

"How are we getting in and out of the country?" Conan asked. "Twice."

"Friends," Boxers said. "We've all got 'em, right? My team's got connections who've got connections."

"Are they trustworthy from the top down and bottom up?" Madman asked. "Seems to me that you and Digger have a certain history with betrayal."

"Well, ultimately you've got to trust someone," Boxers said. "I trust the guy who trusts his guy. Beyond that, it's about keeping everybody scared enough to do the right thing."

"Who are you and what have you done with Boxers?" Jolaine asked. She'd never heard Big Guy be so laid-back about security.

He bristled. "Let's be very clear," he said. As he spoke, his voice dropped a menacing octave. "About the best friend some of us have ever had is caught in a shit storm. There ain't a soul in this room who would be breathing today if it hadn't been for him saving our asses."

"That's not a license to take shortcuts," Madman said.

Boxers' ears turned red, and he looked like he was ready to say something, then swallowed his words. After a couple of seconds, he said, "The locals are likely to think that we're there on anticartel business, but that's only what they've been fed so they'd leave us alone."

"We're not seeking aid from Mexican police or army, are we?"

"Oh, hell no. They wouldn't give it, even if the White House asked, I don't think. They've got no skin in our game at all. And I wouldn't want them, anyway."

"No need to sound defensive," Conan said. "I'm with

you. But somebody in the government has to know we're going to be there."

"If everything goes according to plan, no one in authority will know."

"Jesus, Box," Madman said. "How many chits are you cashing?"

"Every damn one of them. It's *that* important."

"Then it's an honor to be included, Big Guy," Conan said.

Boxers grew uncomfortable with the sentimentality. "I guess this goes without saying, but I'll say it anyway. There's no record of any of this. If we get our asses handed to us . . ." He let the phrase drop away.

"Oh, for Christ's sake," Madman said, with a playful slap to Big Guy's shoulder, which appeared to Jolaine to be a peace offering. "When was the last time any of us fired a shot that we could tell anyone about? Besides, aren't you the one who always preaches that success is guaranteed to those who refuse to acknowledge the alternative?"

Boxers gave a wry chuckle. "No. That's Digger. I'm the one who says that success is guaranteed to those who plan, move, and shoot better than the sons of bitches on the other team."

That got a laugh from everyone.

"So, about these caves you were talking about?" Jolaine said.

"They're storage magazines," Boxers said.

"Okay, then about the storage magazines. Why are they worth all this to the other team?"

Conan said, "We don't know that yet, do we?"

"Not definitively," Boxers said, "but Mother Hen has a theory that I think holds some water." He rested a butt cheek on the edge of the conference table, which issued a loud crack.

A few seconds passed in silence as everyone waited for someone else to make the smart-ass comment. In the end, the moment passed unmolested.

"Mother Hen looks to the timing," Boxers continued. "If what they had was there already, the assholes would have been in and out and done with it. Instead, they're corralling people and hanging around."

"So, you think they're waiting for something?" Madman asked.

"I can't think of another reason."

"Unless the magazines have nothing to do with it," Conan said.

"Yeah," Boxers said, "except for that. And if that's the case, it makes no difference to our mission at all."

"Tell me how you see this going down," Conan said. "In fact, start at the very beginning. What does mission success look like?"

Boxers didn't drop a beat. "Scorpion and Gunslinger come home safe and healthy."

Madman sat up straighter. "What about the hostages?"

"What about them?"

"If we start a war, we can't just leave a bunch of innocents as collateral damage."

"Let them hire their own rescue team," Boxers said. "We go in, we snatch our precious cargo, and we exfil."

"That's bullshit," Conan said. "Even if I agreed with you—which I *absotively* do not—Digger would never go along with that. He won't leave until every one of those tourists is safe."

"Then I'll make him," Boxers said. His words and his body language could not have been more out of sync.

"No you won't," Jolaine said. "I actually agree with you—a smaller snatch and grab is a hell of a lot easier than a big one—but no one says *no* to Scorpion. *No one*. Ever. At least not in my experience."

Madman raised his hand. "Take it from the perspective of a former commanding officer," he said. "She Devil is right. We need to plan for the evacuation of the entire island."

Boxers clearly wanted to press his point, but he equally clearly understood that the rest of the team was correct. Then he sat straighter and smiled. "Not necessarily," he said.

"What are you thinking?" Conan asked.

"We only have to be concerned about the rest of the hostages if their captors, or keepers, or whatever the hell they are, are still around to pose a danger."

Jolaine felt excitement rising even as a look of dread fell over the others.

"What exactly are you suggesting?" Madman asked.

"When we get there, we'll just plan on killing all those sons of bitches."

CHAPTER 18

Jaime led Jonathan and the others to a rock outcropping on the eastern side of the island. Jonathan estimated the elevation to be a hundred, maybe 150 feet above the rocky shore. They had a decent view of the arrival dock, but not much of a view of the roadway that served it. The old minesweeper remained moored where it was, but now a two-man guard detail stood at its side, looking as bored as guard details always looked.

Given the rising body count at Jonathan's hand, he thought it prudent to stay away from areas that could be easily patrolled. He hadn't seen any hunter teams out looking for them yet, but he had little doubt that they would soon be on their way. There was a lot of time to kill between now and nightfall.

Jaime leaned out farther than Jonathan thought prudent and pointed to a spot on the slope to their right. "If you stretch a little, you can see one of the caves," he said. "It's that patch of white over there."

"Pull back in before someone sees you," Jonathan said. "And keep your voice down. We'll get to the magazines in time. I presume there is a road that serves that magazine?"

"Of course."

"And how far away from the road are we?"

"It runs directly below us."

Jonathan exchanged rolled eyes with Gail. Barely above a road was pretty much the same thing as being *on* a road.

"What?" Jaime said. "We can't be seen from here."

"Don't worry about it," Jonathan said. "With any luck, we won't be here that long, anyway."

The *Crystal Sands Express* was within easy viewing range now. About the size of a Coast Guard cutter—half the size of the *Olympia 3*—Jonathan remembered the interior to be more suited to commuting than cruising. It was comfortable enough, with padded benches along the sides of wooden tables. Tended by obsequious white-gloved waiters, it was perfectly adequate for the hundred-mile journey from Zihuatanejo to here, but so far as Jonathan could tell, there were no sleeping quarters and even the kitchen was limited.

In his mind, the vessel was packed with hundreds of soldiers, and he and his companions were righteously screwed.

About fifty yards from the shore, the *Express* slowed to a crawl. Water churned at its aft end as the captain turned the vessel on its axis so that it could back into a dock that ran parallel to the minesweeper's parking spot, and a little bit closer to Jonathan's observation point.

"It's riding pretty high on the water," Tyler observed. "That has to be a good thing, right?"

Jonathan was impressed. He hadn't noticed, but

now that it was called to his attention, the ship was clearly riding high. Assuming that the laws of physics hadn't changed, that was an indication of a lighter load. Soldiers and equipment were heavy, after all. "If nothing else, it means that the load is less scary than it might have been otherwise," Jonathan conceded.

The vessel progressed at what seemed a velocity of inches-per-minute as it backed up to the pier. When it appeared that it might collide with the wooden planks, the driver created another churn with the propellers, and the ship stopped. Two armed soldiers hopped out onto the dock with ropes in hand and tied the ship off to the pilings. The engines stopped, and Jonathan waited.

And waited. Five minutes passed. The soldiers who'd disembarked remained in position on the dock, their rifles at a loose port arms as they scanned for targets. At least Jonathan and Gail were getting under the bad guys' skin. That was something.

"What do you think they're doing?" Gail asked.

"I don't know," Jonathan said. "Maybe they're waiting to receive something rather than deliver." Even as he said the words, he didn't believe them. They already had enough ship moored at the dock to carry pretty much anything they wanted.

"Wait, I see movement," Jaime said, pointing.

"Will you please stop doing that?" Jonathan snapped. "Quick movements and extended arms are going to give away our position."

"But do you see them?"

"Of course, I see them. Just stay still and keep your voice down." Jesus, it was like dealing with seven-year-olds.

Another soldier appeared in the passenger door. He

shouted something Jonathan couldn't make out to his friends on the dock, and when he got a thumbs-up, he moved forward. Behind him, a white-haired man in a beige suit and pink shirt walked tentatively, his hands tethered behind his back. Yet another soldier followed closely behind.

"Oh, my God, Tyler," Jaime said.

"That's Baker," Tyler said. "That's my stepfather." There was an edge of panic in his voice. "What are they doing?"

"Easy, kid," Jonathan said. "Just keep cool. He doesn't look hurt."

"They've tied him up."

"It looks like handcuffs, maybe," Jaime said.

"Same thing," Tyler said. "We need to help him." He started to stand.

"What you need to do is stay put," Jonathan said.

"Can't you shoot them?" Jaime asked.

Jonathan shook his head. "Not from here." They were separated by an easy two hundred yards. Maybe if the rifle in his hands was his own, with sights that he had zeroed personally, but not with these. "I'd be as likely to hit your stepdad as the bad guys."

"Besides," Gail said, "we can't afford that kind of attention with eight hours of daylight ahead. We'll be lucky not to be found, as it is."

The soldiers led Baker to a waiting Crystal Sands pickup truck, where they shoved him into the front seat. He had difficulty getting in without the use of his hands.

"They're going to kill him," Tyler said in a frayed voice.

"No, they're not," Jonathan said. "They could have done that already. They want something from him."

"What kind of something?" Jaime asked.

"Well, that's the big question, isn't it?" Jonathan said.

Tyler slid away from the edge and stood. "I'm going back to the resort to see what they're going to do."

"You'll do no such thing," Gail said.

Jaime added, "Are you out of your mind?"

"Are you going to stop me?"

Jaime stood, as well. "If I have to. Why do you want to go back there and get yourself killed?"

"Because it's better than waiting here to get myself killed," he said. "This is bullshit. There's a whole world down there being tortured and killed, and we're up here smoking weed and not doing anything to help."

Gail turned to Jonathan. "Scorpion, say something."

"Staying safe is not *doing nothing*," he said. "Staying safe is staying safe. There's no shame in that." Even as he spoke the words, he heard how unconvincing they were.

"He's my stepfather," Tyler said. "No, screw that. He's my *father*. He's always been a hell of a lot better to me than the bio version. How can I live with myself if I just do nothing?"

"It's better than not living at all," Jaime said.

"I'm not sure it is," Jonathan said.

"Scorpion!" Gail looked appalled. "He's only nineteen."

"VA hospitals are filled with *eighteen*-year-olds," Jonathan said.

"But what about—"

"Yo, Gunslinger," Tyler said. "At what point, did you become my mother? I'm a big boy. I can make my own decisions."

"What do you have in mind?" Jonathan asked.

Jaime threw up his hands. "I do not believe you're having this conversation."

Jonathan ignored him and kept his focus on Tyler. He hoped the kid would follow his lead and focus.

"I'm thinking I can sneak back in the way I got out," Tyler said.

"In the daylight?"

"Some of it will be tricky," he explained, "but once I get into the maintenance corridor, I'll be below grade and pretty much invisible. That's how I got out in the first place."

"At night," Jaime reminded.

"But we've snuck around there in the daytime, too. If you know where to duck, you can stay out of sight."

"And to get to the maintenance corridor, you have to be out in the middle of everybody."

"We need to distract them," Gail said.

Her words shocked Jonathan, and clearly his face showed it.

"What?" she said. "Obviously, you've made up your mind, and Tyler's determined to be a target, so the least I can do is get with the program."

"What is wrong with you people?" Jaime said. "You act as if this is some kind of game. People are going to die!"

"Yes, they are," Jonathan said. "They already have, and it's entirely likely that others will. What's your point?" He was being deliberately obtuse to force the discussion that Jaime seemed determined to have.

"What's my *point*? What's my *point*! Are you crazy?"

Gail stiffened. "Be careful, Jaime," she said. "*Crazy* is a tough word. A loaded word. These people—these terrorists, whoever they are—are *evil* people, but they're not *crazy*. The people who tried to run and were killed for their efforts were not crazy, either. And when you look at Scorpion and me, you'd be wise never to even consider the deployment of that word. We know exactly what we're doing, even if we don't know where it will go. If you want to hide, hide. But understand that if, at the end of all this, you're still alive, it will have had nothing to do with you. It will have had everything to do with the fact that you hid and let other people do the fighting for you. Only you can decide where you want to be on that curve, but you'd be wise to stay out of the way of those of us who wish to have a say in our own futures."

Jonathan found himself stunned. He'd known and worked with Gail for more than a few years now, and he knew her background as a lawyer and an FBI agent and a small-town sheriff. He'd seen her shoot the wings off a gnat when the chips were down, but he'd never heard her echo his own thoughts so precisely before. For people in their line of work, moments arrived when fate presented a binary choice, where you could work to live or you could hope to live. In a perfect world, those moments didn't arrive in the middle of a vacation, but the world was an imperfect place.

"Here's the thing," Jonathan said. He modulated his voice to take some of the edge off the rancor. "Tyler has just volunteered to do a noble thing. He's willing to go behind enemy lines, so to speak, in order to gather intelligence for the rest of us. Intel that will help enormously when our rescue crew arrives tonight."

"That assumes we will be alive when they get here," Jaime said.

"No, it really doesn't," Jonathan countered. "They'll be here, whether we're alive or dead. Knowing at least two of the personalities who are coming, you should pray for quick ends for those who kill us if it comes to that." He couldn't stop the chuckle at the thought of the waste that would be laid by Boxers if he arrived to find either of his friends dead. Look up *scorched earth* in the dictionary. That would be the first act. Before it got rough.

"Look, let's reset. Jaime, your life is yours to live— however you want to live it. I'm not passing judgment. Gunslinger and I have fought our way out of some pretty nasty dustups over the years. I think I speak for both of us when I say that we have every intention of going home alive. In the short term, though, that means taking some chances, and embracing some danger. If you don't want to be a part of it, that's fine. But for the next few minutes, I need you to be quiet and let the rest of us work out what options we might have."

Jonathan didn't wait for an answer. In fact, he broke off eye contact and drilled back into Tyler. "What's your purpose for going back into the resort?"

"To help Baker."

"How?"

Tyler seemed a bit put off by the question. "By . . . being there."

Jonathan waved him off. "You need to stay invisible," he said. "These dickheads have a history of killing anyone they perceive as having escaped."

"But they don't have to know that."

"You can't determine how others will think," Gail said.

"I've bluffed myself out of a shit ton of bad stuff," Tyler said with a smile. "They don't even know I'm missing. If they catch me, I'll tell them that I was hiding, and then I realized that the best thing to do was to present myself."

"What about the jilted girlfriend?" Jonathan asked. "Annie, right?"

That took some of the wind out of Tyler's sails, but only for a few seconds. "She'll be pissed," he said. "But I don't think she'll get me killed over it. I'll just keep my distance."

Jonathan worried that the kid was vastly under estimating the fury of a betrayed squeeze, but it wasn't his fight.

"You know what happened to the Edwardses," Gail said.

"That's different," Tyler objected. "They were with you. They were with the team that you killed. The terrorists probably thought—"

"That they helped in killing those first two," Jonathan said, finishing the thought. The kid made a good point. "But you can't go into this with the intention of getting caught."

"No, not with the intention, but if it happens, I'm saying that I think I can talk myself out of it."

"And what good will that do for us?" Gail asked, again thinking Jonathan's thoughts.

"Huh?"

"We need you to get in and get back out," Jonathan explained.

Suddenly the expression on Tyler's face dimmed to something less defiant. "I don't understand."

"We need eyes on the inside," Gail said. "We need you to find out where the hostages are being kept and how many captors there are."

Jonathan said, "When our friends get here, the more we know, the more efficient we can be in resolving this."

Jaime raised a hand, as if to tentatively ask a question in class. "These friends of yours," he said. "When they arrive, what will they be here to do?"

"To bring everyone to safety."

"Everyone, or just their friends?"

There was an unstated accusation beneath the words that Jonathan chose to ignore. He turned back to Tyler. "I need you to commit to getting in and then getting out again."

Tyler blanched. "How am I going to do that?"

"You said yourself that you know how to navigate the area," Gail said.

Jonathan added, "For the moments when you're exposed, we'll help provide a diversion so people will be looking the other way."

"You can't know that," Tyler said. "People are going to look where they're going to look."

Jonathan presented his hands in mock surrender. "This was your idea," he said. "I'm just adding some modifications."

"And doubling the danger."

"Tripling," Gail said with a smile. "At least. Maybe even more."

For a second, Tyler seemed confused, as if the words didn't make sense. Then he laughed. "Jesus God, is this really what your life is like?"

"What do you mean?" Jonathan asked.

"You talk about the odds of dying like they don't mean anything."

Jonathan said, "Tell me if you want honesty or sugarcoating."

"Jesus," Jaime said. "Patronize much?"

"I'm not patronizing," Jonathan said. "A lot of people have a very real preference. I'm a facts-in-your-face kind of guy, but lots of people aren't."

"What are we talking about?" Tyler said.

"The odds of dying," Jonathan said. "You want facts or sugar?"

Tyler steeled himself with a big breath. "Facts," he said.

"In the long view, they're one hundred percent," Jonathan said. "Because none of us get out of this life experience alive."

Tyler rolled his eyes. "Oh, good. Word games."

"Not at all," Gail said. She'd heard this speech before. "Listen to him."

Tyler did his best petulant stance, arms crossed, weight on one leg.

Jonathan continued, "Your chances of dying in the next day or two are a lot higher than they were yesterday, but next week, with any luck, they'll have dialed back down to what they were yesterday."

"I have no idea what you're talking about."

"My point is that the odds don't matter in real time. You do your best, you keep your head down, you make smart decisions, and you beat the odds. Fail to do any of those things, and you lose."

Tyler added a scowl and cocked head to his petulant stance. "Was that supposed to be inspiring? You just made the case for me breaking back into the resort and staying there."

"Because that would lessen your odds of being killed," Jonathan guessed.

"Exactly."

"While at the same time increasing everyone else's odds of being killed," Gail said.

The wall of petulance cracked a little.

"We need that information," Jonathan said. "And I'll be completely honest with you. I never would have asked you to do any of this. But you volunteered."

Tyler looked to his buddy.

"Don't do it," Jaime said. "It's a crazy idea."

He looked back to Jonathan.

"I've made my pitch," Jonathan said. "The decision is yours."

Tyler's shoulders sagged. He thrust his hands into his hair and pivoted as he stomped away three paces and then returned. "You know this isn't fair, right?" he said. "All I want to do is lie low, and you pile all this shit on my shoulders."

"Don't do it, Ty," Jaime said.

"Now I have to!" Tyler said. His tone was a muffled shout. "I have to go in, be a spy, and come back out, because if I don't, King Scorpion here will tell the world that I was a coward."

"I won't say a word," Jonathan said, his voice the essence of calm. "Knowing it yourself will be plenty."

Tyler paced in a circle again. "I hate this shit," he said.

"I know."

"And I hate you!"

"Okay."

With a giant sigh, Tyler let his legs fold beneath him and lowered himself onto the ground, sitting Indian-style. "Okay, how are we going to do this?"

CHAPTER 19

Zach Turner left his prosthetic leg on the pool deck as he lowered himself into the water. He didn't want the fabric sleeve to get wet. Sooner or later, wet cotton against flesh would wear a hot spot. When this situation went sideways—as it was bound to do sooner or later—he wanted as few complications as possible.

As time wore on, and the guards endured the same heat as their captives, the guys in the uniforms had allowed their assholery to wane a bit. While the rule against talking still existed, they were enforcing it less zealously. People were social creatures, after all, and they were going to communicate. As the dangling bodies of the man and the woman swelled and festered, perhaps the guards thought that the graphic warning was enough. And for some, it no doubt was.

Zach wanted to explore a little more and see who among them were the very opposite of cowed by these asshats' atrocities. It would be suicide to try to mount a rebellion now, but if the opportunity presented itself, they needed to be ready to pounce.

The other rule the guards decided to lift was the prohibition against getting in the water. Zach figured that decision to be rooted in pure practicality. They'd all been denied food, though they'd been given ample drinking water. As stomachs got rocky, the exacerbating effect of the bright sun and boiling heat would have people dropping out as if struck with the plague.

By allowing the captives to remain hydrated and cool, the captors avoided a lot of heartache.

Of course, Zach noticed that as the flow of people into the pool increased, the flow of people into the bathrooms decreased accordingly. What the hell? He'd swum in cesspools before. What's one more, even if the others were more of a metaphorical variety?

As he splashed about in the water, he kept eyeing the couple he'd noticed before—the ones who looked like firefighters or police. They seemed very into each other, sitting arm-in-arm, each stroking the other in comforting gestures. Zach didn't want to be too obvious in his efforts to get their attention, for fear of attracting unwanted attention to himself, but he didn't want to miss an opportunity, either.

Finally it was the lady of the pair—the wife?—who caught his eye. She poked the guy, and indicated Zach with a subtle nod. When the man connected, he looked angry, and then there was recognition. He gave a quick wink, and went back to his conversation. Maybe a minute later, he stood from his girl, sat on the edge of the pool, and slid into the water. The trick here was to make the upcoming conversation look entirely coincidental, so as not to draw attention.

Finally they crossed paths near the giant planter that

marked the entrance to the Lazy River, a narrow path of flowing water that would float inner tube–clad swimmers in a meandering circuit around the pool.

"Zach Turner." He wanted to waste no time.

"Will Ambrose," the other man said. Zach hadn't expected the heavy British accent. "I'm hating my travel agent right about now. You look like a man with a plan."

"No plan yet," Zach said. "I'm just trying to assemble a team for when the shit gets real. You look like a guy who's won a few fights in his day."

"More than I've lost, I suppose."

"You a cop?"

"No, mate, I'm a firefighter. London Fire Brigade. So's my wife. That's her over there. She thought you were ogling her."

Zach laughed. "Well, she's worthy of a good ogle, for sure. But I'm here with my wife, too."

"It'd be nice to have a plan," Will said. "I'll tell you this, though. Those twats ain't gonna decorate no doorway with my corpse. Nor Lindy's, neither."

"Copy that," Zach said. "I've got another guy over on my side of the pool willing to kick some ass if it comes to that."

"That old guy you were talking to?"

"That old guy was a Navy SEAL back in the day. Maybe he can't run the surf the way he used to, but I'm guessing he knows how to knock the life out of these dickheads."

"I was thinking we could double-team one of those tossers, grab his rifle, and take the fight to them."

"Please don't do that," Zach said. "Too much risk of

shit going badly. What I'd like for you to do is see if you can pick up more recruits."

"You're talking dangerous shite if they decide to curry favor with the lads in the uniforms."

"Do what you think is right, then," Zach said. "Trust your gut. Don't do anything that doesn't feel right."

An angry voice called from Will's side of the pool. "You! You two! No talking!" It was one of the soldiers.

Zach smiled and gave a little wave. "Let's not either of us do something rogue," he said as he rolled to his side and paddled away. "When the time comes, we'll do something coordinated."

"You'll want to stash that rifle and vest," Jonathan said. They'd assembled on the mulchy ground where they were largely obscured by foliage and vegetation. "If they catch you with that, you'll find yourself in the middle of a gunfight for sure."

"That means I won't have any protection at all." If there'd been enthusiasm for this mission in the beginning, it seemed to be dwindling.

"If they see you with a weapon, they'll shoot without asking any questions," Gail said. "That can't end well for you."

"How about if I stash something in the trees nearby? So if I need to run, I can get to it and shoot. At least I'll have something if I need it."

"Sure," Jonathan said. It wasn't worth the argument. In his own experience, there'd never been a time when he cursed life because he had a gun, but there'd been plenty of curses when he didn't have one. The fact that he wasn't sure the kid even knew how to shoot was another troubling factor. But that was for later. If it made him feel better, what the hell?

Jonathan moved to the next part of the plan. "Slinger, please give him your phone and dial in my number." As Gail complied with the request, Jonathan said, "Keep the phone with you, and keep it on vibrate."

"I'll just mute it," Tyler said.

"No," Jonathan said. "Vibrate. If we need you for something, I want to be able to get through to you. Trust me, I'm not going to be calling to chat."

"Only three people in the word know the number, anyway," Gail said as she handed the phone over. "It's a burner phone. I never travel with the real thing."

"Too many secrets on it, right?" Tyler guessed.

"Something like that," Jonathan said. "How confident are you about your final approach into the back side of the resort?"

"Pretty," he said. He motioned for the tourist map and Jonathan gave it to him. "We're way the hell over here on this side of the island."

"There are kill teams out looking for us," Gail reminded.

"We'll provide escort for as long as we can," Jonathan said. He pointed a finger at Tyler. "And you, young man, need to keep me in the loop. What you see, when you're moving, and when you're coming back out."

"Okay, I will," Tyler replied. "If we can work our way down to the golf course"—he pointed to a spot well inland from the northwest coast of the island—"I just need to cross the parking lot, and then I'll be back in the trees and shrubs. I figure I can stay near the empty bungalows, cross behind them, and then drop into the service path, over here behind the pool."

Jonathan sucked in a loud noseful of air. "That's what, three or four hundred yards between the golf course and the pool area?"

"That's a lot of exposure, Scorpion," Gail said.

"Yes, it is," he agreed.

"That's why I want to have a gun."

"No." Gail and Jonathan said it together.

Jonathan explained, "One way or another, it will be a bad day if you get caught. But if you're empty-handed, you'll have a chance to talk your way out."

"Isn't it better to have a chance to shoot my way out?"

"They can take you out from five hundred yards," Jonathan said. "Not all gunfights are like the movies. In fact, none of them are."

"Why don't you go with him?" Jaime asked.

"Same reasons," Jonathan said. "Us getting killed will do nothing to help anyone."

"But Ty getting killed will?"

"I don't put my weapons down for anyone," Jonathan said. There was a threatening rumble to his voice.

"I get it, Jaime," Tyler said. "I really do. The trick is to not get caught, and if I do get caught, the trick is talk like hell."

"I'm going to go with you," Jaime said.

Jonathan recoiled from the words. "Whoa. Come again?"

"I can't let you go alone. I taught you all the back ways that you know, but you don't know all the ones I know."

Tyler looked startled.

Jaime bobbled his head as he hedged. "There are utility tunnels," he said. "They go pretty much everywhere."

"Tunnels?" Tyler said. "And in all this time you never told me?"

"Hey, a guy's got to have secrets, you know?" Jaime sold it with a smile.

Jonathan found himself fully engaged. "When you say 'they go pretty much everywhere,' what does that mean?"

"It means that tunnels bring steam, electricity, and cable TV to every place on the resort," Jaime explained. "We stay pretty much at thirty degrees year-round, but some nights will dip into the low twenties. I remember one whole week where it never got above twenty-two."

Jonathan understood that he was speaking of centigrade. He translated on the fly to hear swings from the nineties to the low seventies on the Fahrenheit scale. "Are these tunnels big enough to enter?"

Jaime nodded. "I don't like going down there, but I will if I have to."

"Wait," Gail said. "How can there be tunnels to every bungalow? Hidden basements?"

Jonathan's mind swam at the opportunities. If they could directly access each of the bungalows—

Jaime dialed back a little. "Okay, no. I see what you're getting at. You can't get to every bungalow, but you can get close. There are central stacks, one for every cluster of bungalows. The final plumbing connections branch off from the stacks and run under the walkways to the bungalows themselves. If something breaks between the stack and a bungalow, all we have to do is dig up the path to fix it. But the main lines run through the tunnels."

"Can we get into the Plantation House from a tunnel?" Tyler asked. "It has a below-grade loading dock. Wait, is that what that locked room is for?"

Jaime explained, "There's a creepy-looking locked room that Ty has been begging to see."

"You said you didn't know what was in there."

"It was better than telling you and then living with your whining when I wouldn't take you there." He turned back to Jonathan. "That is the only access to the tunnels through a door."

Jonathan felt himself deflate. "Well, shit. Under the circumstances, it's asking a lot to break into the basement of the Plantation House."

"You don't have to," Jaime said. "You can get into the tunnels through the stacks."

"I don't know about utility tunnels," Gail said. "What are these stacks you keep talking about?"

"They look like garden houses," Jaime said.

She scowled, then got it. "The little gnome houses in the flower beds?" Each of the bungalow clusters featured a unique, bright-colored little cottage in the central garden with statues of big-eared, smiling gnomes involved with various gardening endeavors.

Jaime chuckled at the phrase. "Yes, the gnome houses."

"Isn't there a concern about children or animals getting in there?" Jonathan asked.

"Animals get in all the time," Jaime said. "But there are heavy grates at the bottom of every stack—*gnome house*—and those are locked."

"Please tell me you have the keys with you," Gail said.

"They're back in the shanty."

Jonathan stood. "Then let's get back to the shanty," he said. As he walked, the others followed. "Okay, listen, guys. I need to make a phone call."

"How come everything in Mexico looks alike?" Jesse Montgomery asked as he watched the sagging pastel buildings pass by.

He'd been expecting a snarky answer from his father, so he was surprised when Davey said, "That's what generations of corruption and poverty do to a place. It doesn't help when that place gets invaded every hundred years or so."

This was Jesse's second trip below America's southern border in just a few months—for much the same purpose—and he couldn't help but notice that there was a hopelessness to the poverty down here. He'd been to South Central Los Angeles, and he'd gotten lost in the slums of Chicago and D.C. and Memphis over the years, but as slummy as those slums were, at least the structures seemed sound, and the water was drinkable. Down here, he got the sense that everybody walked along the edge of death. There was a foreverness to the poverty here that depressed him.

And yet almost everyone he made eye contact with smiled.

"Be careful, kid. They all want something from you." It was as if Davey had read his mind. "It's the cool car and the white skin." At the airport, Davey had sprung for a BMW rag top at the rental-car place. Jesse knew that the words that registered as racism were meant as a practical observation.

As so many racist comments were.

Jesse decided to change the subject. "I thought we were supposed to keep a low profile this time. You know, because of the last time." On their last visit to Mexico—to the northern coast—they'd left a lot of dead people behind. That the dead were all part of a drug cartel actually made it worse because they were the people who ran the police departments.

"You're gonna get an ulcer if you always worry about the little stuff," Davey said, winking at him across the center console. "We haven't done anything wrong, and as far as I know, nobody could possibly know that we were the ones who lit up that night. It's a nice day. Enjoy the sunshine and shit-smelling humidity."

Jesse laughed. The air did reek of shit, and not the herbal cow-and-horse variety. This shit smelled like humans or big dogs. Mixed with the stench of decaying fish that wafted from the marshland behind the sagging buildings. "We're really not stealing anything on this trip, right?" Jesse asked.

"That's the way I understand it," Davey said. "I've got two hundred fifty large in my bag. That should buy us a pretty nice boat."

Jesse wasn't sure he'd heard correctly. He leaned forward and pivoted his head to the left to get Davey's attention. "You've got a quarter of a million dollars in your bag?" Incredulity had spiked his voice higher and louder.

"That's the very opposite of the low profile you were talking about," Davey said through a laugh. "And it sounds like so much more when you use the *M*-word."

"Where did you get that kind of cash?"

"Your inheritance fund."

Whatever Davey saw in his son's face made him laugh.

"I'm kidding," he said. "The only way you'll ever get that kind of money on your own is if you make it. Big Guy wired it to my account, and I cashed it out because I figured the banks down here would choke on it."

"So, you're just going to hand two hundred fifty thousand dollars to a stranger?"

"What are you so shocked about? It's not like it's going to a panhandler. We're going to get a big-ass speedboat in return."

"That's what boats cost?"

"For something fast and durable, yeah. I'm hoping that the greenback nature of the transaction will get us a discount."

"Where are you going to find the boat?"

"Mother Hen already found it for us," Davey said. He pointed ahead and to the right. "That's the marina, right there. We're supposed to meet a guy named Esteban Gris."

Jesse felt a little overwhelmed. "When did all this planning happen?"

"Before I called you," Davey said. "And a little more while you were primping for the mirror."

Davey piloted the rental through the open front gates and pulled to a stop in front of a construction trailer lookalike sporting a hand-painted sign that read, OFFICINA.

"I don't speak a lot of Spanish," Davey said, "but I'm guessing that says office."

To Jesse's eye, the place was less a marina than a boneyard. A few vessels bobbed at moorings, but the majority—powerboats, shrimp boats, and a couple of sailboats, along with three rusting ambulances and a school bus—sat on the ground. Wooden wedges constructed of what looked like scrap lumber kept the landlocked boats from keeling over.

"The beauty just never stops, does it?" Davey quipped.

Jesse opened his door first and stepped out. He could hear the sounds of people working, but none of them were visible to him. He waited for Davey's lead, then followed him up the three creaky steps. He expected him to knock, but he just walked in. *"Hola,"* he said to the man behind the desk.

The guy looked to be in his late forties, with a thick middle and a bald head. "Good afternoon," he said. "I speak English, so you don't have to torture the Spanish language." He closed the smut magazine he'd been reading and laid it in the middle of the other crap on his desk.

"I guess I need to get better at my pronunciation," Davey said. "You know, since all you Mexicans are franchising out to Texas."

Jesse's stomach tensed. Clearly, Davey didn't like this guy's attitude. That said, it was entirely unclear how the trading of insults could do much to further the business of the day.

"You must be the gringos the lady called about. I am Esteban Gris. What kind of boat are you looking for?"

"What did the lady tell you?" Davey asked. There

was a verbal chess game going on that Jesse didn't understand. He knew to stay quiet, though.

"She said that you wanted something fast, and that you were going to pay cash. She wanted to know if I had a problem accepting cash."

"Dare I ask what your answer was?" Davey had shifted to a fighter's stance. It was a subtle thing, but Jesse had seen it before. He kept his arms crossed against his chest, but he bladed his body a couple of degrees and put his weight on both legs.

Esteban seemed to see the shift, too. After only a second or two, he broke out into a big laugh. "I told her that cash is always welcome here." He stood. "Come, let me show you what I have in stock."

Davey stepped out of the fat man's way.

"Please," Esteban said. "Lead the way."

"Nope." As an afterthought, he added, "After you."

As Esteban crossed the threshold and was out of view, Davey leaned close to Jesse and said, "Watch his hands, and don't let anyone get too close to you." He straightened and then followed their host.

Jesse didn't get it, but he knew better than to question it. When he was growing up, he hadn't had a lot of opportunity to hang out with his old man, but now that Jesse was out of prison, and Davey was out of the Navy, they'd had some meaningful time together. Jesse had come to admire the guy's ability to read people, and to respect his ability to bring a quick end to a mortal threat. If Davey sensed that something was out of place, the smart money said that there was something out of place.

"How much range do you need?" Esteban asked as they headed toward the boneyard.

"The most I can get for the money," Davey said. "Count on a thousand-kilo load."

Esteban whistled. "That is a lot of blow," he said.

Jesus, he thinks we're smuggling drugs. "Wait," Jesse said. "We're not—"

Davey silenced him mid-word with a glare.

"You are not what?" Esteban pressed.

"We're not in the mood to chat," Davey said. A second weaponized glare drove his point a few inches deeper.

"If you have ninety-five thousand dollars to spend, I have a cigarette boat for you. The boy can learn what it was like during the *Miami Vice* days." Esteban laughed at his own joke.

Jesse had no idea what the man was talking about. And Davey didn't seem to care. "Bigger than that," he said. "More along the lines of a Sunseeker Camargue."

Esteban turned and started walking backward. "So, you have *real* money," he said, and he bounced his eyebrows, oozing sleaze. "I can make your day. I have that very boat, but she's a few years old."

"How many is a few?"

"About fifteen years."

Davey stopped and planted his fists on his hips, drawing everyone else to a halt, as well. "About?"

"She is nineteen years old," Esteban said with a smile. "I am a salesman, after all."

"Does she float?"

"She floats and she runs—how do you gringos say it? She runs like a top."

Jesse didn't believe a word the guy said.

"I'll take a look at it," Davey said.

Esteban led them to a hard right and Jesse found

himself in a canyon of boats, dozens of them, stacked three-high in some places. Most were pretty small, and a couple would qualify in Jesse's mind as yachts. He saw wooden hulls and fiberglass hulls. Some of the powerboats were missing engines.

"Where do you get your inventory?" Davey asked.

"It's all legal, I assure you," Esteban said.

"That's not even close to an answer."

"Why does it matter to you?"

Davey said, "I like to know who I'm dealing with. Let me tell you what I believe to be the case. I think that when people with boats need money, you take their boats as collateral. Then when people like me come along looking for a boat, you sell them something that does not belong to you in the first place."

Esteban's expression darkened. He stopped again. "You know, many consider it a dangerous thing to wander into a stranger's place of business and accuse him of being a criminal."

"That's another nonanswer, Señor Gris," Davey said. He made no move to escalate the situation, but he did nothing to defuse it, either. "Here's the thing. If you sell me someone's very expensive boat, I don't want to find myself being arrested in the future for being in possession of stolen property."

Esteban held Davey's gaze for a beat, and then gave a hearty laugh. "I'll promise you this," he said. "I won't keep any permanent records of the transaction. If I don't know who you are, then neither can the party who may be upset that his property is missing."

The answer seemed to please Davey, who gave his own hearty laugh. "Let's see what you have for us."

Three minutes later, they stood in front of big speedboat with a long sleek bow and a cockpit that began a little past halfway to stern. The shiny white fiberglass body was crusty with dirt, but to Jesse's eye it look seaworthy enough. In fact, it looked almost brand-new.

"There she is," Esteban said. "Fifty-five feet long, a seven hundred sixty–horsepower Detroit Diesel engine. It has a range of about three hundred fifty nautical miles, and it is a steal at two hundred and thirty thousand American dollars."

Jesse hung back as Davey and Esteban circled the vessel. If it had tires, they'd have kicked them. The entire circuit took maybe five minutes, during which Jesse wished that he'd been allowed to bring his phone along. The burner Davey had given him was literally just a phone. No e-mail, no games, no anything that would distract him from the oppressiveness of the heat and the humidity and the stink.

When the walk-around was completed, Davey said, "Put her in the water for me, please. Let's see if she floats."

"Remember that this is a cash transaction," Esteban said.

"I remember," Davey said.

Esteban's eyebrows danced once, and then he headed off.

"Do you want to tell me what the hell is going on?" Jesse asked in an urgent whisper. "Why are you trying to pick a fight with that guy?"

"To let him know that I'm willing to," Davey said. "We're about to produce a couple hundred thousand dollars in very real money. It's important that Señor Gris be a little afraid of me."

"Why won't he just kill us and take the money?"

Davey gave his son a clap on his shoulder. "Now that's the way you should be thinking," he said. "It would be bad business. I have it on good authority that Mother Hen plays a good game of hardball. If he kills us, he knows that he'll follow soon. Remember, we have his address."

"With a quarter million dollars in his pocket, maybe he'll take the chance."

"Aren't you the cheerful one? Well, if it goes that way, it's been a pleasure parenting you."

Esteban wasn't gone long. Within a minute or two, the roar of a big engine marked his return as he drove a massive forklift around the far corner of the line of stored boats. Gouts of black smoke marked every gear change. Davey and Jesse both stood out of the way as Esteban expertly maneuvered the big machine into the correct angle to lift the boat from its supports, and then transport it across the uneven, pitted yard to the marina's launch ramp.

After twenty minutes, the beast was ready for a test drive.

"Until you buy the boat, I must come along with you," Esteban said. "Unless, of course, you'd agree to leave your colleague here with me as collateral that you will not steal my property."

Jesse's gut tensed as the fat man tossed a thumb at him. For a few seconds, it looked like Davey might be considering it.

"Nah," he said at last. "He came with me. I guess I should go home with him."

Davey had Esteban lead the way down to the boat, and let him board first. Davey went second, and Jesse brought up the rear. It was not lost on him that through the whole transition, Davey never moved his eyes from the fat man.

The throaty engine fired up right away, and after they'd trolled out a little ways from the shore, Davey opened it up wide. The bow rose on acceleration and the stern dipped accordingly as the big engine churned the water and propelled the vessel smoothly across the water.

"Take a look belowdecks and tell me what you see," Davey instructed.

Jesse found the short flight of stairs at the front of the cockpit and lowered himself into the area under the long forward deck. He didn't have a lot of experience with such things, but this looked fairly palatial to his eye. Lots of dark wood paneling and white leather furniture. He found two small bedrooms and one large one at the very front of the boat, plus a bathroom—a head, he remembered—complete with a shower. There was some light staining on the upholstery, and the carpet needed a good shampoo, but everything looked good structurally.

Jesse felt the vessel slowing while he was still below, and when he returned to the others, Davey was carefully but expertly piloting the boat back to the dock. Ten minutes later, they were all back in Esteban's office, and Davey was peeling off greenbacks and stacking them on the desk.

"Two-thirty," Davey said when the count was finished. "Count it yourself, if you want."

Esteban waved the offer off with a flick of his hand. "I watched you count and you seem trustworthy."

Jesse watched for a reaction from Davey, but saw nothing. Maybe this whole thing was about to end.

"It's interesting, though, that you insisted on paying in cash," the fat man went on. "I didn't ask for that. Your girl on the phone told me that was your preference."

"Do you have a problem with cash?" Davey said, straightening his posture.

"I do not, no. As I said. Yes, it is an inconvenience to deal with. I cannot just deposit so much money in a bank. Not without drawing *suspicion*."

Something about the way he leaned on the word raised the hairs on Jesse's back. He watched the muscles in Davey's jaw flex.

Esteban leaned back in his chair, causing it to creak. "Cash is inconvenient for you, too, I'm sure. And certainly it poses security concerns. I always assume that people who prefer to deal with large sums of cash are trying to hide something."

"Do you now?"

"And to invest that much money up front tells me that there is much money to be made by that investment. Much more than just, say, two hundred—"

Davey struck like lightning, launching himself across the desk to grab the fat man's throat and shirt collar. Before Esteban could react, Davey pulled him out of his seat and halfway across the cluttered work surface. He wiped the surface clean with a sweep of his arm and rammed Esteban's face into the flat surface twice, with startling force. Blood spattered the wood as Davey tossed him back into his chair.

"Don't threaten me," Davey said. His tone was harsh, but his volume soft. The fat man's nose and mouth bled freely. "We've made a deal, and you will stick to it. Cross me and the consequences will be dire. Do you under-stand this?"

One hundred percent of Esteban's attention seemed to be focused on stanching the flow of blood from his broken face. He pressed his hands against his mouth and nose, but he bled through his fingers and off the end of his chin.

Davey didn't press for an answer. "Let's go," he said, and he led the way out the door and back toward the car.

"What about the boat?" Jesse asked.

"We need to get the tools out of the trunk."

"You really hurt that guy."

"Nah," Davey said. "Just rearranged his face a little. You can't take even an ounce of shit from people if you're going to play in this league."

"But what—"

"He was going to extort us for more money. I paid a good price, and that should be the end of it."

Jesse was no saint—he'd done his time in prison for taking shit that didn't belong to him—but the ease with which Davey meted out violence and the total absence of remorse startled him. But it also made him proud.

Back at the BMW, Davey opened the trunk and re-moved the heavy bag of tools he'd brought from the airport. He bounced the bag once in his hand to get it comfortable, and then he closed the lid. "Now it's time to get to the boat."

"What are the tools for?" Jesse asked.

"You know all that fancy leather stuff belowdecks on the boat?"

"Yeah."

"It's all got to come out."

"Why?"

"We're going to need all the speed and range we can get, and all those creature comforts weigh too much."

"But you just *paid* for all those comforts." The last boat Jesse and Davey had shared didn't even have a belowdecks area—he still had the signs of his sunburn even after months had passed. He'd been looking forward to some time on all that comfy leather.

"I paid for a way to get people and weapons out to an island and back," Davey said. "And let's not forget the most important thing."

Jesse looked to him, waited for it.

"It wasn't my money."

CHAPTER 20

Venice had no idea how the clock had spun all the way around to one, but such was the nature of things when she lost herself in research. Jonathan's revelation that there was a network of tunnels under the Crystal Sands Resort posed some interesting opportunities for research. She was looking for anything on the construction project—any small detail—that could lead to other small details. Those tidbits, when stitched together, could provide invaluable intel. The fact that she didn't know exactly what she was looking for made the problem infinitely more challenging and deepened her mental rabbit hole.

When her phone rang—the landline, which she almost never used—the noise startled her. It was one of those old-fashioned rings, too, the kind with an actual bell. She lifted the receiver before it could split her concentration a second time.

"Hello?"

"Um, Ms. Alexander, this is Rick Hare at the security station."

Venice's insides tightened. While the phone rarely

rang, the security station at the entrance to the office had *never* called her. She waited for the rest.

"There's a visitor here who says he has to meet with you."

"What does he want?"

"He says he can speak only with you."

"Why?"

"Um, he said he'd only speak with you, ma'am."

Venice chuckled. "That was kind of a stupid question, wasn't it? Does he look threatening?"

"No, ma'am. Otherwise, I wouldn't be calling you."

Another stupid question. "Did he give you a name?"

"Yes, ma'am. His name is Derek Halstrom. He said he talked with you this morning." Hare lowered his voice to a whisper. "But he doesn't know how to pronounce your name properly. Do you want me to tell him to go away?"

A chill rattled Venice's whole body, leaving her feeling light-headed and nauseous. Derek Halstrom was TickTock2. She'd screwed up big-time. This was a power play, and it scared the daylights out of her.

"Ma'am? Are you there?"

Venice shook herself back into reality. "Yes," she said. "Yes, I'm right here. Tell Mr. Halstrom that it's inappropriate to meet here in the office. Tell him to wait on the bench outside and that I'll join him in five minutes."

She listened as the guard covered the mouthpiece and delivered her message. It took longer than she expected. There clearly was some back-and-forth between the two of them. When Hare returned to the phone, he sounded agitated. "Yes, ma'am, I told him. He wasn't happy about it, but he's on his way outside."

Venice closed her eyes. "Okay, thank you, Rick."

"Ma'am?"

"Yes?"

"He told me to tell you that five minutes means five minutes. At six, he said, and I'm quoting here, your life will get very difficult."

The chill returned. "I understand."

"Perhaps you'd like me to go with you?"

Venice smiled, touched by the loyalty and commitment to duty. "No, Rick, that's okay. I'll be fine."

"You can't stop me from keeping an eye on you," he said. "You need something, you just give a wave and I'll be there."

"I know you will, Rick. Again, thanks." She hung up before there could be more conversation. This was bad. No, it was beyond bad. This could be catastrophic. She'd overextended her hand to exactly the wrong person. She'd allowed herself to fall victim to the same hubris for which she'd chastised so many others, so many times.

With the clock ticking, she realized that she had exactly zero control over what would transpire next. TickTock2 had invaded her space because she had invaded his. She didn't know how he'd been able to find her, but at this point, the *how* of it really didn't matter much. He was here, and she was vulnerable to the point of being defenseless. And she had two minutes to get downstairs.

She needed to settle her thoughts, to push the fear away and to rejoin the moment. She was about to embark on a live-action chess game, the stakes were unspeakably high, and her opponent had had at least the length of a long car ride to figure out his plan. He worked for one of the most secure, secretive agencies in the world. He could make her disappear and in the process erase all traces that she had ever been born.

But to do that would require him to kill Roman, as well, and maybe even Mama.

"Computer geeks are not killers," she told herself aloud, but she didn't find her voice all that convincing.

"Stop it," she said. "Just stop it. It is what it is. In about a minute and a half, you'll know just how awful it is."

She'd discovered many years ago that the act of speaking thoughts aloud made them more real. The phrase *just how awful* resonated louder to her ears than any other.

She slipped her cell phone—the one that linked her to Jonathan—into her pocket and left everything else on her desk untouched. As she headed for the door, she stopped and returned to the top right-hand drawer. Years ago, Jonathan had given her a little .22-caliber pistol with the instruction to carry it with her all the time. It was a tiny thing with a Beretta logo on the grip and a weird tip-up barrel for easy loading. Jonathan said it was a girly gun that would make a lot of noise, and was better than going through life unarmed.

She'd never carried it, and frankly, she objected to having it in her desk. Until today. She shifted her cell phone to her left pocket, and slid the pistol into her right. For all she knew, she couldn't hit within three feet of anyone she might shoot at, but for the first time, she understood where Digger was coming from. It felt better to have it than to not.

Venice exited the Cave, passed through the main

work area, and then exited out onto the hallway and the stairs.

Rick Hare was waiting for her. He rested one hand on the pistol in his belt, and the other on the array of spare bullets he carried on the other side. "I really think I need to go with you."

Venice smiled and touched his cheek with her fingers. "You're sweet," she said. "But I'll be okay. I know who he is."

"Then why does he pronounce your name like the city in Italy?"

Venice decided that it made no sense to continue the conversation. Rick Hare had his orders, and he would follow them. She had no doubt that he would try to position himself so that he could watch them from afar, but she also had no doubt that TickTock2 was way too smart to allow that to happen.

With a blossoming sense of dread, Venice descended the long stairway, and stepped out into the heat of the day.

When Jonathan Grave converted the Fisherman's Cove firehouse to his personal residence and office space, he'd gifted the patch of ground at the corner of Church and Water Streets to the town, where he'd planted some trees and installed a bench that walkers or runners could use for respite. He'd also installed a marble pedestal-style drinking fountain. The space was rarely visited, so far as Venice could tell, but it was beautiful.

A thin African-American man sat in the shade on the bench. He appeared to be within a couple years of thirty and he wore close-cropped hair and beard. Wearing a gray sport coat with a blue shirt and a maroon tie, he looked more like a lawyer than a hacker. Not that she had any idea what a hacker should look like. He stood as she approached.

"Hello, Venice," he said.

She corrected his pronunciation.

"How very pretentious," he said. His smile took the insult out of the words. "Do you mind if we walk while we talk?"

"May I ask what we're going to talk about?"

Derek extended his hand. "Let's meet properly. Derek Halstrom."

Venice hesitated, then shook his hand. "You're confusing me," she said.

Derek smiled. "I don't think that's true. It was your security guard who confused you. He's the one who made you nervous."

"Because you said my life would get difficult if I didn't hurry."

He conceded the point with a twist of his neck. "I didn't want you doing something desperate that would get me in trouble before we had a chance to talk."

"Again, what's the topic? I'm busy here and I have a job—"

"Your coworkers are in more trouble than you know," Derek said.

And he started walking up the hill toward St. Kate's and Resurrection House beyond it. Venice wondered if he knew the significance of either one of those buildings and the roles they played in her life—and, by extension, in Digger's life. She quickstepped to catch up.

"Officer Hare is not going to be happy to lose sight of you," Derek said.

"This would be a good time to tell you that this is a

small town," Venice said, "and I've lived here my whole life. I am what you might call connected, so if you think—"

"I'm not a killer," Derek said, cutting her off. "I'm not even a beater-upper. You can relax."

Something about Derek impressed Venice as honest. She'd been wrong before—had the ex-husband to prove it—but not in a long time. She found herself liking this guy. "What are you, then?" she asked. "If not a killer or a beater-upper?"

He looked away from her, and down at his shoes, as he said, "Mostly, I'm a fanboy."

Venice coughed out a laugh. "A *what*?" This was not at all what she was expecting.

"Come on, are you *kidding* me? You're Freak-Face666, for crying out loud. There wouldn't be any Gloomity without you. Though I was a little freaked when I found out you're a girl. A woman, I mean."

This guy was acting like a high schooler with a crush. If it wasn't so scary, it would have been charming. "So, what did I do wrong?"

He cocked his head. He didn't get the question.

"How did you find me?"

"After you and I disconnected, you made a phone call and used some of the same phraseology I gave you. And I have access to limitless NSA resources. I guess you could say I misappropriated some taxpayer dollars."

In retrospect, she realized that she should have expected that. "So, are you here on official business?"

"Oh, hell no. I took a day off."

"To come and do what?"

"To meet you. Well, okay, that's not true. At least it

wasn't at first. I wanted to get even somehow. You'd scared the shit out of me, and I wanted to do at least as much to you."

"You just spoke in the past tense," Venice said.

"Yeah, I did. After I blow off the initial layer of steam, I'm not a very vindictive guy. You caught me being stupid once, and I paid the price. It's not your fault that I was stupid."

Venice gave him a long look. "Is that the polite way of saying that it's my fault that you're here?"

He giggled. No, really. He *giggled.* "A gentleman would never say such a thing."

She had to laugh, too.

"So, as I was driving out here—what a pretty drive, by the way. And a gorgeous little town. Anyway, as I was driving out here, it hit me that I was going to actually meet FreakFace666. I've admired your work for, like, forever."

Venice pulled up short. "Wait a minute," she said. "When I touched you this morning, I wasn't Freak-Face666."

"No, you were BadThings."

"So, how—"

"You didn't see the SMS I sent you, then?"

Venice answered with a scowl.

"I was so freaked out by being outed by BadThings and I reached out to FreakFace666 for advice. Then, after I intercepted your phone call, I traced things down and I saw that the Hacker King—excuse me, the Hacker *Queen*—had a lot in common with BadThings."

Venice brought her hand to her forehead as reality hit her. "Oh, crap," she said. "You didn't know for sure

that we were the same person until I just now confirmed it for you."

When Derek smiled, his whole face lit up. "Weren't
you the one who posted that social hacking is nothing
more than one big poker game?"

She felt her ears get hot. "Well, damn," she said.

"Don't worry about it," Derek said. "It's a good
feeling when you know you've bested the best."

Venice closed her eyes and shook her head. She'd
been an idiot.

"Take it easy on yourself," Derek said. "Sooner or
later, hubris takes all of us down."

"Have you told the rest of Gloomity who I am?"
She could have danced around the question, but decided to shoot for the heart.

Derek looked hurt. "I wouldn't do that. I don't think
that you've grappled with the fact that I'm not here to
hurt you. In fact, I'm here to help you."

"By telling me how my colleagues are in deeper
trouble than we understand."

"Exactly."

"So, tell me."

"Agree to have dinner with me first," Derek said.

Without thinking, Venice reached out and grabbed
the fabric of his sleeve. "Wait. What?"

"I want to take you to dinner."

"A date?"

He deflated a little. "You can call it whatever you
like. But I want to spend time with you."

"You don't even know me."

"But I know about you."

Another warning bell.

"Oh, shit, I'm sounding creepy. I don't mean to, but when you've got skills like mine, you know how to learn about people. Are you going to tell me that you don't do the same thing?"

She really wished she could. The fact of the matter was that she'd unintentionally (or maybe intentionally) sabotaged a boatload of relationships over the years by digging into pasts and discovering stuff she wished she didn't know. "What do you know about me?"

"I'll tell you over dinner," he said.

"That can't happen," Venice said. "Certainly not tonight. I have work to do."

"Because Jonathan and Gail are in trouble on the Crystal Sands Resort."

Data point: Derek didn't know all that he thought he did. No nicknames, no code names. As she ran through the telephone conversations she'd had with Jonathan today, she was certain that no real names had been mentioned. That meant that while Derek knew that calls had been made, he didn't know what had been discussed.

"That's exactly right," Venice said.

Derek's eyes narrowed. "I missed something," he said. "I see it in your face."

"The essentials are there," Venice said. "The essentials are spot-on. But I cannot possibly meet you for dinner tonight."

"Tomorrow, then."

"We'll see how this all works out." She sensed him digging an emotional trench for himself and she launched a peace offering. "But later this week, I promise."

Derek's whole being brightened. "You *promise* promise?"

Again, back in high school. "Yes."

"Okay, then," Derek said. "Good. That's very, very good."

They strolled up the long hill, past the perpendicular walkway that led to Saint Katherine's Catholic Church, and soon they would be at the walkway to Resurrection House. Venice couldn't articulate why, but she didn't want them to get that close to her home. And her mother. And her son.

"You said that my coworkers are in jeopardy."

"Yes, I did," Derek replied. He pulled to a halt and turned to face Venice full-on. "Look, I recognize that you own me, okay? You know about me and Gloomity, and you know that by doing what I have done, I have committed felonies that could end my life. Certainly, life as I know it. I'll be honest with you. I wouldn't do well in prison."

"I'm not sure any of us would," Venice said.

"So, what I know—what you want to know—is just another lock on my prison door. If I tell you, it'll be for all the right reasons, so that the people you care about won't get themselves in trouble that they can't get themselves out of."

"Okay," Venice said.

"So, you won't rat me out?"

Venice crossed her heart and held her hand up, hoping that there were no witnesses. "I'll pinky swear if you want me to."

Derek looked at her for a long moment, then shoved his hands into his pockets and started up the hill again.

"Derek, listen to me," Venice said. "I'm knee-deep in something very important here. I don't have time to play games."

"Are your friends there on the island to steal munitions?" He asked the question quickly, as if it had been burdening him.

Venice recoiled from the thought. "*What? No!* Good heavens, no."

"Why, then? Why was it so important for you to know what goes on there?"

It was time to be careful. Derek knew too much as it was, but the genie wasn't yet entirely out of the bottle. "I can't tell you that," she said. "But I swear to you that we're the good guys."

"Why was it important for you to know about the storage magazines on the island?" He continued to stroll as he talked, mostly addressing the ground in front of his feet.

"I can't tell you that, either." As she heard her own words, she realized how evasive and suspicious she sounded. "You, above all others, should know about secrets. How important it is to keep them."

Derek stopped and turned to face her. "Do you understand the risk I'm taking by being here? I'm risking a lifetime in prison."

"And that's a choice you made," Venice said. She moderated her tone to be calm, entirely reasonable. "You clearly thought that you could trust me with your secrets. I don't know that I can do the same. Not yet. We just met. And what's at risk for me goes far beyond jail time. Lives are at stake. Many lives."

"You're not a government contractor," Derek said. "You're a private investigation firm. I've done the research, trust me. That's all you do, at least officially. How can a private investigation take you to a Costa Rican island off the coast of Mexico?"

She waited for him to connect the dots for himself.

Derek's eyes grew wide. "It's a resort," he said. "Your friends were vacationing there, weren't they? And something bad happened." He started walking again, this time looking at the sky as the pieces fell into place. "I'm guessing some kind of attack."

Venice followed at a distance, admiring his intensity.

"It *had* to be an attack," he declared. At this point, he was engaging entirely with himself. "What else could be so urgent? But how did Security Solutions get the call? Why not the local . . ."

He spun on his own axis and pointed his finger at Venice. "Got it. Your friends are involved in some kind of a fight, and they can't get any help because Costa Rica doesn't have any troops or cops to send." He looked to the sky again, and then back at her. "Your friends figured out that it must have something to do with the old Soviet storage facilities." He grinned. "Am I right?"

Venice grinned, too. There was a whole lot to like about this guy. "I can't tell you," she said.

"Of course you can't." Derek laughed. "Damn, that felt good."

"But if you *were* right, what is the bad news that you have to share?"

"Let's go walking back to your office."

"I can't let you into my office."

"That's okay," Derek said. "But you have some serious warning to do. There's a shipment of weapons coming to the island tonight. That's what I thought your buddies were hunting for, but now I think it's what their enemies are hunting for."

"What kind of weapons are they?" Venice asked.

"Agent VX," Derek said. "You probably know it as nerve agent."

Venice's chill returned. "No, I know it as Agent VX," she said. "That stuff's been outlawed for years."

"Yes, it has," Derek said. "All that means is that our government—and about a dozen others—have been working very hard to hide it."

"Where's the shipment coming from?"

"That's the tricky part," Derek said. "The cool thing about the Crystal Sands as a weapons depot is that everybody gets plausible deniability for what they do."

"You're being obtuse," Venice said. "Where is it coming from?"

"I actually don't know the specific port of origin, but I do know that the shipping company is a cutout for the Central Intelligence Agency."

It was Venice's turn to stop short. "*Our* Central Intelligence Agency? Why?"

"I don't know for sure," Derek hedged, "but there's been a lot of chatter in official Washington over the past couple of weeks. President Darmond has decided that the time has come to level the playing field for the Ukrainian rebels."

Venice couldn't believe the words she'd just heard. "We're going to use nerve gas against the Russians?"

Derek looked back at the ground. "We're not going to gas anyone," he said. "That decision will be up to the Ukrainians."

CHAPTER 21

One of the guards had thought to bring along games for the children to play. Erin Talley thought that was a good idea, but there simply weren't enough games to go around. She also questioned the sanity of pitting underage strangers against each other in competitive games like Monopoly and Risk. Thanks in part, she thought, to the general discomfort of the surroundings, tempers had begun to fray, and the children had begun to act out. A lot.

The guards seemed uncomfortable with their mission here. It was almost as if they were afraid of the kids, instead of the other way around. They knew how to bark orders and demand quiet, but they seemed unnerved when it came to the task of actually taming the noise. She had no doubt that they were willing to shoot if it came to that, but with any measure short of that, they seemed sort of clueless.

Erin decided the one who called himself Mike was the one in charge, at least for this shift. The guards had turned over at least once—and maybe another time, since she did fall asleep for a while. Mike seemed to be the one everyone listened to. He was also the only one with a real name. Unless parents actually named their kids Whiskey or Tango.

Erin arose from a game of rummy, which she'd lost interest in ten minutes ago, and decided to brave an approach. Mike's posture stiffened as she approached, so she was careful to show a smile.

"Please go sit back down," he said. His accent was the same as the others, but thicker.

"I need to speak with you, please," Erin said.

"Sit."

"No, sir. Not until we can talk."

The soldier looked to be in his late twenties, though Erin was not the best judge of grown-ups' ages. Her words clearly surprised him, and she tried not to laugh. She intended to keep their conversation private, but when she got inside three feet of him, his hand moved to the grip of his rifle and she stopped.

"I don't want to make you nervous," she said. "I want to talk about the children. You need to let them outside to play. They need to run around. Either that, or you've got to get some movies to show or something."

"That is not possible," Mike said. "Now go sit down."

"That's just the thing," Erin pressed. "I'm tired of sitting. We're all tired of sitting. It's not as if we're going to run away. There's no place to go even if we wanted to. You can see as well as I can that this isn't working. Maybe we could even go to the pool."

"Absolutely not. No pool."

That answer came with such emphasis that she didn't push. The pool was out. "Then what about some fresh air?"

"No," Mike said. "I am not authorized to let you outside."

She pointed to the microphone Velcro'd to the front of his vest. "You've got a radio. And we need food and drinks."

"You had breakfast."

"We had dry cereal and water. That's not breakfast. It's almost noon, and everyone is hungry."

"The world is full of hungry people," Mike said.

Erin saw a dangerous opening, and she decided without thinking to go for it. "Not in this world," she said. "Look around. I don't know what our parents paid to bring us all here, but it was a lot. These kids are *rich,* Mr. Mike. They've never spent a single hungry day in their whole lives. And they're not used to being told what they cannot do. If you keep treating them like adult prisoners, it's going to come to the point where you have to actually use that rifle. Is that really what you want to do?"

"I will do my duty," Mike said.

"I'm just saying that it doesn't have to come to that," Erin pressed.

"You have made your point," Mike said. "Now, please go sit."

Erin wanted to press more, but the vibe coming from Mike had changed with that last comment. He was getting pushed into a corner where he didn't want to go. She'd seen teachers get to those corners before—a lot of times—and she understood that it was time to back away.

She had no interest in returning to the rummy game, so she wandered toward the living room. "I'm hungry,

Erin," said Isaac, the eleven-year-old who'd come to her at dawn.

"I know," she said. "I told them. Try not to think about it."

"I have to think about it," Isaac said. "There's nothing else to do."

Erin moved on, scanning the rest. Nicholas was still asleep, or pretending to be, curled up in a corner near the door. What a lazy son of a bitch. And to think she'd thought he was hot when she saw him at the pool. What was the sense of having muscles if you were going to spend all the time hiding?

The sound of a droning man's voice drew her attention back into the hallway. Mike was talking to someone on his radio. When he made eye contact with her, he turned so she couldn't see his face.

Maybe she'd gotten through, after all.

Forty-five minutes later, the front door opened—the one that led to the road, not the slider that led to the beach—and a crew of three soldiers brought in plates of sandwiches and cases of sodas. In a second wave, they brought a stack of books and DVDs. Erin recognized them from the so-called TeenTreat, which was appended to the Plantation House, on the opposite end from the English Bar.

She smiled as the food was piled up and winced when she saw the kids all rushing.

Mike yelled, "Take your time, everyone! Take your turn!"

No one listened.

It was Erin's turn. "Hey!" she shouted, and everybody jumped. "Indoor manners, everybody. I know we're all hungry, but the soldiers won't let us get hungry again, will you, Mike?"

He deferred to a man Erin hadn't seen before.

"That's right," the man said. "We've fixed the system."

Erin didn't know what that meant, but she continued speaking at an elevated tone. "Please take your turn and take one sandwich at a time. If you want another, you can come back for it when you're done with the first. Those of you who are twelve or older should help with the smaller ones. Come on, everyone. Let's make our parents proud."

Her words did the trick, at least for the time being. She stood close, ushering them through the procedure of getting food. "Take a plate first," she instructed. "Put your sandwich on the plate, and then grab a can of soda. If you need help, look to one of the others. Remember, you older ones, make sure the little folks are taken care of."

Ten minutes into the herding process, everyone had food, and now it was Erin's turn. The only sandwiches left were tuna fish on rye bread. She didn't hate it, but it would not have been her first choice. Now she just hoped that the mayonnaise hadn't been left in the sun all day.

She remained standing while she ate, resting her ginger ale on the TV stand in the living room. Her grandfather always joked at Thanksgiving that you could tell how hungry the crowd was by how much conversation there was at the table. By that standard, this crowd was starving.

"You're very good with the children," a voice said from behind her.

Erin turned to see the man she didn't recognize.

"I told your man that they were hungry," she said.

"I know," the man said. "And he told me." He extended his hand. "I'm the man they call Alpha," he said. "I'm in charge here."

She looked at his hand and then took a two-handed bite out of her sandwich. "I'll shake your hand when I see my parents again."

Alpha smiled. His eyes looked kinder than she expected. "You're a feisty one," he said.

"I'm tired and I'm scared," she said. "We all are. I don't know why you're here, but you're being cruel to the children. I can only imagine what you're doing with the adults."

Alpha didn't reply at first. "We all have jobs to do," he said at length. "Some are uglier than others. As long as everyone behaves, then there should be no more violence."

Erin opened her mouth to say something, but then took another bite of sandwich, instead.

"You may speak freely to me," Alpha said.

"You don't want to hear what I have to say."

"Listen to my words . . . Erin, is it? Erin Talley?"

Something icy shot through her belly at the mention of her name.

Alpha continued, "I am a man of my word. If I tell you that you are free to speak, then that is exactly what you are."

Erin put the remains of her sandwich back on her plate and faced Alpha full-on. "You say you want everyone to *behave*. If we *behave*, then you'll stop shooting people. Well, if that's the case, then your soldiers can't wait for the opportunity to shoot everyone in this room."

She scanned Alpha's face for a reaction, and found that he looked interested, fully engaged in what she was saying. A gentle nod urged her to continue.

"I don't know how you're dealing with the grown-ups," she said. "Grown-ups confuse the hell out of me. But I'm telling you that by keeping all these kids locked up like this, you're begging for a junior riot."

"We brought books and games and movies," Alpha said.

"And that's fine," Erin agreed, "but only for a little while. They're kids. They need to stay occupied. It's beyond cruel that you and your soldiers won't let them outside to play."

"I thought that children didn't play outside anymore," Alpha said. It appeared to be a serious observation.

"Do you have any children?" she asked.

"That's none—"

"Oh, for God's sake. Do you *know* anyone who has children?"

Alpha recoiled and laughed. "My goodness, I bet your father has his hands filled with you. Yes, I know people who have children."

Erin was vaguely aware that she was using much of the same attitude and body language that could launch her father into orbit. He called it being sassy, while her mom called it being bitchy. "Then you know," she said, "that children need options. If you want the little ones to stay inside, you tell them they have to go outside. Right now, this place smells like a dirty toilet. It's too hot and there's no breeze. Half of them will probably want to stick around inside and watch movies, but a chunk of the others will want to go outside and do something. Even if it's only a change of place where they can sit and talk."

"You seem to be an expert in these things," Alpha said.

"Duh, I'm a kid."

Alpha launched a big laugh. "All right," he said. "You win. I will tell my men that your children will be allowed to go outside, and I will tell them that you are responsible for all of them."

"Excuse me?"

Alpha held up his hands. "Hey, you want the role of mother, and you've got it. Roll will be taken every hour, and also on a random basis. There are thirty-five children here and—"

"Thirty-four," Erin corrected. "I've counted many times."

"Did you count yourself?"

She blushed.

He winked. "I count on you to make sure that the count remains the same. If anyone goes missing, I will hold you personally responsible."

She gaped. This wasn't a responsibility she'd signed on for.

Alpha continued to smile as he leaned in close and said, "You do not want to disappoint me. I would hate to have to deliver a daughter's corpse to her parents."

Venice decided that the office could wait. When they got to the bottom of Church Street, where the firehouse was on the left, she swung a turn to the right, down Water Street toward the fishing piers. "This nerve agent thing," she said. "Is it a strategy from the top, or some rogue action within the CIA?"

Derek made a waving motion with both hands. "Not my pay grade," he said. "I am strictly an implementer of plans. They don't let me within a hundred yards of policy, and the politics bore me."

Normally, Venice's warning bells would be clanging like a carillon, but the more time she spent with Derek, the more she liked him. The more she trusted him. Yes, she understood that was a dangerous place to be, but sometimes chances had to be taken.

"Why are you doing this?" she asked.

"I already told you."

"You told me you were a fanboy for FreakFace666," Venice said. "That doesn't explain your willingness to share what is probably highly classified information."

"Oh, there's no *probably* about it," Derek said with a wry chuckle. "Off-the-charts classified. Go-to-jail classified."

He seemed to want additional prodding, but Venice waited for the rest.

"You said you'd read my personnel file," he said. "I'm not cut out for the NSA. I know too much shit that I wish I didn't know. I've seen too many decisions made that hurt people for the sole purpose of advancing some bureaucratic asshat's career. Everything's so goddamned secret that the assholes who run the place know that they can do whatever they want, essentially without consequence, because nobody can talk about the shit they're doing without committing a felony."

"Are you talking about the political appointees?"

Derek puffed a laugh for dramatic effect. "Oh, God no. Those guys are lost. It's the career guys that run the place. The politicos are scared shitless of being exposed as the ignoramuses they are. They posture and make noises at press conferences, spouting carefully-crafted bullshit that's been fed to them by the SES pukes who essentially run their own government." Senior Executive Service.

"That's pretty harsh," Venice said. "They can't all be like that."

"No, of course they're not all like that. In fact, in my experience, the vast majority of them are exactly the good soldiers and patriots that you'd hope they would be. The problem there is that good soldiers follow orders and do what they're told. And, if I might throw in a little cynicism, they know that Fort Meade is a good gig, and they don't want to screw that up for themselves."

"So, you're a modern-day Don Quixote," Venice said.

"Fine, make fun if you want."

"I'm not making fun," Venice said. "I've always admired Don Quixote." She didn't bother to add that the true modern-day Señor Quixote was her boss.

"Then yes," Derek said. "I'm that naïve guy who believes in doing the right thing because it is the right thing to do."

Venice smirked. "Like sharing top secrets with relative strangers?"

Derek didn't drop a beat. "Yeah, exactly like that. It's all in the timing. I knew that your friends were somehow in trouble, and then I found out about the VX. At least I'm not turning it over to the press. I know you have no tangible reason to believe this, but you really can trust me. I really am not trying to screw you."

The phrase hung in the air. Then they both laughed.

"Okay, maybe later, but not that way," Derek said.

Venice had not blushed in a very long time. In any of a thousand different circumstances, she would have struck a posture of righteous indignation, but not today. Not with Derek.

Over to the left, the docks of the fishing pier were fairly quiet. The morning boats had all gone out, and only a few had returned. There was an aroma to this part of town that Venice had come to realize that people either loved or hated, with no room for a middle ground. To her, the smell of fish and the river was the perfume of home. She loved it.

"How much do you know about Security Solutions?" she asked.

Derek gave her a sideward glance. "Have we crossed into the truth-telling phase of our relationship?"

Relationship? "Um . . . sure."

"Remember," Derek hedged, "I knew where to dig, and you left me some bread crumbs that others wouldn't have."

This sounds like it's going to be bad, Venice thought.

"You look like I'm going to hit you," Derek said.

"I feel a little that way, too," Venice said.

He sighed deeply. "Look, I don't want to freak you out. Let's just say that I know that there's a secret side to Security Solutions that creates a pretty wide swath of violence. I know there are a few unsolved murders in this country and others that more than likely have your team's fingerprints on them. Please don't confirm or deny."

Venice felt a little ill. Everything they did depended on absolute secrccy.

"Don't look like that," Derek said. "You didn't screw anything up. Really. Nobody else is going to be able to find the trail, I promise you."

"You can't know that," Venice said. The words were already out before she realized that she'd just confirmed his suspicions.

"Yes, I can," Derek said. "What little trail used to be there is all gone now." He beamed.

Venice truly didn't know what to make of this. "This is what you do to people who piss you off? You cover their tracks for them?"

"Only for FreakFace666," he said. He pointed at his face with both forefingers. "Fanboy."

They walked in silence for twenty yards.

"You guys do what I want to do," Derek said.

That earned him a look. "What is that?"

"You create mayhem for all the right reasons. Hostage rescue, right?"

"Holy crap."

"That's okay," Derek said. "I told you, you can trust me."

"You know that none of this is my decision, right?"

"No, that would be up to retired First Sergeant Jonathan Grave, formerly Gravenow."

Venice's sense of dread deepened.

"Oh, come on," Derek teased. "That's public record. He owns the friggin' company."

Venice's pulse raced and she felt light-headed. This

was all too much. This was the nightmare. *The* nightmare.

"Audition me," Derek said.

"Excuse me?"

"Audition me. There's bad shit going down in the Pacific, off the coast of Mexico, right? You've got a lot to do, right? Palm some of it off on me."

"I can't let you in the office," she said. "I've already told you that."

"I don't need to go into your office," Derek shot back. "You know what I do. You know my skills. Give me a decent Internet connection and I can do pretty much anything."

Venice's mind raced as fast as her heart now. Digger was going to be furious when he got wind of this. Boxers was likely to kill Derek and Venice both.

Jonathan's voice materialized in her head. *What's done is done. Irrelevant. Correct the course and solve the problem.* She'd heard him say it a thousand times. It was the verbose corollary to, *Shit happens.* Derek knew what he knew about their operations. That couldn't be undone. Jonathan had trusted people before, and they'd never turned on him. Probably because of the overt threat of shattering retribution if they ever tried. No one pulled off intimidation better than Big Guy.

Venice ran through her options. If Derek was as reliable as she thought (hoped?), then she could use his help. But if this was a Machiavellian power play— playing the long game—then his effort to help could screw everything up.

Which he could easily do without any permission from her. She reminded herself that Derek was Tick-Tock2, for crying out loud. The guy had mad skills.

With what he already knew, he could wreak havoc on everything if he was of a mind to. In the end, the decision was obvious. It was even easy.

"Remember the electrical-grid play Gloomity did a few months ago?"

"When we blacked out the rich guy's private island?"

Venice grinned and made her eyebrows dance.

Derek grinned, too. "Ah," he said. "You want me to black out a rich guy's private island."

"Exactly. Can you do it?"

"Oh, please. Do Leprechauns poop green? Of course I can. I can have them blacked out in a couple of hours, max."

"Just put the pieces in place," Venice said. "We'll need to wait for an order to actually make anything happen."

Derek giggled, kicked the ground, and clapped his hands. "This is going to be fun. What a great day!"

CHAPTER 22

Henry West watched out the gulfstream's tiny window as the Pacific Ocean grew closer and closer. These were the trying moments when you simply had to trust that the pilot was competent, and that his view included the image of a runway. A quick glance across the aisle showed an equally tense Boxers, who, as Henry understood things, would normally be flying the plane instead of sitting in the back. As it was, he'd enlisted a couple of recent retirees from the 160th SOAR—Special Operations Air Regiment—to sit in the drivers' seats so he could participate in the mission planning.

The satellite imagery that Mother Hen had scared up was helpful, but only to a point. It was always nice to know the terrain and the possibilities for infiltration and exfiltration, but without current data on where the hostages were being held, it was all an academic exercise. They knew that they needed to get to the island via a point on the eastern edge, and then they had to rescue people and kill bad guys. Those were the details that remained murky.

If the bad guys could be eliminated, there'd be no

need to evacuate any of the hostages. That was the preferred outcome. Henry and the rest of his team—they'd adopted the moniker Team Yankee—could leave as quickly as they'd arrived, presumably with Digger and Gunslinger in tow, and the rest of the vacationers would be left wondering who those masked men were.

It all got stickier if good guys were wounded in the inevitable gunfight. They'd arranged to have another off-duty SOAR crew in the air with a rented medevac chopper orbiting off the area of operation. Was there anything in Mexico that could not be rented? Those medics could fly in anywhere to scoop and swoop a wounded operator, and they were capable of some pretty advanced medical care. For more advanced needs, there were some covert medical connections left over from the days of the Drug War, where a patient could be stabilized before being flown back to a *real* hospital in the States. All of that would be handled off the books, without official records.

Dead civilians would be left behind to be dealt with by whatever poor suckers were going to be tasked with cleaning up this mess. That was a no-brainer. The real head-scratcher of a problem was what to do with wounded civilians, particularly those with severe wounds. As a practical matter, they were no more difficult to medevac than a wounded operator, but then what? Covert worlds were covert for a reason, and those covert medical facilities were not accessible to people outside of the Community. Hard stop. So, how do you drop off somebody with a bullet wound or shrapnel injury at a local hospital and disappear? A lot of questions would be asked for a lot of very good reasons.

At the moment, they didn't have an answer for that one. Boxers was rolling the dice that the fact of an infirmary on the island meant that there was a medical staff. Even if that were true, Henry questioned the ability of the resident medical team to handle major trauma, but that was not his call.

The Gulfstream touched down without so much as a bump, and as they decelerated, Henry caught sight of a line of vehicles racing down the tarmac. It wasn't clear that they were there for Team Yankee, but Henry thought that's where the smart money would take him.

"Hey, Big Guy," he said. "I think we have company on the right."

"On the left, too," She Devil said.

Madman muttered, "This can't be good."

Over the intercom, the pilot announced, "Hey, team. I'm getting word from the tower that we need to stop on the tarmac and be boarded."

Henry craned his neck to look at the cache of weapons stacked up in the rear of the aircraft.

"This should be interesting," Boxers grumbled. He unclipped his seat belt and unfolded himself from his white leather seat. He walked at a steep bow as he made his way up to the cockpit door and knocked. They opened it and Boxers went into the flight deck and chatted up the pilots.

As they rolled to a stop, the vehicles stopped with them. Henry saw black SUVs and gray SUVs. None of them displayed any flashing lights, and they bore no markings that labeled them as government officials.

"Any thoughts?" Henry asked to the others.

"I am not going to jail," Madman said.

"That's not an option in the first place," She Devil

said. "Big Guy would burn the whole country to the ground before he let himself be taken into custody."

"I'm not sure that's entirely reassuring," Henry quipped. He rose from his seat and wandered to the cockpit. "What's going on?"

Boxers looked impossibly scrunched in the small space of the flight deck. He peered back at Henry through the A-frame formed by his armpit. "A bit of a power struggle," he said.

"Who are the players?"

"People I've already paid, and people who want me to pay them, instead."

Henry waited for the rest of the explanation.

"Some government minister is tweaked that we flew in without proper clearance and vetting," Boxers explained. "That translates in this swamp of a bureaucracy to he didn't get his slice of the pie. But my guy is a more important minister and he has access to guys with guns. Shouldn't take too long."

"So, they're not really going to board?"

"Um, no. That wouldn't be good or healthy for any of them."

"Or us."

Boxers didn't reply.

In the end, the crisis ended—however such things play themselves out—and the vehicles all pulled away.

"Score one for the good guys," Boxers said.

"How are we going to off-load all this stuff?" Henry asked.

"I rented a private hangar and a couple of trucks."

"Holy shit," Henry said. "What's the final price tag on this operation?"

The question seemed to annoy Big Guy. He exited the flight deck, and as he squeezed past Henry, he said, "My friend's life."

It was hard to judge travel distance from the back of a plane while taxiing, but it felt like a mile or more as the Gulfstream drove from one slice of tarmac to the other, over and over again, for every bit of fifteen minutes. Finally, the pilots eased the aircraft across a threshold into a space that looked just like many other spaces of its kind that Henry had launched missions from over the years. As the engines spun down, Boxers pulled the lever for the door and the self-deploying stairs. He looked anxious to be able to stand straight again.

For no particular reason, Henry chose to bring up the rear as they deplaned. The humid heat hit him like a two-handed push as he climbed down to the hangar's concrete floor. The equipment could wait for a while. In fact, they all had to wait for a while. For nearly five hours, in fact, until it was time to depart for the rendezvous with Torpedo and Bomber, the boat driver and his son. This was the most out-of-sight location for them to kill time, and with nighttime being key to their mission, there were no bonuses for arriving at the embarkation spot early.

"I don't suppose anyone knows where the thermostat is for this place," Madman said. All of their faces were already glimmering with sweat.

"Hey," Jolaine said, pointing out the open doors. In the distance, a tiny blue car approached at a speed that seemed too high for the space.

Henry's hand moved reflexively to the pistol on his

hip. He didn't draw it, but he was ready to, if needed. The others all braced for their own fight with the incoming driver.

"What the hell is he doing?" Henry thought aloud.

"Making dangerous people very nervous," Boxers said.

As it closed in, the car revealed itself to be a little Fiat, and it slowed as it closed to within fifty yards, and then stopped completely twenty yards out.

"If that's an IED, we're toast," Madman said.

"Different Sandbox," Big Guy said.

The driver seemed to understand that he'd put people on edge. When he opened the door and climbed out, he led with his hands, fingers splayed. "I'm a good guy!" he yelled in English.

"I recognize that voice," Boxers said.

Madman added, "You're shitting me."

As the new arrival rose to his full height and stepped away from his vehicle, he held his arms out, cruciform, his fingers still splayed. He was about six-two, sported a battle beard, and still had the physique of the operator he used to be, all compressed into a T-shirt and faded Levi's.

"Boomer Nasbe," Jolaine said. "I thought he was dead."

"Not dead, She Devil," he called. "Just disappeared."

Dylan Nasbe, aka Boomer, was a former D-boy who'd gotten seriously sideways with Uncle Sam when he took it upon himself to mete out justice on some CIA shitheads who righteously deserved what they got. The intelligence community could forgive a lot of sins, but that was not one of them. He'd taken to the mattresses, as the Mob liked to say, a while ago, after the same

West Virginia op that got Jolaine fired from Jonathan's team.

"What are you doing here?" Madman asked. His tone was leaden, 100 percent disapproval.

Dylan let his arms drop to his sides and he walked toward Team Yankee, a big grin decorating his face. "Ah, come on, Stanley. Bygones and all that." He stopped in front of Boxers and offered his hand. "Howya doin', Big Guy?"

To Henry's eye, there was genuine affection when Boxers said, "It's good to see you, Dylan. Glad you're still breathing."

"I heard that Digger needed help," he said. "And I happened to be in the neighborhood."

"The family?"

Dylan looked away. "Don't see them anymore. This is no life for a teenager. I want Ryan to run *toward* his life, not away from mine."

Jolaine stepped forward to shake his hand, as well. "Nice to see you again."

Dylan grinned as he said, "You still a batshit-crazy killer of innocents?"

She smiled through pressed lips. "I'm here by specific request," she said.

Henry figured the jab hit a little too close to home. When it was his turn, he shook the newcomer's hand. "Henry West. Conan."

"You're not a Unit guy." It sounded a little like an accusation.

"DEVGRU," Henry said.

Dylan shook his hand aggressively. "A squid!"

"I'll try to use small words," Henry said.

Dylan gave a hearty laugh. "I like working with you

SEALs. We never run short of mirrors or hair gel when you guys are on the team."

"How'd you hear about the op?" Boxers asked.

"There's a watchful hen in Virginia who may or may not have my contact information," Dylan said. "And not because I gave it to her."

"Is this where you've been serving your exile?" Jolaine asked.

"I'm a no-fixed-address kind of guy these days. As luck would have it, I happened to be in Mexico when your balloon went up." He held his arms out again. "So, do you have room for another shooter or not?"

"Always got room for you, Boomer," Boxers said.

Dylan held up a finger. "Nope, remember the rules. I'm not Boomer anymore. For that matter, I'm not Dylan anymore, either, but for your purposes, Dylan is fine."

Henry knew there was a backstory here, but he also knew that it was none of his business. What mattered was that the others seemed to get it, and they, likewise, seemed cool with it all.

"So, do we have a plan?" Dylan asked.

"We were just about to get to that," Big Guy said.

Jonathan asked, "Is there any high ground we can occupy that will let us look down on the resort itself?" They were progressing slowly and carefully through the jungle, intentionally staying off the paved areas. He knew from overheard radio transmissions that hunter-killer teams had been dispatched to find the people who had been killing the invaders. Given the disparity in numbers, invisibility at this point was hands down their strongest weapon.

"Not really," Jaime said. "I mean, there are areas where you can look down on one cluster of bungalows or another, but there's no place that will give you a complete view."

"When you design a resort, you want all the sight angles to be interesting," Tyler added. "I guess the good news is that all green stuff keeps people from seeing us, too. Cuts both ways. How come we haven't seen any of these killer teams yet?"

Jonathan had been wondering the same thing. "I'm gonna guess that they don't care a lot if we stay on the marina side of the island. As we get closer, I expect security to get tighter."

"That's how I'd do it," Gail agreed. "Are you boys sure you want to do this thing?"

"Less sure all the time," Tyler said.

Three minutes later, the flora thinned quickly, and they were on the edge of the golf course. Impossibly green grass covered gently-rolling hills far to the left and far to the right. Jonathan wasn't much of a golfer—in fact, he hated the game—but to his eye, this looked like a pretty tough course.

This was about to get a thousand times more intense. From here forward, they'd be in the open, moving in the daylight, clearly visible to anyone who happened to be looking.

"Okay, listen up," Jonathan said. "First things first, you two ditch the guns, the vests, anything that'll make you look like anything other than wayward guests."

"Can we leave them here?" Tyler asked.

"Sure. Stash everything under leaves and stuff. Be sure to pull the flashlights."

As they did just that, and Gail supervised, Jonathan looked out over the course, planning his next move.

"Do you know exactly where you are?" Jonathan asked.

Both of them nodded.

"Show me on the map." Jonathan unfolded his copy and they pointed at the correct spot. That had been a test and they'd passed. "Now show me where the nearest stack is, where you're going to enter."

Jaime pointed to a spot in the middle of a cluster of bungalows that were hidden by the tree line on the other side of the golf course.

"You're sure you can get anywhere you want within the utility tunnels from that spot?"

Jaime dangled a ring of keys from his finger. "With these, I can get through anything to go anywhere."

"And there's no security down there?" Gail asked. "No alarms to set off?"

"If there are, I've never seen them."

"Not the most comforting response," Jonathan said under his breath.

"What about making noise?" Gail pressed.

"We'll be careful," Tyler said.

"Noise shouldn't be a big problem until we get in close to where the hostages are."

"Don't get cocky," Jonathan warned. "Fact is, we only think we know where the hostages are. And to really put a fine point on it, we have no clue where the children are being kept. That's the info I need you to get. That, and anything else you learn."

"Anything else like what?" Tyler asked.

"Anything like anything," Jonathan said. "I don't know what we don't know."

"And communicate in real time," Gail added. "If you uncover an interesting something, let us know right away."

Both kids gave the same cocked-head, puppy-dog look of confusion.

"You can't forget to tell us if you communicate it right away," Jonathan said. What he didn't add was the reasonable likelihood that they wouldn't be coming back out, once they went in. "This guest map will be the key. All locations need to be communicated as they are represented here. This is the only point of reference we have in common."

"Got it," Tyler said.

Jonathan continued, "So if there's something important we need to know about under the ground in the tunnels, that needs to be conveyed relative to the things we can see aboveground. Observations are useless if they can't be tied to a place."

Jonathan saw the fear and anticipation in their young faces, and the cautious enthusiasm brought a kind of sadness. There was so much that they didn't know, so much that they were on the brink of learning in the hardest possible way.

"All right," Jonathan concluded. "Here's the way it will work. Slinger and I will move out first, and we're going to take cover in those sand traps—"

"Bunkers," Jaime said.

"What?"

"They're bunkers. There's no sand in them."

"I deeply don't care," Jonathan said. "We're going to go out there and establish a position from which we can cover your advance across the open spaces. When I tell you to move, you move. When I tell you to stop, you stop. If I tell you to get down, do it quickly and stay down. That will be your clue that bullets may be about to fly, and you won't want to catch any of those. Are you with me so far?"

Tyler and Jaime nodded to each other.

"To me," Jonathan said. "I'm in charge, you address me."

"I'm with you," Jaime said.

"Me too."

"Which one of you is working the phone?" Jonathan asked.

"I am," Tyler said.

"Okay, then let's establish that connection now." Jonathan dialed Gail's number and the phone in Tyler's hand buzzed.

"Hello?" he answered, bringing it to his ear. Then he smiled an assurance that he knew he was being stupid.

"Keep the earbuds in and the line open," Jonathan instructed. "That's your lifeline back to us. If we lose the connection when you're underground, I will work to reestablish it. If you need to sign off in a hurry, say the word *red* and get off. I'll know what that means."

"You're giving them a lot to remember," Gail observed.

"Because there's a lot to remember," Jonathan said. He hoped that his tone did not show the irritation he felt. He hated to be interrupted in the middle of a briefing. "Has anything I've said confused you?" he asked the guys.

"A little bit," Jaime said. "If we get caught with a phone, they're going to be very upset."

"If you get caught at all, there's going to be hell to pay," Jonathan agreed. "The best I can offer is to advise you to dump the phone the instant you think capture is on the way."

"Then what?" Tyler asked.

"Then you wait for us to come and get you."

Gail said, "If that happens—if you get caught—say nothing about having seen us. Your cover story should be that you heard shooting last night, and that you've been hiding ever since. If they link you to the deaths of their colleagues . . ." She let her voice die away.

"You've got to resist the urge to run," Jonathan coached. "You can walk with purpose, but if you're seen running, all the assumptions will stack against you."

"We're not going to get caught," Tyler declared.

"I like the attitude," Jonathan said.

"We're going to have to mingle," Jaime said.

"Not the same thing," Tyler said. "If we can slip back in with the crowd, then we should be able to slip back out again. Especially after dark."

"You know," Jaime said, "I just want to say there's merit to staying in, once we get there."

They all waited for it.

"It cuts our exposure in half. It'll be hard enough to get inside without getting caught. That's the big risk. If we can avoid having to get out again, that's a big deal."

"But they're *torturing* people in there," Tyler said.

"And you can be the eyes that help us stop the torture," Gail said.

Jonathan held up his hand. "Enough," he said. "You know the ups and the downs, the pros and the cons. Decide. We're going to move out to the *bunker*. We'll let you know when it's safe to approach. If you come,

you come. But I'm not flaying this cat any more than
it's been flayed." He looked to Gail. "You ready?"

She adjusted her vest and did a press check on her
M4, pulling the charging handle back half an inch to
make sure that a round was in the chamber. "Ready."

Jonathan rose to his haunches. "Now."

They dashed together out of the concealment of the
tree line and out across wide-open rolling hills of the
golf course.

"How come they can run and we can't?" Tyler
asked. It was more an attempt at levity than a real
question, but Jaime answered, anyway.

"Because they can shoot back. Are we really going
to do this thing?"

Tyler's heart pounded, and he wasn't sure he was
breathing right anymore. He'd never been this scared.
This . . . *amped.* "Yeah," he said. "I am. I think I have
to." He looked to his friend, praying that his eyes did-
n't show his fear. "And I'd really like for you to come
along."

"If it's so damned important to those guys, I don't
get why they don't do this themselves."

"Because we're *meant* to be the ones," Tyler said.
As he heard his own words, he realized that he'd just
articulated something he'd only *felt,* something that
was lurking beyond his consciousness, but was the
root of why he proposed this insane mission.

"Think about it," Tyler continued. "All the shit that
we've done together. Not the weed, but the exploring
and troublemaking make us the ones who are qualified
to do this. It's like that was our training ground. We

know all the hiding places. If we don't do anything stupid, I think we can sneak back and blend in."

"And if we don't, we'll get killed."

"One way or another, people are going to die tonight, Jaime. Maybe we can help keep that number down. You never know."

The phone earbud startled him when he heard Scorpion's voice say, "We're set if you are."

Tyler and Jaime each waited for the other to say something. Finally Tyler said, "Do it for Baker?"

Jaime's shoulders sagged and he rolled his eyes. "For Baker, then."

They stood together, straightened their clothes, and set out onto the golf course for a nice afternoon stroll.

Baker Sinise sat alone on a straight-back wooden chair in his executive dining room, his hands cuffed behind him and his right ankle shackled to the pedestal of the fabulous granite-topped mahogany table. His captors had not said a word to him since he'd been kidnapped. How long had that been? He honestly didn't know. He'd spent too much of it unconscious. His head still boomed from whatever they'd done to him.

He'd never seen any of these men before, and he could only guess what mission brought them here. As they paraded him from the boat dock to the Plantation House, they made sure that he saw the evidence of their atrocities. Bodies of guests lay where they fell, clad in nightclothes or perhaps nothing at all. Birds of prey had already begun to feed on them, and the image of that alone was forever stenciled on his brain. As his captors did not speak, neither did Baker. He stifled his gasps and swallowed his bile if only to deny them the pleasure of hearing him.

Then there was the vilest atrocity of all, the bodies dangling at the entrance to the pool deck. That gasp could not be suppressed, and as he'd predicted, the soldiers who guarded him smiled at the sound.

These men were animals. Brutes. Bullies. And for reasons known only to them, it was important that they be perceived as such. Perhaps that was to maintain order, or perhaps they were a troupe of serial killers. Whatever justification they could find for themselves, he wanted them all to die.

And somewhere out there, Tyler was toiling amid all the misery and cruelty. If, in fact, he was alive at all.

No, Baker thought, *don't think such things.* Karma was a very real thing, and it was important—it was *essential*—that he keep his thoughts as positive as he could for as long as possible.

Baker knew that this was the end for him. If not his life, then certainly his future. He'd invested everything in the Crystal Sands Resort—everything, and then some. He'd built a reputation of obsequious service and dream fulfillment. Even if these animals didn't burn the place down, no one would ever come here again. The reputation he'd worked so hard to build, one customer at a time over the course of two decades, would be trumped in the minds of the world by the lurid, vile events of a single day.

The door to the dining room opened, and a soldier entered. Within a few years of fifty and less than six feet tall, the man was on the soft side of fit. The ring of salt-and-pepper hair around his bald pate needed a trim, and the heat and humidity had imparted it with a

Bozo the Clown unruliness. He was alone, but he kept the door open. The only weapon Baker saw was a pistol clipped to the vest he wore over a camouflage-patterned T-shirt.

The soldier helped himself to the chair on the opposite side of the table from Baker, his back to the door. He leaned heavily on folded arms propped on the granite tabletop and stared at his prisoner. Baker wished that he had the fortitude to stare back, but he knew he didn't have it in him. He concentrated on a shiny spot in the granite, about halfway across.

"Are you afraid of me, Mr. Sinise?" The man had a subtle Eastern European accent.

"You killed my guests."

"They did not obey orders. They left me with no choice."

Baker switched back to silence. What was there to say?

"You never answered my question," the man pressed. "Are you afraid of me?"

"Of course I am," Baker said.

"That's good, because you *should* be afraid of me. You should be afraid of all of us."

This conversation, such as it was, had a schoolyard-bully feel to it. It was as if the soldier wanted to get a rise from Baker, who would be happy to give the guy what he wanted, but he felt that there likely was no right answer, but only wrong ones.

"What is this all about?" Baker asked. He kept his eyes focused on the shiny spot. "And what have you done with my staff, my workers? All I see outside are tortured guests."

"Your workers are taken care of," the man said.

"Like the guests, some are safe and some are dead. We are keeping them in their dormitory building. As for why we are here and you are there, I think you can guess," the man said. "I'll give you a hint. It has nothing to do with the side of your business that is advertised in your brochures."

Baker's racing heart jumped into a higher gear. "I see," he said. "Who are you?" His first thought was that perhaps he was dealing with an unhappy customer. In that line of work—the illicit trade of weapons—even the smallest slights could be blown far out of proportion. "I'm sure we could just talk and work through—"

"I am quite sure that we could not," the man said.

"Surely, this isn't just a robbery," Baker said. In his fear, he'd been able to tap into his voice. "This much violence. This much death."

"You trivialize events by calling them a 'robbery,'" the soldier said. "Corner stores are *robbed*. Banks are *robbed*. This is retribution."

Wait. This wasn't right at all. "For *what*? No one is more politically agnostic than I," Baker proclaimed. Not only was it a statement of pure fact, but it was the key element that allowed him to operate as he did. He did not take sides. He was a businessman, pure and simple. "If I sold to someone you disagree with, that is not my—"

The soldier pounded the table with the flat of his palm, making a noise that was loud enough to summon another soldier to the door. That young man peeked in and immediately retreated. "You will not trivialize!"

Baker yelled, "I don't know what you're talking about!"

"Tonight's shipment!" the soldier yelled.

Baker's world stopped. No one knew about that shipment. No one *could* know about it. He'd been assured of it. For half an instant, he considered denying knowledge of what the man was talking about, but he knew that would be a mistake.

"Yes, you do know what I'm talking about, don't you?"

Baker tried to form a response, but defaulted to a nod.

"You tell me that you are—what was your phrase?— politically agnostic, yet you do business with the American Central Intelligence Agency."

"I do business with everybody's intelligence agency," Baker said. "And cartel leaders and revolutionary groups. This is not a sporting-goods store. And why are you terrorizing my guests? If you wanted to kill me, you could have killed me in the hotel you snatched me from."

"I need you alive," the soldier said.

And then he explained why.

CHAPTER 23

The fairway bunker Jonathan had selected as his observation point looked like an asymmetrical bomb crater, a giant U with raised sides, ten feet wide and forty feet across at its widest dimensions. It provided perfect defilade from the direction of the bungalows. He and Gail lay on their bellies with their rifles perched on the top edge, scanning for anything that might look like a threat. So far, all he saw were a regiment of flamingos. He wondered if they did to golf courses here what geese did to golf courses in America.

Peripherally he saw Tyler and Jaime walking like a normal day toward the far woods line and the residential part of the resort that lay beyond.

"Should we have gone with them?" Gail asked.

"I would have liked to go instead of them," Jonathan said. "But as the guy who *actually* killed their friends, that couldn't possibly end well. By staying out here, maybe we can take out a few more of their friends. Make it easier on Boxers and company when they finally arrive."

The boys made it across the wide-open expanse without incident. When they were gone from view, Jonathan said, "Let's go explore the magazines."

"Let's wait a few more minutes," Gail said. Her eyes never stopped scanning left to right, right to left.

"What for?"

"In case."

"Of what?"

Finally she drilled him with a glare. "I said I want to stay for a few more minutes."

Jonathan didn't try to argue. They were staying for a few more minutes.

Not running was hands down the hardest part. It's not until you're trying your hardest to look natural that you realize you have no idea what "natural" looks like. At that moment, everything, from the length of your stride to the swing of your arm, feels entirely false. Tyler and Jaime said nothing as they walked, the jingle of the keys in Jaime's pocket providing their own personal sound track.

"Do you think you can muffle those things?" Tyler asked.

"I've already got my hand in my pocket," Jaime said. "There's a lot of them."

A thought flirted through Tyler's mind. "They *are* labeled, right?"

"Nope."

"But the locks to the grates in the stacks are all keyed the same."

"Nope."

"You've got, like, forty keys."

"Yep. Still feeling like a good idea?"

"Look, Jaime, if you still want to—"

"Careful, Ty. Don't say it if you don't mean it. I'm scared shitless. I'm here because I told you I'd do it. I'm not sure I'd release me from that if I was you."

Tyler assumed that he was kidding, but he couldn't be sure. He cast a glance back over his shoulder. "Scorpion and Gunslinger can't see us anymore."

"Then let's move a little faster, okay?" Jaime didn't wait for an answer before he picked up speed by half. They weren't running yet, but they were walking *fast*.

It felt good, Tyler had to admit. It felt less like they were posing for target practice. They were among manicured gardens again, where the grass was meticulously cut, still wet from the automatic sprinklers.

Jaime pointed ahead. "There's the stack we're using."

To Tyler's untrained eye, the stack was a four-foot-tall green-red-and-white cottage that might have been part of the movie set for a Mother Goose story. The cottage's chimney rose high above the charming structure, culminating in a similar-colored birdhouse. To get to it, they crossed behind and between two bungalows. It occurred to him just how easy it would be for the terrorists to be hiding behind any one of those windows, watching them from obscurity.

"You're creeping yourself out, Tyler," he said aloud.

"Talking to yourself kinda creeps me out, too," Jaime said.

The stack cottage was surrounded with three-foot hedges behind three ranks of red and yellow flowers. "Be careful not to crush the flowers," Jaime said.

"Really? That's what you're worried about?"

Jaime gave him a hard look. "Because if we leave tracks, the terrorists can follow us."

Tyler let Jaime lead the way. Clearly, this was not his first time. He contorted his body just the right way to place his foot parallel to the ranks of flowers, and then he twisted his whole body sideways to create his own passageway between the flush edges of adjoining bushes. Tyler started to follow.

"No," Jaime said. "Not yet. I need a little room to maneuver. Keep an eye out for trouble."

Tyler felt an inexplicable jab of jealousy. Why should Jaime be able to be under cover while he had to stand out here in the open? As if a waist-high barrier of greenery could save anyone's life. He watched as Jaime squatted low and hugged the circumference of the cottage and pressed up with his legs. As it rose, the house made a scraping sound, which was probably nowhere near as loud as it sounded. It rose on rails, exposing a three-foot-high opening between the bottom edge of the house and the sidewalk. Jaime twisted the house a few degrees, and it stayed in place.

"How could I not have seen this before?" Tyler asked.

"If you're watching me, you can't be watching for terrorists," Jaime said.

Tyler wanted to argue, but he'd made too good a point. Still, that tingling sense of exposure was almost crippling, as if every sound was a threat, every movement of foliage an impending disaster. Every smell—

What the hell was that smell? Equal parts floral and rancid, the stench was carried on the breeze. Instinctively, Tyler knew what it was. He moved ten feet forward of the gnome house, where he could see more of the surrounding area, and he was confronted with the bodies. Two of them, a man and a woman, lay perpendicular to each other in the grass. He was naked, and she was nearly so. Each had bloated up in the heat, their legs stiff and suspended above the ground as if to mimic the posture of dead deer along the side of the road.

"Take a good look," a voice said from close behind.

Tyler yipped and spun around to see Scorpion and Gunslinger not fifteen feet away. "Jesus, you scared me!"

"Those are the stakes," Scorpion said.

"What are you doing here?" Jaime asked.

"You guys head to the hills," Scorpion said. "On further consultation with my team, I can't in good conscience send you in to do the job that we're better suited to."

"How do you figure that?" Tyler asked.

"Shut up," Jaime snapped. "Don't talk him out of it." He left the gnome house shell suspended in the air and slid out through the hedges to step across the flowers onto the grass.

"I need the phone back," Scorpion said. He held his palm up and wiggled his fingers.

"We'll have no way to contact you," Tyler objected.

"There'll be no need to. You guys need to head back up into the hills and stay out of sight."

As Tyler handed back the phone, he couldn't put his finger on why he felt so slighted.

Scorpion continued, "Stay predictable, and I'll find you when it's time. Remember the plan if you get caught. You're relieved from your intelligence-gathering job, so if you get nabbed, all you have to do is talk your way out and stay alive. If you want my suggestion, I'd tell the bad guys that you were up at your den in the woods, smoking pot, when the balloon went up. You didn't know about anything but the shooting."

Scorpion shifted his attention to Jaime. "Make me smart about this tunnel system."

"Let me see your map," Jaime said.

They kneeled on the ground. Scorpion removed the tourist map from his pocket and spread it out across the grass.

"Let me see your pen," Jaime said. He clicked it open and started drawing on the map. "These are the stacks," he said, drawing little circles. "And this is how the tunnels connect them." He drew lines. "When you get to the bottom of this stack, from where you're facing the ladder, turn left to head this way toward the Plantation House. There are two branching places. Here and here." He drew *X*'s. "As long as you're headed toward the Plantation House, you should never take a branch to the left. The branches to the right will take you closer to the bungalows."

"Where do the branches to the left take you?" Gunslinger asked.

"To staff dormitory and lower-priced bungalows, but mostly to some of the maintenance areas. Feel free to go there if you want, but I don't think you'll find anything there you want to see."

Scorpion gathered the map and returned it to his pocket. He held out his hand. "Can I have your keys?"

Jaime hesitated.

"That, or you come with us. I think we're past the time where you have to worry about me stealing from you." He gave him a smirk.

"Take care of them," Jaime said. He handed the ring to Scorpion. "Lose those, and I'm fired."

"I'll guard them with my life," Scorpion said. "Now you guys take off for the hills. Stay out of sight."

Tyler didn't know what to say, didn't know what to do. He'd amped himself on the whole idea of doing the right thing, and now this. "I want to go with you," he said.

Gunslinger answered forcefully, "No. This one's on us. Head back. Collect your weapons and gear and get out of sight. We'll see you when it's over."

"I at least want to be in the fight," Tyler said.

Her tone softened. "Who knows?" she said. "Maybe there doesn't need to be a fight. Let's take it a step at a time."

Scorpion had already made his way to the gnome stack and was disappearing into the ground. No good-bye, no good luck. He just climbed down.

"Do me a favor and put the house back down for us?" Gunslinger asked. "Scorpion tends to break things when he doesn't know how they work."

Tyler waited for her to finish her climb down into the darkness, and then, with Jaime's help, the house slid into place above them.

Then they were alone.

"Let's get out of here," Jaime said.

Gail knew that Jonathan was angry, and she knew that he had every right to be. Boxers and his team were coming here for the specific purpose of liberating them and the other hostages, and whatever battle plan he'd put together depended on aid and support from both of them. If they got caught, then the entire mission could turn out to be a disaster.

But this was necessary intel, too, and she didn't think it was right for those inexperienced young men—those *boys*—to take on that kind of responsibility. The way she'd sold it to Digger was that both he and she knew what to look for, what was important and what was not. When the intel was finally put into use, it would be 100 percent reliable. There was no way they could depend on that kind of reliability from the boys. Everything would have to be second-guessed.

The top priorities would have everything to do with numbers and locations. How many hostages were located where? How many guards? If possible, where were the off-duty guards when they rested? They needed to know as much as they could about as many details as they could determine.

It was a job the boys were simply not up to.

The tunnel was as claustrophobic a setting as Gail had ever encountered. Maybe five feet tall and as many wide, the low ceiling made it impossible to walk upright, so she moved with her waist bent and her chin tucked into her chest.

"Big Guy would not have been a happy camper in here," she said.

Jonathan chuckled, a sound she was happy to hear. "Give him a fuse and three minutes. He'd just make the hole bigger."

With little else to do as they waited for the next go order, Henry West stripped and cleaned the weapons he intended to carry on the Team Yankee mission. He'd taken his M4 down to its component parts, cleaned every part down to the trigger spring, and oiled the shit out of it. Big Guy walked by as he slid the bolt carrier back into place.

"Jesus, Conan. We'll be able to follow you by your oil trail."

"The only good rifle is a wet rifle," Henry said.

He'd seen countless failures in the field over the years from under-oiled firearms. He got that they were messy, but that's what rags were for. Blood was messy, too, and in his experience, spilled blood was the inevitable result of a weapon malfunction in the middle of a firefight.

He closed the receiver, slid the pin into place, and cycled the action a few times. Perfect. The M4 got a fair amount of hate among the gun porn crowd—not enough stopping power was the biggest hit—but Henry had always liked it. Never once had he shot someone in the face and witnessed him not fall down dead.

Big Guy had thought the load-out through pretty carefully. In addition to an M4 for everybody and enough 5.56-millimeter ammunition to start an army, he'd brought an array of handguns, grenades, and carrying gear. And because Big Guy was Big Guy, he'd brought sixteen pounds of C4 explosives and a smorgasbord of detonator options.

"I know you're intending to float all this shit ashore," Henry said, "but what the hell are we going to do with it all from there?"

"We're gonna hump it," Boxers said. "We'll work that office-boy slump outta your shoulders and get you to standing tall again." The comment drew approving laughter from Madman and Boomer, the other D-boys of the team.

Henry locked the M4's bolt back, inserted a full mag, double-checked the safety and snapped the dust flap closed. Time to move on to his pistol. He'd chosen a nine-millimeter Glock 19, in part because he liked the Glock platform, but mostly because he liked the fifteen-round magazine. There was a reason why the gun world revolved around Glocks, and it had every-thing to do with the fact that they virtually never failed. Back in his snake-eating days, he'd played with many different platforms. Maybe if Big Guy had packed a Sig, he'd have loaded up with that, but woulda, coulda, shoulda.

"You said we hook up with the boat boys at sixteen hundred?" Madman asked.

"That's the plan," Boxers said.

"It's fourteen-thirty now. How long is the transit?"

"We'll depart at fifteen-fifteen," Boxers said.

Jolaine offered, "That's still a lot of daylight to kill."

"Torpedo and the Chief haven't heard word one about the plan," Boxers said. "I'm hoping that Mother Hen will have some improved sat intel by then, and that Digger will have some hard intel about the is-land."

"It *would* be nice to know where the bad guys are warehousing the good guys," Conan said.

A few seconds passed in silence, and then Boxers cleared his throat. "I think we need to get a couple of things straight from the beginning. We touched on it before, and I don't want to pick that scab, but our pre-cious cargo on this op number is exactly two. Scorpion and Gunslinger. They come home, period. The only way they stay on that island is if we all go cruising for Haji's virgins. Are we clear on that?"

Henry noted how uncomfortable Boxers looked in

the role of commander. It's not that he didn't have the chops, and God knew he had the skills, but he was clearly out of his comfort zone.

"I asked if we were clear."

"Clear," they answered in a ragged, imperfect unison.

Big Guy continued, "When we're feet-dry and we make contact, Scorpion will no doubt assume command."

"Try to stop him," Madman said, sparking a laugh.

"And he's gonna go all altruistic and shit," Boxers continued. "He's gonna put every one of those damn hostages ahead of him, and I'm fine with that . . . till I'm not."

Dylan cocked his head. "What are you saying, Box?"

"I'm saying that this is my party and we play by my rules. The fact that Dig proclaims himself to be in command will not put him in command."

"Oh, Christ," Madman said. "You're gonna knock dicks with Digger? What the hell?"

"It's not dick-knocking," Boxers snapped. He was losing patience, so his voice dropped an octave. "It's saving his goddamn life. And Gunslinger's. If I give the order, I don't care what you have to do—zip-tie him or just lead him by his ear—you're going to get him the hell to safety."

"I can't do that," Dylan said.

"Then get the hell out," Boxers said.

"You're serious."

"Damn straight I'm serious. There'll be other saves, and I'm not expecting any of you to be a human shield for Scorpion. He's gonna shoot the shit outta bad guys just because he's pissed, and I don't care about any of that. But if things go to shit and he goes all Nathan Hale about regretting only but one life, I'm gonna cut that shit off. He gets home, period. So does Gunslinger. I want your word."

Henry watched as the others stewed over what they'd just heard. He feared that some saw it as a power play, but Henry knew exactly what Big Guy was up to. Digger was yin to Boxers' yang. As such, it was more important to Big Guy that Digger live than Big Guy did.

"You have my word," Henry said. "But here's the rest: As long as I am breathing, none of us gets left behind on the battlefield. Not one."

Boxers smiled. "Not one," he said. "I can live with that." He looked out to the rest.

This time, the unison chorus was perfect. "Not one."

CHAPTER 24

Scorpion had just delivered a gift to Tyler. he didn't have to risk his life to find information he didn't know how to collect. Why did he feel so . . . guilty?

"Will you give it a rest?" Jaime said. They were crossing back across the golf course. Moving slowly and *naturally,* just as Scorpion had instructed them. "I, for one, am a devoted coward, and I don't see how dying for a bunch of—"

Dirt erupted from the ground in front of their feet as gunshot pounded the air from behind them. "You!" a voice shouted. "Stop!"

"Shit." They said it together.

"Get down on your knees!" the voice yelled. "Get down or I will shoot you."

It took no further convincing. Tyler raised his hands and slowly lowered himself to his knees.

"What are you doing out here?" the voice asked. "How did you escape?" The soldier who owned the voice emerged into his field of view. He held a rifle, but it was pointed more around Tyler than at him. He sensed, but could not see to confirm, that another soldier stood behind them.

"W-we didn't escape," Tyler said. He never thought he'd have to practice their lie so soon. "We were never captured."

"We were smoking weed," Jaime added. "Out in the woods. We heard the shooting, and then we panicked and stayed away. Until now."

The soldier said, "Take off your clothes and toss them to me."

"Excuse me?" Tyler said.

"Do what you are told," said a second voice, this one from behind.

"They want to search our pockets," Jaime said. "Can we stand?"

"Shirts first."

This was more than a little weird. Tyler stripped his polo shirt over his head and held it. "There?" he asked, pointing to a spot on the ground in front of the guard he could see.

"Right there."

Tyler underhanded the shirt, and then Jaime's landed on top of it.

"You may now stand," said the guard from behind. "Now the rest."

"*All* of it?"

"Shoes, pants, underwears, all of it."

Tyler noted the odd plural for *underwear*. Why not? he supposed. They were Russian, after all. As soon as the thought crossed his mind, he tried to force it out. He wasn't supposed to know that detail. He wasn't supposed to know *anything*.

As he stood naked in the fairway, he tried reminding himself that if the night had gone the way he'd wanted, he'd have been naked, anyway. But under much better circumstances. The thought of sex with Annie caused a stirring *down there* even now, and he panicked a little. The last thing he needed was to pop an erection in front of his kidnappers.

The front guard swung his rifle on its sling until the muzzle was pointed at the ground and the stock rested behind his back. He picked up the articles of clothing, one at a time, sifted them through his fingers, and turned the pockets inside out. The pockets were all empty. He tossed the garments back on the ground between the boys. Neither moved to pick them up.

"They have nothing," the guard said. "No phones, no identification, nothing."

"I work here," Jaime said. "Jaime Bonilla. I run a maintenance crew. I don't need identification. Everyone knows me."

"And what about you?" Tyler felt a poke between his shoulder blades. In his mind, it was the muzzle of the man's rifle. "Where is yours?"

"I-I'm Jaime's friend," Tyler said. "I come here a lot. He lets me visit when I want. I don't need identification, either."

"Are you American?"

"Yes," Tyler said. "Sir."

"Then where is your identification? You need a passport to board the boat to come to the island."

The truthful answer, of course, was that the terrorists already had all of his stuff. They just didn't know it yet.

"What's your name?" Another poke between the shoulder blades.

"Ben," Tyler said. It was the first name that popped into his head. "Ben Jackson."

"Where do you live in America?"

"Springfield, Virginia." That bit of truth popped out before he could stop it. He couldn't think of a fictional town fast enough.

"That is a long way to travel just to visit a friend."

"Can I put my clothes back on, please?"

"Not yet. When we are done talking. It is, what? Six thousand miles from this place to your home? Please explain that to me."

"I spend summers with my uncle in Los Angeles," Tyler said. He was beginning to feel a little as if he were drowning. *Shit, what did I say my name was again?*

"Only one thousand five hundred miles, then," the guard said.

"His uncle was a guest here a few weeks ago," Jaime explained. His voice was utterly calm. "He left Ben behind to hang with me. He'll be going back in a couple of weeks."

Tyler intentionally did not look at Jaime for fear that his face would give something away.

"And where were you last night?" the guard pressed.

Jaime pointed up the hill, and the guard snapped, "Not you. I want to hear it from your friend."

Tyler raced his options through his head, and again came up only with the truth. He pointed ahead toward the hill. "There are old staff structures up there," he said. "Most of them are falling apart, but Jaime and I fixed one of them up as kind of a hangout."

"Where you can smoke drugs," the guard said.

"Yes, sir."

"And sometimes take the ladies?" This from the guard in front, complete with a lecherous tone.

"Um, no, sir," Tyler said. "It's not the kind of place you'd take a lady to. It's . . . rustic." He wasn't 100 percent sure that was the word he was looking for, but *rustic* seemed to work.

"How old are you?"

"Nineteen," Tyler said.

"Twenty-two," Jaime said.

"Young men your age live on your phones," the rear guard said. "Where are yours?"

Jaime said, "I don't have one. I have no one to call, and I couldn't afford one, anyway."

"How do you communicate for your job?"

"Two-way radios. I keep mine in my room in the staff dormitories."

"And what about you, Mr. Jackson?"

"Mine's in his room, too," he lied. "That's where I sleep when I visit." A fly landed on his dick and he shooed it away.

"When you heard the shooting last night, what did you think?"

"I thought we were under attack," Jaime said. "We both did."

"So, what did you do?"

"We hid. Stayed out of the way, trying to be invisible."

"Why did you come out?"

"We were hungry," Jaime said.

"Not you," the guard snapped.

"We were hungry," Tyler said. "We went searching

for food." As soon as he heard his words, he knew he'd tripped a trap.

"Where, exactly, did you expect to find it? Ben Jackson, that is for you to answer."

Shit. Shitshitshit. "We, um, thought we could maybe take something from the bungalows. Jaime has all the keys, so we thought—" He stopped short, but there was no taking anything back.

"And did you find what you were looking for?"

"No, sir," Jaime said. He spoke quickly, as if to steal the conversation away from Tyler. "We found a bloated dead body and lost our appetites."

For a long time, the front guard looked past them, presumably waiting for direction from the guard behind them.

Finally the front guard nodded and said, "All right, then. Put your clothes back on. We'll take you back to see what will be done with you."

Tyler went for his boxer briefs first. "What does that mean, *what will be done with us?*"

"The order is to shoot you," the rear guard said.

Tyler turned at those words and saw the man for the first time. He was short and stocky and looked mean as hell. He needed a shave, and not in the way of the cool *GQ* dudes who can pull off the perpetual five-o'clock shadow. This guy's beard grew in splotches that gave the impression of a hairy rash.

"Perhaps, given the circumstances, you will be given a reprieve because you did not have a chance to be warned. That is not my decision to make."

"But you're not going to shoot us now, right?" Tyler asked.

The soldier smiled. "The day is still young," he said.

Tyler looked to Jaime, whose jaw muscles had begun to twitch. He seemed intent on not making eye contact. Tyler had seen the look before, but rarely. The pursed lips and locked jaw meant that Jaime had been pushed beyond his limits.

Tyler picked up his pants next. As he stuffed his foot into the first pant leg, the guard said, "A lot of my colleagues have been killed since last night. What do you know about that?"

Tyler didn't say anything. He didn't know if he could trust his voice.

Jaime said, "What a shame. Who on earth would want to kill a bunch of asshole—"

The bullet blew out his face and his legs folded. His body hit the ground butt-first and then pitched over onto its side.

Blood splashed Tyler's face and he screamed. "Jesus! Jaime! Oh, Christ!" He dropped to his knees to help and fell over as something hard hit the top of his head. Blood flowed immediately from a gash in his scalp beneath his hair. "What the hell!"

The guard grabbed Tyler by his hair and pulled him up. He almost fell when his feet got tangled in his flopping pant leg. When he was standing, the guard yanked his head back until he was looking at the sky.

"Killing is easy, Mr. Jackson," he said. "I don't know who your friend thought he was talking to, but he'll never talk to anyone again. Do you have to learn the same lesson?"

"No, sir," Tyler said. He thought he might cry and he thought he might vomit.

The guard let go of his hair and launched him forward with a shove that sent him face-first into the grass. Three feet to his right, blood poured from the ragged hole that used to be Jaime's mouth and nose. He looked away.

"Get dressed," the guard said, and Tyler scrambled to finish pulling on his clothes.

"And Papa," the guard said.

The other guard perked up, and Tyler was reminded again of the phonetic alphabet, in which *papa* doubled for the letter *P.*

"While our friend Ben Jackson gets dressed, do me a favor and grab those keys from Jaime Bonilla's pockets. We might need those."

As he spoke those words, his eyes never left Tyler. And he smiled.

"There were no keys," Papa said. "The pockets were empty. They had nothing in them at all."

Tyler's hands trembled as he fumbled with the button and zipper to his pants.

"What a surprise," Short Man said.

Tyler froze in midaction, his shirt in his hand, unsure what to do next.

"I said to get dressed," Short Man said. "We have to get you up to the boss and see what he wants to do with you. Unless, of course, you want to change any of your story before we get there."

Tyler knew this was a trap. Everything about this encounter was a trap. A deadly one, at that. His mind wasn't even racing anymore. It was as if it had seized and was no longer capable of meaningful thought. There was only fear.

"Put your shirt on," Short Man said. Something changed behind his eyes. This man wanted nothing more than to kill him.

"I won't tell you again," the guard said.

The thing about putting on a polo shirt is that there is a moment of blindness when the fabric passes over your eyes. That was the precise instant when the full-on kick took him in the balls. The next blow was somewhere near his ear.

And then the beating started.

Jonathan despised tight spaces like this, and he knew that Gail's back must be killing her. He thought about suggesting that she take a break and that he'd get back to her, but he knew that there was no way that she would go along with that. She'd be pissed that he suggested it.

They'd been in here for nearly fifteen minutes, and he was becoming less convinced that the exploration was going to yield anything useful. He told himself that if nothing else, he'd make himself familiar with the space in the hope that maybe they could utilize it somehow when Boxers arrived after dark with the reinforcements.

"What, exactly, are we looking for?" Gail asked.

Jonathan was about to answer when he heard something. He held up his hand. "Did you get that?"

"Get what?"

Jonathan slowed his painfully slow pace even more, hoping to reacquire—

"I heard it that time," Gail said. "Children's voices?"

"That's what I got," Jonathan agreed. "And to answer your question, this is exactly what we were looking for." He smiled. "We just didn't know it yet."

The darkness down here was pretty absolute, but once his eyes adjusted, Jonathan could be guided by the dim circles of light that filtered in through the ornament-covered stacks. Best he could tell, the tunnels ran in straight lines down here, as opposed to what looked like randomness from ground level, thanks to the gardens and landscaping. So far, the floor had been fairly free of tripping hazards, but you had to be pretty close to the circles of light before you could even begin to see your feet.

They were approaching the fifth stack since entering the tunnels. By Jonathan's calculation, they were approaching what the tourist map referred to as Bungalow Cluster D, which would make it the fourth cluster up from the swimming-pool complex. And the closer they got, the clearer became the sound of chattering children. Conversations, it sounded like. Some laughter, but not much.

Jonathan stooped down on his knee to get a better view of the map, moving as close to the dim circle of light as he could get without actually entering it. He couldn't imagine the circumstance where someone would peel off the gnome house to peer directly down at him, but on days like this, anything that was not impossible needed to be considered likely. Gail stooped next to him.

"How're you holding up?" he asked.

"Nothing wrong yet that another couple of rounds with the physical therapist can't take care of."

Jonathan gave the map some serious study. "I've been making marks as we go along," he whispered. He pointed to a spot on the map. "I know that this is where we came in. That would put us right here." He moved his pen to the first unmarked space.

"So, this is where they're holding the children," Gail concluded.

"That's what I think, too," Jonathan said.

Gail hedged, "Or at least one of the places."

"Maybe," Jonathan said, marking the map with a big circle, "but I don't think they'd want to split their forces like that, especially given the dwindling numbers we've handed them. Guarding a lot of kids in one place is hard enough. Splitting them between two locations would be a real drain on manpower."

An adult male voice yelled, "Playtime is over for you." It startled the crap out of them both. "Get inside and make room for the next group."

It was a data point, but Jonathan didn't know what to make of it. There were enough kids that they could not be allowed outside all at once, but so what? It wasn't possible to extrapolate a whole number from that.

There were some words of objection from the kids, but not a lot. Mostly, they just became silent among sounds of rustling and footsteps.

"Wait!" a little voice yelled. "I dropped my flip-flop."

"Someone else can get it for you," the adult said. "Get back in line."

"It'll just take a—"

The sound of a slap silenced the voice, and then the sound of a wail replaced it.

Another voice—an older girl, it sounded like—protested, "Hey! You didn't have to do that. He's only nine years old."

"That's old enough to follow instructions," the adult said. "You get in line now, too, unless you want the same."

"You guys are so stupid," the girl pressed. She didn't sound the least bit intimidated. "You treat these kids like shit, and they'll—"

Another slap. "I warned you," the adult said.

"It didn't even hurt," the girl replied.

Jonathan glanced back at Gail. "Oh, I like her," he said.

CHAPTER 25

Tyler could barely see through his left eye, and his right was blurry. He hurt everywhere. He knew that his guts weren't right, but he couldn't articulate why. They'd bound his hands in front of him, probably because of the way he howled when they tried to bend his arms behind him. He feared they'd done something to his shoulders. When he touched his face, everything felt out of order. Not rearranged so much as asymmetrical.

He had only a dim memory of his walk back to the Plantation House. He knew that he did it under his own power—that no one had carried him—but large chunks of that walk just weren't there. The memories weren't blurry, mind you, they did not exist.

He remembered a focused awareness blooming somewhere about the time they crossed through the maintenance trench behind the swimming pool. He remembered forcing himself to concentrate on what he saw, and to inventory it all with as much precision as possible. Scorpion would want to know. He was depending on him to gather important information. No, intelligence. Intel. That's what he wanted. Intel.

So, what had he seen? Lots and lots of people clustered tightly around the pool, all of them stressed, but the terror had subsided. Maybe they had just accepted a certain inevitability. Maybe they were all prepared to die.

In that crystal-clear moment, Tyler realized that he was *not* ready to die. He was, however, ready to kill. At the first opening. In fact, for the first time in his life, he *wanted* to kill, and his fantasy target had a face, but no name. He was the man who had turned Jaime's face into ground beef.

The Plantation House had clearly been transformed into their command center. They'd planted Tyler in one of the upholstered, yet still impossibly uncomfortable, visitor chairs that lined the wall opposite the desk that used to belong to Peggy Nelson, the pruney old lady who was Baker's secretary. In every meaningful way, it was she who ran the resort, not Baker. His name was on the corporation and on the paychecks, but Peggy was the one whose wrath people feared.

Now that he was seated, Tyler found himself drifting in and out of awareness. He was more aware of activity than of purpose. Whatever was happening, it seemed to be very important to the players. They moved with efficiency and focus, mostly oblivious to the fact that he was even there.

He didn't know how long he'd been sitting in that chair when a soldier materialized in front of him. "You still alive?"

Tyler rocked his head up and looked at the soldier

with his good eye. He said nothing, in part because he wasn't sure that his tongue and lips worked anymore. There was a numbness about the pain in his face that made him think that his smile would be less charming to the ladies than it used to be.

"Can you stand?"

Interesting question. Without hesitation, and keeping his eye on the soldier, lest he reported back to his friends that he'd looked away, Tyler stood to his full height, all six-one of him. He ignored the fact that he weighed only 175 pounds. It felt good to tower over his captor.

"Follow me," the soldier said. He led the way into what once was Baker's office. The surroundings were so familiar—so locked into his brain as a pleasant place to be—that the presence of these murderous assholes felt even more awful.

Tyler took pleasure in knowing what these assholes did not: that many, if not all, of them would die before morning. Even if they did not die at Tyler's hand, they would die at the hands of people he knew. At an intuitive level, he knew that these thoughts were wrong, but at an emotional level, he didn't care. People who talked of peaceful negotiation had never been on the hard end of an ass-kicking.

The soldier led Tyler to the conference table and said, "Sit." It was identical to the tone that they'd use for an errant pet.

Tyler continued to stand, his nod to defiance. His nod to Jaime.

"If I break your legs, you'll sit," the soldier said. The calmness of his delivery made the ugliness of the words even more terrifying.

Tyler sat.

"Alpha will be here in a minute."

There was something deeply unsettling—something deeply *wrong*—about the faux normalcy of this office environment juxtaposed against the murders these men had committed. He found himself imagining his captors with their faces blown out, their brains spilling out onto the grass. He hated them.

"I said, Mr. Jackson," a voice said. He seemed annoyed, and from the tone alone, Tyler could tell that this had not been the first time he'd been addressed.

It took a couple of seconds for Tyler to remember that he was Ben Jackson. "Oh," he said. "Yeah?" His voice was clearer than he'd feared, and his lips and cheeks still appeared to be in working order.

The man who addressed him wore the same uniform as the other soldiers, without any extra stripes or regalia, but he clearly was the man in charge. There literally was nothing about him to distinguish him from any other fortysomething guy in a uniform. Average everything, even down to the brown eyes.

"I'm sorry that my colleagues lost their temper with you. Are you in a lot of pain?"

"I'm fine," Tyler said. He wasn't going to give them the satisfaction.

The soldier grabbed another one of the visitor chairs and pulled it across from Tyler. He spun it so he could hug the padded back. "X-ray is a problem to me sometimes. He is very good at his job, but sometimes he enjoys violence too much. I am sorry about your friend."

Tyler eyed him, but otherwise did not acknowledge the comment. This guy wasn't sorry about shit.

"Are you thirsty? Can I get you anything? X-ray mentioned that you were hungry."

Fully aware that conversation is what got Jaime killed, Tyler said, "Is X-ray a person?"

"Yes, he is," the soldier replied. "You may call me Alpha. These aren't real names, of course, but you probably understand." He took a deep breath and shifted in his seat. "Young man, I confess that you pose a problem to me, and I am not one to get stumped very often."

This didn't sound like an introduction to anything good.

"When X-ray and Papa brought you up here to the Plantation House, did you by chance see the bodies hanging by the pool?"

Something dissolved in Tyler's gut. Whether it was a stab of fear or merely lingering damage from his ass-kicking, he wasn't sure.

"Those are the bodies of a husband and wife who escaped after I announced that anyone who escaped would be killed. They challenged me and they paid the promised price. Perhaps you knew them, the Edwardses, Hunter and Lori?"

Tyler tried to look Alpha squarely in the eye. "Never heard of them."

"That's interesting," Alpha said. "Because Lori told me that she had run into two young men, and that they had been hiding together."

The pain in Tyler's gut was now undeniably fear. He fought to control his breathing, to show no fear, whatever that meant. Did fear have a look?

"That seems like an outrageous coincidence, don't you think?" Alpha pressed. "Answer me."

"That was not me," Tyler said. The *S* slurred a little.

"Ah, but that's what you would say if it *was* you," Alpha said. "Can you see my dilemma? And the people that Hunter and Lori were wandering with killed a number of my men. What do you know about that?"

"I heard a lot of shooting. All through the night."

"I bet. Being as close to it as you were, it would be hard not to hear it, wouldn't it?"

Tyler tried to look confused.

"You told X-ray that your little hideout was up on the other side of the mountain. Wouldn't you know, that's exactly where the bulk of my men were shot."

"I-I had nothing to do with that," Tyler stammered.

"To tell you the truth, I never thought that you did." Alpha leaned in closer. "But I bet you have information you can share." He arose from his chair and disappeared into Baker's office for a few seconds before returning to view with a hammer in his hands. Nothing exotic, just the same kind of nail pounder that a carpenter would use.

As he reapproached, he spun the hammer playfully in his hand, along the axis of the handle. "What does the number two-oh-six mean to you, Ben?"

Focused as he was on the spinning head of the hammer, and on the damage that could do to him, Tyler wasn't hearing words anymore. Just hollow sounds. It took a second or two to decipher their meaning.

"That's a rhetorical question," Alpha said. "It's the number of bones in the human body. Every one of them hurts when it is broken. And then, when the broken ends are moved around, it gets excruciating." He approached the conference table again. This time, instead of resuming his seat on the other side, he dragged one of the chairs from the end over to Tyler's side, to where they were nearly touching.

He laid the head of the hammer gently on his captive's knee, and Tyler jumped.

Alpha smiled. "Here," he said, offering the hammer. "Hold it. Feel the weight of it."

When Tyler hesitated, Alpha moved the hammer closer. "I said *hold it.*"

Tyler was embarrassed that his cuffed hands trembled as he reached out for the tool. He'd held hammers just like this dozens if not hundreds of times in his life, but this one felt twice—no, three times as heavy as any he'd felt before.

"I wish I could tell you that I have never seen a man tortured with a hammer, Mr. Jackson, but that simply would not be the truth. And if torture were an art form, let me tell you that your friend X-ray would be a modern-day Michelangelo. I've heard men scream their vocal cords bloody over the course of three, four, five days. Alas, we don't have time for that, do we? My needs are more urgent."

Alpha slouched in his chair and extended his legs, crossing his ankles and arms. "Another trivia question for you, and I bet you can answer this one, if only by extrapolation. It's another significant number. Thirty-two. Can you guess?"

Tyler stared at the hammer, his stomach churning. He couldn't make his voice work.

"Answering is not optional, it's required," Alpha said. "Guess, if you don't know. What is the significance of the number thirty-two? Especially today, especially for you?" He gave a hideous artificial smile and clacked his teeth together.

Tears flowed and his battered lip trembled as Tyler guessed, "That's the number of teeth," he said.

Alpha reached out and gave Tyler's knee a playful slap. "You're exactly right. Have you ever broken a tooth, Ben?"

Tyler shook his head.

"Oh, I have," Alpha said. "A couple of times. Once on an unpopped bit of popcorn. Split the tooth all the way down to the gum line. Exposed the nerve. Oh, my goodness that hurt. Tooth pain—man, it's the worst, isn't it?"

Tyler couldn't control it anymore. He turned in his seat and vomited onto the oriental carpet.

"Oh, my," Alpha said. "What a mess. I must be up-setting you. Tell you what. Let's change the subject." He snatched the hammer from Tyler's hands and the boy yelled.

Alpha laughed. "You are a loud one, aren't you? We haven't even touched you yet. But since you have such a nice smile—I bet you wore braces on your teeth when you were younger. Since you have such a nice smile, when the time comes—*if* it comes, because there's always a better way to share information than to scream it—I'll give you control of one of the very important decisions. Do you prefer to have your teeth broken off one at a time, or would you prefer to have them driven back into your jaw? Truthfully, I've seen it done both ways, and from my perspective, they are equally effective."

Alpha stood, and beckoned for Tyler to do the same. "I think you need a few minutes to think," he said. "You have so much to gain from being reasonable, and so much to lose by being difficult. You have your whole life ahead of you at nineteen. And such a handsome young man. Please don't make me cripple you and turn that fine face into something ugly. I lose a little bit of myself every time I am forced to do such a thing."

Tyler tried to stand once, but the balance wasn't there. His ribs and his gut really hurt, and his scrotum felt swollen. Alpha placed an arm on his biceps to help him up. The gentleness of his touch surprised Tyler.

"As I said," Alpha continued, "you will have some time to consider your options. Come with me."

Alpha led the way across the lobby to a closed door, which Tyler knew led to Baker's private dining room. "You can have a seat in here while you consider your options."

As the mahogany door swung open, Tyler saw that another prisoner had already been stashed here. This one sat at the dining table, slouched in the chair, as if he were sleeping—or, God forbid—

The sound of the door seemed to startle the other hostage. As he turned around, Tyler instantly recognized that it was Baker Sinise. As the flash of recognition crossed his face, Tyler did his best to project an urgent *Say nothing*. Baker registered a flash of confusion, and then he got it.

"You two know each other?" Alpha asked.

Tyler advanced a lie before Baker could say anything. "He yelled at me the other day," he said. "Ben Jackson. You didn't like the fact that I was crashing with Jaime Bonilla."

Without dropping a beat, Baker said, "I thought I told you to get off the island."

"Now I wish I had," Tyler said. Finally a refreshing taste of the truth.

Getting out of the tunnels required a careful, choreographed pivot that put Gail in the lead. The strain of the hunched-over walk was beginning to light up Jonathan's back. Too many parachute jumps and hard landings over too many years. These had been among the most uncomfortable thirty-five minutes of that entire career.

"Nice ass, Ms. Bonneville," Jonathan whispered.

"Oh, yeah," she replied. "Perfect time to dazzle me with romance."

"Just stating a fact. Raising the mood with a little chauvinistic objectification."

"Ever the charmer."

Jonathan could hear the smile in her voice. And he was happy with the intel they'd been able to pick up on the location of the kids. When Boxers arrived in a couple of hours and this op went hot, Jonathan would consider it a nonfailure just if they got the kids to safety. Parents were important, too, but if someone had to die, he'd made his choice who it would not be.

"We're gonna need to hit that bungalow first," he thought aloud.

"No argument from me," Gail agreed.

They decided to exit the tunnel via the same stack through which they'd entered, if only because it was a known quantity. When they reached the ladder that led to the grate, Jonathan said, "I'll go first and check for hazards."

"The hell you will," Gail said. "I'm happy to engage

any ten bad guys if it gets me out of this hellhole thirty seconds faster."

Jonathan couldn't argue with a word of that. He watched from below as Gail ascended the short ladder and then used a kind of modified military press to lift the gnome house out of the way. She scanned for targets, and then beckoned for him to come up and join her.

Once clear of the stack, Jonathan lowered it back into place. With their rifles at low ready, they made their way back through the trees and bushes to the near edge of the golf course, where they stopped together and dropped to a knee.

Jonathan pointed. "Look." What appeared to be a body lay in the middle of the fairway, maybe a hundred yards in the distance.

Gail gave a little gasp. "The blue T-shirt," she said. "Isn't that what—"

"Jaime was wearing," Jonathan finished. "Shit. Stay here."

Gail protested, "But I—"

"Stay *here*!" Jonathan didn't wait for an answer. *This* was why the kids were better in the tunnels and then hiding in plain sight among the hostages. *This* was why the adults with the guns and the training were supposed to be in a position to use them. He'd let Gail talk him into changing the order of things, and now Jaime was dead. He knew that it was unreasonable of him to lay his death on her, and he needed this time, this walk across green grass in bright sunlight, to clear his head of the terrible thoughts.

Jaime was most definitely dead, a hole blown through

his face. From the level of damage, Jonathan figured they'd shot him with a rifle and at close range.

"That means they have Tyler, doesn't it?" Gail asked from very close by.

"I thought I asked you to stay," Jonathan said.

"No, you *ordered* me to stay. But this is my doing, and I won't hide from it."

Jonathan looked to her.

"I know you were right," she said. There was no defensiveness in her tone. "And I know I was wrong, and that makes me responsible for Jaime's death."

"Bullshit," Jonathan said. "You didn't pull the trigger."

"And you know that doesn't matter," she said. "What do we do with the body?"

"Nothing," Jonathan said. "Not yet, anyway."

"We can't just let him roast in the sun."

"I imagine there'll be a lot of bodies to take care of before tomorrow morning. We don't need to telegraph to these assholes that we've been here."

"What are we going to do about Tyler?"

"We're going to hope that they keep him alive long enough for us to rescue him later."

"You know they're going to kill him," Gail said.

"All I know is that's what they've promised to do. There's a difference."

"But we can't just—"

"Jesus, Gail, what would you have me do? I think it would be great to go storming over to the pool with guns a-blazin' and yank him away, but we can't do that, can we? Not and survive. We don't even know where the hell he is."

Gail looked wounded by his words. She recoiled. And he didn't care.

"We've all got one job here, and that's to survive," he went on. "No make that two, to survive and to gather whatever intel we can find that will make tonight be something other than a shit show. Big Guy is going to come onto the island, and he's not going to want to take any punishment to the bad guys beyond what it takes to get you and me out of here. In his mind, *we're* the precious cargo. If we don't have some kind of an action plan to present to him and whoever else he's bringing, then our shit is going to be pretty stinkin' weak. He's going to toss us onto his boat and drive home." Jonathan didn't know where this well of anger came from, but he'd tapped into something big that didn't want to stop.

"So, that's what we're going to do," he said. "We're going to gather as much intel, and do as much damage as we can, so that when the cavalry arrives, we'll be ready to go." He started walking toward the jungle on the other side of the fairway. "Just like everybody else, Tyler's going to have to fend for himself for a while."

This was new territory for both of them. Being in need of rescue was a whole different animal than being the guy in charge of the rescue. The sense of helplessness—of *victimhood,* for lack of a better word—unnerved him. He didn't like being in a position of having to wait for others in order to stay alive, but the reality of his situation was that he had no cards left to play. Until darkness fell and reinforcements arrived, he was in the business of keeping hidden and staying alive.

"So, where are we going first?" Gail asked as they crossed from the open into the jungle.

"Let's take a look at their power plant," he said.

His phone buzzed in his pocket. He took it out and answered, "Joe's Pizza."

"Where have you been?" Venice was nearly yelling. "I've been trying to get hold of you for over an hour."

Jonathan scowled. "Whoa, what's up?"

"What's up," she said, "is a delivery of VX agent to your island tonight."

CHAPTER 26

"What's going on here, Baker?" Tyler asked. "Why is this happening?"

They'd determined when Tyler was first planted in the same room with Baker that it would be best to say nothing for fear of being overheard. For their captors to know that they were related would tilt the balance of power in a way that couldn't help either one of them. But after more than a half hour of silence, Tyler couldn't take it anymore.

"It's a very long story," Baker said.

"Does it have anything to do with the storage caves on the back side of the island?"

Baker looked stunned.

"Yeah, I know about them," Tyler said.

"Then you know everything," Baker said. "The Crystal Sands is an expensive facility to run. It won't work without the extra revenue."

"Revenue from what?"

"I really don't want to go into all that."

"Baker, when that Alpha asshole comes back in

here, he's going to bust me to bits with a hammer. I think I have a right to know why."

"What do they think you know?" Baker's demeanor changed in an instant. His face was a mask of concern.

"They don't believe anything I've told them."

"Should they?"

Tyler gave him a look. "I don't know what to do. I know that as soon as they start smashing my teeth—"

"Oh, my God."

"—I'm going to give them everything they want. But if I cave outright, I'll never be able to live with myself."

"But you'll be able to live," Baker said. "What secrets do you have to hide?"

Until this day, Tyler had regarded his stepfather as one of the noblest men in the world. But that was before he learned stories of illicit arms sales and activities that could inspire the kind of violence that Alpha and his army brought with him.

"You first," Tyler said. "What do these terrorists want?"

"You wouldn't understand."

"I'm brighter than you think."

"That's not how I meant it."

"Baker, don't you get what's happening here? People are dying because of whatever secret you've kept. You've already admitted that it has everything to do with selling arms to people who shouldn't have them."

"Wait," Baker snapped. "Who's to judge who should and shouldn't—"

"No. Don't. Don't even try. The guys who kill tourists to get weapons are the ones who shouldn't have them. I mean, come on. That's not even debatable." Tyler watched Baker's eyes, and as the subject drilled in on weapons, his stepfather couldn't bear to look at anything but the floor.

"It wasn't supposed to be like this," Baker said. "It was supposed to be *nothing* like this. You know, bad people do bad things, with or without the involvement of good people. If group A wants rocket launchers, they're going to get them, one way or another. Or rifles or hand grenades, or whatever. That exchange is *going* to take place." When he looked to his stepson, he seemed to be searching for approval. Understanding, maybe.

Tyler tried to give it to him, but wasn't sure that he pulled it off.

"But those kinds of transactions are dangerous when they happen on the street or in the jungle," Baker went on. "When someone from the CIA wants to pass a load of Sidewinders or AMRAAMs to a group of insurgents with an air fleet that they barely know how to fly, that can't just happen in the middle of an alley, you know? The Crystal Sands provides a safe point of transfer. We're a service."

"I get that," Tyler said. "How long have you been providing this . . . service?"

Baker keyed in on the hesitation. "You're judging me," he said. "Don't you dare do that. The money that this place has generated—through the front door and the back—has provided you with a lifestyle that other young men would sell their souls for."

Except for this part, right here, Tyler thought. "I don't mean to offend, Baker. Hell, I don't know what I mean to do anymore. I'm sorry."

Baker said, "The arms business predates the hospitality business by probably six, seven years. It's the reason I bought the island."

"Is it legal?"

"Under whose law?" Baker asked. "That's the beauty of the place. There's probably a subparagraph of some international law that we're breaking, but who's going to enforce it? And even if they wanted to, *how* are they going to enforce it here? We're essentially an island without a country. At least, not one that matters. Our business works because all sides of every conflict know that we are a safe haven."

Despite his pain and his fear, Baker's words broke through and Tyler recoiled from what he was pretty sure he'd just heard. "What does 'all sides' mean? You do business with our enemies?"

"I don't have *enemies*," Baker said. "I have *clients*. Not all of my clients get along with each other, but that is not my problem."

Tyler considered that for a few seconds. "So, you're like a living Switzerland? Neutrality all around?"

"Exactly. Exactly."

"So, what happened here?"

"I'm not sure," Baker said. "There's a shipment coming in tonight that Alpha and his team do not approve of."

"From where?" Tyler asked.

The door slammed open and Alpha stormed in with two other soldiers. One was X-ray, Tyler's nemesis from the golf course. Alpha held a wallet and a phone in his hand. Tyler recognized both of them. It's entirely possible that he stopped breathing.

"Tyler Stratton," Alpha said. "Does that name ring a bell with you?"

Tyler said nothing. What was there to say?

"Swollen as you are, I couldn't put my finger on it, but I knew you looked familiar to me. Then one of my colleagues gave me exactly one wallet and one phone that had not been claimed." He held one in each hand at shoulder height and width. "Do these look familiar to you?"

Again, there was nothing to say. Now he was going to die.

"Tyler Stratton, you are going to tell me everything you know about the animals who are roaming this island killing my men. I know you know, so don't bother trying to deny it."

"I know that they are here," Tyler said, trying hard to hedge his bets. "I know that they have guns and that they are shooting your people. But I don't know anything about them." Most of that actually felt like the truth.

Alpha smiled without humor. Smiled with menace. "Well, liars lie, don't they?" he said. "I have no way of knowing the actual truth, do I? Not without a trial by pain." He turned to X-ray, who, Tyler just now noticed, was holding the hammer. "Start with the teeth," Alpha said.

"Stop!" Baker boomed, startling everyone in the room. "Don't touch that boy."

Alpha stared at him for a few seconds, then threw his head back and laughed. "Or what?"

"Or you fail," Baker said.

Tyler thought he saw a crack in Alpha's badassery. "Bold talk for a man who's tied to a table," he said.

"Do your research," Baker said. "Tyler Stratton is my son. Okay, my stepson, but as a practical matter, there is no distinction. If you touch him—if you so much as muss his hair—you're on your own. I won't give you anything you're looking for. That shipment will arrive off the shore, hear nothing, and then sail away again."

"If that happens, you die," Alpha said.

"I won't let you hurt my son. Hard stop."

Tyler watched the exchange through blurring vision. Was Baker really willing to die for him?

X-ray seemed most disappointed of all, like a child who'd been told he couldn't play his favorite game. He focused his gaze on Alpha, who dismissed him with a subtle flick of his head.

Alpha leveled a finger at Tyler. "This isn't over," he said. "If one more of my men is killed at the hands of whoever is wandering out there, it won't matter what your stepfather does or does not give to us. I will burn out your eyes personally."

The intensity of Alpha's glare was such that Tyler didn't doubt that his threat was not an idle one.

Then Alpha turned to Baker. "And your time is coming sooner than you think. Do yourself a favor, and do not overplay your hand. If you don't give me what I want, I will lay waste to everything and everyone on this island. It will be a bloodbath."

Baker listened stoically. He glanced to Tyler, and then looked squarely at Alpha. "I'm not going to let you hurt my son," he said.

Jonathan found a deadfall to use as a seat, and Gail sat down next to him. He put the call on speaker, and dialed the volume down till it was barely audible. "You're sure it's the CIA making the delivery," he prompted.

"That's what my sources tell me," Venice said.

"Who are your sources?" Jonathan asked.

"I can't tell you."

"Can't or won't?"

"Whichever you're most comfortable with."

Jonathan looked to Gail for ideas. Got nothing in response. "How confident are you that your sources are correct?"

"Very."

"How can you be?" Gail asked. "That's a pretty big secret just to stumble onto."

"Let's talk about the last time I got something this big wrong," Venice said. She hated it when she had to justify her conclusions to Jonathan or anyone else.

Jonathan said, "Okay, you got me."

"Thank you," Venice said. "Now let's talk about why they're bringing the nerve gas to you."

"I've only got so much battery power," Jonathan said. "Please don't make me guess."

"The CIA plans to give it to the Ukrainians."

Jonathan felt a chill. "To use against the Russians," he said.

"That's what I'm told," Venice confirmed.

"So, that explains everything," Gail said. Her eyes were huge. "The Russians are here to nab the shipment."

"And that begs the question of what *they're* going to do with it after they get their hands on it," Venice said.

"Well, we know they don't plan on destroying it,"

Jonathan said. "Else they wouldn't have brought that big ship."

"But why the attack?" Venice asked. "Why take everybody hostage?"

"I can only guess," Jonathan said. "But I think I've got a good one. Whoever's running this for the Company is using Baker Sinise as a broker for a reason. I'm guessing it's the deniability factor, but the motivation matters less than the fact of it. If the Russians battle it out with the Agency pukes, there'll be a lot of official paperwork to fill out, if only to cover for all the undercover shit. So, the Russians want the spooks to think that everything is working the way it's supposed to."

"You mean business as usual," Gail said.

"Exactly," Jonathan said. "But I'm guessing this'll be the end of his gunrunning business. That's a small world, and small worlds have wicked rumor mills."

Venice concluded, "By taking hostages, they'll have the leverage they need to force Sinise to commit financial suicide."

"Exactly," Jonathan said. "If not actual suicide. I've dealt with a few gunrunners in my day, and they are not a forgiving lot. Whoever was slotted to make the run for the Ukrainians was due for a hunk of cash, I'm sure, and they're gonna be perturbed when they find out that their payload has gone bye-bye."

"Do you want me to call Wolverine and find out what she wants us to do with the shipment if we can get our hands on it?" Venice asked.

"Whoa, wait," Gail said. "We don't know anything about how to handle nerve agent."

"What's this *we* shit, *kemosabe*?" Jonathan said

with a grin. "I know plenty about it. And the most important takeaway has always been to stay the hell away from it."

"Thank you," Gail said.

"Except in this case, we can't do that."

Her jaw dropped.

"It's friggin' nerve agent," Jonathan explained. "There's a reason why that shit's been declared illegal. If I get a chance to keep the Russians—in particular—from getting their hands on it, I'm going to take it."

"Don't they already have a lot of it on their own?" Venice asked. From her voice alone, Jonathan could tell that she did not approve of whatever plan was blooming in his mind.

"Not officially, but of course they do. We don't officially have any of it, either, but I could name the facility in New Jersey where we store shit tons of it. And we don't need it getting in the hands of Ukrainian terrorists, either."

"I thought the Ukrainians were freedom fighters," Gail said.

It took a couple of seconds for Jonathan to realize that she wasn't joking. "Sure, they're freedom fighters now, but wait till they get their hands on some WMDs. Labels like terrorist and freedom fighter are heavily dependent on which end of the missile you're looking at."

"So, why don't I call Wolverine and ask for her input?" Venice said.

Jonathan rolled his eyes. "The short answer is because I already know what I intend to do," he said. "The longer answer is that if it is the policy of President Tony Darmond to solve our problems with Russia by arming their enemies with nerve agent, the FBI director will have nothing to do with it. The whole operation will be beyond her purview, so she won't have a vote."

"So, now you're making policy for the United States government?" Gail asked.

"It's not like I could screw it up a lot more than it is," Jonathan said. "I didn't ask to be involved in any of this, but here I am. Now that I know, I can't just look away. This can't be a surprise to you."

"What if Uncle Sam finds out?" Venice asked.

Jonathan laughed. "If he finds out that a couple of private citizens interfered with their illegal plans to supply forbidden weapons to a foreign nation? He'll be equal parts scared and pissed. If he found out before the fact, he'd make every effort to kill the citizens who held the secrets. After the fact? He has a massive PR problem to manage. Do Big Guy and his crew know this detail?"

"Yes, they do. They're calling themselves Team Yankee, by the way."

"I like the ring of that. And how far out are they?"

"Your official sunset tonight is six-eleven. They plan to reach the shore precisely at seven p.m. It will be full dark by then."

In a perfect world, that was still too early to launch an op. Midnight or later granted the best combination of fatigue and complacency in an enemy. But in this case, Jonathan agreed that earlier was better.

"I need to figure out a way to kill the power to this place to prepare for their arrival," Jonathan said.

"No, you don't," Venice said. "I've got that covered

from here. Their electrical grid is an easy hack. They essentially have done nothing to protect it."

"You were able to do that in a day?" Gail asked. She looked flabbergasted.

"I cheated a little," Venice said in her coyest tone. "And no, neither of you wants to know what that means."

CHAPTER 27

"You can't stay here," Baker said.

"I have options?" Tyler asked with a wry smile.

Baker strained forward and cocked his head to look at the door. "How badly are you hurt?"

"I don't know," Tyler said. He wasn't being evasive, merely stating the truth. "Everything hurts, but I don't think anything's broken."

"Can you move fast?"

"What do you have in mind?"

Baker pivoted in his chair to point with his forehead to the corner of the room to his far left and slightly behind. "There's a passageway back there," he said. "The bookshelf pivots on its own axis and there's a stairway there that will take you down to the wine cellar. A clever little feature that never failed to impress visitors."

How could he not know this after all the times he'd been here? Tyler stood, pausing for a second and wincing against pain from too many places on his body to identify. It didn't matter whether he could make the trip down the stairs or not. Going anywhere was better than staying here.

"Come on," Tyler said. "Let's go."

Baker said, "I can't." He rattled a chain from under the table, out of sight for Tyler. "They got me shackled to granite and mahogany. You'll have to go it on your own."

Awareness of the obvious broke like a wave over Tyler's head. "I can't just leave you," he said. "They'll kill you."

Baker's eyes glistened as he manufactured a humorless smile. "I think we all know I'm not seeing tomorrow," he said. "But I want you to. You don't deserve any of this."

"Jesus, Baker, *nobody* deserves this."

"You know what I mean. Save yourself. Once you get to the wine cellar, buttonhook around to behind the stairs. That blank panel you see is a door. That'll take you to the loading dock. It's the door we use to bring in the wine for the cellar. After that, do your best to survive." He looked to the floor. "I'm truly sorry, son."

Tyler didn't know what to do. He knew what he *had* to do, but he didn't know how to begin. "I love you, Baker," he said. "I love you, Dad."

Baker smiled. "There you go. I like that word. I love you, too, Ty. Now get the hell out of here."

Tyler hesitated for a couple of seconds more, and then made his way to the back corner.

"There's a little latch in the upper right corner," Baker said. His tone was hurried, just as Tyler's hands were trembling.

Tyler pushed aside a *Reader's Digest Condensed Books* volume from 1996 and slipped his hand behind.

The latch wasn't much, just a lever, maybe three inches long. He tried pushing it up, and it didn't move. Then he pressed it down and was rewarded with a satisfying click.

"Push on the shelf," Baker said.

The bookshelf was hinged in the middle, along the top and the bottom, so the entire section of bookshelf rotated vertically. As the space opened, it revealed the shadowy outline of the top landing of a tight spiral staircase, which seemed to disappear into the blackness below.

"There's a light," Baker said, "but don't use it unless you absolutely have to. The glow shows from around the edges of the shelf. Just keep spiraling down. When the stairs stop, you'll be in the wine cellar. Trust me."

Tyler's heart was racing again, but this time it was different. This time, he had a sense of hope, a sense that maybe this might end better than terribly. He stepped into the darkness, and when he looked back, he watched a tear track down Baker's face.

"Look," Tyler said in an urgent whisper. "I shouldn't tell you this, but help is on the way. After dark. Try to keep faith."

With that, he disappeared into the shadow and pushed the panel closed behind him. An additional shove produced another click as the latch seated itself. The blackness was absolute, save for the hair-width seam of light that outlined the edges of the bookshelf. Using his cuffed hands to feel his way along, he found the steel rail, and he held on tight as he felt with his toe to find the edge of the top step. To fall down this vertical shaft would be like falling off the roof, with a hard stop against a concrete floor.

The stairs formed a helix that rotated to the left around a center post. By staying to the right-hand edge, where the wedge-shaped risers were thickest, Tyler could keep a firm grip on the rail. If his feet did slip, at least he'd still be hanging on.

He had no sense of distance or depth here in the darkness, and he hadn't had the presence of mind to count his steps as he began his descent. After what felt far too short a time, the steps came to a hard stop. He tightened his grip on the rail as he explored again with his toes. It turned out only to be a landing, with more steps descending from the far side. He encountered three more such landings before he hit the bottom of the stairway. This time, there was no doubt because the surface under his feet felt entirely different. Felt like concrete. Maybe the trip up and down was faster and easier when you had the use of your hands and you could see where you were going, but Tyler found himself feeling sympathy for the poor staff members who had to negotiate the climb while carrying cases of wine.

So, now what? What was his next move? Somewhere in here—behind the stairs, if he remembered his instructions from Baker—there was a door that would take him to . . . where? Sure, onto the loading dock, and beyond that lay the rest of the island, but the rest of the island was where all the death and danger were. Could he stay in here, he wondered, and avoid all of that?

What was it that Scorpion had told him? That it's always best to keep as many options open as possible. That was the benefit of maneuverability. If danger is coming in the front door, you always have the option to flee out of the back. That was the problem here. On the one hand, Tyler felt safe for the first time since the initial shots had been fired. No one but Baker knew he was here, and what was the likelihood that the terrorists might stumble upon it?

Actually, he thought, the chances of that were fairly high. Once Alpha and his hit men discovered that he was missing, and they reasoned that there was no way that he exited through the doors where guards were stationed, they would know that he had to have found some hidden means of escape. They would tear Baker's office apart—hell, they would tear Baker apart—to find that stairway. If he was still here when they connected the dots, he would die.

He had no intention of dying today.

"I hate this shit," he whispered aloud. Still keeping his cuffed hands on the stairs to keep himself oriented in the dark, he set about searching for the door. It was behind the stairs.

The stairs were circular. Where was the back of a circle?

You're overthinking this. The back of the stairs would be the direction opposite of the way he was facing when he reached the bottom. To get it right, he stepped back up onto the final riser and pressed his heels into the step above.

Now you're facing forward. He stepped back down onto the concrete and kept his hands in contact with the stairs until he figured that he was looking at the back wall. The darkness was total. As soon as he let go of the stairs and stepped forward, he became disoriented. He inched forward in tiny, shuffling steps, with his hands outstretched at what he figured to be eye level. If something were on the floor in his path, he knew he would fall, and with any luck at all, he'd catch himself with his hands rather than doing a face-plant. By the same logic, when he got to the wall, his hands would be the first part of his anatomy to arrive.

The toes of his left foot made contact with something. When it made a chirping noise and scampered off, it was all Tyler could do to keep from yelling out.

"It's the jungle," he mumbled. "You're not the only species living here." If it were a different jungle, one whose indigenous wildlife hadn't been so carefully curated, he'd be even lower on the food chain.

Though moving slowly, his knuckle still cracked when his fingertips found the wall. As before, he had no sense of distance or orientation. Suddenly, though, getting out of this place—getting back to where he could see things again—had become very, very important to him.

He splayed his fingers and pressed his palms against the surface of the wall. It felt like wood. Swaying his upper body from left to right, he swept the surface with his hands in a giant arc, looking for some indication that he'd found the door. And what would a door feel like?

There'd be a crack. A vertical seam that marked the location of the jamb. And then by following the seam, he'd discover either hinges or a latch. From there, it would be either push or pull. And then it would be the next step, whatever that might be.

He'd just completed the thoughts when his fingers found the crack he'd been hoping for. He traced it with his fingers to about waist height, and there he found the lever-style handle. He pushed it down and leaned forward, but the door didn't move. The he pulled back, and nearly fell over when the panel opened. He'd expected it to move from left to right, and was startled when it pulled the other way.

The open door revealed nothing but a seam of light a few feet ahead of where he stood. He recognized the air lock for what it was. He walked to the next door, easily found its knob, and placed his hand on it.

This was it, the point of no return.

He took a huge breath and held it for a few seconds before letting it go. "Oh, what the hell?" he mumbled. "Go big or go home, right?"

He straightened his shoulders, stood tall, and pushed the door open onto whatever lay ahead.

Tyler didn't have it in him to run. Bruised as he was, and still essentially blind in his left eye, he worried that he physically couldn't make it back to the hideout in the hills—if indeed, that hideout was worth hiding in anymore, after he and Jaime had tilted their hand to X-ray and his friend.

But he had to go somewhere other than here, and he had to get there quickly. The window of opportunity for him to escape summary execution—if he was caught again—had slammed shut. The only chance he had for surviving, he decided, was to put as much distance between him and the terrorists as quickly as possible.

The door from the wine cellar air lock opened onto what was essentially a subterranean loading dock—not underground, per se, but below the view of the guests. It was the door, in fact, that Jaime had told him led to the utility tunnels, which must have explained the second door in the wall of the air lock.

Um, no. Tyler was not going into the tunnels. Not now. He'd had his taste of tight dark spaces, and he didn't care for more.

He eyed the golf carts that were lined up at their charging stations. They were one solution, to be sure. They were faster than walking, and they were quieter than a gas-powered vehicle, but they were slow, and there was no shielding. If terrorists could see the vehicle, they would know at a glance who was behind the wheel.

And assuming they were actively looking for him, that seemed like a bad idea.

Tyler's eyes were drawn to one of the landscaper's trucks that sat idly at the end of the ramp. He knew these dump-bed trucks were real workhorses, and he'd driven in them with Jaime, but they were standard transmission. Tyler wasn't very good with those. He could work the gears enough to get the vehicle moving and get it stopped, but he was no one's version of smooth in his actions. Moving from a stop in the middle of a hill was particularly challenging for him.

But the trucks could ford streams and climb any hill. That was how he would get away from Alpha and X-ray. At least for the time being. Maybe if he got away, they would just forget about him. Maybe they'd determine that finding him wasn't worth the drain on their resources.

Yeah, and maybe pigs will fly.

Screw it.

Better to take a chance and lose than stick around and have your bones broken one at a time. The truck he saw bore the number *0014* on its fender.

Now he just had to hope that the keys were in the

storage cabinet. It was Jaime's rule that any landscaper should be able to access any vehicle at any time, and that meant having the keys accessible 'round the clock. If it had been left up to Jaime, the keys would remain in the ignitions, but Baker had overruled that idea for fear that guests would help themselves while in a drunken stupor—or while underage—and cause real problems. The compromise had been to put all the keys in one storage cabinet, where every vehicle had a corresponding hook from which its ignition key dangled.

Tyler opened the front of the cabinet and was delighted—though not surprised—to find that the key on the peg labeled *14* lay between those labeled *13* and *15*. He snatched the key into his fist and limped to the driver's-side door.

He settled into the seat, inserted the key, kicked out the clutch, and cranked the ignition. The engine turned and caught in two seconds. Jesus, it was loud. But he was on his way. With his hands cuffed, shifting would be a challenge. He leaned far over to his right as he used both hands to pull the transmission into second gear, then sat up straight up behind the wheel again. He over-revved the engine as he searched for and found the engagement point for the clutch. The truck lurched forward, but it didn't stall. He was on his way.

Baker Sinise realized now that there's a level of fear that exceeds the body's ability to cope. As he sat shackled in the conference room, he felt certain of two things. First, by urging Tyler to leave, he had performed one of the noblest fatherly acts of his life. Second, that same act of nobility guaranteed that Baker would die in pain sometime before the next sunrise.

The certainty of his death brought an odd peace. Yes, the fear was still there, boiling out of control in his gut, but with his options eliminated, the trembling and the pressure of tears behind his eyes had subsided. He wasn't a religious man, but he hoped that there would be something on the other side. It seemed wasteful that a man could occupy a few cubic feet of the universe for nearly sixty years only to then evaporate.

He'd know soon enough, one way or the other.

That sense of peace evaporated the instant Alpha reentered the room. He'd brought two other goons with him, and they all paused in unison when they took in the view of the interior. Alpha pivoted on his own axis, as if Tyler had somehow slipped in behind him. Next he stepped outside the door through which he'd just entered, and Baker heard him ask if anyone had sneaked by. Baker couldn't hear the answer, but what else could it be?

When Alpha returned, his face was a mask of rage. He'd pressed his lips tight, till they looked like a single thin line, and his face glowed red.

Alpha strode over to Baker and lifted him out of the chair by his shirt collar. "Where is he?"

"Who?" Baker's attempt at aloofness earned him a savage punch to the solar plexus and he crumpled.

"Do not toy with me, Mr. Sinise!" he yelled.

Baker couldn't have spoken even if he'd wanted to, as his diaphragm seized and struggled to draw air.

Alpha lifted him again by his hair, and Baker closed his eyes as he saw the cocked fist aimed at his face.

"Alpha!" a voice yelled. "Stop!"

The blow did not come. Baker dared to open his eyes.

"Why? This man betrayed us."

"He's our enemy," the other man said. "And we are his. There is no such thing as betrayal among enemies."

But Alpha wanted to hit him. Baker saw it written on his wide red eyes.

The other man continued, "We need him functional for later. And we need him not to look beaten. The *Katie Starling*'s captain and crew are not stupid. They will notice a broken face. If the vessel refuses to dock, then all of this has been wasted."

Alpha's face was close enough that Baker could smell his breath. The man wanted to kill him.

In the end, he threw Baker back into his chair.

As Alpha's glare cut his prisoner in half, he said in a barely audible voice. "Find that boy and bring him to me in pieces."

CHAPTER 28

Within three seconds of hanging up with Venice, the terrorists' radio net lit up with traffic. Jonathan had removed the earpiece a while ago because of the incessant chatter about stuff that didn't concern him. Now, however, even though the bud rested on the shoulder of his vest, he heard the buzz of something big happening.

Gail heard it, too. It was that emphatic.

Jonathan pressed the piece back into his ear. Within three seconds, he'd gotten the gist of it.

"Tyler escaped," Jonathan said, snapping to his feet. "I'm not sure where he escaped from, but he's not where he's supposed to be and the bad guys are going apeshit."

"What does 'apeshit' mean in the practical sense?"

"It means lots of people coming after him. Ready to go give him a hand?"

"You've got a plan?"

The answer came to him in the form of another transmission from whoever the terrorist was who needed to learn how not to shout into the radio. The speed of electricity was not affected by shouting.

"He stole a landscaper's truck," Jonathan reported. "That must mean that he's back at the pool deck and plantation area. Let's see if we can help." He gave Gail a hand rising to her feet. "You up for a bit of a run?"

"You lead and I'll follow," she said.

"Just remember that the bad guys are on higher alert than they were," Jonathan cautioned. "We don't want to get sloppy."

It wasn't until he was moving that Tyler realized he had no idea where he was going. The words, *anywhere but here,* resonated like a chorus in his head. This place right here meant certain death, and that certainty became less certain with every bit of distance he put between himself and Alpha.

It was time to break the rules. In Baker Sinise's world, footpaths were not roads, and roads were not footpaths. Today, right now, that was all bullshit.

As far as Tyler was concerned, if a surface was wide enough to allow this truck to pass, it was fair territory. He was going about twenty miles per hour when he crested the hill onto the path that led away from the pool. As he leaned over to shift into third, he tried his best to ignore the angry voices in the distance. He was in it, now. He'd entered live-or-die territory. Black or white, no room for gray.

He'd reached the dogleg in the path that took him up the hill toward the first cluster of bungalows when he heard a heavy *thock, thock, thock,* which rippled through the steel frame of the truck, followed an instant later by the sound of gunshots.

When he finished the turn, he was shielded from view from the pool by a massive magnolia tree and surrounding hedges. The shooting stopped. At least he thought it did. He'd bought himself some time.

He stepped harder on the gas and the engine screamed. He knew it was time to shift again, but he also knew what he had planned up ahead, and he thought third gear was about the best place to be. He was headed to the golf course and beyond—the only place he could think of— and even the walking paths provided too circuitous a route. He was connecting two points the geometric way, via the shortest route—a straight line. A lot of very expensive decorative shrubbery was about to pay with its life.

The four-foot row of flowers and shrubbery raced toward him and he pushed the truck even harder. Tyler figured he was doing nearly thirty miles per hour when he hit the shrub line, and the impact tossed him up out of his seat. He landed sideways in his seat and his bruises yelled in a rebellious symphony of pain.

"Ow! Dammit!"

He got his foot back on the gas and the tires spun in the dirt and the undergrowth. He saw shit flying into the air behind him and to the side, but he never let up. Then the tires found traction, and he launched out onto the cart path around the golf course. Far off to his right, he saw another vehicle and brief flashes of light before the *thock* of a bullet hit somewhere on the truck's body.

* * *

"Those are gunshots," Jonathan said. He pointed to the left. "I put them over there." It was hard to tell with the acoustical tricks played by the open spaces.

"That's where the Plantation House is," Gail said.

They took off at a controlled jog. If Tyler was still alive, and he was in a vehicle, whatever running they did was going to be of marginal use. The kid was either coming their way and closing the distance quickly, or going the other way and opening the distance quickly. They'd know soon.

More gunshots.

"They sound closer to me," Jonathan said. Maybe that was hope talking. Sometimes it's hard to tell the difference.

"There!" Gail said, pointing. "Isn't that a landscaper's truck?"

All the way on the other side of the fairway, a flatbed truck barreled down the cart path, bouncing and yawing, on the edge of being out of control. Behind him by about fifty yards, a smaller, far more agile resort pickup truck was closing in. Whoever was in the passenger side of the pickup stuck a rifle out the window and fired.

Jonathan brought his M4 to his shoulder and ripped a five-round burst at the pickup truck. The distance was too great and his sights were too uncalibrated. He saw two of the rounds hit the sidewall and another one hit the pavement behind the vehicle. He did his best to correct, but at this range—two hundred yards, give or take—what should have been an easy shot was rendered impossible when the weapon's sights were bad.

He cursed.

Two seconds later, both vehicles were obscured from view by the rise of a fairway bunker.

Jonathan took off at a run, chasing them. At least he knew the direction they were headed.

Now on hard pavement, the truck accelerated quickly. Within a few seconds, it was screaming down the cart path three times faster, five times faster than the course designer could have anticipated. Where the path narrowed, Tyler aimed for a clear spot in the middle. His mirrors tore branches from trees even as roots, which had erupted through the pavement, repeatedly bounced the vehicle into the air, and Tyler into the roof of the cab.

Through his mirrors, he saw the other truck closing the distance. They'd fired a few shots at him, but they went wild. Now, he figured, they were waiting till they could fire point-blank. He did the math in his head. At the rate they were closing, this whole thing would end in a minute or two.

He swung a series of S curves, first to the left and then to the right. On the final swing to the left, his tires lost traction for an instant, and he had to slow to maintain control. That's when the shooter behind him made his move. Whether it was a better truck or a better driver, the active word was *better.* They were better at this car chase thing than he was.

A hundred yards ahead, the tunnel of leaves and trees would open up into the wide expanse of the fourteenth fairway. In a flash, he realized that would allow the shooters to accelerate and then they'd be alongside him and he wouldn't have a chance. In his mirror, he saw that they had thought the same thing and were already making their move.

Tyler slammed his brakes, stood on them. The flatbed screeched and Tyler was thrown forward against the steering wheel. A fraction of a second later, an even greater lurch threw him back into his seat and then down onto the floor as the pickup with the terrorists slammed into him from behind.

He found himself under the dashboard among the pedals and food wrappers and he sensed that his truck was still moving. He needed to get it stopped, and he needed to find his feet and get out of here. Making them wreck was the whole idea to buy time, but here he was wasting it.

The truck lurched again, and the driver's-side window shattered as yet another impact brought him to a halt. He was oriented on the floor with his head facing the passenger side. The challenge of wriggling past the floor-mounted stick shift was too daunting, so he chose to sit back up into his seat and climb out the door.

He estimated that he'd lost a critical twenty, thirty seconds of his lead.

Upright now, he pulled the handle on the door, and drove it open with his shoulder. At first, it wouldn't budge. On a second and third try, it moved a little. Then, on the fourth, it finally flew open, and he damn near tumbled out.

He rolled from the cab to the ground, landing on his feet and ready for a fight. Using his cuffed hands as a single claw, he grabbed a folded shovel, which was clamped under the driver's seat, and held it as if it were a baseball bat. His heart hammered, and virtually every body part screamed, but he saw no one to swing at.

Where were they? His truck had come to rest at an angle that obscured his view of the road. The portion he could see was clear, but the smell of a leaking radiator was undeniable. Certainly, the massive palm tree he'd hit had cut a pretty deep dent in the grille.

Before he could run, he needed to know where the shooters were. As soon as he showed himself, they'd mow him down.

By now, he'd lost all elements of surprise. He wouldn't allow himself to be captured, just to be tortured, and he wasn't going to give these assholes an easy target. That left no option but a fight. The last time he'd fought anyone was at a football game last year, and that one hadn't gone all that well for Tyler.

Of course, the stakes weren't as high.

Where the hell were the terrorists with the guns?

Keeping low and to the driver's side, Tyler inched down the length of the truck, ducking even lower when he crossed from the cab to the flatbed. He really had no cover at all, just the twelve-inch depth of the flatbed and the girth of the wheel wells. He was entirely exposed from the road to the undercarriage.

So, why weren't they shooting at him?

Tyler dared a look through the gap under the truck, and drew a quick breath when he saw the damage that had been done to the front of the pickup that had been chasing him.

The trailing edge of the flatbed's lift had all but decapitated the pickup truck, shearing through the windshield and all the way back to the B-post. Unless they'd ducked, there would be nothing left of the people in the cab. Even from here, Tyler could see smears and flashes of red. He had no desire to see it more closely.

Judging from the volume of foul-smelling liquid

that was spilling from under the cab of his landscape vehicle, he didn't bother to try and start it up again.

If the dead guys had had a chance to get out a radio call, then there'd be more soldiers on the way soon. Keeping the shovel in his hand for good measure, he started the long jog across the golf course and back up the hill to the other side of the island.

Jonathan had just regained sight of the car chase when the impact happened, and it was epic. The good news for the bad guys was that they didn't feel much pain. "Holy shit!" Jonathan exclaimed. "Did you see that?"

When he didn't get an answer, he turned and saw that Gail had fallen behind. She'd developed a distinct limp, too, telling him that her old injuries were becoming new ones again. He knew she was tough and that she'd endure, but he couldn't wait for her. That kind of impact could have injured Tyler. Jonathan wanted to get to him before he had a chance to bleed out.

He'd closed the distance by half when he saw the kid emerge from the wreckage and start to jog back across the fairway.

"Tyler!" Jonathan yelled. When the kid didn't respond, Jonathan yelled again.

Still, no response.

Jonathan fired two rounds into the grass, and Tyler reacted immediately, first ducking, and then turning to see who was shooting at him.

* * *

"Shit!" The gunshots came from very close by.

Tyler pivoted to confront the threat, and was shocked to see the shooter waving at him. Big, bold arm movements that were more appropriate to signaling aircraft than waving hello.

And he was yelling Tyler's name.

"Scorpion?"

In the distance, behind Scorpion, Tyler could see Gunslinger running to catch up.

"Scorpion!" Tyler ran toward him, then slowed to a jog as the distance closed to within a few yards. He wasn't going to die, after all. Not now, anyway.

When Scorpion caught up to him, the commando grabbed him by both shoulders and beamed. "Jesus, kid, are you okay?"

That's when the emotion hit, breaking like a wave and drowning him. "No," he said. Or at least he tried to. It came out more as a sob. Embarrassed, he pressed his hands to his eyes and tried to push it all back, but it wouldn't stop.

"They . . . Jaime." Words wouldn't work. Nothing would work. The sobs escaped his throat and made sounds that he'd never heard himself utter before. He'd seen too much. He'd hurt too much. He'd killed people. He was sure he was dead, and now—

His legs folded until he was kneeling in the grass. He tried so hard to stop. So hard—

And then someone folded him into an embrace. He knew without looking who it was, and as Gunslinger hugged him, he hugged her back.

* * *

Jonathan had no idea what to do as he watched the kid fold in on himself. It was the kind of emotional meltdown that never happened outside the world of violence. It was all-consuming, paralyzing.

And far outside Jonathan's wheelhouse. That kind of emotion had no place in the middle of an emergency. As they stood out here, they were exposed. When Gail arrived and went to the ground to embrace Tyler, Jonathan was relieved that she'd taken control of the emotional first aid, but he was even more aware that there was one fewer rifle in play.

And they were still out in the open.

"Can we take this to the tree line?" he asked.

Gail nailed him with a glare.

"We're in the kill zone here. The jungle is right over there." He worried that the dead guys might have friends on the way. One thing was for certain—they were not in friendly territory here.

"I'm okay," Tyler wheezed. He eased away from Gail and took a swipe at his eyes. "I'm sorry. I don't know where that came from."

"Don't worry about it," Jonathan said. "These are stressful times that bring awful things." He grasped the kid's hand in a thumb grip and helped him to his feet. Then he did the same for Gail. He looked Tyler in the eye. "I really need for you to be okay. Don't just say it if you don't mean it."

Tyler snuffled and wiped his eyes again. "Then how's this. I'll *be* okay."

"Works for me," Jonathan said. "I think we're all a little worse for wear. Let's find a place to hole up and rest. We've got a few hours before the night gets *really* interesting."

The voices from the radio bud in his ear were sounding agitated as they called again and again for Quebec and Uniform to answer up. Jonathan kept that detail to himself. He figured that Tyler didn't need to know the names of the guys who had just beheaded themselves on his bumper, even if those names weren't names at all.

Nobody asked Jesse Montgomery for his opinion, but if they had, he'd have told them that it would have been a hell of a lot cheaper and easier just to buy a boat that had already been stripped of all its goodies. They'd peeled this boat like it was an orange. Seats, tables, everything. They were all gone.

"My orders were to make a fast boat faster," Davey had said, "and less weight means more speed."

And, as he'd pointed out so eloquently before, it wasn't his money.

Now Jesse understood why. First there were the people. He and Davey didn't know how many had been invited along on this party, but now that they numbered six—and one of them was the size of three more—the need for extra room made more sense. On the way back, there'd be a minimum of two more people, for a total of eight. Add them to the arsenal of weapons the team had brought with them, and he could see how lighter was better.

They'd met Team Yankee on an isolated dock on a tiny river north of Zihuatanejo at around four in the afternoon. The land-based team was already assembled and waiting, their SUVs parked along a tree line, and their gear stacked all around them. Davey told Jesse to stay with the boat and he stepped aground to meet them. From where Jesse stood, the greeting had the feel of a reunion of old friends. Lots of handshakes and fist bumps. A few bursts of laughter.

There was even a girl in the mix—a lady? Jesse couldn't put his finger on why that struck him as odd, but it did.

If Jesse remembered correctly, the Lurch impersonator preferred to be called Big Guy, and *really* did not like being called Lurch. Of the others, none looked familiar to him, though all of them had a similar thick-necked bearing about them, including the girl. He found her She Devil nom de guerre a little over-the-top. Of the four, she was the one who said least. In fact, Jesse wasn't sure he'd heard her voice at all yet.

"Permission to come aboard," said the youngest and most cheerful of the operators as he carried an over-stuffed duffel bag over the gunwale and stepped down onto the deck. "You must be Torpedo. You've got the physique for it." As the guy spoke, his smile took the edge off the insult. "I'm Conan," he said.

"But your friends call you Barbarian, right?" Jesse replied.

Surely, it wasn't the first time the guy had heard that, but he gave a hearty laugh, anyway. "I'm gonna like you," he said. "Where can I stow this stuff?"

Jesse pointed to the opening that led to the cleared-out lower deck.

Conan thanked him and disappeared.

She Devil boarded next, with a stuffed canvas bag

in each hand, followed by a much older guy who despite his age—fifty, maybe?—still carried himself with that operator swagger. "Madman," he said by way of introduction. He appeared to be about Davey's age, but a little less haggard. The load he carried seemed heavier than what the others bore, and Jesse wondered if the difference was really the weight of the load or the strength of the man who carried it.

Not surprisingly, when Big Guy hefted his load, he didn't look strained at all, but the vessel shifted significantly when he boarded.

"Jesus, Big Guy, don't capsize us at the dock," Conan said. "We've got work to do."

Big Guy made a sound that resembled a growl, and the growl triggered a laugh from the others. Davey brought up the rear with a duffel that clattered with the unmistakable sound of firearms rubbing against each other.

"That's okay, son," Davey said as he passed. "We've got this."

"I figure you older guys need the exercise," Jesse replied.

As Big Guy passed on his way for another load, he said to Jesse, "Kid, a shark could eat you whole and not even fart."

So, it was going to be that kind of trip.

The loading process took all of ten minutes.

"Okay, Chief," Big Guy said, "fire this thing up and let's head out. How long a ride do you figure?"

"Three hours, give or take," Jesse said as he moved to the controls.

Big Guy raised his eyebrows. "So, you've been promoted to boat driver?"

"Big Guy, I'd hang on if I were you," Jesse said as

he started the engines. "A guy your size could keep a frenzy of sharks busy for days."

He saw Big Guy look at Davey and say, " 'Frenzy'?"

"Apparently, that's what they're called," Davey said with a big smile. "I wouldn't argue with him. If it's in a book, the kid probably knows it."

CHAPTER 29

Anatoly felt his command slipping among his troops. They wanted to find and kill the infiltrators, whoever they were. Two more were dead now, and those were killed by a teenager! The marauders were still free, still roaming the jungles, and the men wanted them dead. Anatoly shut that down. It simply did not make sense.

He'd pushed hard to release the first hunter teams against the counsel of his lieutenants, and now one of those teams was dead. The remaining members were angry. They wanted revenge. But the men needed to stay focused on the mission they came here to do. When that was accomplished, if they wanted to stay behind and wreak havoc, he wouldn't get in their way. But for now, he needed all hands for the transfer. Their intel told them that the CIA shipment would arrive at or around eight o'clock this evening.

Baker Sinise would greet them, just as he always would, and his dockworkers would off-load the shipment, just as they always did. By dawn, the delivery vessel would be gone. By eight, the *Olympia 3* would be loaded, and Anatoly and his team would be on their way.

He stood on the veranda outside Baker's office, watching the approaching sunset and enjoying the breeze from the overhead fan.

"What are we going to do with all of them when this is over?" a voice asked from behind. It was Gerasim.

Anatoly continued to watch the ocean and the horizon beyond. "Those who behave, we will leave to recover the cost of their vacation. Those who do not behave, we will leave for a future overworked coroner."

"What about the staff?"

That drew Anatoly's glance. "What about them?"

"Are we going to let them live?"

"Why would we not?"

"They will know details," Gerasim said. "They will know what we took, and let's be honest, not all of us have perfect English. Some will figure out our nationality. We have specific orders not to let that happen."

"How could it possibly be in their interest to talk?" Anatoly asked. "They are guilty of the international trade of chemical weapons. They will be praying that *we* will not reveal *their* identities."

"Think it through, Tolya. There are Americans and British citizens here. The FBI and MI6 will turn the world upside down to solve what happened here. Do you think an underpaid resort worker is going to withstand the kind of pressure those agencies will inflict? They are certain to talk. Certainly, some of them, and we will never know which of them will be the problem."

"Are you suggesting that we kill them all?"

"That is exactly what I am suggesting. Not the guests—at least not the compliant guests. When we leave, they will eventually build the nerve to go searching for their children, and all of this will feel to them like a very bad dream. But the staff—especially the staff who help us at the docks—need to be killed."

Anatoly had not thought the plan out that far, perhaps because he didn't want to. He was not opposed to killing when it was necessary—certainly, Baker Sinise would see a bullet through his brain when this was over—but Anatoly was a loyal man who liked to reward loyalty in others. "Do you think we should give the workers an opportunity to come with us when we leave?" he asked. "Would that perhaps be a way to spare some of their lives?"

"Our men would not stand for it," Gerasim replied. "We mercenaries are not a trusting lot. They would be seen as spies." He gave a wry chuckle. "You know yourself, Tolya, that once a man has been held as a prisoner, his loyalty can never be trusted. We have killed their friends. We have frightened them, and they will be working on the docks under threat of death. Even a man with so big a heart as you could not let yourself trust them after that."

That was an undeniable point, Anatoly thought. But the thought of a group massacre conjured images of some of the tasks he was forced to perform during the unpleasantness in the Balkans, and he had little desire to repeat those sins.

People will allow themselves to be herded into tight groups, and they will even allow themselves to be shot—something that Anatoly never understood, no matter how many times he witnessed the phenomenon—but they could not will themselves to die quickly. The pitiful wailing and screams of panic still fueled his nightmares, even after all these years.

"What must be done, must be done," Anatoly said. "But only those who help us at the docks."

"But, Tolya, those workers at the docks will all have friends. How do we know who they have confided in over what happens on the dark side of this island? That is all it will take. One person who spreads a story to one investigator, and then the secret is out."

Anatoly felt his resolve slipping.

"As unpleasant as it is, it is the only way, my friend." *So many lives,* Anatoly thought. *Too many lives.*

"We knew that this was going to be messy when we started," Gerasim pressed. "We knew it was going to be violent. Frankly, the hostages have on the whole been more compliant than I anticipated, and the violence has been less than what I expected. I really think this is the only way. The staff must be eliminated. All of them."

Anatoly gave a loud sigh and returned his gaze to the horizon. "What will the men think of that level of brutality?" he asked.

"They are the ones who asked me to have this discussion with you," Gerasim replied.

Jonathan was annoyed that Tyler and Jaime had shared the location of the shantytown, but grateful that Tyler had remembered to share the fact that he had. There was no evidence that the information had been repeated, but they had to assume it had, and that location was now out of play. Between now and Boxers' arrival with Team Yankee, they'd have to shelter in the jungle like real soldiers, making the best of natural cover and trying their best to be invisible.

Once they were deep enough into the undergrowth that Jonathan thought it was safe to stop, he ordered a halt.

"So, what do you think about life in handcuffs, kid?" he asked.

With his hands still pinioned in front of his body, he moved through the jungle with an awkward, halting gait that clearly belied a continual sense of falling.

"I kinda hate it," Tyler said. "I don't suppose you have a key."

"Of course I do," Jonathan said.

Gail gave him a look. "You do?"

"Well, I will. Take a seat."

While the others watched, Jonathan opened his knife and went hunting for the perfect branch. He wanted something hearty, but not too stiff.

"What are you doing?" Gail asked.

"Just pay attention," Jonathan said playfully. "Don't get ahead."

With the twelve-inch section of branch separated from the tree, he used his blade to nick off a couple of straggling leaves, all the while ignoring the gooey coating of gore that remained on the blade and the hinge from last night's initial attack.

"Handcuff locks are among the easiest locks in the world to pick. It's easiest with a paper clip or a bobby pin—I should have asked first. Do either of you have a bobby pin or a paper clip?"

Gail said, "Oddly enough, in our haste to leave . . ." She didn't bother to finish the obvious.

"That's why I didn't ask," Jonathan said. He whittled both sides of one end of the stick down to the dimensions of a flat toothpick.

"Stand up, Tyler," he said. "Hold your hands out."

Tyler did as he was told.

"The locking mechanism is actually a spring with ratchet teeth that bite into the teeth on the bracelets." As he spoke, he lifted Tyler's wrists a little higher. He shifted the bracelet on Tyler's right arm to expose the opening where the male and female elements of the assembly joined. As he continued, he demonstrated his words. "I'm going to slip this shim into that slot. I'm gonna have to tighten the ratchet to get it to work."

As he squeezed the bracelet tighter, the shim was drawn into the mechanism. When he was in about an inch, he said, "Okay, here's the hard part. You stand still. One . . . two . . ."

On three, Jonathan pushed the shim deeper as he yanked the bracelet open. Tyler yelped at the suddenness of it, but then he grinned.

"Mission accomplished," Jonathan said.

"How do you know how to do shit like that?" Tyler asked, clearly impressed.

"Chalk it up to a misspent youth," Jonathan said. It took maybe three minutes to whittle down the other end of the stick and repeat the process on his left cuff.

"Thank you," Tyler said as he rubbed his wrists. "That feels a lot better."

"What do we do now?" Gail asked.

"Let's get to a higher point, where we have a better view. If they do have hunter-killer teams deployed, I'd like to be in a position to see them coming, know what I mean? Do you know this part of the jungle, Tyler?"

"I'm sorry, I don't," he said. "If it's not on the resort or in the shantytown, I don't know it."

"All right, then. Let's head uphill and see what we find."

They walked in a cluster, without a lot of effort made to control noise. When they spoke, they spoke in a whisper, and they tried to avoid the noise of traversing thickets of vegetation, but compared to a lot of other walks Jonathan had made in hostile environments, this one was pretty tame.

"They've got Hunter and Lori's bodies hung up on display," Tyler said. Those were his first words in two or three minutes. "They're naked and hanging from the archway to the pool."

Jonathan exchanged glances with Gail. Together, they chose to say nothing. If the kid needed to vent, the least they could do was let him.

"That's not right," Tyler went on. "I mean, Jesus, they were human beings."

"I'll be honest with you, kid," Jonathan said without turning to look. "I'm a shitty philosopher on these things, but I'll share something I've learned over the years. There are whole swaths of this world where evil is bred into people. Killing a person and swatting a fly occupy the same spot on the spectrum of morality. It's always been that way, and always will be."

Another moment of silence passed before Tyler said, "Um, don't take this the wrong way, but did you just describe yourself? You don't seem to have too hard a time killing people."

"You want to be careful here, Tyler," Gail said. "False equivalencies and all that."

"No, I'll take it," Jonathan said. "And no offense

taken. A little while ago, you killed a couple of people with your truck. Did you do a wrong thing?"

"I didn't kill them," Tyler objected. "They killed themselves. And yeah, I feel bad about it."

"Do you feel better or worse than you would have felt if they captured you and tortured you?"

Tyler didn't offer an answer, and Jonathan didn't wait for one.

"But you're right," Jonathan went on. "I don't have a hard time killing people when they are trying to kill me. I don't enjoy it, but sometimes people make stupid choices."

"So, in real life, are you an assassin?"

"God no," Gail said. It warmed Jonathan's heart to see her so defensive of him. For him.

"I've already told you that we won't discuss what I do in *real life*." He leaned on the words to signify his displeasure with the turn of phrase. "But I will tell you that I am on the side of the angels in everything I do. I endeavor to save lives, not to take them."

"And sometimes you have to kill to save a life," Gail added.

"Especially when you're saving your own?" Tyler asked.

"Sure," Jonathan said. "If it comes to that. But for others, too. Those assholes back on the resort are the very opposite of me. They kill for sport. They kill to terrorize, and those kinds of predators are everywhere."

Another quiet spell lasted for maybe thirty-five yards. "What are we going to do when your friends arrive?"

Jonathan started to answer, but Gail raised her hand to signal silence. "What should we do?"

Tyler's silence drew Jonathan's gaze. The kid had

gone dark. His jaw was locked and his eyes were focused on a spot in the air that did not exist.

"Tyler?" Gail prodded.

"They blew Jaime's face off," he said. "God only knows what they did with the body. My stepdad told me to run away. That wasn't my choice." He rocked his gaze to Jonathan. "That wasn't my idea. I wasn't a coward."

Jonathan brought them to a halt. "I never said that you were."

"Yes, you did. Before. When I left Annie. I wasn't the coward then, either. *She* was."

The kid was on the verge of unraveling, and it made Jonathan nervous. He chose to say nothing. Tyler seemed so deeply entrenched in his own brain that he wouldn't have heard his words, anyway.

"I *wasn't* a coward, goddammit!" He yelled this, startling Jonathan.

"Stop!" Jonathan yelled back, and Tyler jumped accordingly. "You have all the meltdown you want, kid, but you keep your voice down, you hear?"

Tyler dropped his voice to a desperate whisper. "But that's what they're going to think of me, don't you see? Why should they all be hostages and I'm not?"

"Because you had a less shitty day than they did," Jonathan said. "This isn't complicated, Tyler. On a battlefield, when the whole world is shooting at you, people on all sides of you fall dead. Front, back, left, right, but because your stars aligned, you get to breathe to see another day. That's just life."

"But what—"

"Wait," Jonathan said. "What you need to ask yourself is how are you going to tip the Reaper who spared you? How are you going to make it good for those poor bastards who never even heard the bullet?"

Tyler gaped. He had no clue.

"You pay that shit back by avenging the lives the Reaper took. And you do that by sending him a shit ton of corpses that are wrapped in the enemy's uniform."

"You're talking revenge."

"I'm talking justice. And there's a big difference. I apologize for the things I said to you about your girl. I was out of line. It did take a lot of courage to escape when you did, and it took twice that amount to escape a second time. Tyler, buddy, you're a survival machine." He sold that with a big smile, which went unreturned.

"But there are other brave men and women down there. Your stepdad showed huge balls when he encouraged you to get the hell out, and every one of those parents who are tortured every second by not knowing where their kids are, are brave as hell. So, answer Slinger's question. What do you think we should do when Team Yankee gets here tonight?"

The hard look on Tyler's face transformed from a look of despair to a look of resolve. "We bring justice," he said.

"Damn straight."

CHAPTER 30

As the sun dipped below the horizon, Jonathan silently catalogued all of the technology he wished he had access to, chief among them night vision and telephoto optics. They'd chosen an outcropping of rocks on the eastern side of the island. It was new territory for all of them, and it afforded a reasonably unobstructed view of the area where Team Yankee planned to make their landing. Jonathan had walked down to the beach and back again, just to make sure that there were no insurmountable hazards between here and there.

Unfortunately, they'd planted themselves on the wrong side of the breeze again, and mosquitos and other ravenous insects were chowing down on all of them.

"How long do you think it will be?" Tyler asked.

Jonathan checked his phone. "If they stick precisely to the schedule, they'll be making landfall in about thirty-five minutes."

"How will we know?"

Gail said, "They'll contact us when they're in place offshore. Then they'll swim in and we'll meet them at the beach."

"They're going to *swim*?" Tyler said. He seemed horrified. "At night? How far?"

"That's up to them," Jonathan said. "Probably about a mile. The trick to pulling something like this off is stealth. If the bad guys are alerted to the sound of an approaching boat, we're screwed."

It was near full dark now, and Tyler's features had morphed to shadows. "I thought they were bringing guns and ammunition and stuff," he said. "How are they going to swim a mile with all of that?"

"It all goes into inflatable bags," Gail explained. "As they swim, they tow it all behind them. Takes very little effort."

As if on cue, Jonathan's phone buzzed. He connected and said, "Yep."

"Hey, Boss!" Boxers' voice exclaimed. "You ready to light up the night?"

"What took you so long?" Jonathan said.

"Just because God and I are close friends doesn't mean He listens to me all the time. I offered to flip Him for a sunset at sixteen hundred hours, but He said I was behind on my confessions."

"Hell, if you kept up with your confessions, you'd never get anything done. You still planning to make landfall at the same coordinates?"

"That's the plan," Boxers confirmed. "But I got some lightweights on the team with me, so the current might take them to Peru or some friggin' place."

Jonathan heard the requisite griping in the background and smiled. Just hearing Big Guy's voice had a soothing effect. "So, who exactly is on Team Yankee?"

"You sure you want me to ruin the surprise?"

Jonathan waited for it.

"We've got some of the usual suspects. Madman and She Devil—"

Jonathan bristled at the thought of teaming with Jolaine Cage again. A fine fighter, she was just three clicks too close to psychotic serial killer. Madman wasn't his favorite, either, but over the last couple of years, he'd done a lot to redeem himself. Certainly, he was not the raging asshole that he'd been during his Army days.

"—plus Torpedo and Bomber—actually, he prefers Chief now. And you remember our spooky friend, Conan?"

"Of course." Jonathan had always liked Henry West. They'd only worked together a few times, but he always found the man to be smart, mission-focused, and lethal. "Glad to have him on board."

"The big surprise for you will be Boomer."

"Whoa," Jonathan exclaimed. "Glad to hear he's still alive." He covered the mouthpiece and relayed that news to Gail, who was equally shocked. Dylan Nasbe had been a living recruitment poster when he was an operator. A few years ago, he went off the rails, though, and killed some CIA pukes who had betrayed and killed a favorite asset of his. Boomer made the spooks pay with their lives, and then he disappeared. Everybody in the Community thought Boomer Nasbe was dead.

"I got word that you picked up a couple of stragglers," Boxers said. "Four, right?"

"Just one," Jonathan said.

A beat. "Was there a time when there were four?"

Jonathan avoided looking Tyler's way, even though

the kid couldn't possibly see any more detail than Jonathan could. "There was a time, yes."

Boxers gave a low whistle. "Yikes," he said. "Bad friggin' day."

"I've had better."

"Well, we'll have bang sticks to spare," Boxers said. "I'm not unpacking all that shit until I have to."

"Too many guns and NVGs," Jonathan said with a chuckle. "Words never spoken."

"I can't stay on the phone and chat with you all day," Boxers said. "Don't cry in the dark. Think happy thoughts and do your best to stay alive till I get there to rub your tummy." He clicked off.

"So, when do we knock out the lights on the island?" Tyler asked.

"Sometime after they've swum to it. When you're in the middle of the ocean, it's always nice to have a target to aim for."

"When do we head down?" Gail asked. "This darkness is pretty absolute. Even with shielded flashlights—"

"Yeah, that could get pretty hairy," Jonathan agreed before she could finish her point. "Plus, the sooner we meet up, the sooner I get out of this victim mode and I can gear up to make something happen." He turned in Tyler's direction. "What do you say, kid? You ready to go?"

"Probably not," Tyler said. "But I sure as hell am not staying up here alone."

They rose together. As they were about to start the walk down the steep incline, Tyler said, "What do you think that is over there?"

"Pointing in the dark is only marginally helpful,"

Jonathan said, though he could see the stain of Tyler's silhouette pointing out toward the horizon. It took a few seconds to find it, just as it had the previous night, but those were clearly the lights of an approaching ship.

"Do you think that's the nerve agent?" Gail asked.

"Given the luck of the day, how could it be anything else?" Jonathan said.

"What does that mean?" Tyler asked. "Okay, I know what it *means,* but what does it do to our plan?"

"I don't know," Jonathan said. "Other than make it a hell of a lot more complicated."

Baker Sinise called it the "Red Phone," but it was black, just like any other landline. The fact that it was ringing meant only one thing, and somehow Alpha knew exactly what it was.

"This is the moment when you can be smart, or you can sentence all of your guests to death," Alpha said. "That would be the *Katie Starling,* would it not?"

"How do you know these things?" Baker asked.

The phone continued to ring.

Alpha walked to the credenza, lifted the phone from its charger, and handed it to Baker. "If you do your job correctly, the *Katie Starling* will tie off at the dock, their crew will work with your team to off-load their cargo, and we will be on our way. If they do not, then everyone on this island dies." He pressed the phone closer. "Answer it."

Baker took the phone with his free hand and looked at it. The counter on the ringer told him that it had been ringing for thirty-two seconds.

"Answer the phone, Mr. Sinise," Alpha menaced.

"It has to ring for at least a minute," Baker said. "It's part of the security plan." The nature of the clandestine shipments that arrived at the Crystal Sands required a carefully controlled flow of information. Only hand-picked workers were allowed to handle the shipments and interact with the ships' companies. The chosen workers had been with Baker since the beginning, and they were both trustworthy and well-compensated. They worked like a fine-tuned machine to take delivery of the contraband and then transfer it to the storage locations, only to repeat the process in reverse when customers arrived.

The entire process started with a phone call that could be answered only by Baker. It's difficult for people to allow a telephone to ring unanswered for an extended period. The sixty-second-plus delay in answering was a hedge against an unauthorized person picking up the Red Phone. If that were to happen, the shipment would turn around and alternative plans would be made.

Baker let it ring for a minute-ten before he pressed the CONNECT button. He'd been thinking about this moment for hours now, and a part of him wanted nothing more than to repay Alpha's atrocities with a mission failure, but he couldn't do that. Not with so many innocent lives in the balance.

"Four seven, seven, three," he said into the phone.

A voice on the other side said, "Kilo, alpha, juliet, hotel." Translation: This is the *Katie Starling* awaiting instruction.

"Papa, papa common timing." Everything's ready. Use the regular piers. How far out are you?

"Due west, break four-zero."

"Charlie uniform." C.U. As in, "See you." Internet phonetic bullshit had invaded everything.

Baker disconnected the call and handed the phone back to Alpha. "They'll be here in fifty minutes," he said. "I told them to come to the common piers to keep the transfer simple."

Alpha clearly didn't trust him. "What did 'due west, break four-zero' mean?" He asked the question as if it were a trick.

Baker explained, "Due west is ninety degrees. Break means minus, and four-zero means forty. Ninety minus forty is fifty." The trick with any radio code was to be cryptic enough not to be immediately understood by eavesdroppers, but not so cryptic as to confuse the targets of the conversation.

"Give me the names of the workers you wish to be transported to the dock to unload the ship."

Baker hedged. These men had been his first employees. They were the ones who helped him build his fortune. "You're not going to hurt them, are you?"

"Of course not," Alpha said. "I've said from the beginning that those who cooperate will be treated fairly. I have no need, and certainly no desire, to harm you or your staff or your guests. Those who I *have* harmed left me no choice."

Baker hated this guy. Was it possible that a mass murderer could truly self-justify his barbarity?

"Don't get all self-righteous on me now, Mr. Sinise," Alpha said, as if reading his mind. "At least my men and I are soldiers for a cause. We kill to achieve a goal. You, however, kill for the money. You kill for profit."

"I've never killed a soul," Baker protested.

Alpha laughed as he indicated to one of his men to

unchain Baker from the table he was shackled to. "You tell yourself that, Mr. Sinise. You tell yourself that all those guns and bombs you broker do no harm. Tell yourself that they kill no children. You tell yourself that the chemical weapons you are about to receive were not going to be used to choke the life out of innocent men and women, boys and girls."

Baker rubbed his freed wrist as his ears burned.

"You do what it takes to allow yourself to sleep at night." Alpha moved closer, as if daring Baker to throw a punch now that his limbs were free. "But in those quiet moments, when your guard is down, you know the truth. You know who you are and what you are. If you are a religious man, you know that you will never see the Gates of Heaven. They say that soldiers go to Heaven because they kill for what they believe to be just causes, but who is to know? Personally, Mr. Sinise, I don't care. I don't believe in religion. I believe that we become fertilizer when we die. One day, I will know if I am right or wrong, but in the meantime, I have no difficulty sleeping at all."

Tears burned behind Baker's eyes as anger boiled in his gut. This man—this stranger—had pressed a raw nerve. Everything the man said was true. Baker did have difficulty sleeping some nights when the truth of his life sneaked through the protective barriers of his mind. He'd tried in the past to talk himself into believing that what he did was no different than what the owner of a gun store did. He'd told himself that he was no more responsible for the lives taken by the weapons he processed than a bar owner was responsible for the deaths caused by drunk drivers.

But there was a big difference. A *huge* difference.

He didn't sell to sportsmen and citizens who wanted to protect themselves. He was the equivalent of the guy who sold weapons to known criminals out of the trunk of his car at outrageously inflated prices. He was the treacherous, lecherous old man in the alley who sold bad booze to pitiful drunks who didn't mind that their product was filtered through an old car radiator.

Baker did believe in God, and if there was a second certainty in his life—beyond the fact that he would die tonight—it was that eternal damnation lay in his future.

Baker didn't resist as the soldiers led him out of his opulent dining room and across the beautiful office to the once-hidden stairs.

One way or another, this would all soon be over.

CHAPTER 31

Fewer than five minutes after Team Yankee slid into the water with their gear, Jesse Montgomery felt a crushing sense of isolation. The ocean was a big, dark, silent place when you're all alone. For a while, he could hear the faint splashing of the team's progress toward shore, and for a while more, he talked himself into believing that they hadn't yet disappeared. But ultimately, reality sneaked in and the fact of his aloneness could no longer be denied.

The night vision goggles helped give some definition to the otherwise blank landscape, but combined with the rolling action of the boat, they added a strange level of disorientation. Not dizziness, necessarily, but not far from it.

If Davey's estimates were correct, it would take somewhere between thirty and forty minutes for them to reach the shore. Once on dry land, they'd unpack their stuff, and one of the first official acts would be to give him a shout on the radio. Not to give him instructions—he already had those—but to let him know that they were safe.

While they fought their little war, Jesse's responsibility was to keep the boat ready for immediate exfil. He was also to keep an eye out for unusual things, whatever the hell that meant.

This whole adventure felt too much like déjà vu for him. The last time—the only time—he'd worked with this Boxers guy and his friend Scorpion, the floor of the boat they'd brought became slick with blood. As Davey had explained, when people throw hot pieces of metal at each other, somebody's going to bleed.

Who knew that his father was such a philosopher?

Because of the need for quick action when the time came, no anchor had been thrown, which meant that the boat was essentially adrift and subject to the vagaries of currents and tides and fish farts. With the engines just above idle, he was to keep his eyes focused on a single spot on the island in order to keep from losing his bearings.

When the time came to pull them out of there, they'd light up an infrared strobe to serve as a beacon, but if he'd floated too far in any direction, he might not be able to see it.

To makes things even more challenging, there'd be a time pretty soon when all the lights would go out on the island, making night vision dependent on starlight. This, of course, would be at the same time when cloud cover was rolling in. To keep his position when darkness came, his sole focus would be on his GPS coordinates. As long as he stayed a click or two with an imaginary circle drawn around that precise point on the globe, then everything else should work out perfectly.

Problem was, this maritime shit was all pretty new

to Jesse. His specialty was stealing stuff, which was what led him into this weird clandestine world to begin with—but not before getting jammed up by a prison term that was shortened without warning by the intervention of the FBI. It was a long story, but the short version was that if he stole stuff for Uncle Sam, then stealing was okay.

Except Team Yankee and Scorpion were not Uncle Sam. He wouldn't be surprised if they did occasional work for Uncle—in fact, he'd be shocked if they didn't—but those were questions he'd learned a long time ago never to ask.

So, when the roulette wheel of his life settled down this time, all he had to do was stay stationary in the middle of a moving sea, waiting for the opportunity to save lives. All the while, he'd be contemplating that the consequence of his failure would not just be the death of his father, but that of the entire insertion team.

Yeah, good times.

Something moved in the darkness behind him.

He whirled to see a ship about ten times the size of his boat carving a Rorschach blotch out of the horizon. Through the NVGs, it looked like some kind of cargo vessel, and he could see movement on the deck. He didn't think he was in danger of being rammed, but they were going to pass within seventy-five yards of him.

What would they think, he wondered, when they saw—

A floodlight came to life near the ship's aft end, washing out his NVGs. In that instant, Jesse knew he was in trouble. Without hesitating, he slapped the throttles to idle and dove for the opening to the lower deck, pivoting in midflight to land on his back to prevent breaking his face with the night vision goggles. He landed hard, driving the air out of his lungs, but he didn't think he did any harm.

A couple of seconds later, the bright white light swept his boat. It started from the aft transom and then painted the entire length of the craft. Shadows swirled around him as the impossibly bright beam played through the windows of the cockpit to bring even interior details into high relief.

"Ahoy!" someone yelled. "Everybody okay?"

Jesse pressed himself against the bulkhead, wishing that they hadn't removed so much of the interior.

"Is anyone aboard?" the voice yelled. It didn't sound threatening in the least.

Jesse didn't breathe. He just watched the contours of the shadows as the ship moved to the bow, and projected the blinding light from the front.

Then darkness returned.

Jesse scrambled to his feet and returned to the cockpit, slapping the NVGs back down over his eyes. The activity on the ship's deck seemed to be disbursing, leading him to believe that his boat had been the reason for the activity in the first place.

As he reengaged the transmission, he made a mental note of the ship's name as it was stenciled along the aft end.

The *Katie Starling*.

Jonathan stood among the trees at the edge of the beach with Tyler and Gail, scanning the breakers for some sign of Team Yankee. His line of work didn't involve a lot of amphibious landings—though he'd done a few—but he was reminded of what a blessing the sound of the surf was to cover the sound of battle rattle. Now that he was on the flip side, that same masking effect was annoying.

Because the sand was as white as it was, Jonathan felt it was important to hang back so as not to be silhouetted for casual observers. The downside of that decision was limited visibility. They could see only the section of beach that played out in front of them—maybe fifty yards of it, max. It was the section where Boxers and company were supposed to land, but pinpoint accuracy seemed a bit of a stretch under the circumstances.

Then the surf gave birth to Team Yankee. Their glistening silhouettes rose from the water one and two at a time. Most were hard to distinguish at this distance, but there was no mistaking Boxers, who was literally head and shoulders taller than the second tallest member of the team.

"Holy shit," Tyler whispered. "That guy's huge."

"Yes, he is," Gail said. "That is Big Guy."

"But he's sensitive about his size," Jonathan said. "I wouldn't mention it if I were you."

"Okay."

Jonathan added, "And he's deaf in his left ear, so stay to his right to talk to him." As he spoke, he led his team out onto the beach, scanning above and behind them for any sign of bad guys.

Gail whispered, "I didn't know Big Guy was deaf in his left ear."

Jonathan couldn't contain his grin. "He's not."

"Then why—" She got it. "Good God almighty. Really? Rookie games? Here?"

Jonathan didn't answer. There was never a bad time to have a little fun.

Up ahead, the arriving members of Team Yankee dragged their equipment bags out of the surf and across the sand toward the tree line.

"Let's make sure we have their attention before we get too close," Jonathan warned. "This is a bad time to startle people."

But Boxers had clearly been looking for them. He raised his arms high and waved.

Jonathan waved back.

Boxers detached himself from his float gear and met them halfway. "Evenin', Boss," he said when they were close enough. "What the hell have you gotten yourself into?" To Gail: "How's that romantic getaway working for you, Gunslinger?"

He laughed.

She didn't.

Boxers pointed to Tyler. "What's this?"

"My name is Tyler." As he spoke, he pivoted around to Boxers' right side, earning an odd look.

Jonathan explained, "His stepdad owns this place."

"That so." Boxers' voice dropped an octave.

"He says he doesn't know anything about the dark side of the enterprise and I believe him." Jonathan knew that Big Guy would catch the personal endorsement as a cue not to pursue it further. "Let's meet the rest of the team."

Jonathan recognized everyone, but Gail needed to

be introduced to Conan and Chief. Tyler needed to be introduced to everyone.

While Team Yankee divested themselves of their dry suits and straightened out their clothes, Jonathan led the effort to unpack the bags. He had to chuckle. If explosives were like cupcakes, then Boxers packed like a twelve-year-old heading off to camp. They'd brought grenades, a couple of claymore mines, a shit-load of GPCs, and detonators for everything.

The gun bag contained a bunch of suppressed M27s—a Marine Corps modification of the Heckler & Koch Model 416 (which itself was an improvement on the M4)—and a couple of suppressed H&K 417s chambered in 7.62 millimeter, Boxers' favorite choice in rifles.

"Just eyeballing, I'm guessing a thousand rounds?" Jonathan said.

"Fourteen hundred," Boxers corrected. "But a thousand are for the five-five-sixes."

"We've got another four hundred to add to the five-five-six pile," Jonathan said.

"Well, shit," Conan said. "We won't even have to aim."

In seven minutes, they were ready to roll. When Jonathan slipped the night vision over his eyes and fired them up, it felt like he had come home. Honest to God, sometimes he wondered if he didn't prefer the comfortable green glow from the NVGs over the romance of starlight.

He was grateful to change out of the bloodstained chest rig he'd taken from the dead terrorist and slip into the plate carrier he was more accustomed to. This one even had plates installed, which surprised him because Boxers was not a big fan of them.

That's when Jonathan remembered that in Boxers' mind, his status had changed. Big Guy saw him and Gail less as team members than as precious cargo. And you always provided optimum protection for the PCs.

When his gear was in place and his rifle was slung, he found the coms gear and wired himself up.

"Hey, Boss," Boxers said. "Check a little deeper into the ammo sack. Go to the outside pocket. There's a present for you."

It was Jonathan's go-to sidearm, a heavily modified Colt 1911 in .45. It was as close to a kiss on the lips as Boxers could give.

"Ah, you like me," Jonathan said. "You really like me." He strapped on the pistol's thigh rig, and he felt soldierly again.

Team Yankee had brought a set of everything for both Gail and Tyler. Gunslinger knew her way around the gear blindfolded, but the kid needed some help. "Jesus, this thing is heavy," Tyler said as Jonathan settled the plate carrier on his shoulders.

"Nah," Jonathan said. "It won't be heavy for another couple of hours."

"Then it'll be really friggin' heavy," Madman said. They shared a chuckle.

The last thing for Tyler was the NVGs array, and Jonathan took a minute or two to explain their operation. There actually wasn't a lot to it, once you got the four-tube array balanced on your head. "It'll take a few minutes to feel normal," he explained, "but just keep them in place and your brain will adjust."

Tyler stood still as Jonathan adjusted the eyepieces. "A couple of things to keep in mind," Jonathan said. "First, these things cost about sixty thousand dollars apiece, so I'd appreciate it if you'd take care of them."

"Holy shit."

"And second, remember that when we kill the generator, it's going to be blacker than black. Keep the lenses as close to your eyes as you can, to limit the amount of light that leaks out. I'll try to keep an eye out for you to remind you, but still."

Tyler grinned as he pivoted in a circle, taking in his surroundings. "Wow, you really can see everything, can't you?"

"Hey, Big Guy," said Chief. "Let's give my boy a call. He's gonna get worried soon."

"So, Scorpion," Big Guy said. "You want command?"

It felt like the natural order of things, but . . . "I don't want to step on your toes."

"This isn't friggin' high school," Boxers scoffed. "You might as well take command, because you're gonna tell people what to do sooner or later, anyway."

"Okay," Jonathan announced, "I'm taking command. Chief, what channel is your boy on? He's Torpedo, right?"

Davey answered, "Yeah, Torpedo. He's expecting to hear from us on Channel Two."

"Copy Channel Two," Jonathan said. "Our tac channel will be three, Mother Hen will be Channel One. PTT only, please, unless I say otherwise." PTT meant push to talk, as opposed to VOX, which would broadcast everybody live.

Jonathan dropped to Channel Two. "Torpedo, Torpedo, Torpedo, this is Scorpion. The team is in place and safe. Acknowledge."

"Oh, yeah, I acknowledge," Jesse said over the radio. Jonathan recognized both the voice and the stress in it. "Where the hell have you guys been?"

Davey's voice said, "Ease up, son. This is Chief. What's going on?"

"There's a big ship on the way in toward you—"

Jonathan could see the lights in the distance. It was still far enough away that it wouldn't cause a problem.

"—and it came really close to me. They saw the boat. They lit it up with a searchlight, but I don't think they saw me."

"I copy," Jonathan said. "Be advised that Scorpion is in command now. I don't know what your orders are yet, but stay close to the radio in case we need you."

"Got it," Jesse said. "Good luck to all of you."

The words made Jonathan cringe. He refused to admit that luck played more than a passing role in hot operations. Success and failure hinged on skill and marksmanship alone. "Thank you," he said over the radio. "Now stay off the air unless there's an emergency, in which case you go to Mother Hen over on Channel One. Scorpion out."

He switched over to Channel One. "Good evening, Mother Hen," he said, knowing that she'd likely been plugged into the net for a couple of hours.

"Now, there's a nice voice to hear," Venice said. "Gunslinger, are you there, too?"

"I am," Gail said. "Along with all of Team Yankee. Any new developments we need to know about?"

"Negative," Venice said. "But let me know when you want the lights turned off."

"That'll be about thirty minutes from now," Jonathan said. "But wait for the order."

"I understand," Venice said. "Shoot straight, everybody."

Jonathan turned back to the team. Everyone was kitted up and ready to go.

"Hello, She Devil," Jonathan said. "You're kind of quiet."

"I'm very quiet," Jolaine said. "I'm getting into my Zen killing place."

Given her past, Jonathan couldn't swear that she was kidding. He could hope, but he couldn't swear. He noted that she alone among the group had affixed an M203 forty-millimeter grenade launcher to her rifle.

"We need to get off this beach," Madman said. "We look like a bunch of ants in the sugar bowl."

Jonathan laughed at the imagery. It was especially true given the prehistoric-insect look of the NVGs.

"Shouldn't we get briefed on the plan?" Dylan asked.

"We'll do that at the top of the hill," Jonathan said. "Everybody ruck up and we'll move."

In addition to their plate carriers and ammo vests, each of the operators split up the supplemental gear—explosives, medical gear, extra batteries, and such—into surplus Army rucksacks and hung them on their backs. That still left a lot of spare explosives, food, and medical gear staged at the infil/exfil site as a hedge against the possibility of the operation taking longer than planned.

"Gotta carry your load if you want to play," Jonathan said to Tyler.

"Does the kid know the round end from the flat end of his bang stick?" Boxers asked loudly enough to get a laugh from everyone but Tyler.

"I've had extensive training on the safety switch," Tyler said without dropping a beat.

"Can't ask for more than that," Boxers said. Jonathan knew that if Big Guy could run the world, every one of its residents would receive a week of training in firearms safety and marksmanship as a requirement to attend first grade. He didn't like it when Jonathan armed the newbies.

It was one of the reasons why Jonathan so rarely asked for a show of hands on any decision.

When they were ready to rock, Jonathan said, "Okay, Tyler. You know this island better than anyone. Lead us back to the overlook."

"Me? Okay." He pivoted and headed back toward the path they'd just traveled down from the top.

Jonathan let the others follow in line before he and Gail fell in with Boxers in the rear.

"It's great to see you again, Box," Jonathan said. "It's nice to be able to bring the fight back to these assholes."

"So, how bad is it?" Big Guy asked.

"These bad guys are *bad guys,*" Jonathan said.

Gail talked about the bodies that had been draped at the pool entrance.

"We'll make quick work of that shit," Boxers said. "How many hostages we working with?"

"A lot," Jonathan said. "I don't want to go through it

all twice, so we'll share info when we get to the top of the hill."

"How's Jolaine?" Gail asked.

"Still crazier than a shithouse rat," Boxers said. "But you gotta like that Zen of killing line. I might have to steal that one."

At the top of the path, Jonathan laid out the tactical plan. "We secure the kids first," he said. "Then the adults."

He spread out the tourist map and hit it with the beam of his infrared flashlight. "I know this isn't much of a map, and it's a lot of scribbling, but it's the only map we've got. We're here." He pointed to a spot on the northwest arc of the island. "This is the resort down here. From what I can tell, the children are being held here, in Bungalow Seven. The adults are here in the area of the swimming pool—"

"The groups are too close for separate ops, Boss," Boxers interrupted. "That's only, what? A hundred yards separating the two groups? Somebody hears a single scream or a single gunshot from the kids' house, and they're gonna start shooting up the swimming pool. We've got to hit both at the same time."

"We don't have the manpower for that," Gail said.

"I agree," Jonathan said.

"We've got all the manpower we're gonna have," Boxers pressed. "If we had *fifty* operators and we screwed up the timing, a lot of good guys would die."

"And let's not forget about that shit they're bringing in on the ships," Rollins said.

"That's not our problem, Madman," Jonathan said.

"The hell it's not. What's the point of saving a bunch of rich tourists and then letting a bunch of peasants somewhere choke to death on VX?"

"We've got to avoid mission creep," Jonathan said. "VX is not the precious cargo."

"Neither are the tourists," Boxers said. "You and Gunslinger are the PCs. This mission has already creeped."

"You know what I mean," Jonathan said.

"I don't think I do," Jolaine said. "Are we here to save lives, or aren't we?"

Dylan said, "VX is really, really nasty shit, Scorpion."

Jonathan looked to Gail for an ally, but she said, "I'm with them on this one."

"Okay," Jonathan said. "What's the mission with the VX? What does victory look like?"

"The bad guys don't get it," Rollins said. "Can't get less complicated than that."

"You know this is an Agency operation we'll be getting in the middle of, right?" As Jonathan spoke the words, he realized they'd been a mistake.

"Since when have you been worried about getting between Secret Squirrel and his nuts?" Boxers said.

Jonathan chuckled at the imagery.

Rollins said, "When the lights go out, there'll be those first moments of panic on their part. With our NVGs, we'll have absolute supremacy for ten or fifteen seconds. Most of the bad guys will be dead before they know they're in danger."

Jonathan knew that he'd lost his argument. "So,

we'll have *three* simultaneous assaults going on," he said.

"Better than a running gunfight," Boxers said. "*Bang, bang,* get it over with fast."

"It also pushes back our timeline," Jonathan said. "We need for the ship to settle into place before we can do anything." He looked to Davey. "Chief, how long does it take to get a cargo vessel ready to be off-loaded?"

"Once she's berthed and tied off, they can start right away."

"You're not going to shoot the resort workers who are moving the stuff, are you?" Tyler looked horrified as he asked the question.

"Of course not," Rollins said.

"Then who are you going to shoot?"

"These guys are terrorists," Gail said. "And the shipment is an illegal load of chemical weapons."

"That they intend to steal," Jonathan added.

"Exactly. That they intend to steal. There's no way that invasion force is going to trust them. They're going to have to assign someone to watch what they're doing."

An upbeat thought occurred to Jonathan as Gail was speaking. "And for every soldier who's down at the dock, that's one who's not guarding the hostages," he said. Just like that, he found himself in favor of the third front. "We're not the only ones who will have to split our forces."

There was a general rumble of consensus. They were going to do this.

"Now, there's the matter of teams," Jonathan said. "Madman, you've got the jones for VX, so you're on that, along with Conan and She Devil. We good with that?"

Nods and thumbs-up.

"Good. That will make you Yankee One. Slinger, you take charge of the kids, okay?"

"Okay," she said. "Tyler, I want you with me."

The kid didn't argue.

"Dylan," Jonathan said, "you make up the third member of the nursery team, Yankee Two. That leaves Big Guy and the chief with me at the pool and we'll be Yankee Three." He paused for a few beats to allow for questions.

"Where are we taking everybody?" Tyler asked.

"In a broad sense, we're not taking anyone anywhere," Jonathan said. "We want to neutralize the bad guys and go home. The faster, the better."

"What about the dead and wounded?" Dylan asked.

"To hell with the bad guys," Jonathan said. "And, hopefully, there won't be any casualties among the good guys."

"Not likely," Henry said.

"Probably," Jonathan conceded. "We'll do the best we can for wounded good guys, but our priority really needs to be to neutralize and leave."

"Shoot and scoot," Boxers said. He looked proud of himself.

"There's an infirmary on the resort," Tyler said. "The medical people are probably among the hostages. Where else could they be?"

"Tyler, listen carefully," Jonathan said. "The children are *your* responsibility. Gunslinger and Dylan will handle the bad guys, but once they're down, you've got to keep the kids contained. Once the shooting is done, I'm going to need them as reinforcements up at the pool and the Plantation House."

"How am I supposed to *contain* them? They'll have just seen a bunch of people get shot. There'll be blood everywhere. They're gonna go nuts."

"Not if you stay calm," Gail said.

"*Calm!* How the hell am I supposed to stay calm?"

"Because it's your friggin' job," Boxers said. "Because they're kids and you're not, and if you *don't* do your job, they're likely to wander off and get hurt. And that will be on *you.*"

Big Guy's words seemed to take the oxygen out of the air. Everyone looked at Tyler, and Tyler looked at the ground.

"Oh, don't look so butt-hurt," Boxers said. "The truth is the truth."

Jonathan held up a hand. There were days when Big Guy could be less than calming. "Sometimes the dealer slings bad cards, Ty," Jonathan said, deliberately using the familiar form of his name. "Don't ever take offense at direct communication. The kids are going to want to scatter. Some will hunker down and freeze, but others will run like frightened deer. You need to keep them from wandering off."

Tyler thought for a few seconds. "I can get them into the utility tunnel," he said. "We'll make it a game."

"I like that idea," Gail said. "That will put them out of harm's way."

"What about the darkness?" Tyler thought aloud. "Kids are afraid of the dark."

"Oh, hell," Jonathan said, "Big Guy's afraid of the dark. Isn't that right, Big Guy?"

Boxers grumbled, "You know I could have just

stayed home, right?" As he spoke, he dug into one of the pockets of his ruck and produced a handful of thin foil packets. "These are glow sticks," he said. "Do you know how to use them?"

"Break 'em and shake 'em," Tyler said.

"Yup. Stuff some of these in your pockets. They won't give you a lot of light, but they'll take the edge off the darkness."

Tyler accepted the packages and shoved them into his pants pocket. "They'll give the kids a cool toy to play with, too."

CHAPTER 32

As Baker Sinise approached the dock, he noticed for the first time that the secondary cargo pier was already occupied by what appeared to be a World War II–era warship, minus any guns. "What the hell is that?" he asked Alpha, who led a team of three other soldiers to serve as the staff's security detail.

"Nothing you need to concern yourself with," Alpha said.

Of course, it could only be one thing: the vessel that would transfer the stolen weapons to wherever these terrorists were taking them. "How will I explain it to the crew of the *Katie Starling*? These are people who do not like surprises."

"Tell them that one of your guests has quirky tastes in yachts," Alpha said.

Baker supposed that could work. If the crew dug deeper and wondered why rich guests would ride in such an ugly vessel, he'd just have to feign ignorance. His was not to question the tastes of his guests.

"How am I going to explain you?" Baker pressed.

"Uniformed men with guns will most certainly spook them."

"Only you will know we are here," Alpha explained. "But we will be watching. If anything out of the ordinary happens—and I mean *anything*—you and your staff will be the first to be shot."

Baker didn't know the crew of the *Katie Starling* personally, but he understood who they represented. He had no doubt that any violence started by Alpha and his army would be finished by the ship's company. It had been Baker's experience over the years that the illicit-arms industry was a group not to be messed with.

It was a lesson Baker would learn firsthand soon enough if he were fortunate enough to live to greet the Ukrainian operatives who would arrive in two days to pick up the shipment they had already paid for.

The pier burned white-hot with the lights turned on. Baker and his staff waited midway down the dock as the ship went through its berthing procedures. He stood with his feet planted and his arms folded while the other workers sat in idling fork trucks.

"Remember, gentlemen," he coached his workers. He had to find the right volume level that would allow him to be heard over the idling engines, yet not so loud as to be overheard by others. "This will soon be over. Treat this shipment just like any other, and the terrorists will be on their way. The crew of the *Katie Starling* has no need to know that anything is amiss. Are we clear on this?"

He looked around and got nods from all five of his workers.

"Good. Now smile, everyone."

Within a couple of minutes, the *Katie Starling* had slid along the dock. Baker fastened the mooring line to the aft cleat, while his foreman, Peter Angelos, took care of the bowline. When the gangplank was deployed, Baker stood at its base to receive whatever crewman wanted to greet him.

It didn't take long. An overweight man with close-cropped hair and a gray beard walked down the incline to the dock. The man carried himself in a way that told Baker he was in better shape than he appeared. As he came close enough for eye contact, a predatory bearing about him nearly chilled the air.

"Walter White," the man said as he extended his hand.

Baker accepted the handshake. "Baker Sinise," he said. What he didn't say was that "Walter White" was quickly replacing "John Smith" as the ask-no-questions pseudonym among spooks.

"What's with the other ship?" Walter said.

"One of our guests enjoys cruising the old way," Baker said. "And I'm happy to say that he pays his hotel, food, and beverage bills in full and on time."

"Speaking of which," Walter said. "Don't you have a bag of cash for me?"

"In a virtual sort of way," Baker replied. "If you check the account you gave me, you will find that half of the agreed-upon amount has been deposited."

"I was told that there'd be cash," Walter said. His tone raised hackles on Baker's neck. These were details this man should know about. Had something gone wrong?

Then he decided it didn't matter. "You'll get the rest of the payment in cash when the material is off-loaded and an inventory taken."

Walter seemed to sense that something was wrong, and he craned his neck to take in the surroundings. It was the kind of movement that no doubt put Alpha and his trained dogs on edge.

"What's with the other boat I saw floating out there offshore?" Walter asked.

Baker cocked his head, genuinely surprised. "What boat is that?"

"About a mile out. It appeared to be just sitting there. I didn't see an anchor."

"Late-night divers?" Baker guessed.

"Is that one of the programs you offer?"

"No, but you never know what the locals are going to do." As soon as those words left his mouth, he remembered Tyler's parting words: *"I shouldn't tell you this, but help is on the way."*

Was that really possible?

"I'm not liking this," Walter said. "Maybe I should just leave."

"Once you have off-loaded the cargo I have already paid for, you are certainly free to do whatever you wish." Baker added a smile as an afterthought. "You bring the cargo to the dock, and my crew and I can take it from there."

Walter hesitated, clearly not at ease.

"It's unprofessional to make me ask yet another time," Baker said. Another common denominator in the illicit-arms sales racket was the importance of a reputation for honesty. The irony was not lost on Baker that the proffered honesty dealt almost exclusively with stolen materials, but that was the nature of the business.

After one more scan of the surroundings, Walter unleashed a two-finger wolf whistle and people on the deck went to work.

Henry West and the rest of Yankee One hadn't counted on the sudden illumination of floodlights, and the brightness and number of them startled him. They were hunkered down among crates and assorted stuff along the apron of the pier when they jumped to life, and now they were stuck about a foot inside the boundary where the division between light and dark was the most harsh. They weren't entirely exposed, nor even entirely illuminated, but Henry and Jolaine, in particular, were on the feather edge of being visible.

Madman, on the other hand, was well-concealed. In a few minutes, when Team Yankee cut the power and the lights went out, none of that would matter.

Peering through a gap that existed between two wooden crates, Henry's field of vision was annoyingly narrow. Mostly, he could see handling equipment and mingling workers, but he didn't see any of the soldiers he'd been expecting to encounter. He was confident that they were there somewhere, but they were well-hidden. The only reasonable place for them to be staying out of sight would be in the shadow of the tree line. That assumption, in fact, was the reason why Yankee One itself was not in the tree line.

Until the lights went out, and/or the shooting started, they would remain utterly silent unless something urgent required them to make noise.

Henry even suppressed his urge to look at his watch—
knowing, as he did, how unusual motion drew attention. At this point, the time didn't matter.

At this point, time would begin when darkness fell.

Jonathan and Yankees Two and Three had moved
down the side of the mountain to stage at the edge of the
golf course. From here on out, it appeared that every
other tree and flower had its own light. Last night, they
were atmospheric and romantic. Tonight, they were just
bright.

The radio bud in Jonathan's right ear popped to life.
"Scorpion, this is Torpedo."

Jonathan pressed his TRANSMIT button. "Go ahead,
Torpedo."

"Yeah, I wanted you to know that I think the ship
has parked at the docks. They just turned on a whole
shitload of lights down there."

Jonathan craned his neck to look at the night sky on
the far side of the island, where he saw a subtle yet distinct glow of artificial light.

"Okay, thank you, Torpedo. Mother Hen, did you
copy that?"

Venice's voice said, "Loud and clear. The lights are
on. Are you ready for me to turn them off?"

Jonathan looked to his team.

"There's gonna be a lot of panic down there when it
goes dark," Boxers said. "Lots of shooting. We're not
in position."

"We'll give it a few more minutes," Jonathan said to
Venice. "Yankee One, are you in position?"

The radio broke squelch one time in his ear. *Affirmative.*

Jonathan addressed the rest. "Okay, here's where irony meets stupid. Despite the availability of night vision—one of the world's greatest force multipliers—we've got to get across a brightly-lit golf course before we can go hot."

"That sounds like something we'll regret later," Davey said.

"Yeah, well, actions have consequences," Jonathan said. "As Big Guy pointed out, the guys on the docks are gonna go apeshit when the lights go out. That shooting, plus the fact of the darkness, is going to make our targets go nuts. Makes no sense for us to maneuver safely just to have to scrape up a bunch of corpses."

He was a little surprised when he got no pushback.

"We'll cross the golf course in twos," Jonathan said. "When you get to the cart path on the other side, take cover and break squelch twice. Then we'll send the next group. Questions?"

Silence.

"Gunslinger and Boomer, you go first," Jonathan said.

"I'm not Boomer anymore. I'm Dylan."

"Oh, my God, words cannot express how little I care," Jonathan said. "Three . . . two . . . one." The "go" was always silent because it was the cadence that counted.

Dylan and Gail took off at a low sprint. They didn't scan for targets, because that was the job of their cover team. Within ten seconds, they were out of sight.

The radio bud in Jonathan's ear rasped twice.

"Chief and Tyler," Jonathan said. "It's your turn."

"To do what?" Tyler asked. His face was a mask of confusion. "The talking hole in your face makes noise, but I don't know what the sounds mean."

Jonathan laughed. You had to like this kid. "In the simplest of terms, run like hell until you're on the other side of the cart path, and then make yourself invisible."

"Just follow me, Tyler," Davey said. "When I run, run. When I drop, drop."

Jonathan counted it down, and they took off.

In each iteration, as the teams ran, Jonathan and Boxers scanned every compass point for any sign of a bad guy, but they came up with nothing.

"And here we are again," Boxers said. "In that awkward moment when we're all alone, but we know people are watching."

Honest to God, Big Guy was the only person he had ever known who found his center—his calmest self— on the precipice of a firefight.

"Yeah, that," Jonathan said. He counted it down, and they made their dash across the wide-open space.

As they slid to a halt at the cart path, Boxers said, "I'd consider it a personal favor if you never asked me to do a thing like that ever again."

"When did you become a big pussy?" Jonathan asked.

They were close now. The roofs of the bungalows were visible through the trees.

"The rules of engagement couldn't be simpler," Jonathan said. "If they're a bad guy and they have a gun, drop them. If they approach a hostage, drop them. Speed and overwhelming violence are the only advantage we have."

"You don't ask them to put their hands up or anything?" Tyler asked.

"I just stopped liking you, kid," Boxers said.

"Absolutely not," Jonathan said. "They've already declared their intent to kill, and we have to take them at their word. We're just turning their own plan against them."

"I don't know that I can do that," Tyler said.

"We'll all find out together," Jonathan said. "Think of that rifle as a tool of last resort. Your job in this isn't about shooting, anyway. Just don't get in the way of others who are willing and able."

Jonathan pulled his map from his pocket again. He lit up his IR flashlight.

"Tyler and Gunslinger," he said. "You know where the access points are for the utility tunnels. If you need big cover, go there."

Jonathan reached into his pocket and produced the jumble of keys that Jaime had given him earlier. "Tyler, opening the grate is your job. I never got a chance to do that."

The assortment of keys filled Tyler's hand. "Which one is it?"

"When you know, so will we all," Jonathan said.

"Chief and Big Guy, you're with me," Jonathan said. "The signal to go will be when everything goes dark. At the bungalow, Tyler, I can't stress enough to you the importance of speed and leadership. The rest of your team will take care of the bad guys, but it'll be on you to get the kids underground and to safety. The rally point for everybody is the exfil point on the beach." He pointed to it for the twentieth time on the map.

"All right," Jonathan said. "You've got your plan. I don't think the bad guys thought to put IR reflectors on their kit, but I can't swear to that, so be careful."

"I'm not understanding you again," Tyler said.

"Take a look at Big Guy," Jonathan said. As the kid turned his head, Jonathan lit him up with his IR flashlight, and patches on Boxers' vest and helmet came to life. "Those patches are only visible through infrared light," he explained. "In a perfect world, we're the only ones on the island wearing the patches."

"Don't shoot me, kid," Boxers said. "And if you do, either make it count or run like hell."

CHAPTER 33

The terrorist named Mike said, "Erin, go with him."

Little Isaac looked horrified. "I'm eleven years old! I don't need help to pee."

Mike remained unmoved. "Go with him."

Erin stood from her spot against the wall and walked to the boy.

"I'm not going to pee in front of a girl!" he protested. "I've been going alone all day."

"It's nighttime now," Mike said. "I'll let Erin explain."

"It's because Mike is an *asshole*," Erin said as she crossed in front of the guard. More quietly, she said, "I promise I won't look," but she rolled her eyes as she did. What was it about boys that made them think that every girl wanted to stare at their penises?

Isaac was not happy. "I think this is stupid."

"Just don't run away," Erin explained. "They've promised to kill us all if even one of us runs away. Now that it's nighttime, I guess they're especially nervous."

"That's stupid, too," Isaac said. "Where would I run to?"

As they crossed the threshold from the bungalow out onto the veranda, Isaac said, "You stay there." He wandered into the shadow beyond the halo of light and turned his back. "This vacation sucks," he said. Then she heard the stream start.

If there was one thing Erin admired about boys, it was that no matter where they were, they could always—

Darkness.

It came instantly and silently and was so absolute that for a moment Erin wondered if she had been struck blind.

Cries of panic blossomed among the children behind her. She thought she recognized the scream of the little brunette girl with the glasses whose name she forgot.

The guards yelled commands. "Everybody, stay calm. Don't get up." Beams of white light erupted from the front of their rifles and they darted back and forth through the night. "You, outside! Come back in here."

Somebody back there said a string of words in what sounded like Russian.

"Isaac, you've got to—"

It was as if Isaac could fly. One second, he was standing there, taking care of his business, and then he gave a little yip and he was gone—lifted off his feet and sucked into the leafy ferns in the garden.

There was movement back there, too. Voices? Who would—

A man and a woman yelled together, "Everybody, down! Down! Down! Down!"

And then the shooting started.

The instant the lights went out, Zach Turner knew that their ordeal was coming to an end. As a reflex, able to see nothing, he reached out to Becky and locked her neck in the webbing of skin between his thumb and forefinger. He pushed her head down and pulled her onto the concrete. He knew right away that he'd used too much force, that she hit the ground too hard, but there'd be shooting soon, and he could always apologize later.

He dropped to the concrete and spread himself out on top of her. "Stay down," he said. "No matter what, stay down."

"What's happening?" Becky asked. Her voice sounded strained against the weight he'd put on her.

"I think the cavalry just arrived."

All around him, hostages started to yell. He heard the sound of frantic movement as lounge chairs overturned. People fell or dove into the water. And, good Lord, the yelling! He'd watched people panic before, but he'd never experienced it strictly as a sound track. *Bedlam* was the only word he could think of.

"Stay in your seats!" one of the guards yelled. It felt as if the night itself were moving as muzzle lights swept the crowd. "All of you stay in your—"

He fell silent as an even louder cry of panic bloomed from the crowd near him.

"Everybody, stay down!" a voice yelled from up around the restrooms. "We are Americans and we are here to rescue you!"

Then the shooting started.

CHAPTER 34

From the shadows at the end of the dock, Anatoly had wedged the barrel shroud of his M4 carbine into the spot where a stout tree branch met the even stouter trunk. As the off-loading operations were carried out, he practiced the motions that would be necessary to kill everyone he could see. It wasn't the outcome anyone desired. Moscow specifically forbade a shooting war with CIA paramilitary operatives, but in a situation as dynamic as this, it was impossible to predict how people would react. He needed to have a plan for every variable.

He'd dialed his scope to 3X—his preferred magnification in situations like this. He found it to be the perfect compromise between telephoto and sight acquisition.

Baker Sinise would die first under any scenario, and Anatoly wondered if the man somehow understood that to be his fate. He stood completely still as the forklifts and the crews performed the complex choreography that was the movement of cargo. Baker kept his back turned to the tree line and his arms folded across his chest, providing the perfect target for a center-of-mass kill shot.

From there, Anatoly would pivot to the CIA boss Baker had chatted with. It was clear that the CIA man was suspicious that something wasn't right. Like Baker, he hadn't moved from the spot where he had the broadest view of the activities swirling on the dock. That man—Anatoly had not heard his name—had a military, predatory look about him. Pressed into a corner, that man would fight, which meant he would have to die before the chance to fight presented itself.

Anatoly calculated that the others within his view— the resort staff and the cargo workers from the *Katie Starling*—would pose little risk. They looked more like runners than fighters, which meant that they could be handled with less urgency. The one advantage Anatoly had now, which he did not have a half hour ago, was that the *Katie Starling* was firmly and securely moored to the pier. A quick escape was not possible.

Come to think of it, if the ship's crew decided to hole up in their vessel and pose no overt threats, he'd be inclined to let them live. He might have trouble convincing the rest of his team, but maybe he could talk them into it.

In his peripheral vision, ahead and to the left, Anatoly caught sight of what might have been movement. If it was there, it was beyond the wash of the floodlights. He moved only his head to take a closer look. When that revealed nothing, he pivoted his rifle. Oh, so slowly, he moved his body with the barrel, never leaving the support of the tree branch. He kept his eye in direct line with his scope as his red dot swept open pavement, and then the utility and maintenance vehicles, which had either been brought tonight or stashed in the past.

Then there were the crates of boat bumpers and other dock equipment that had likely been there for years.

It occurred to Anatoly that if he were inclined to sneak up on an operation such as this, those crates would make for the ideal hiding place. He scanned the area, stared at it, willing himself not to blink as he looked for any abnormality. If he'd finally encountered the people who'd murdered his team, he didn't know if he'd be able to marshal the self-discipline not to shoot them on the spot and risk the larger mission.

His men would love it, but his bosses would be furious.

Something was out there.

Yes, *there*. It was as if a shadow moved.

Anatoly slowly and carefully moved his left hand to the magnification ring on his scope and clicked up to 5X. It brought him closer, while at the same time narrowing his field of view.

Yes, there, behind the crate. Was that a bird resting on top of the nearest crate?

As soon as a gloved hand reached up to what wasn't a bird, he recognized the object to be a night-vision array that had been pushed up, and now was being brought down.

It's them, he thought. He looked back to the offloading operations. He only needed a few more—

Blackness.

The mission was lost. He didn't know how or why

or by whom, but they were under attack by a force that brought night vision and was able to control the power supply.

Everything that followed from here would flow from the confluence of opportunity and pure luck.

Anatoly activated his muzzle light, and opened up on full auto.

Henry West recorded the darkness and the incoming fire as simultaneous. He dropped to the concrete as the crate they'd been using for shelter disintegrated under a withering fusillade of bullets.

"I'm hit!" Jolaine said. "Ah, goddammit, I'm hit bad, Conan."

"I didn't see where it came from!" Rollins shouted from the left and behind.

The world around the ships had become a chaotic mix of dancing muzzle lights, running and shouting people, and two-way gunfire.

"Where ya hit, She Devil?" Henry asked.

"Gut," she said. "Oh, Jesus, that hurts."

Henry dared a peek above what was left of their cover as he keyed his radio mic. "Team Yankee, Conan. She Devil's hit," he said. "Details to follow."

The leading edge of the jungle, right where it transitioned to the pier, pulsated with muzzle flashes and rifle fire.

No one seemed to be shooting at them anymore, but they'd declared their intentions and Henry wasn't going to wait. Where there was a muzzle light or a muzzle flash, a shooter resided two or three feet behind it. He shouldered his suppressed M4, rocked the selector to single-fire, and fired at the voids behind the flashes. He fired groups of two.

"Get She Devil out of here," Henry said. "I'll give you covering fire if you need it."

"I can stay," Rollins said. "You take her."

"We're not having this conversation. I was first to sign on. That gives me seniority, now follow orders." Even as he spoke the words, he didn't know if there was any logic in them, but that was his decision.

Rollins hesitated, but Henry kept his eyes focused on the threats. "She needs to be out of here."

"I'm fine," Jolaine said through a groan that exposed her as a noble liar. "You can't fight them alone."

"I'll join you after you're secure," Henry said. It was probably a lie, but with luck it would get them off the X. He keyed his mic again. "Break, break, break. Torpedo, you there?"

"Still here. Sounds like things are getting bad."

"Keep your traffic to a minimum," Henry scolded. "Fire that bucket up and bring it to the exfil point. We have a wounded operator."

"Oh, shit," Torpedo said. "Who is it?"

"You have your orders," Henry said. "It's pedal to the metal time, kid."

For a few seconds, Gail thought that the little boy had spotted them. She thought they were well concealed behind the shrubbery, but as he emerged from the open slider at the back of the bungalow, he walked directly toward them. He even made eye contact, she thought. But when he told the girl to stay at the door and not look, she understood the mission.

When it became apparent that he was going to piss on Tyler, she whispered, "Don't you dare move." *And don't you dare laugh,* she told herself.

Through the radio bud in her ear, she heard Jonathan's voice say, "Mother Hen, make it dark."

Gail snapped her NVGs down over her eyes the instant blackness fell like a hammer.

In that same instant, Tyler reached through the foliage, grabbed the boy, and pulled him out and down. "We're here to save you," he said. "Stay here and stay down."

"You stay here, too," Gail said. "Keep him down and out of trouble." Through the green light of her NVGs, Gail saw blooming pandemonium on the other side of the doors. The children yelled and cried, and she heard adult voices yelling at them to be quiet, but she couldn't see a target to shoot.

"Advancing," she said. She and Dylan moved together toward the doors, their suppressed rifles pressed into their shoulders.

An older girl, maybe thirteen or fourteen, stood stunned on the patio, her hands pressed to her mouth.

"Get down!" Gail yelled at a whisper. "We're rescuers."

"There are three of them," the girl said as she lowered herself to the ground. "They like to smoke cigarettes out front, too."

Gail smiled. The kid had a future ahead of her as a spy.

"I don't see a bad guy yet," Dylan said.

Gail didn't bother to answer. They were there somewhere.

Then one of the soldiers had the decency to switch on his muzzle light. "I said, everybody—"

Gail shot him in the face through the open door. He dropped straight down and landed hard on at least one child at his feet. The kid yelled. The fight was on.

She fired two quick shots into the ceiling of the bungalow through the tempered glass of the stationary panel of the door. The glass spiderwebbed and collapsed into a pile. Now Yankee Two had unfettered access to the interior.

"Everybody, stay down!" Gail yelled. "We are Americans and we're here to rescue you." In the cacophony of the screaming children, she wasn't at all sure that she'd been heard. They were in the bungalow's bedroom. She recognized the layout of the bungalow because it was the reverse design of the one she and Jonathan had occupied much more recently than it felt.

Yankee Two crossed the threshold together, with Dylan on Gail's right.

Ahead and to the left, from what Gail knew to be the hallway that led to the rest of the bungalow, a soldier peeked around the corner, fired two quick shots, and ducked back again.

Dylan returned fire through the wall.

"No!" Gail said. "Aimed shots, for God's sake."

Children were everywhere, on the floor, on the bed. All of them were crying. Two crawled toward Gail's feet. "Down, down, down," Gail shouted.

They moved quickly, their IR lasers tracing lines in the air. A closed door lay straight ahead. Gail pointed to it. "Bathroom."

Gail swung left and dropped to her knee. The soldier

who'd shot at them was still there, but with his muzzle light off, he could only shoot at movement and his two rounds went high. Gail's return fire took him in the throat and the point of his chin. He sat back hard, but didn't fall, so Gail shot him in the forehead.

"Check that bathroom," she ordered. There were a lot of nightmare scenarios to play out during operations like this. Among the worst was having a shooter emerge from a room you didn't check and shoot you in the back.

Dylan kicked the door.

She aimed steadily down the hall, trying her best not to be distracted by all the terrified children. They were everywhere, even on the floor of the hallway. The gunshots had spun them into a fury. "Children, stay down!" She really belted it out this time.

"Bathroom's clear."

"Moving," Gail said. She led the way down the hall, stooped lower than she normally would, in order to give Dylan a clear firing lane.

The wall to her left erupted as the bungalow shook with the sound of rifle fire. The shooter was firing blindly, through the wall. Gail dropped to the floor. And made herself small as another full-auto rip tore through the wall.

"Where the hell is he?" Dylan yelled. He'd also hugged the floor.

"That's the dining room," Gail said.

"This is bullshit," Dylan said. He rose to his haunches and duckwalked down the hardwood, firing long, full-auto bursts high along the hallway wall into the ceiling of the dining room.

Gail thought it was a brilliant way to keep the

shooter's head down without endangering any of the kids.

When Dylan got to the archway that led to the dining room, he rose to a knee, leveled his M4, and fired four shots.

He turned to Gail. "That's three," he said.

Jonathan led Yankee Three to the edges of the decorative plants around the upper pool and hunkered down. He broke squelch three times and heard two sets of two in return. He keyed his mic again and said, "Mother Hen, make it dark."

The instant the lights went out, Yankee Three rose in unison, stepped over the planters, and fanned out. They still moved as a team, but with space between them so they never presented a unified target. Bad guys needed to know that to shoot one of them was to be shot by two others.

The first two were easy. A pair of soldiers had gathered near the tiled bar just off the edge of the pool. The sudden loss of light had alerted them, but they clearly didn't know what they'd been alerted to. Jonathan double-tapped them both and they dropped.

"Don't be selfish," Boxers said. "Leave some for the rest of us."

All around them, guests in various stages of undress and wakefulness surged in panic.

"Everybody, down!" Jonathan yelled. "We're Americans and we're here to take you home."

Boxers fired twice and killed a guy Jonathan hadn't seen.

"Keep yellin', Boss," he said. "Give 'em something to shoot at."

Davey took out a soldier who'd been lounging against the lifeguard chair.

"Down!" Jonathan yelled, but his words seemed less than soothing to the hostages. Then he realized that those were exactly the instructions the terrorists had been shouting. These poor people were literally blind, and their world was coming apart. Maybe they didn't need people yelling at them on top of it.

Besides, they weren't listening, anyway.

"We're the goddamn cavalry!" Boxers boomed. "Stay down and let us kill these assholes!"

His words brought instant compliance and more or less silenced the crowd. At least they knew now what was going on.

As they advanced toward the lower pool, Jonathan swept his IR laser over every face he saw, making countless *shoot/don't shoot* decisions. How could he know if a bad guy had decided to camouflage himself as a hostage?

On Jonathan's far right, Davey fired five or six shots in rapid succession, then ducked as return fire chewed up the trees and decapitated a statue of a Greek goddess.

"They've formed a skirmish line at the wall," Davey said. "They can't see a thing, but they're shooting, anyway."

"Good people are gonna die, Scorpion," Boxers said.

He and Jonathan advanced on the line. The wall Davey talked about was a tile-and-seashell decorative piece that marked the beginning of the long, shallow-riser stairway that led ultimately down to the beach.

Jonathan swept the wall with his laser and keyed his mic. "Do you see my sparkle on the wall, Chief? Is this the spot you saw the bad guys?"

"Affirmative. But some good guys have sneaked into the mix. I've seen some taking off down toward the beach."

They're the smart ones, Jonathan thought. He keyed the mic again. "I'm going to bang 'em. Make them move and show themselves." A flashbang grenade was a nonlethal noisemaker that was designed to disorient the enemy. One hundred eighty decibels and a million-candlepower flash will do that.

Jonathan ripped open the Velcro of a pocket on his vest, pulled out the tubular grenade, and pulled the pin. He keyed his mic. "Banger away." He heaved the grenade in a lofting arc that sailed over the heads of the assembled bad guys. Even amid the gunfire, the explosion was world-rocking.

The five soldiers behind the wall all jumped. Two of them tried to bolt. All five of them died within seconds as Yankee Three's bullets tore into them.

An unsuppressed gunshot from behind startled the bejesus out of Jonathan and he whirled in time to see a soldier grab a lady's jaw in the crook of his elbow and lift her out of the chaise where she'd been sitting.

"I'm hit," Davey said over the radio.

Shit!

"I swear to God, I'll kill her!" the soldier yelled. He held the woman in his left arm while he swept the crowd blindly with the rifle he held in his right.

Jonathan said nothing as Boxers' IR laser settled on the soldier's right eye. The 7.62-millimeter bullet misted the soldier's head. He dropped and the lady screamed.

"Talk to me, Chief," Jonathan said.

"Got me in the plate," Davey said. "I was stupid enough to silhouette myself, and he took his shot. I'll be okay."

"Hey!" Jonathan yelled to the crowd. "Where are the rest of them?"

"Who are you?" a lady asked.

"Inside the Plantation House," a man's voice yelled. Jonathan recognized the guy as Zach, the peg-legged vet that he'd chatted up at the pool. "Get me a light and I'll come with you."

"Roger that," another voice said. This one belonged to an older guy. His name was Dan.

"Everybody just stay down," Jonathan instructed as he led his team toward the beach. "This isn't over. But if you want to do something truly noble, please cut those bodies down."

CHAPTER 35

Henry West had already dropped two of the Russians, but there were more. They'd all taken to ground in the darkness as they fired randomly into the night. The working lights from the Katie Starling provided enough illumination for the workers to scatter, but probably not enough to provide solid target pictures. The result was a wasteful spray-and-pray approach, which did little harm but wasted a lot of ammunition.

With the benefit of night vision, Henry could take his time and—

Madman's voice in his ear said, "Conan, I need your help. She Devil's in bad shape. I need help carrying her to the exfil site."

There wasn't a choice to be made. A team member needed his help. The guys on the dock would get a bye.

Pressed as tightly into the mulchy floor as he could, Anatoly listened through his earpiece as his team came apart. Rescuers had somehow arrived and the body count was rising with startling speed. The pool had fallen, no one could raise Mike, Tango, or Whiskey from the children's bungalow, and now this. The mission was a total disaster. It was time to switch to survival mode. He'd brought three of his men with him to the pier—Romeo and Sierra and Two-Bravo—and they were all dead now, though he was not sure who their killers had been.

The CIA team continued to pour fire onto his location, though they were not aimed shots, so they went wide. He sensed that the sustained fusillade was intended as covering fire to keep heads down and prevent retaliation.

And then the shooting stopped.

The pounding impacts of rifle fire had been replaced by the deep rumbling of heavy diesel engines. When Anatoly dared to peek up, he saw one of the heavy mooring lines arcing through the air and landing on the dock. None of the crew members of the *Katie Starling* were on the dock anymore. The ship was pulling out to sea.

In that instant, Anatoly saw his way out of this mess.

He keyed the mic on his radio. "Home Base, Home Base, Home Base, this is Alpha."

He waited for the skipper of the *Olympia 3* to respond, but got only silence in return.

He tried again. More silence.

Anatoly dared to stand, then stepped out onto the pier. He saw deckhands on the *Olympia 3* moving about. The bridge was occupied.

The cowards were abandoning him.

The hell they are! Anatoly started running toward his ticket to safety.

She Devil had been hit. Jonathan didn't know what that meant, but from the tone of Madman's voice over the radio, it was serious. "Mother Hen, Scorpion," he said over the radio. "Launch medevac protocol. We have an operator down. Conan will provide updates."

And that was all he could do. There was still a lot of mission left to complete.

Jonathan led Yankee Three cautiously and slowly toward the Plantation House. This war was now eleven minutes old—plenty of time for the soldiers inside the building to build a strategy to keep Jonathan and company out. They'd still be blind, but their eyes had had plenty of time to adjust. Shadows and silhouettes that would have been invisible a few minutes ago would now be discernible.

The sheer size of the building was their first problem. Venice had sent them a fairly detailed floor plan, but that mostly validated Jonathan's concern that there were so many rooms, doorways, nooks and crannies that they could never be entirely sure that they got everybody.

"You sure you're up to this, Chief?" Jonathan asked.

Davey moved like a man in a lot of pain. "Don't worry about me," he said. "I'll get the kinks worked out."

They kneeled among the decorative ferns off to the side of the five steps that led to the grand veranda.

"Okay, Big Guy," Jonathan said. "If you were them,

and you knew we were coming to get you, what would you do?"

"I'd surrender," Boxers said. "I'd be really friggin' afraid of me. But, assuming they're not as smart, I think they'd try to find a way to bring the fight to us."

"You talking booby traps?" Davey asked.

"Sure, why not? They haven't had time to put anything elaborate together, but that's for sure the direction I would go."

Jonathan's radio popped. "Scorpion, Gunslinger. The kids are secure. Three tangos are sleeping. Need help?"

"That's affirmative," Jonathan said. "And good timing. I'll use whatever I can get." He told her where they were.

Three minutes later, Dylan and Gail joined Yankee Three. And they'd granted their opposition force three extra minutes to plan.

"Choke points are going to be the issue," Jonathan said. "If they're tactically aware—and I think we have to assume that they are—then they know that their best chance to stop us is to slow us down or force us into a position with limited movement."

Gail said, "That means our best chance is to go strictly by the book. Room by room, floor by floor."

"Here's what we'll do," Jonathan said. "Chief, I'm promoting you and your busted ribs to Yankee Two, and, Gunslinger, you're coming back with us. We'll split our forces. Chief, you and Dylan take the first floor, and Slinger, Big Guy, and I will take the second floor. I want us out of here in five minutes or less. It's taking too long as it is."

"Copy that," Dylan said.

"Fast and hard," Jonathan said. "On my count. Three . . . two . . . one . . ."

She Devil had been hit in the gut—one of those impossibly lucky shots that slipped under her ballistic plate—and the wound was pumping blood at an alarming rate.

"The fireman's carry was killing her," Rollins said.

"I get it," Henry said. "No problem." He grabbed Jolaine's legs so that they straddled him like the handles of a wheelbarrow. Still loaded with her weapons and ammo, she wasn't a light burden.

"When we get her evacuated to the boat, we can go back and take care of the VX."

"You're not evacuating me anywhere," Jolaine said. Her NVGs had slid sideways on her face, and her voice was weak and raspy.

"We left trauma gear at the rally point, I hope," Henry said. "We've got to get her leaker plugged. Look at the blood trail."

In their night vision, the stream of blood registered as a shiny intermittent stripe along the ground.

"Yankee One, this is Torpedo. I think I'm in the right place. Where are you?"

To respond would require one of them to let go of Jolaine, so they said nothing. They did pick up their pace, though. If Henry calculated correctly, the distance back to the rally point was about half a mile, and he reckoned that they'd traversed better than half that distance.

"Yankee One, Yankee One, can you hear me? This is Torpedo."

With what appeared to be considerable effort, Jolaine brought her hand to her chest and keyed her mic. "Cool your jets, Torpedo. We're on our way. Get in as close as you can."

"I'm afraid of running aground."

"If that happens, we'll *un*-run you," Jolaine said. "Look for the light. It'll be a few minutes still."

When she was done talking, she folded her arms across her vest and M4 with its M203 grenade launcher under the barrel.

"How ya doin', She Devil?" Henry asked.

"It's beginning to sting," she said through gritted teeth.

"We're almost to the exfil site," Rollins said. "Then we'll be able to put you down. And evaluate you."

"Sounds like Scorpion and the gang are giving somebody hell," Jolaine said. "Sorry I kept you from the action."

"Yeah, I don't get shot at nearly often enough," Henry said.

"I think I'm officially too old for this shit," Rollins added.

Jolaine tried to laugh, but the effort created a coughing spasm that launched blood from her nose and mouth. "Oh, that can't be good," she said. A spasm wracked her at that instant, causing her to yank her knees up and pull Henry off-balance. "Oh, God, that hurts," she said.

"We're almost there," Henry said. In the near distance, he could hear the sound of the boat idling close to shore.

"We're going to put you down now," Rollins said.

Together, they laid her as gently as they could onto the rocky sand. While Rollins went for the stack of staged equipment and the med kit, Henry pointed his IR flashlight toward the water and flashed it three times. He got three flashes in return and then heard the engines throttling up.

"Let's see what we've got here," Henry said. "I'll take your weapon." He reached for her M4 and tried to lift it away.

"I'll keep it," Jolaine said. "I don't want to be the only one without a gun."

Henry wasn't going to argue. "Then pull it up out of the way. I need to open your vest and see how big a hole they made."

He ripped open the Velcro closure on her vest. As it clamshelled open, he lifted her shirt to expose the wound. Not an inch above her belt line, the bullet hole was the diameter of a pencil, and it pumped blood at an alarming rate.

"I need QuikClot, Madman!" he yelled to Rollins.

He checked for an exit wound, but didn't find one. Night vision was not the optimal choice when evaluating traumatic injuries, where the nuances of skin color and the shades of blood were important diagnostic tools.

Madman kneeled at his side, tore open a package of QuikClot, and handed it to Henry. "Gonna need two?" he asked.

"I'll let you know in a second." QuikClot gauze was one of the world's most lifesaving inventions. It contributed to the plummeting battlefield mortality rate. Impregnated with kaolin, an inert substance that increased the rate at which blood clotted, it bought hours of survivability for soldiers in the battlefield, for whom trauma surgeons were often hours away.

"Okay, She Devil," Henry said. "This is going to be uncomfortable." In order for QuikClot to be effective, the surface of the gauze needed to touch as much of the surface of the wound channel as possible. That meant stuffing the gauze deeply into the bullet hole.

Henry used his forefinger. Jolaine howled like a wounded animal.

"Oh, goddammit, that friggin' *hurts*!"

"I'm sorry," Henry said, but he continued to jam his finger and the gauze as deeply as he could into the hot wetness of the wound cavity. "Open another package," he said.

"Oh, God . . . no," Jolaine said. "Please."

"Better in pain and alive than bled out and dead," Henry said. To Rollins, he said, "Get me a trauma dressing and a roll of Kling, please."

Madman dug through the med bag and produced a twelve-by-twelve-inch package, which was about half an inch thick. He tore it open, and when Henry was ready, he handed it to him.

Henry folded the dressing over itself twice, then pressed it against the stuffed bullet wound. "We're almost done," he said.

Madman handed him a fat roll of Kling, a kind of gauze bandage that was designed to adhere to itself, allowing for an effective pressure dressing.

Holding the pad against the entrance wound, Henry lifted Jolaine's shirt out of the way, and with Rollins's help, they rolled the Kling around her torso six or seven times, until the entire roll was expended.

"It's too tight," Jolaine grunted. "It *hurts*."

"It's gotta be tight," Henry said. "And pain makes you tough."

"Stupidest thing I've ever heard," Jolaine grunted.

Before Henry could ask for tape, Madman had already presented it to him. He secured the running end of the Kling, and they were ready to go.

"Hey, She Devil," Henry said. "Any chance at all that you can walk with assistance?"

"Oh, Christ," she moaned. "I guess we'll find out, won't we?"

"There's the spirit," Henry said.

He positioned himself on her right arm while Rollins took the left. "Lift by the armpits," he said. "Ready, set . . ."

Jolaine yelled a grunt as they lifted her to her feet. For a second, her legs buckled, but then she seemed to find them again. "I don't have to do this for long, do I?"

"Just to the boat," Henry said. He keyed his mic. "Do you have eyeballs on us, Torpedo?"

The response came instantly. "Yes, sir. How bad is she?"

Jolaine keyed her own mic. "You know I'm right here."

For the next sixty seconds or so, Henry's greatest concern was to keep Jolaine's dressing dry. The introduction of seawater into open wounds spiked the possibility of infection. Until she saw a surgeon, they'd have no real idea of how badly wounded she was. Henry would take whatever advantage they could get to keep her chances of survival and recovery as high as possible.

When they were maybe ten yards from the boat, the sea bottom fell away. As they waded to their waists,

Madman and Conan locked their wrists under She Devil's butt and half carried, half floated her out the rest of the way.

Finally they were at the boat. "Hey, Torp," Henry said. "Grab her by the shoulders of her vest and pull. She's gonna yell, but it's better than drowning."

And yell she did as Jesse pulled while Henry pushed. She landed on the deck with a satisfying thud. And another yelp of pain.

Henry smiled. He didn't wish pain on anyone, but he'd learned a long time ago that trauma victims who had enough strength to yell were a hell of a lot healthier than those who did not.

"I'm going back for the rest of the med bag," Henry said.

"I've got it," said Madman. "You take care of She Devil. Your medic skills are better than mine."

With Torpedo's help, Henry hauled himself aboard and wrestled Jolaine into a comfortable, partially reclined position against the boat's cockpit wall.

"Where are the others?" Jesse asked.

"They're still working," Henry said. "This injury kind of knocked my corner of the plan out of kilter. When Madman gets back with the med bag, I want you to take us out to sea far enough that we're out of range so I can deploy white light and see how bad She Devil really is."

The boat rocked severely, and the med bag tumbled onto the deck. "I could use a hand," Madman said.

Jesse and Henry each grabbed a shoulder of his vest and heaved Rollins up and in.

"Okay, Torpedo," Henry said. "Take us out to sea.

About a mile should do it. That way, if Yankees Two and Three need exfil, we'll only be a few minutes—"

"Look!" Jesse said, pointing back toward the darkened docks. "The ships are getting away."

Jonathan and Boxers led the way, shoulder-to-shoulder, up the grand staircase, while Gail covered their six o'clock. It was good to be back with the team he'd worked with so well for so long.

The top of the stairs opened up on a lavish lobby that led to the formal dining room and the second-floor veranda that lay beyond. Gail held the hallway while Jonathan and Boxers did a cursory search of the dining room. It made no sense for anyone to hunker down in there, but by the book meant *by the book,* and they couldn't afford to cut any corners.

Closed double doors blocked the archway to the normally open hallway that led to the business and executive offices.

"Those door aren't normally closed," Gail said, voicing Jonathan's thoughts. And they were locked.

"I believe that's a tell," Boxers said. "Shall we make some noise?" Even as he asked the question, he'd pulled a Slap charge from its quiver on his MOLLE gear, peeled off the Stickum, and pasted it to the latch on the right-hand double door. Next he attached his Skin-Pack detonator and ran the line out about fifteen feet, allowing them to back off into the dining room.

"Fire in the hole," he said with a grin. He pulled the pin, and the second floor bounced with the detonation that tore the door apart.

They moved as before, with Jonathan checking the offices on the left, while Boxers cleared the offices on the right. Gail kept her eye out for stragglers and ambushes.

From downstairs, they heard the sounds of forcible entry, but no gunfire. Three minutes after Jonathan and his team had exploded into the executive offices, they realized that the spaces were empty.

"Maybe we got them all," Big Guy said. His disappointment was palpable.

"There has to be a command post somewhere," Jonathan thought aloud.

He heard movement. Nothing overt or obvious. More like a creaking floorboard.

"Did you hear that?" Gail whispered.

"Sounded like it was from overhead," Boxers whispered.

"Did we miss a stairway?" Jonathan asked.

"Tyler said something about a back stairway," Gail said. "That's how he got away. It led to the basement."

"Where there's a back stairway, doesn't there have to be a front stairway?" Boxers asked. "Kind of by definition."

"We've missed something," Jonathan said.

They needed to retrace their steps.

How do you hide a stairway? Well, you'd put it behind a wall, wouldn't you? But for it to be truly hidden, there could be no knob.

"We need to look for some kind of hidden latch in the wall," Jonathan whispered.

From downstairs, Chief yelled, "Hey, Boss, we're all clear down here. The sons-a-bitches all took off."

"We're clear, too!" Jonathan yelled. Then he whispered to his team, "Why let the bad guys hear they've been made." Into his radio, he whispered, "Yankee Three, come to the top of the grand staircase and stack up at the end of the hallway. We might have something."

As he felt along the wall for irregularities—a place for a latch to be hidden—he discovered a hinge.

"I've got it," he whispered. On a hunch, he leaned on that section of wall and it flexed. With an audible *snick,* the latch unseated. "Bingo."

"What's our play?" Boxers asked.

Stairways, like narrow hallways, represented a "cone of death" for assault forces. They were the one mandatory choke point where bad guys knew that good guys had to go to get from point A to point B. They were ready-made ambush zones.

"We don't know the layout and we don't know their strength," Jonathan said.

"We could always burn them out," Boxers said. He smiled, but Jonathan understood that he spoke only in jest. Okay, mostly in jest.

"We don't know if there are good guys up there," Jonathan said. "Scorched earth won't work."

"We still have the advantage of darkness."

"And they've had time to plan," Boxers observed. "If I were them, I'd wait for the guys with the NVGs to show up and then hit them with a ton of white light. Turn it into a shooting gallery."

"How about bangers and strobes?" Jonathan said. Combined with flashbang grenades, strobing muzzle lights were disorienting as hell.

"Works for me," Boxers said. "Slinger?"

"God, I hate strobes," she said. "They make me feel like I'm falling up."

"Oh, and I brought some new toys," Boxers said. He reached into his flashbang pouch and handed two grenades to each of them. "Nine-bangers," he said with a grin.

Literally, they were flashbangs with nine individual charges in them, and the nine bangs were not symmetrical.

Jonathan slid them into the pouch on his vest, which held his other flashbang.

"Okay, stand back. Here we go." With his back pressed to the wall, and with the rest of the team clear of the doorway, he pulled on the panel and let it swing open.

If there was a shooter at the top of the stairs, he was a disciplined one, because no one fired a shot.

Rocking his NVGs out of the way, he pulled the pin on the nine-banger and heaved it up the stairs without looking. After the first bang, someone returned fire from upstairs. The fight was on.

Jonathan activated the strobe on his M27 and swung into the stairwell. A soldier at the top of the stairs winced against the bright light and fired a wild shot. Jonathan shot him in the forehead.

"Moving up!" he announced, and he climbed up the narrow stairs as quickly as he could, with Boxers right on his heels. At the top step, Jonathan dipped to a knee and swept the hallway to his left. No targets.

Boxers dropped somebody on the right with a double tap.

Up here, everything looked far more opulent. This was more of a ceremonial office, Jonathan figured, a place to entertain investors. It consisted of a reception area and another closed door. With fewer places to hide, they cleared it in just a few seconds.

Which left them with the closed door.

"Slap it," Jonathan said, calling for another explosive breach.

Before Boxers could respond, the door and the wall around it erupted to the sound of automatic-weapons fire.

Two unseen sledgehammers nailed Jonathan in the shoulder blade and the kidney, dropping him face-first into the carpet.

"God *damn* it, I'm hit!"

Boxers didn't hesitate. He switched his 7.62-millimeter cannon to full auto, and he raked the wall and the door with a thirty-round rip. Then he dropped his empty mag, loaded a fresh one, and sent thirty more downrange.

The wall and door were both shredded when Big Guy kicked the door open and casually tossed in two M67 fragmentation grenades.

"Frags friggin' away!" he said, and then he sprawled himself on top of Jonathan.

The grenades tore the office apart blowing out the windows and toppling artwork.

Boxers did a push-up to rise off Jonathan, and said, "Be back in a minute." Big Guy strolled into the devastated office. "Okay, who else wants to mess with me?" he boomed. "Who else wants to die tonight?"

Jonathan rose to his hands and knees, reasonably confident that his plates had protected him, and watched as Boxers examined the devastation. Big Guy saw someone that Jonathan didn't and shot him twice at point-blank range.

Boxers keyed his mic. "Yeah, we're pretty goddamn clear here."

CHAPTER 36

Henry strained to see. "That's not the CIA ship, is it?"

"The *Katie Starling*? No. It's the other one." Torpedo looked back at the others. "But the *Katie Starling* looks ready to pull out, too. Did they get the nerve agent stuff transferred?"

Henry and Rollins exchanged looks. "I can't say for sure one way or the other," Rollins said.

Jolaine adjusted herself to a more comfortable position. "Follow her," she said. "Follow the terrorists' ship. I'm good or I'm not. We'll all know sooner or later."

"Follow her to do what?" Jesse asked.

"I vote we blow her up and sink her," Jolaine said. She hoisted up her M4 and grenade launcher as best she could. With a feigned Cuban accent, she said, "Say hello to my little friend."

Now that was a good idea. "How many rounds do you have for that thing?" Henry asked.

"Four. HE." High explosive.

"Not enough," said Rollins and Henry in unison.

* * *

Yankee One needed to wade back to shore one more time for the grenades, C4 and detonators, and then bring them back to the boat. "Big Guy is gonna be *so* pissed that we blew up a ship without him," Rollins said with a laugh.

"Don't get cocky," Henry warned. "We haven't done anything yet."

Yankee One approached the *Olympia 3* at full throttle, closing the distance quickly. They kept their lights off, as did the larger vessel, but again, night vision won the day.

"Is it safe to run up on them this fast?" Jesse asked.

"There's nothing about this night that is safe," Rollins said.

"I mean, won't they see us and start shooting?"

"A distinct possibility," Henry said. "But the machinery in that old bucket is so loud that unless they're looking for us, they probably won't notice until it's too late."

"Probably," Jesse said. He clearly didn't like the taste of the word.

"No guarantees in the shooter's life," Henry said with a smile. He pulled a digital rangefinder out of a pocket on his vest and scoped the distance separating them. "We're at about three hundred yards," he said. "You can slow down, but keep closing the distance."

"How close do we need to be?"

"A hundred fifty yards or less," She Devil said.

"So, you're still with us," Henry said. "Want to take the first shot?"

"I'd love to," she said, triggering a bloody cough.

"But I don't trust my marksmanship skills so much right now."

"How about you, Madman?"

"I'll take some shots if you need me to, but I haven't used an M203 in a long time."

Henry chuckled at the irony. There was no greater sign that you've been out of the game a little too long than realizing that your familiarity with the toys of the trade was slipping. "Well, you know the old saw, right?" he said as he opened the launcher's breach and slid a stubby round into place. "Close only counts with horseshoes and hand grenades."

"What are you loading with?" She Devil asked.

"HEDP." High explosive, dual purpose. "We brought twenty rounds. I figure to just lob them aboard and hope we hit something important. Maybe set it on fire."

"What about the nerve stuff?" Torpedo asked. "What if you blow that up?"

"We're not even sure they got any aboard," Rollins said.

"And even if they did, it wouldn't do much harm out here."

"What about to us?" Torpedo pressed.

"You're driving the boat," Henry teased. "Don't let us get that close."

Jesse turned to face Henry. There was something ridiculous about the way he looked in the four-tube night-vision array. He looked so skinny and young that the NVGs looked like they were heavier than he was. "This is about to get serious," he said. "I don't know if you're shitting me or if that's the actual plan."

That was a fair point. "Okay, that's sort of the plan,"

Henry said. "The rest of it is we're going to pull up and run parallel to the *Olympia 3*. Yes, I'm going to lob grenades, but we're going to do it like an old-fashioned broadside. We'll make our range about a hundred yards."

"And you're really just going to lob them and hope?"

Henry explained, "According to Scorpion, they've got munitions topside, near the bow. I don't know if they're still there or not, but if they are, I'm going to try to hit them. That should make for a pretty respectable bang."

"And then what?" Torpedo asked.

"And then we see where we are."

Anatoly stood at the rail on the starboard side and told himself that he was not a coward for leaving. His men were not his men at all. They were independent contractors to whom he owed no allegiance, just as they owed no allegiance to him. Had any of them been in the same position as he, they would have done exactly the same thing. Even Moscow wanted no official involvement in any of this.

The Kremlin would be upset that the larger mission had failed, as none of the VX made the transfer. Would the Ukrainian dogs get their chemical weapons? Who knew? He couldn't imagine that the crew of the *Katie Starling* would be anxious to stick around.

As for the crew of the *Olympia 3,* they were grateful to be under way again. Did they mourn the loss of their shipmate? Perhaps. Or perhaps theirs was a crew of soldiers of fortune, as well—men with skills who were willing to sell those skills to the highest bidder.

This was what the world had become in these days of diminishing honor. Anatoly himself had no true memory of the days before the Wall fell—he was barely a teenager at the time—but he had heard stories of the way things used to be when his home was feared by the world and known as the Soviet Union. Those were the days before the oligarchs and their special breed of corruption. Anatoly's father told him time and time again about the devotion that Soviets felt toward their Motherland. Now people cared only about money and prestige.

Anatoly regretted that he had allowed himself to be pulled in that very direction, but it was simply the way of things. The Russian government wanted things done that no government may cause to have done, so they turn to people like Anatoly and his team.

But again, it *wasn't* a team. Teams trained together and shared common goals. And those goals needed to be something loftier—more noble—than merely money deposited in a bank. He didn't lead this operation so much as he herded mercenaries.

If the men he'd left behind on the island survived, many of them would not rest until Anatoly paid with his life for abandoning them. This did not concern him. Many, many people on this planet wanted to see Anatoly Petrovich Ivanov planted in the ground—or ground in a wood chipper. He'd gotten used to it. But as the list grew, he knew that his odds for long-term survival shrank accordingly. Soon a day would come when he simply would not be able to afford to sleep.

But those were concerns for the future. For the present, he would convince the *Olympia 3* to sail to Colombia, where he had many covert contacts who could help him disappear and start a new life. For a price, of course. Always for a price.

The explosion startled him, drove him to his knees, his hands covering his head. A bright flash and a simultaneous boom that sounded, for all the world, like a grenade. It came from the far side of the superstructure, and after a second or two, debris rained down on him.

Who the hell was shooting at them?

A second explosion erupted much closer, shattering the glass in the bridge. Alarms sounded. People shouted. He did not understand their language, but he understood the fear that compelled it. Anatoly started to run, but then he stopped himself. Where would he go?

The third grenade landed on a container of flammable liquid somewhere on the other side of the vessel and spewed flaming debris in every direction. A stripe of burning liquid splattered across his path, spattering his pant leg and setting it ablaze. He dropped to the deck and patted out the flames, but not before burning the skin of his shin.

They were under attack again. Or was it still? At sea. In international waters, against the laws of every nation in the world. He didn't know who was mounting the attack, and he sensed that he never would.

The next grenade sailed over the superstructure itself, hit a rail, and bounced onto the deck about twenty feet behind the spot where Anatoly stood. He threw himself onto the wooden deck as he saw the grenade ricochet off the rail. When it detonated, the deck pulsed with the concussion, and shards of hardwood launched into the air. Something tore a hunk of flesh from his ear.

Where do you go when your boat is under attack? Surely, it was more dangerous to be inside where spaces flood than outside, where you always have options. He could not have been more aware of the fact that this vessel was built of wood. How would the fires be extinguished?

The fire on the port side was growing quickly, though Anatoly still could not see the source of the flames. A grenade pierced the window of the bridge and detonated inside.

The smoke obliterated the stars and the moon as Anatoly made his way aft to the open deck, where he crossed to the other side to take in the destruction. Another explosion tore up the bow, just forward of the ruined bridge. In the glow of the fire, he saw the final arc of the next incoming round. He turned and shielded himself from the explosion. As he stood upright again, he finally had some idea of where the assault was coming from.

He couldn't see the vessel itself through the darkness and the smoke, but it was out there somewhere.

He slid a fresh magazine into his rifle and fired randomly in that general direction. The chances of hitting anything were minuscule, but it gave him something to do.

Just as his bolt locked back on an empty magazine, he again caught sight of the arc of the incoming grenade. As he extrapolated the angle, he knew what they'd been aiming to hit.

The munitions.

And this one was going to be close.

* * *

The explosion whited out their NVGs, and launched a massive pressure wave across the open water.

Henry was able to pull Jesse to the deck the instant the pressure hit hard, shattering the glass of the cockpit, and lurching the light craft far over to its port side.

"Stay down!" Henry yelled. "It's not over yet."

The wave of water came next, lifting the boat high out of the water, and then dropping it back into a deep trough.

"Cover your heads! Don't get up!" As he yelled, Henry dove for the throttles and jammed them forward and he turned the rudder hard to the left to gain distance between them and what was left of the *Olympia 3*. Its bow all but gone, the burning hull listed hard to its port side. In minutes, it would slip below the surface.

Debris fell like rain for the better part of a minute, starting maybe ten seconds after the detonation. Nothing heavy, thank God, but that wasn't their fault.

"Everybody okay?" Henry asked.

"I'm good," Madman said.

"Me too," said Torpedo.

"She Devil? You okay?"

No answer.

"Torpedo, take the helm," Henry said.

He and Rollins moved to her together. "Hey, She Devil, come on," Rollins said. "This is no time to nap."

She'd slumped to the deck to lie on her left side. Blood pooled on the deck around her.

Henry shook her. "Come on, She Devil. Time to get you fixed up." He pulled her night-vision array off her face, and then pulled off his own. Next he pulled a standard flashlight out of a pocket on his sleeve and lit her up with white light. With the light gripped in his teeth, he rolled her onto her back as he yanked his glove off to feel for a pulse.

The fixed stare said everything. The absence of a pulse confirmed it.

Tyler didn't have the heart to make the kids go down into the utility tunnels. They were scared enough, as it was, and despite all the panic and the blood, they were pretty calm. He had a girl named Erin to thank for that. She was the designated mother, the one they seemed willing to listen to. The one who made Tyler's job doable.

The shooting seemed to go on and on, and from all different points on the island. He told the children that they were safe now, that the rescuers were here and that all the bad men would be killed. But what if that turned out to be a lie? What would happen to the children then?

What would happen to Tyler then?

As he thought back on all that had happened, he wondered how it was possible for so much to change so quickly. Even if Scorpion and Team Yankee won, and none of the other guests or staff were killed, Tyler's life would never be the same. Not ever again. Baker was either dead or he would go to jail. The Crystal Sands couldn't possibly survive after this.

But guests *had* died. Guests had been *murdered*. None of them deserved that. Hell, no one deserved that. He felt ill when he thought of Hunter and Lori Edwards. The way they'd died, and then how their bodies were defiled. How was Tyler going to *un*see that? How was he going to wake up in the morning and feel sane in a world where such awfulness could occur?

All Jaime had ever wanted to do was what he was doing. He wanted to run the maintenance shop, meet a girl, and father babies. He'd have been a good dad. Now that would never happen. Those well-raised kids would never be born.

What the hell was Tyler going to do?

He had no idea if Baker was still alive, and a part of him hoped that he wasn't. All this suffering lay at Baker's feet, even though he never pulled a trigger. How many people had died over the past two decades at the hands of murderers who used the weapons Baker provided?

He was such a nice man. Kind to his employees, dedicated to his guests, tolerant—no, *supportive*—of his often-wayward stepson. How many other nice people in the world were truly monstrous in the other aspects of their lives?

Even Scorpion and Gunslinger and the rest of their team—caring people who yet were capable of such unfettered violence.

Maybe waking up in the morning wasn't such a good idea.

Something changed in the rhythm of the night as the kids milled about differently, and sounds of distress bloomed like a rose.

Then he understood why. Scorpion and his team members were approaching from the ocean side. Scorpion and the guy they called Chief moved funny, as if every step hurt. Seeing them made him realize that he no longer heard shooting.

Tyler stood as they approached. "Are you okay?"

"Been better," Scorpion said. "The resort is safe again. The terrorists are all dead, at least as far as we know. I see you didn't take the kids to shelter."

Tyler felt himself blush. "I didn't think—"

"I don't care," Scorpion interrupted. "It'd be a good idea to reunite these children with their parents as soon as possible. They're all a little shell-shocked, but I think a reunion—"

The horizon flashed like daylight. Six seconds later, an explosion shook everything. Everyone flinched.

"What the hell was that?" Scorpion said.

Big Guy replied, "I think somebody just made a big hole in the water."

CHAPTER 37

Jonathan keyed his mic. "Yankee One, Yankee Three. status report."

The reply came slowly. Jonathan was about to transmit a second time when squelch broke, and Conan said, "Yankee Three, Yankee One. The *Olympia 3* and her crew are gone. The *Katie Starling* has put out to sea. The status of the victor x-ray is unknown."

"What's the status of your team?"

Another long pause.

"Yankee One?"

"Uh, Yankee One's headed in to exfil."

Jonathan heard the dread in Conan's voice. All of them heard it. If it were appropriate to furnish further detail, he would have done it. Jonathan knew instinctively that Jolaine was either dead or beyond hope. He looked up at Big Guy.

Boxers' jaw had set, and he stared out at a spot that was probably far beyond the trees—a spot that only he could see, perhaps. As far as Jonathan knew, Big Guy hadn't had many relationships in his life. While the one he had with Jolaine was fleeting, and it ultimately failed, there'd been something.

Gail put a hand on Boxers' arm. It was an offer of tenderness that was beyond the vocabulary of anyone on the team. In fact, there *was* no vocabulary for a moment like this.

"Quit staring at me," Boxers said. "We've got a job to do. Let's find us a truck."

Word spread quickly among the parents. Tyler was still trying to wrangle the kids for the trek to the pool area when the first mom arrived. She looked like hammered hell in the moonlight, her face shiny and her hair a wreck.

"Landrum!" she yelled. "Landrum Parnell! Where are you?"

"Mom! Mommy!" The voice came from the middle of the rough line that Tyler had tried to assemble.

More parents followed, and then it was a flood of reunions. Hugs and tears and an unnerving chorus of wailing that Tyler didn't understand. Within a minute, kids who hadn't been claimed started to run toward the pool area where the parents had come from. It seemed like a recipe for disaster to Tyler to have kids running blindly into the night, and he tried to keep them at the bungalow. But it was like trying to block an outgoing tide. Those he couldn't stop just flowed around him, and then he realized that to hold on to a child physically was to hurt the kid even more.

Five minutes into his mission to keep order, he gave up. The reunions were going to happen.

The reunions *should* happen.

Instead of blocking the tide, he decided to go with it. He walked instead of running, keeping an eye out for stragglers.

Fifty yards into the journey, the flood of terrified parents met the flood of terrified children head-on in a massive roiling scrum of reunions. It was heartbreaking. And heartwarming.

Tyler watched for a minute or two, but then it felt like voyeurism, an invasion into private moments where he wasn't welcome.

Also, he didn't want to be present when the inevitable happened and there was an odd child out, a little one who didn't have a parent to reunite with anymore. He wasn't ready for that. Not yet. Maybe not ever.

And that's when the full force of reality hit him. He *was* that odd child out, even if childhood seemed so very far away. As he wandered back toward the pool, toward the rancid odor of sweat and death and smoke, it was hard to remember how beautiful such an awful place had once been.

As he walked past the bodies of the dead soldiers, and the bodies of the dead guests, he wished that he could muster some element of the detachment that Scorpion and Gunslinger and Big Guy and the others seemed to access so easily, but it was not there. All he felt was a hollow sadness.

At the decorative archway to the pool, only frayed ropes dangled from the places where the Edwards bodies had hung, but the bodies lay close by. Someone had thought to cover them with towels, but they were still naked and still dead.

Dead forever.

There was happiness in the sadness, too. A palpable sense of relief that the worst part of the nightmare was over, free from the realization that the literal nightmares of this ordeal would never end. Future descendants of these terrorized vacationers would speak of the horrors their grandparents endured twenty, fifty, a hundred years from now.

And Tyler was truly heir to it all. To the property, to the misery that Baker inflicted. Even if Baker was still alive—and for now, Tyler hoped that he wasn't—and shouldered all the responsibility for what had transpired here, his indelible stain of inhumanity would color the world's opinions of Tyler and any future progeny for all time. The fact of a different last name might cushion the blow, but the shame and the horror would still endure.

Tyler stood to the side, apart from the grieving and the happiness and relief. He'd never really been one of them, and now he truly was alone. In the outdoor dining area, under the dark pergola with its invisible lights and flowers, Tyler chose a table by himself, as far away from the living and the dead as he could find. The metal chair scraped against the concrete as he pulled it out. As he sat, the exhaustion struck. He crossed his arms on the table and laid his head on his wrists, wishing that he could cry.

Wishing that he were among the dead.

"Tyler?"

The voice came out of nowhere, perhaps out of a dream. Was it possible he'd fallen asleep?

"Is that you?"

He looked up and squinted at the slender silhouette

against the slats of the pergola. It was Annie Banks. "Oh, my God," he said, jumping to his feet. His knees knocked the chair over backward. "You're still here! You're alive. Oh, thank God."

He spread his arms wide and moved to embrace her.

He never saw the blow coming. She threw a round-house punch, closed-fist, he imagined, and it landed precisely on the spot that had closed his eye before.

"Asshole!" she yelled. And she hit him again.

He saw that one coming from the other side, but let it land. He turned his head a little to present an un-bruised spot. The attack was vicious enough—loud enough—to silence nearby conversations.

"You left me!" she screamed. "Those people were animals, and you left me with them while you saved yourself!" She tried to knee him in the balls, but he got his hip shifted in time.

He had nothing to say.

Annie spun around and stormed off into the now-attentive crowd, no doubt to out him and ruin him forever.

As he stood there, now the focus of so many eyes, so much hate, he wanted simply to disappear. He wanted to . . . not be.

"You're the one who went to get help," said another voice from the darkness. A short, round woman of a certain age stepped closer. "Tyler, right?" she said. "The owner's stepson."

Oh, shit, he thought.

"It's me," she said. "Muriel Hartwig. I created the diversion that let you escape. Did you bring the rescuers?"

The question made him feel off balance. "No," he said. "Well, sort of. Maybe. I helped them. But they saved everybody. They saved me too." It was as if his mouth were answering questions on its own, without influence from his brain.

"Did you kill any of those sons of bitches?" a man asked from the crowd.

Tyler nodded, even though he doubted that people could see the gesture in the dark. Even though it wasn't like that. They kind of killed themselves. But that wasn't what the crowd wanted to hear.

"Where are they?" someone asked. "Where are the people who rescued us?"

"They're gone," Tyler said.

That wasn't what they wanted to hear, either.

CHAPTER 38

Jonathan was grateful for the weather. it was nice to be stranded in the country as snowflakes pelted the glass and the wind howled. It was the perfect end to a painful day. It had been nearly two weeks since Jolaine's cremation, and he'd decided that his 225-acre getaway in the Blue Ridge Mountains, near Charlottesville, would be the perfect spot for her to rest. As the weather rolled in, and the snow accumulated, they'd jointly decided to fill the guest rooms of Jonathan's hunting lodge. With dinner done, they gathered around the massive stone hearth in the great room.

"Thanks again for those kind words, Padre," Boxers said as he took a long swig of twenty-five-year-old Lagavulin. "Though I can't say I agree with all of them. There's a lot of evil in the Valley of the Shadow of Death, but God's rod and staff aren't why I don't fear it."

"Not to put too fine a point on it," Dom D'Angelo said, swirling his Maker's Mark. "But they really weren't my words. Gotta give credit to David, and I think he was being a bit less literal than you."

"I think it's sad," Gail said. She sat on the sofa in a

bulky cable-knit sweater, her legs pulled under her. "She really had nobody? No relatives?"

"None that we could find," Venice said. "And I'm pretty good at rooting out such things. But I'll keep looking."

"If there's a relative, I'll find a way to see that they're taken care of," Jonathan said. He swirled his own Lagavulin. "I don't know what else I can do. I've never lost a team member before. Not since the Army, anyway, and they had a VA to take care of their kin."

"I think she knew this was her time," Boxers said. "Just the way she held back. I'm gonna tell myself that she's happier now. I don't know that I believe that, either, but I know she wasn't a happy camper in this life. I thought there was something beautiful in the way the wind took her ashes this afternoon. I think maybe that's how I want it to go for me when the time comes."

Jonathan said nothing. Those words were more poetic than he was used to hearing from Boxers, and he didn't want to ruin the moment. He sipped his scotch and let the smokiness settle on the back of his tongue before swallowing.

"Are you okay, Dig?" Dom asked.

Jonathan didn't know there was a way to answer that question. Given what he'd devoted his life to, the word *okay* was a difficult one to grasp. The answer was always some variation of both *yes* and *no*. "As well as I ever am, I suppose. I've never expected fairness out of life, but it bugs the hell out of me that one of my operators died while a guy like Baker Sinise got away."

"We don't know that," Gail corrected. "All we know is that nobody found his body. I like to think he was killed when the ship blew up."

"I like to think the Agency pukes got their hands on him and gave him their special breed of love," Boxers said.

Venice took a sip of her pinot grigio and cleared her throat, clearly ready to change the subject and make an announcement. "Do you all remember David Kirk?" she asked.

"The reporter," Jonathan said. "We gave him a hell of an exclusive on the Canadian thing."

Venice smiled. "Exactly. Well, I have a confession to make. I spoke to him on deep background today."

Jonathan felt a sense of dread. "What did you do?"

"I gave him the name and address and job title of the CIA guy who decided to ship nerve agent to the Ukrainian rebels. Pretty much everything he needs to build the whole story."

Boxers gave a low, rumbling laugh. "Oh, that's gonna piss some people off."

"Where did you get that information?" Gail asked through a smile.

"I have my own sources on deep background," Venice said.

Jonathan narrowed his eyes. "These new sources you keep mentioning—are they reliable?"

"One hundred percent."

"Well, who are they?" Jonathan pressed. "Given what's at stake, at least give me a clue."

Venice tipped her glass and winked. "Have another scotch," she said. "You're not nearly oiled enough yet to hear that."

ACKNOWLEDGMENTS

Like every day, every book begins and ends with my lovely bride, Joy. She is the consistent, ever-reliable source of everything that makes life wonderful. I love you.

One of the coolest parts of doing what I do for a living is meeting wonderful people who do (or have done) in real life much of what Jonathan Grave and his team do on the page. I am forever grateful to U.S. Navy SEAL Jeff Gonzales, president of Trident Concepts, LLC (www.tridentconcepts.com) and director of training at The Range Austin, for his help with tactical considerations and his hands-on lessons in night vision. I am equally grateful to Special Agent Chris Shaw of the FBI's Hostage Rescue Team for the behind-the-scenes tour and capabilities demonstrations. As always, when I need help in the technical or practical elements of deploying edged weapons, there is no better expert or nicer guy than Steve Tarani (www.SteveTarani.com), the managing member at Global Resource Services, LLC. It's an honor to have friends like these in my Rolodex.

There's a reason why Jonathan and Boxers (and so many of their real-life counterparts) prefer Heckler & Koch weapons, and it has everything to do with superior engineering design, quality, and performance. H&K's Robert Reidsma has been enormously (and repeatedly) helpful to me in my efforts to get the details right, and I am very grateful.

On the issue of firearms, I make it a point never to give Jonathan and his team a weapon that I have not shot personally, and that requires the space to do so. I am especially grateful to C.R. Newlin and his very special Echo Valley Training Center for providing an exceptional range and training experience.

Thanks also to Lori Edwards, whose generous donation to Trinity Lutheran School earned a character to be named after her husband, Hunter. I'm very up front with the organizers of these charity events that the story rarely ends well for the characters named in such auctions, but rarely do things go as badly as they did for the fictional Lori and Hunter Edwards. If an apology is in order, I hope this suffices.

Many thanks yet again to my buddy Claude Berube, who is my go-to source for any information I need on the subject of ships.

When it comes to critique groups, you know you're involved in something special when writers' conferences build panels around them. Such is the case with the Rumpus Writers, the group of friends and fabulous writers with whom I gather every month to share our work and our real-life triumphs, tragedies, and frustrations. Over the course of seven years, we've never once missed a meeting, and that's pretty special. So, thank you, Donna Andrews, Ellen Crosby, Alan Orloff, and Art Taylor, for your help and friendship.

In the grand scheme of bringing a novel to the marketplace, mine is in many ways the simplest job. All I have to do is sit in a quiet room and make stuff up. The real heroes of every book are the ones whose names never make it to the cover. No one on the team works harder than Michaela Hamilton, my editor at Kensington, whose eye and ear are perfectly tuned to what my books need to make them many times better than I can make them on my own. Lou Malcangi is the art director who designed this book's kick-ass cover. Steve Zacharius runs the show and Lynn Cully is my publisher. Publicist extraordinaire Claire Hill took over the reins from Morgan Elwell, and together with Vida Engstrand and the rest of the marketing department, they work wonders in spreading the word about my books. Alexandra Nicolajsen is my Internet and social media sensei at Kensington, and a continuing resource for cool new ideas. A thousand thanks to all of you!

Finally, there's my one career constant, my dear friend and agent, Anne Hawkins, of John Hawkins and Associates in New York. We continue to share this ride together.

*Turn the page to read an exciting excerpt
from the next Jonathan Grave thriller
by John Gilstrap . . .*

TOTAL MAYHEM

Coming soon from Pinnacle, an imprint of
Kensington Publishing Corp.

As Jonathan Grave piloted his BMN M6 through the winding flats of Virginia's Northern Neck, the slate gray winter sky reflected his mood. Anger boiled in his gut. He wanted nothing more than to mash the throttle to outrun the demons, but now was not the time. High speeds required concentration, and his mind was all over the place.

"It's very sad," Gail Bonneville said from the shotgun seat. "He was so young."

"Young men die all the time," Jonathan said. He instantly regretted his words. Cody Johnson was too good a kid—too good an investigator—to be dismissed like that. "That came out wrong," he said.

Gail looked at him for ten, fifteen seconds. "Are you okay, Dig?"

Jonathan forced a wry chuckle. "What does 'okay' even look like on a day like today? We just buried a twenty-seven-year-old who was murdered in front of his infant daughter."

Five days ago, Cody Johnson, Security Solutions' newest hire, had been running behind his jogging stroller when an unknown party killed him with a single bullet through the ear. Powder burns indicated that the shot had been from bad-breath distance, but no bullet was recovered from the scene.

"The police are working hard, I'm sure," Gail said.

"These yay-hoos out here don't know a bullet from a rock," Jonathan said. "They settle bar fights and write traffic tickets."

"That's hardly fair to the state police," Gail countered. "Their crime scene techs—"

"Took too long," Jonathan said. "They didn't get to the scene till after it had rained. The shooter is in the wind. I'm just glad I don't ever have to explain the world to a child."

The hardest part of any funeral—and Jonathan had been to too many to count—was the grieving spouse, and the younger they were, the more excruciating it was to endure. Amanda, Cody's wife of only two years, endured the ceremony with the stoicism of a soldier until the very end. When it came time to walk away from the gravesite, she came unglued. Her legs folded under her as she sobbed into hands pressed to her face. Jonathan couldn't imagine the burden she must feel today, how black the world must seem.

No one brought violence to Jonathan's team without consequence. No one.

"I'm worried about Megan," Gail said. "Did you see her? So upset." Megan Bobbins and Cody worked many cases together. They weren't partners, exactly, but it was close.

"Does she have people?"

"Her parents live up in Philly."

"Give her as much time as she needs," Jonathan said.

"It was a nice turnout," Gail said, a clear effort to find a little brightness. "Even Boxers came."

Jonathan gave her a knowing look. "Well, he's a sensitive guy," he said with a genuine chuckle this time. Brian Van de Muelebroecke, aka Boxers, was many things, from loyal to lethal, but sensitivity, at least in the sense that most people understood the meaning of the word, was not in his repertoire.

"It was a nice show of respect," Gail said. "The investigative team knows that Big Guy is important to the company, but they don't get to see a lot of him." At just under seven feet, with a neck like a truck tire, Boxers had been Jonathan's right hand for many years, going all the way back to their Army days, where they shared a spot at the very tip of Uncle Sam's spear.

The rearview mirror revealed Boxers' Ford F-150 pickup only fifty yards behind them. "I wonder how he and Ven are getting along on the drive," Jonathan said. Venice (pronounced Ven-EE-chay) was in many ways the brains of Security Solutions—the resident cybergenius—and since forever, Venice Alexander and Boxers had never gotten along very well.

"I don't imagine there's a lot of conversation," Gail said. "What is it with those two, anyway?"

"Don't know, don't care." Jonathan understood that Gail wanted to distract him with small talk, but he wasn't in the mood.

"You're not a vigilante, Dig," Gail said, reading his mind. "You've got to give the System a chance to work."

Jonathan didn't answer. At times like this, brooding was better than being honest. As long as *the System* got to the bastards before he did, then *the System* could run the show. A race was on, and the cops didn't even know they were competitors.

Up ahead, a burst of dust erupted just beyond a wide curve in the road, and Jonathan hit his brakes.

"Did you see that?" Gail said.

"I think there's a wreck up there," Jonathan said. He eased on to the throttle again while Gail fished into her purse. "What are you looking for?"

"My phone," she said. "In case we have to call—"

"Oh, shit," Jonathan said. "Hang on!"

It was an ambush. He'd seen enough of them over the years to recognize it in an instant. A red ragtop sports car had been pushed off the road by a copper-colored Suburban, which had positioned itself across the pavement, blocking passage along the highway.

"Oh, my God, that's Megan Bobbins's car!" Gail said.

Jonathan jammed the gas pedal, then stood on his brakes as he twisted the steering wheel hard to the right, triggering a skid that settled his BMW likewise across the road, with his side facing the wreck up ahead. "Stay down," he said.

"Jesus, Digger, what are you doing?"

Before he could answer, two men clad all in black rushed from the far side of the Suburban with AR15 clones pressed to their shoulders.

Jonathan was still opening his door when the gunmen opened up on the wrecked Miata. Each rifle was fitted with a thirty-round magazine, and they seemed intent on emptying them. The tiny car rocked and spit glass under the onslaught of bullets.

Jonathan drew his Colt 1911 .45 from his belt, thumbed the safety off, settled his front sight on the nearest shooter's center of mass and pressed off three shots. The shooter dropped in his own shadow, and Jonathan turned his attention to the second bad guy, who'd only just dialed in to the fact that somebody was shooting back. He ducked below the roofline, disappearing from view, and leaving Jonathan without a shot.

Jonathan advanced at a low crouch, his pistol clasped in a two-handed grip. The first guy he'd shot hadn't moved, so he was out of the fight, and blood spatter on the Miata's windshield and side window told him that he was too late to save Megan. That left no other focus than to engage the remaining gunman.

But the angles were bad. There wasn't much to the structure of a Miata—certainly not enough to stop rounds as hot as the ones Jonathan had loaded, but he didn't dare shoot through the car for fear of hitting Megan with fragments. He was ninety-nine percent sure she was dead, but that remaining one percent drove his decision.

Behind him, he heard Boxers' truck skidding to a stop behind the BMW. A door opened, and footsteps were on the way.

Jonathan saw a flash of movement on the far side of the Miata, and he knew that the remaining bad guy was maneuvering to get back into the Suburban.

Shit! I'm going to lose him.

Acting without thinking, Jonathan pitched himself

onto the pavement, on his right side, and that's when he saw his shot. Peering under the Miata's undercarriage, he caught a glimpse of the gunman's feet as he tried to sneak back into the Suburban. Jonathan fired twice. The first bullet hit the gunman above his ankle, buckling the leg under him, and the second bullet hit somewhere around the knee.

The Suburban's driver, who'd never engaged in the fight, revved the engine and pulled out with the wounded man hanging halfway out of the driver's-side passenger door. Somehow, the guy hung on.

Jonathan jumped to his feet to reengage, but he saw that he didn't have a shot. He broke his aim.

Behind him, he heard Boxers skid to a stop on his feet and reverse his direction. "He's mine," Big Guy said. Boxers had impressive speed for a man his size, and he was back behind the wheel in seconds. Next to him, in the shotgun seat, Venice looked terrified as the F150 accelerated as if shot from a cannon. As the truck disappeared around the curve, Jonathan advanced on the shattered Miata, vaguely aware of the mixed stench of burned rubber and gunpowder that clung in the air.

"Oh, my God," Gail said as she approached at a jog. "What the hell just happened?"

"You check on Megan," Jonathan said. He approached the dead shooter, his front sight locked on the man's head, but as he got closer, he saw the brain matter on the pavement, and he reholstered his .45. Only then did he dare to look over to Gail as she approached the bullet-riddled sports car.

Her body language confirmed his suspicions before she spoke. "Megan's dead, Dig."

Jonathan walked to the passenger side of the Miata

and made himself look long and hard at the bloody corpse of his second-youngest employee. She sat straight up in her seat, her chin on her chest. A flap of skull and hair hung over her eyes, and brain matter was everywhere. He forced himself to stare at the minute details because he wanted the anger. When they caught up with the gunmen who did this, that anger would fuel the retribution he would bring.

He pulled the passenger-side door open as he shrugged out of his suit jacket and kneeled in the broken glass that littered the passenger seat.

"You're ruining evidence," Gail said.

"I don't care." Jonathan draped his jacket over Megan's devastated head. "Nobody deserves to be seen like that." With her wound covered, Jonathan patted her arm and then backed out of the car.

Gail said, "We need to call nine-one-one."

Jonathan moaned. "Oh, Christ, we'll be here all day."

"We can't just drive off," Gail said. "They're going to connect her to Security Solutions, and we'll have a hell of a time explaining—"

"Call 'em," Jonathan said. While it was his instinct was to avoid interacting with police, Gail was right. There was no getting around it this time. But he had work to do before they arrived. Or before another car tried to pass. This was a pretty rural stretch, but somebody had to be behind them somewhere.

"One question," Gail said. "The police are going to impound your pistol. Is it clean?"

"And freshly oiled," Jonathan replied.

"That's not what I'm talking about."

Security Solutions, Jonathan's company, officially

made its living as a high-end private investigations firm, doing the kinds of intelligence gathering for which large companies and wealthy people were willing to spend great sums of money. But there was another side—a covert side—that dealt primarily with off-the-books hostage rescues, and not infrequently, those operations left kidnappers and assorted bad guys dead in Jonathan's wake. Absent official government cover, those deaths were considered homicides in their respective jurisdictions.

"Trust me," Jonathan clarified. "This Colt has never been fired in anger before. And yours?"

"Ditto," Gail said. "But I didn't fire mine."

While Gail walked back toward the BMW, presumably for her phone, Jonathan turned his attention to the gunman's corpse. He kneeled on the pavement, careful to avoid the pooled blood, and relieved the dead man of his phone, wallet, and other pocket junk. He carried these things back to his car in time to see Gail hanging up.

"They're on the way," she said. "Locals and the state police."

"Lovely," Jonathan said. "How far out?"

"Dispatcher said six or seven minutes."

"When seconds count, help is only minutes away," Jonathan grumbled.

"I told them that the situation was stable," Gail said.

Jonathan opened the center console between the front seats, then pulled open its false bottom to reveal a stack of cash and another pistol. He added the stuff from the dead man's pockets to the custom-made compartment and closed everything up again. When he saw Gail's confused look, he said, "I figure they're going to frisk me," he said. "But they won't have probable cause to search the car."

"You can't know that."

"Sure I can," he said. "You're my lawyer, aren't you?"

"How are you going to explain that the dead guy's pockets are empty?"

Jonathan shrugged. "It's not my place to explain anything. I was in fear for my life and I had no choice but to shoot this man. He was a stranger who killed one of my employees. I have no idea what he would or would not have in his pockets."

"Please tell me that you'll be forthcoming with details," Gail said. "Tell me you'll answer their questions."

"Are you speaking as my girlfriend or as my lawyer?"

"You know I hate that term," Gail said.

"There's nothing wrong with being a lawyer," Jonathan said. He knew damn well that that was not the term she was referring to, so he sold his words with his most charming smile. "At least you're a reformed one." Society needed to come up with a better word to apply to adults who are involved in unmarried relationships.

"I don't want you picking a fight with the locals."

"If they play nice, I'll play nice," Jonathan promised. It hadn't been that long since he was arrested on a gun charge in the middle of his efforts to stop a massacre in progress. The arresting officer—a fed, and admittedly well-meaning—inadvertently cost a lot of lives. That incident, combined with the impossibly slow rate at which the wheels of justice churned, left a bad taste.

On the other hand, some of his best friends were cops of various stripes. Life was complicated that way.

When Jonathan's cell phone buzzed in his pocket, he knew it would be Boxers, and a glance at the screen proved him correct.

"Hi, Big Guy," he said after connecting the call. "The news here is bad. The worst. Megan's dead. Cops are on the way."

Boxers said, "Shit. And we lost our guys. I don't know if they pulled into a farm, or what they did, but they've disappeared. We'll be back with you in a few."

"No," Jonathan said. "You keep going. No need for you to be tied up here forever. Did you get a license plate number?"

"Yeah, I did. You ready to copy?"

Jonathan looked over to Gail, then turned his back and lowered his voice. "No, keep that to yourself. I'm going to have to tell the cops that you were here, if only to explain the tire tracks, so that means they're going to want to talk to you."

"I didn't see anything," Boxers said. "And I was alone in the truck. Not my first run around the track, Boss."

"I'll see you back at the ranch," Jonathan said, and he clicked off.

When he turned back to Gail, she was not happy. She'd shifted he weight to her left leg, and she stood with her hands planted on her hips. "You know, sometimes it's actually easier to follow the rules," she said.

Jonathan said, "Let's wait in the car. It's cold out here." When they were seated and the doors were closed, he said, "Gail, I promise that I won't get in the way of the police investigation—at least not intentionally." He patted the center console and smiled. "Other than taking the dead guy's stuff. They have their jobs to do, and they're free to do it. But I've got a job to do, too. Those killers targeted *my* people, and I have every intention of tracking them down myself."

Gail scowled. "You act as if the police are the bad guys."

"No," Jonathan corrected, "the police are the good guys. Until they're not. You know as well as I that there are corners of what we do that will turn the cops against us in a heartbeat if they get a peek. I'm going to make those dots damned difficult to connect."

"And when we catch the shooters?" Gail prompted.

"I don't know exactly," Jonathan said. "I haven't thought that far ahead. It'll be ugly, though."

Connect with Us

Visit us online at
KensingtonBooks.com
to read more from your favorite authors, see books
by series, view reading group guides, and more.

Join us on social media

for sneak peeks, chances to win books and prize packs,
and to share your thoughts with other readers.

facebook.com/kensingtonpublishing
twitter.com/kensingtonbooks

Tell us what you think!

To share your thoughts, submit a review,
or sign up for our eNewsletters, please visit:
KensingtonBooks.com/TellUs.